Before You Say Goodbye

before you say goodbye

sarah gate

Choc Lit
A JOFFE BOOKS COMPANY

Choc Lit
A Joffe Books company
www.choc-lit.com

First published in Great Britain in 2024

© Sarah Gate 2024

This book is a work of fiction. Names, characters, businesses, organizations, places and events are either the product of the author's imagination or are used fictitiously. Any resemblance to actual persons, living or dead, events or locales is entirely coincidental. The spelling used is British English except where fidelity to the author's rendering of accent or dialect supersedes this. The right of Sarah Gate to be identified as author of this work has been asserted in accordance with the Copyright, Designs and Patents Act 1988.

Cover art by Emma Rogers

ISBN: 978-1781897812

For my friends, Cat and Laura, and my little sister, Melissa, who read this book first and helped bring it to life.

And for Charlotte. Thank you for sharing your own story with me so candidly.

CHAPTER 1

Autumn didn't like 8 a.m., but she loved the way it looked on New York. She enjoyed the predictability of the corporate coffee-shop-chain client base. Powerful and stressed-looking business types, sleepy teenagers, and bleary-eyed revellers dressed in snazzy outfits who looked like they hadn't been to bed yet. Their auras collided dramatically and Autumn — a writer — *loved* drama. It made the morning worth the effort. It fizzed from her fingertips and across her pages for the rest of the day. Almost everyone she saw at this hour ended up represented in her writing in some way, even if she only wrote about the creases on their faces, or the poise of their nostrils at the whiff of a freshly baked bagel. She was frequently tempted to announce to the crowd how deliciously their extraordinary normalness inspired her — to declare them the only reason she dragged herself out of bed at this time — but she doubted they'd appreciate it.

She drank them in silently instead, eagerly waiting for her turn at the till, stifling a yawn and wishing she enjoyed the morning itself half as much as she enjoyed the spectacle it brought with it.

Bored, she took time to admire a pretty blonde woman waiting beside her. Autumn winced. She wished she too could wear her hair up in a messy top knot and still look like a diamond. She wished she had the confidence to wear curves like this woman did. She wished she had feet so disproportionately small it was a wonder they could hold her upright. She wished she was the type of person who could commission a tattoo of a semicolon behind her ear without feeling like an attention-seeking idiot.

She felt a familiar wave of sadness and forced herself to stop. There were lots of things she liked about being Autumn Black, she reminded herself. She was ambitious and independent, attractive, clever and funny. She was not obsessed by social media or driven by love.

Temporarily satisfied, Autumn watched the exceptionally animated coffee server and swallowed nervously. Autumn had forgotten her purse and was planning to manipulate this man into giving her a free drink by pretending she hadn't realised before now. She went back to wishing again — this time that she was a better actress. She felt guilty and worried it would be written all over her face. She shook her head slightly, banishing her negativity by reminding herself all women used femininity to get their own way every now and then. She wasn't sure how that aligned with her feminist values, whether it was empowering or — given she didn't believe her prettiness should be considered a trade-off for special treatment from men — hypocritical. She only knew she'd been awake most of the night with a man who'd shown her over and over again that he very much liked the way she looked — her waist, her feet and every other part of her — and she needed energy in the form of caffeine. An almond-milk latte, to be exact. She hadn't intended to avoid paying — she wasn't doing it on purpose — she just didn't have time to go back to her apartment. She really did intend on settling her tab next time she was here, though she knew not everyone would believe that when the time came to declare it aloud — she just hoped the server might. Luckily, he was a man, and almost certainly a straight one. Autumn suspected he would give her a drink temporarily free of charge if she got the timing between ordering her beverage and declaring herself cashless just right.

When it was her turn and he asked for her name — a permanent marker poised readily over a large paper cup — she gave it to him in the same sickly-sweet voice she used when talking to people on the telephone.

"Like the season," she added.

"Beautiful name," he said, flashing her a smile.

"Thank you."

She fished through the contents of her bag as though she had every intention of paying him. He seemed really nice and the feeling of guilt deepened, but not enough. She needed this coffee. The prospect of not having it had increased her desire.

"You know, I love seasonal names," he said. "My favourite girl's name has always been Summer." He was flirting with her. It was really bad flirting, but it was flirting. Encouraged, she shoved her hand deeper into her bag, forcing an expression of mild irritation across her face.

"Really?" she asked. "Is that your favourite season, too?"

"No." He shook his head, placing her drink on the counter. "That's got to be autumn, I think."

She flipped her hair dramatically and smiled, wondering if she'd spent an unnatural amount of time looking. She reasoned she'd definitely done enough to do the trick.

"Oh, damn, I've left my purse at home." She wrung her hands in fake frustration. The barista looked down at her drink, then up at her. She worried she might have overdone it. An actress she was not. The blonde woman in dungarees with the envy-inducing waist stirred beside her, throwing her side-eye and a smirk. It was a supportive gesture, Autumn could tell, and this stranger's encouragement made her feel empowered. She fought the urge to look at her because she knew she wouldn't be able to maintain her composure.

"Oh," the barista said. "Well, I already made it now. You can have it."

He held it out for her to take.

"Really?" she asked. "Are you sure?"

"Yes, quite sure, Autumn."

"Thank you. I swear I'll pay for it next time I'm in."

She meant it, too. Forgetting her purse had been a genuine mistake. Autumn knew how to use her pretty eyes and complexion to get her own way — it had been necessary for her growing up — but that didn't mean she was comfortable doing it.

"No need. This one's on me."

She thanked him again. He nodded kindly, turning to the next customer. The dungaree woman. Autumn expected her to sound like a bird, but she didn't. Her voice was deep and came straight from her chest. She spoke with an eloquent British accent, loud enough to drown out the hum of the coffee grinder.

"I'll have a green tea, please."

"Two Brits in five minutes." The barista smiled, nodding between the woman and Autumn. "My lucky day. What's your name, sugar?"

"No, it's Bluebell," the woman said snippily. Autumn stifled a laugh, but Bluebell was not smiling. The barista winced, but didn't argue. Autumn suspected this was not the first time he'd been challenged over a gender-based microaggression. She thought it was a pity he hadn't learned his lesson. Bluebell watched him make her drink without another word, mumbling a courteous 'thank you' when he handed it to her. Autumn hid a smirk from the line of riveted people and made her way to her favourite place to sit, right by the window. She was pleased to see her first choice of seat — one that allowed her to watch customers inside and commuters outside at the same time — was free, despite the fact there was hardly an empty chair in the entire place.

"It's my lucky day," she murmured to herself. She took off her coat and sat down, reasoning she'd allow herself a few moments of unproductivity before she settled down to write the morning away. She crossed her legs and sipped her drink, content. Across the room, the woman in the dungarees was searching for somewhere to sit. She spotted Autumn and smiled, marching towards her with such friendly purpose Autumn worried they'd met before and she'd forgotten who she was. No. It wasn't possible. Bluebell's smile — framed by lips Autumn was certain had led her in and out of all sorts of trouble — was one she would remember, she knew.

"Hi there," she said.

"Are you free?" Bluebell asked. Autumn didn't know if Bluebell meant unpreoccupied or single. Luckily, she was both.

"Yes," she said, a little stupidly.

"Good, can I sit beside you?" Bluebell asked. "I have to warn you, I'm a talker."

"Sure," Autumn said. Like most writers, Autumn loitered in cafés, but not usually this one. She was alone in New York and she liked it that way. Her quest for solitude was the reason she'd moved as far away from home as she could get. She hardly ever haunted the same place for long because she was afraid people would try to get to know her. She had a whole day of writing planned and rarely broke away from her routine. But there was something about Bluebell. She looked like a dream and felt like an answer. Autumn wanted to be near her. She'd never felt like this about a woman before. She was sure it wasn't romantic attraction, but there was something there Autumn could not explain. A pull. Some sort of draw.

"I hate it when men do that." Bluebell pulled Autumn from her reverie. "He seemed like such a top bloke at first, giving you that drink when he knew your purse story was bullshit."

Autumn frowned in confusion.

"He winked at me when you finally admitted you didn't have it. I thought the whole thing was sweet. Then he called me 'sugar', and I just . . . ugh! It's one step too close to patronisation station and it makes my skin crawl."

Autumn laughed at her phraseology, making a mental note to use it in a book one day. Bluebell smiled.

"You don't think I'm being a prick, do you?" she asked. "Overreacting or some shit?"

"Absolutely not," Autumn replied reassuringly. Bluebell looked relieved.

"The pet-name crap annoys me more than catcalling and the other stuff," she continued. "It's so subtle that half the female population don't even think it's an issue. Some of them even *like* it. It's lazy domination and quiet condescension. I can't stand it."

Bluebell had a real way with words. Autumn wished she had a notebook.

"I agree," she said.

Bluebell beamed again.

"I like your shirt," she said, gesturing to Autumn's plain white blouse. "I wish I was the type of woman who could wear stuff like that, but anything white I wear always ends up covered in coffee or food."

Autumn wished *she* was the type of woman who could approach strangers in cafés and strike up a conversation, but she didn't say that aloud. She wanted Bluebell to think she was friendly and inquisitive. That wouldn't happen if she was her usual self, right away. Autumn had a talent for speaking to men, but not to women. She always felt as though they were judging her. If she wanted Bluebell to like her, she really needed to concentrate.

"I don't eat a lot," she said, admiring the bright white of her favourite piece of clothing. "But I do drink a lot of brown drinks."

"Ah." Bluebell nodded her understanding and Autumn thought she saw a flash of recognition in her eyes. "I get it. I used to 'not eat a lot', too."

Autumn tensed, but then Bluebell smiled, flashing dimples so flawlessly formed they were almost a cliché. Autumn was relieved. She'd expected her new acquaintance to launch into some sort of recovery speech. That had happened to her before and Autumn hated it. It was the reason she'd learned to hide her issues so expertly.

A few moments passed, just long enough that Autumn was starting to panic about what they would discuss next.

She opened her mouth to say something — anything — but before she had a chance to say something stupid, Bluebell mercifully heaved herself into conversation.

"I don't know." Bluebell sighed. "Maybe I overreacted a bit with the barista. But I read something once that said rape starts with microaggressions and so I've been calling them out ever since."

"I think you did the right thing," Autumn said encouragingly.

"He looked confused." Bluebell giggled. "But I suppose they always do."

"Right." Autumn nodded. "He would, having all of the privilege that comes with being a man."

"How lovely it must be—" Bluebell sighed theatrically — "to never have to worry about the intricate social journey that starts with calling someone 'sugar' and ends with femicide."

"Passing 'friend zone', 'bitch', 'Karen', 'submission', and 'she's a slut' on the way."

Despite the seriousness of their conversation, Bluebell laughed.

"Where have you come from?" she said. "I think you might be another version of me."

Autumn smiled, inexplicably overtly pleased to have received a spontaneous appraisal. Bluebell sipped her drink thoughtfully, then continued.

"It's easy to claim language doesn't facilitate oppression when you're not part of an oppressed group. Being from the UK, you'll have seen the deplorable way the British press talks about immigration?"

The mood had changed and Autumn got the impression she was being interviewed. She hoped so. She was a solitary creature, but she wouldn't mind having a friend or two. She was sick of meeting people she thought were cool, then realising six weeks later they hated transgender people or didn't think climate change was real, so she nodded in a way that was, on reflection, a little too enthusiastic.

"That seems mad to me," Bluebell continued. "I think immigrants are absolutely, one hundred per cent entitled to go wherever the fuck they want."

Autumn agreed. "I've never understood borders." They tumbled into comfortable silence. Still, Autumn wished Bluebell would say something. She was enjoying their conversation, but was too habitual to lead it. She'd discovered a long time ago that her opinions on sexism, racism, homophobia and other social-justice issues often invited an argument, so she'd learned to keep them mainly to herself.

"I noticed you ordered almond milk." Bluebell nodded at Autumn's drink. "Are you vegan or just feigning being woke as fuck?"

"I'm vegan." Autumn laughed. She braced herself for an onslaught of irritated questioning, but Bluebell grinned.

"I was raised vegan," she said. "And I'm still vegan now because I really, really love animals."

"How cool," Autumn said. "I've been vegan for six years and I don't think my mum knows what a vegan is."

"My parents are as liberal as they come." Bluebell shook her head as though she was embarrassed. Autumn could tell somehow that she was not. "Compared to some Gen Xers, I mean. They're opinionated and unafraid. Strange and unashamed. They forced us to think about the serious stuff. That's why I'm crammed full of verdicts, I guess."

"Even cooler," Autumn said. "I don't know where I got my opinions from. I don't want to be anything like most people I know."

"And I bet you're not." Bluebell raised her cup to Autumn, who was thrilled by the gesture. She hadn't felt this comfortable in the presence of a stranger for a long time. She hadn't given a great deal away — she tried not to because she worried people might judge her based on her family and their behaviour — but Autumn felt like Bluebell knew her. She felt seen.

"I'm really lucky." Bluebell was sounding a little sheepish. "I'm dripping in privilege and I don't take it for granted. I was raised in a house full of love."

Here, Autumn nodded through her jealousy. Her experience of youth had been entirely different. Her mother barely bothered with her kids, her sister loved her but didn't understand her, and Autumn was quite sure that her father could not possibly care any less about her. That was fine. She didn't like him either. She'd had a stepfather once. He'd cared about her a little *too* much. Autumn shuddered at the memory of his perverted glances, wandering hands and fag-ash breath. She distracted herself from her painful musings by paying closer attention to Bluebell, who was watching her, concern spreading slowly across her features. Autumn didn't like that. She didn't want — or need — any pity from anyone. Desperate to change the subject, she blurted out the next thing that came into her head.

"I'm a writer."

"Cool," Bluebell said. She looked relieved, like she'd been avidly searching for something else to talk about too.

"I'm from the north-east of England," Autumn continued. She knew she was babbling irrelevant facts, but she was terrified they'd slip back into silence.

"Hertfordshire." Bluebell pointed to herself.

"Why are you here in New York?" Autumn asked.

"I live here. With my brothers. Bowie works here."

"That's nice," Autumn said. There was a franticness to their conversation now and Autumn suspected she and Bluebell hated conversational awkwardness with equal ferocity.

"Yeah." Bluebell nodded. "We have a lot of fun."

They stared at each other, passing understanding, reassurance and respect back and forth. Autumn wasn't sure how she knew that was what they were doing — she'd never been able to do it before — but somehow she knew that they were. She felt inexplicably understood. Safe, even in their silence. Still, she would prefer it if they could carry on talking the way they had been before she'd accidentally revealed that her soul was unsettled. Luckily, her brand-new friend was on hand to distract her. To wrench her brain from a pit of torturous thoughts. To calm her fluttery guts with friendship.

"So," Bluebell said, swirling her tea. "Tell me what you read."

* * *

They talked about books, then bloggers, then books again. Veganism. The environment. Jobs they'd done. Politics and the news. How much it irritated them that life for most women their age revolved around finding, keeping and pleasing men. Once she was sure Bluebell had no plans to force her to talk about her choppy childhood and troubled teenage years, Autumn relaxed again. They tumbled effortlessly into new conversations, consumed with each other in that inexplicable way people sometimes *just were*. They talked all through the morning, across lunchtime and all afternoon, until the early evening presented itself, cool, orange and pleasant.

There were no more awkward silences. In fact, Autumn and Bluebell found they were so desperate to chat they were constantly interrupting each other. They paused their conversation only half a dozen or so times so that Bluebell could skip enthusiastically to the counter and replenish their refreshments, insisting every time Autumn winced guiltily that it was no big deal, they'd square things up next time they were together. By the time the barista was packing up the café to close, Autumn had been pitching her positive traits for almost ten hours. Her independence, her drive, how well-read she was, plus how different she was from her family. She found that conversation surprisingly easy now.

"Ah," Bluebell said. "I'm different, too. It makes me feel strange when people tell me that, because I'm not driven by a desire to be like or unlike anyone else — it's just that I am. My family are all for it, though, so that helps."

"Mine aren't. They wish I was like them. They'd be happier if I'd stayed living in our town, met a boy, had a kid, and perhaps got a council house."

"That's because you make them uncomfortable. You make them realise they had a choice. Not much of a choice, mind you, because privilege is real, but it isn't your fault you broke the mould and they should be proud of you."

Autumn nodded. She was really glad they'd met. She'd given up an entire day of writing, something she never did for anyone, but she was so bewitched by her new friend she'd hardly noticed she'd done it. When Bluebell checked her watch, Autumn wondered if she could read minds.

"We've been here all day. Did I keep you from something?"

"Writing." Autumn smiled. "Basically the only thing that matters to me."

She expected Bluebell to take that as a joke — people usually thought writing was silly and pointless — but she didn't.

"Oh, I'm sorry!" she said. "I appreciate you giving me your time. I'm having fun, though. Are you?"

Autumn nodded. She *was* having fun. Bluebell paused to check her phone, read a text message, replied, then dropped it idly back into her bag.

"Do you want to go for dinner?" she asked. "I really want pad Thai."

Autumn hesitated. Fresh from a night of no-strings sex with a stranger, she'd been planning on an early night. At around this time yesterday, untempted by a night on the couch by herself, she'd headed out to look for a willing New Yorker to pound her against it. She'd chosen the third bar she'd passed, one she hadn't been in before, and had spied a tall, dark-haired man sitting at the bar by himself. She'd noticed him right away. He looked unthreatening, like an elementary school teacher. Pretty eyes, nice hair, a sweet smile. She was afraid of him at first, not because she felt like he posed any physical threat to her, but because she already knew he was the type of man who heard wedding bells whenever he saw an attractive, well-presented female. Five foot six and slender, with thick dark hair cut just below her shoulders and deep green eyes, she was exactly the type of woman men like that liked. She was very pretty, and she knew it. She could tell by the way he changed his posture when he saw her that he would have been looking for someone like the woman he thought she was for at least a little while.

Autumn usually avoided these men. They were never content with one evening of her attention, and that was all she was willing to give. But the bar was full of older, less attractive males, and it was raining and cold outside. He would have to do.

"Thomas," he said, holding out his hand for her to shake. He looked relieved and she knew he would have been working up the courage to introduce himself. Autumn didn't have time for games. She already knew what she wanted from him. The worst thing he could do was decline her advances, though she already knew he wouldn't. She introduced herself.

"Pretty name." He nodded. "It suits you."

She let him talk about himself for half an hour, then asked him if he'd like to come home with her. He said exactly what she thought he would say.

"Are you sure?"

"Yes." She ran her hand across his chest. "I'm sure."

He tried to be gentle with her at first, but she steered him into rampant sex. He was a little too kissy for her liking, but his physique was good and he tried desperately to please her. He listened to her body and reacted to her praise. She rarely asked for much more from a lover.

But, in the morning, he did exactly as expected. He stroked her hair and tried to stare into her eyes. He told her that she was amazing. He said he felt a connection to her, something celestial, and he hoped she felt it too. He told her he was sure this was fate and he thought she might be 'the one'.

Autumn tried hard not to openly cringe. She hated the idea of destiny. It implied you didn't need to work hard for everything you had in your life, that good fortune fell from the sky. It reduced everything anyone ever achieved to nothing more than a series of preordained events, instead of a mixture of hard work, unshakeable curiosity and fortunate coincidence.

"Thomas," she said. "You're lovely. Any woman would be lucky to have you. But I'm not looking for anything beyond what we had last night."

She could have tried to spare his feelings, but knew through experience with dozens of lovers that this only prolonged the inevitable. She didn't want him to spend all day thinking about her only to be disappointed when she ignored his calls. Perhaps he would turn up at her apartment, like so many before him, with flowers and a hopeful grin, and would need to be told in person that she wasn't interested in seeing him again. Maybe he would cry, like some, or become violent, like some others. They rarely accepted her words and left. Autumn couldn't be bothered with the drama.

"Why not?" he asked.

"I'm just not ready," she replied. At this point she wasn't sure she'd ever be ready, but she refrained from telling him that.

"You're not getting any younger," he said.

Back-handed nastiness. Despite her experience, Autumn was always surprised by how vicious even the nicest of men became when they were rejected.

"Goodbye, Thomas," she said.

And, now, to her delight, that seemed to be that. He hadn't bothered her since. Autumn had completely forgotten about him until he'd crossed her mind only long enough for her to remember she was supposed to be exhausted. She was surprised to note that Bluebell had stimulated her away from writing and into a level of spontaneity she typically mustered up only when she was searching for satisfaction from men. Continuing their conversation over dinner felt like a splendid idea, though she had no means of paying.

"It's on me," Bluebell reassured her.

"Are you sure? I feel awful."

"Don't," Bluebell said. "You can pay next time."

"Yeah." Autumn nodded. They hadn't eaten properly all day. "Let's do it."

"I'm not keeping you from creating stuff, am I?"

"No." Autumn laughed. "I mean, maybe."

"Screw it." Bluebell grabbed her hand with effortless and admirable affection. She tossed a twenty-dollar tip on the table, and they left.

* * *

Bluebell took them to a restaurant Autumn had been to before, with a man whose name she could not remember. They'd had good sex twice that night. She'd never heard from him again, but that had been all right with her.

"These guys do the best tofu," Bluebell said, ordering a peanut stir-fry. Autumn asked for the same. "So, what's the dream?" Bluebell asked.

Autumn thought about that. Her dream was that her second book be at least as popular as her first. She didn't think any further ahead than that. She didn't feel as though she had the right to. It was the way she'd always operated and it had worked well for her so far. She lived day to day. If someone had told her three years ago she'd be here, in New York, she wouldn't have believed them, but she wouldn't have been surprised, either. She'd learned life had a habit of unfolding when you let it. In the most practical way possible, of course. If you took chances. If you did what was required. If you were in the right place at the right time. *Not* through fate. She didn't say that last part. Bluebell was wearing a rose-quartz crystal around her neck. Autumn was almost certain her new friend believed in hocus-pocus.

"That's so fucking cool," Bluebell said. "I wish I could make stuff. My brothers are musicians and I'm always in awe of the music they make. I just never had that level of talent."

Autumn smiled. "You're a good talker. Perhaps you should do something like that."

"If they paid people to rant, I'd be raking it in."

"They do," Autumn said. "You should start a social media page."

Autumn was serious, but Bluebell laughed.

"The world according to Bluebell," she said. "Who on earth would pay attention to that?"

"Plenty of people. You're really interesting."

"Thank you." Bluebell chuckled. "My brothers would love it. Marley teases me enough as it is. The louder and more opinionated I get, the more sarcastic he is. I might tell them I'm going to do it later, just for kicks."

Bluebell talked about her brothers a lot. There was great love between the siblings, Autumn could tell.

"What about love?" Bluebell asked Autumn. "Is there a person on the scene?"

"No." Autumn shook her head. She hoped Bluebell — who had alluded to same-sex attraction several times — wasn't interested in her romantically, because Autumn had deciphered that wasn't the way she felt. "I've never had much interest in relationships. They're a waste of time. People fall stupidly in love for a year or so — adamant they're more in love than anyone else has ever been — but they all wind up complaining in the end that he or she doesn't do the dishes."

Bluebell laughed. "True," she said.

"I take what I need when I need it. That's good enough for me."

Bluebell dropped all chat about romance after that. Autumn was glad. She hated it when women let their love lives consume their conversations. There were so many other more interesting things to talk about. Over dinner, Bluebell regaled Autumn with tales of her family, who sounded entertaining and lovable. Autumn didn't mention her own family this time and Bluebell didn't press her. They talked about sex and how much they enjoyed it, amusing each other with their best and worst experiences. They talked about feminism, focusing particularly on the invention of virginity and its value. The restaurant was closing by the time they stood to leave. It was the second venue that day to interrupt their relentless friendship-building by pointedly switching off the lights. Autumn was enthralled. This type of platonic obsession had never happened to her before. Bluebell was the most interesting person Autumn had ever met. Funny, clever, friendly and interesting.

But then, as she walked Autumn home, Bluebell blurted something silly.

"Do you believe in fate?" she asked. Autumn stopped herself from rolling her eyes. She wanted to give Bluebell the benefit of the doubt, something she did not award to many.

Her new friend was dripping in privilege. Autumn supposed it was easy to assume life had been designed for you when it had always been perfect, so she shoved aside her annoyance at the question to answer.

"I don't think so. Do you?"

"Absolutely." Bluebell nodded. "And I listen when it sends me a message. Something told me I should talk to you. I had a feeling, right here in the pit of my stomach. Don't you ever get that?"

"No. But I spend most of my time trying to shut myself up." Autumn was an introverted overthinker. If she paid any attention to her head she'd never get anything done. She wouldn't have written her book or published it online. She wouldn't be here in this busy city by herself.

"That's no good. You should listen to your gut. If I hadn't listened to mine when it told me to talk to you, we wouldn't be here."

Fortunate coincidence. Autumn internally explained their chance meeting away.

They stopped beside her apartment building. She wasn't ready to say goodbye yet.

"Do you want to come up?" she asked.

"Are you trying to get me into bed?" Bluebell asked. Autumn laughed.

"No," she said. "You're not my type."

"Well, this was a waste of a day," Bluebell said teasingly. "Sure, I'll come up. Do you have wine?"

"Always."

Giddy from more than enough merlot, they giggled their way towards Autumn's top-floor apartment. The lift, which only went part way up the building anyway, was broken today and they had thirteen floors to climb. Luckily, they were not short of conversation. Bluebell raved through hiccups and howls about things that were 'meant to be'. They were *supposed* to meet today she was quite certain. The reason would become clear in due course. Despite Autumn's dramatic groans and comical eye-rolls, Bluebell paused on the sixth floor and turned. She stared straight into Autumn's face.

"Can't you feel it?" she asked in earnest. Her expression was deeply serious. Autumn let her cheeks fill with air, then guffawed. "Don't laugh!" Bluebell scolded her, hitting her playfully. They turned to continue their ascent.

"Sorry," Autumn said. "But it's all bollocks."

Bluebell ignored her. "The universe is sending you signs. I really believe that. Pay attention, Autumn. Listen to that feeling you get in your chest. You know the one I mean. We all have it. It tells us when someone is dodgy. It lets us know all isn't as it seems. Let it guide you. Why don't we climb quietly for a bit and focus really hard on it?"

They tumbled into silence. Autumn resolved not to speak until they reached her apartment. Even in her drunken haze, she knew letting Bluebell think she'd won was the easiest way to get her to shut up about what was essentially magic. They climbed quietly for a minute or so.

"My gut is telling me you're not actually doing it." Bluebell smirked.

Autumn sighed. Well, why not? What was the worst that could happen? It was all hocus-pocus, anyway. Mumbo-jumbo. The climb was long and boring. Slightly fatigued — and looking for a distraction from the dull ache in her legs — Autumn took a deep breath and asked her inner self, a little irritably, how she felt.

She was surprised. There was something there. A little glow. A feeling of safety. And, buried deep somewhere in a place she hadn't known existed, the dim knowledge that she'd never be lonely ever again.

CHAPTER 2

Eight weeks into their glorious friendship, Autumn answered the door to find Bluebell on her knees, her hands clasped dramatically before her.

"My mum is in New York and she's making me go to a concert tonight to watch my brother because nobody else from the family can go. I know you have that big meeting with your publisher tomorrow and you said we can't hang out, but please come. There'll be boys. And booze. Please come. Please. They're really good, but it's no fun when I'm alone there. Nobody wants to play with me because I'm Marley's sister."

Autumn had once promised herself she would stop doing things she didn't want to do for the benefit of other people, but she couldn't say no to Bluebell. Her new friend knew it, too. She sighed. She was bored anyway, she reasoned. A little break from writing might do her good. And she'd yet to meet any of Bluebell's family, a group of people she knew more about than she did her own relatives. So she agreed to go, but with stark warning.

"No boys. And no drinking. And no after-parties. And no drugs."

"Yes, yes, I get it, no fun. Please come."

In less than five minutes, she'd thrown on a flowery tea dress and a pair of matte black heels, a smidge of lipstick and some smoky eye make-up. All the while, Bluebell chatted about her brother.

"You'll like Marley — he's really confident and funny. He and Bowie are total opposites. Bowie's so sensible and quiet. He's really contemplative and careful. Marley is a party animal. He's even worse than I am. I can't believe we've been friends all this time and you haven't met him yet."

"We've only been friends for two months."

"Fuck me, is that all it's been. I feel like I've known you for ever."

Autumn felt the same. Hardly a day had gone by since they'd met when they hadn't seen each other or spoken in some capacity, either over the telephone or via text message. Autumn had quickly come to rely on Bluebell for comfort and entertainment. She was undoubtedly her very best friend. Autumn felt like nobody knew her better. She'd told Bluebell all about her university days, and how disappointed she'd felt when she'd realised higher education was not bursting with people who wanted to discuss politics and human rights, but largely kids who'd just wanted to escape home. At least, that was the case for the peers she had met. She'd elaborated further on how disconnected she felt from her family and the way they wanted to live. She'd told this woman all about her insecurities and how they sometimes made her feel strange. In return, Bluebell entertained Autumn with tales from her childhood, of everyday life with her quirky, loving parents, sister, and three brothers, throwing in the odd story about her time at college, where she'd studied musical theatre, not because she'd had any desire to act, but because her privilege had meant there was no immediate pressure to work. Drama had been her favourite subject at school and she'd thought it would be fun.

She'd told Autumn all about the interesting friendships she'd forged and then lost through the years, not because she was a bad mate, but because she was quick to lose interest.

Bluebell loved to talk and she was good at it. She could start a conversation about absolutely anything at all, which meant being in public with her was often an adventure. Wherever they went, Bluebell would find someone to talk to about something, effortlessly charming the object of her attention until they were as shamelessly hooked on her as Autumn was. That was always as far as it went, though. Bluebell was choosy about who she let in her life and Autumn felt incredibly lucky their initial conversation had progressed into full-blown friendship.

Despite not being able to relate, Autumn didn't even mind Bluebell talking obsessively about her family, whom she obviously adored. Their proper home was in England, but two of her siblings, Marley and Bowie, lived with her in New York, in an apartment that belonged to a friend of their parents. When she wasn't with Autumn, Bluebell was usually with one or both of her brothers. Still, since Bluebell didn't work, there was plenty of time for shared frivolity. When they met during the day, they drank hot drinks and talked. When they met up at night, they drank cocktails and danced. When Autumn had work to do, they spent time at her apartment, where Bluebell would watch television while Autumn wrote drafts of her second book. Autumn had worried at first that her unemployed friend might try to dissuade her from working, but Bluebell was extremely supportive of Autumn's career. She bragged about it on Autumn's behalf to everyone they met and forced Autumn to celebrate achievements she'd previously had nobody to celebrate with.

"Come on." Bluebell hurried Autumn along, as excited as ever to dance and drink. "Or we'll miss the first number."

They took a taxi to the venue — a small theatre with a grubby floor — bulk-bought drinks to avoid queuing at the bar, then perched on seats in the front row.

"They're good enough that people come to see them, but not so good people fight to be at the front." Bluebell shouted the end of her sentence because the lights had dimmed and the crowd was cheering. Autumn turned her attention to the stage, where five men were happily picking up instruments. It wasn't hard to spot which of them was Bluebell's brother. He was tall, over six foot, with the same dimples and big lips she had, the same messy blonde hair, and eyes so blue Autumn could see their unmissable shade from where she was sitting. His features weren't as attractive on him as they were on Bluebell, but she enjoyed the way he held his guitar, his crotch tilted suggestively towards the audience, as well as the obvious strength in his shoulders and hands. Autumn could tell he had the same unabashed confidence his sister did.

They launched into their first number and, less than ten words into the song, Autumn dragged her eyes from Marley to raise her eyebrows at Bluebell.

"He's really good, isn't he?" Bluebell beamed with pride. "He's so talented. Honestly, he's wasted doing this — they're never going to make it. He's carrying everyone else, but he loves it so who are we to tell him what to do?"

Bluebell's wealthy parents had an unusual attitude to their children working, it seemed. Bluebell lived off an allowance they gave her. In return, they wanted only her assurance that she'd work when she found something she really loved to do.

The music was a little mix of everything considered cool. Bluebell proudly told Autumn that most of what they sang had been written by either Marley or her other brother, Bowie. There were love songs and tunes about partying, songs about sex, drugs and politics. Since live music wasn't really her thing, Autumn had worried she might be bored, but the interval rolled around quickly and then, before she knew it, the show was over.

She'd hardly taken her eyes off Marley all evening. She wondered if Bluebell knew. She hoped not. She wasn't sure how that would be received.

As the band took their bows, Autumn clapped as heartily as everyone else. She felt an inexplicable amount of pride. Beside her, Bluebell screeched her brother's name. He heard her and laughed, but didn't look over. The lights came on without warning and with unnecessary enthusiasm. Autumn winced. She felt sticky and unattractive.

"Here, take my pass." Bluebell passed Autumn a lanyard. "Wait backstage and grab Marley if you see him. I'll be back in ten."

Autumn didn't like the idea of standing backstage on her own, so she took her time in the toilets in the vague hope her friend might be there before she was. She reapplied her make-up and carefully tried to tidy her hair. She realised she was nervous about meeting Marley. She wanted him to like her, not just because he was her best friend's brother, but also because he was exactly her type. She didn't think Bluebell would approve of her sleeping with him — and she definitely would not do that unless she had her best friend's express permission — but she wanted to look nice when he saw her just the same.

She'd been standing backstage for fifteen minutes or more — waiting for Bluebell or Marley or both — when he appeared from behind a curtain. He was walking with absolute purpose, as though he was going somewhere, but he saw her and stopped dead, loitering with obvious discomfort three or four strides away. They stared at each other for a few seconds.

"I'm a friend of Bluebell's," Autumn said. "She told me to grab you—"

"Ah." He shook his head. "Sorry. You think I'm Marley. I'm not. I'm Bowie. His brother. His twin brother. Obviously."

She hadn't known they were twins, but it made sense. The man in the band had been really sweaty by the end of his performance, but the man in front of her looked like he would smell like clean laundry. It also explained how he'd managed to transform from a guitar-wielding, musical genius into a man who could barely maintain eye contact with her.

"I'm really sorry," she said.

"Don't worry. It happens all the time. It has its benefits. We're not identical, but, as I'm sure you can see for yourself, we look very much alike at first glance. Women throw themselves at me at these gigs because they think I'm him. He's sexy, apparently."

Autumn laughed. Bowie was bashful and awkward. She liked him.

"Are you waiting for Bluebell?" he asked.

"Yeah, she asked me to wait and to grab Marley if I saw him. She said she'd be back in a minute."

"Yeah," Bowie said, trying and failing to conceal an apologetic smile. "I'm sorry, she's not going to be back for a while."

Autumn waited for him to elaborate.

"She's sleeping with one of Marley's trumpet players. Adam, I think he's called. I was just back there and I think they're in his dressing room. Sorry to be the bearer of bad news."

"Great." Autumn sighed. She could have been in bed by now. She tried not to be irritated. She and Bluebell had an agreement — it was fine for either one of them to bail if they met someone they liked, but Bluebell had begged her to come tonight, and she didn't normally have an important meeting to get to the next day.

She was a little annoyed this time. She made a concerted effort to hide her irritation from Bluebell's brother and hoisted her handbag onto her shoulder, turning to pick up her jacket from the table behind her.

"Where are you going now?" Bowie asked, readying himself to leave too. He was wearing jeans and a plain white T-shirt. He picked up a dark-grey duffle coat and a scarf from a stack of chairs in the corner and started to put them on. It was March, and freezing cold. His coat looked warm.

Autumn had an unsettling desire to climb into it with him.

"Home. I have a meeting in the morning."

"Have you eaten?"

Was he asking her to dinner? She was surprised. She hadn't sensed any hint of an attraction to her while they'd been chatting. She was wearing a dress that showed a little cleavage and a lot of leg, but his eyes had been firmly fixed on hers, except when he was looking at the floor. She'd be lying if she said that hadn't been alluring. Autumn was pretty. Men usually let her know that they thought so. She found herself smiling and shaking her head.

"There's a place around the corner that makes great cake," he said.

Not dinner. Cake. Was that the same thing? She found herself hoping so. Despite her looming meeting, she wasn't ready to go home yet and she had no desire to be out by herself. She opened her mouth to answer, but Bowie broke their lingering eye contact to watch an approaching rabble. His twin brother was among a small group of jovial men and women. The siblings caught sight of each other and grinned.

The resemblance between them was breathtaking. Autumn searched frantically for differences. Marley was slightly taller, but not by much. Bowie had a small freckle beneath one eye, and Marley had one ear pierced several times against the single, delicate silver hoop in Bowie's left lobe. Marley had slightly longer and darker hair, and his demeanour was much more relaxed than his brother's. He was quite clearly a man who was very comfortable with who he was and how he looked. Bowie, despite their likeness, didn't seem so sure. They embraced.

"This is Bluebell's friend, Autumn." Bowie gestured. She liked the way he said her name. As though she was a really big deal. Urging herself not to blush, she took Marley's hand and shook it.

"We've heard a lot about you," Marley said.

"Nice to meet you." Autumn smiled.

"You too." He dropped her hand. "My sister says you're the most liberal woman she's ever met. That's a lot, coming from Bluebell."

Autumn laughed. Bowie agreed with a nod. He opened his mouth to speak, but Marley jumped in again before he could.

"They don't make many women more liberal than Bluebird." He grinned. Bluebell had told Autumn once that her brothers called her that to annoy her. It was interchangeable with 'blueberry' and 'bluebottle', depending on how they were feeling.

"That's definitely true," Autumn said.

"If you're even half as liberal as she is—" Autumn knew Marley was working hard to hold her attention. Beside him, Bowie was looking at the ground — "New York had better look out."

"It's far too late to save New York," Autumn said jokingly. Marley laughed.

"Good for you."

They were silent while he looked her up and down. Autumn was used to the eyes of men upon her, but she found herself blushing under his gaze. She wondered if he was imagining her naked. When he was done, he turned to Bowie.

"Have you asked her out already?"

Bowie laughed nervously.

"We're going for cake," Autumn answered for him.

"Damn," Marley said. She could tell he didn't really care. He was attracted to her, but there was a gaggle of girls waiting eagerly for him by the door. Autumn found herself wondering which one of the women he would sleep with tonight. If Bowie hadn't shown up, it might have been her. The tension between them was palpable. Still, she wasn't sure Bluebell would approve. And she was not there to ask. So, though Marley was undeniably sexy, eating cake with Bowie was a much better idea.

"I'm bailing," Marley said. "I'll handle your absence with Mum if you need me to."

"Thanks." Bowie blushed, smiling a little sheepishly at Autumn. The brothers embraced again. Autumn wasn't sure if she'd had two hugs in her entire life from her own sibling.

"Don't do anything I wouldn't do," Marley quipped as he left.

"That doesn't leave much," Bowie called after him, waiting until his brother was gone before he met her eyes again. Despite being the eldest of Bluebell's five siblings, he was obviously the less dominant twin. How was it she knew useless information like that but had not known they were twins?

Bowie was silent, so Autumn brought the conversation back to cake.

"I'm vegan," she said. She expected him to say something sarcastic about cows. Men usually did.

"Of course you are." Bowie chuckled. "You're Bluebell's friend."

He smiled and moved towards the door, holding it open for her. "I'm vegan, too."

She supposed she should have worked that out for herself. Bluebell had been vegan almost her entire life. Her parents were vegan, Autumn knew. It made sense that her siblings would be vegan, too. Herbivorous men were hard to come by, and that made them impressive to Autumn. She liked him a little bit more.

"So. This café . . ." she said, stepping out into the corridor and waiting for him to fall into step beside her. He grinned and blushed, and Autumn was floored. There it was again, the same fuzzy feeling she'd experienced the day she'd met Bluebell, stronger than it had been then, and a little dizzying this time.

***

Bowie took her to a tiny café. They ordered a pot of tea to share and a piece of cake each. Autumn would usually be drunk or high by now, but was surprised to find she was enjoying this just as much. She liked the atmosphere. The place was almost empty, except for a few trendy-looking couples. There was a man playing piano in the corner, and the walls were adorned with music posters and adverts for guitar lessons.

They'd met less than an hour ago, but Autumn, enraged by a man on the street who'd automatically expected her to get out of his way and bashed into her rather than move himself, was already setting out her stance on women's rights. She did so over the first thing she had eaten all day, which happened to be the best lemon drizzle cake she had ever tasted. Bowie listened to her intently, waiting until she was fully finished before he offered his own opinion. Such manners were not a given in conversations between men and women. It was a small thing, but Autumn found herself grateful.

"My mum and my sisters are always complaining that men have it easier than women," he said. "It's hard to put yourself in that position when you have all of the privilege that comes with being a man, but I believe them completely. My sisters are cool. They don't make finding husbands and having kids and taking care of men their priority, and I think they sometimes struggle to meet people like them. I guess that's why Bluebell likes you so much."

Though she had already known how Bluebell felt about her, his words made Autumn beam. Her new best friend was not, as promised, a person who hid her feelings when she loved a person, but it was nice to hear it from someone else.

"Your sister is the only person who makes me feel like I can be myself," Autumn said, dropping her one-woman tirade against nameless men everywhere.

"She says the same thing about you." Bowie smiled. "Most women think she's nuts. She's too confident for them, I guess, too shameless. It's good to finally meet you because she never stops talking about you and we were starting to think you might not be real."

Autumn grinned at him, an authentic gesture she normally suppressed around strangers. She was having an unusually good time. She had to be up at seven, but she didn't want to leave. She could barely believe she hadn't known Bowie an hour before. She felt, as with Bluebell, as though she had found someone really special. She searched for a new branch of conversation.

"Bluebell didn't tell me you and Marley were twins," she said.

"Yeah, we don't look that much alike to her anymore, so I think she forgets. It might also be the drugs."

Autumn laughed. Bowie smiled.

"Going back to feminism, do you read?" he asked. Autumn nodded. "I read a book recently I think you'd like, about a gap in data that means women are literally dying because important things, like seat belts, are tested on crash dummies designed like men. I can't remember the name of it, but I'll give it to Bluebell to give to you."

She was a little perturbed by his insinuation they might not see each other again soon. She didn't know if it was because her ego didn't like the idea the decision to meet again might not be solely hers — since she was typically the one who did the rejecting — or because she genuinely liked him.

She was still trying to work it out when they finished their cake and saw no alternative except to give herself more time to decide by inviting him back to her apartment to watch a movie *or something*.

Autumn had no idea what 'or something' meant and immediately wished she hadn't said it. It was too open to interpretation and she was worried it might be misconstrued. Most men saw an invitation home as a penetration invitation. Why else would you invite someone back to your house in the middle of the night? *She* only did that when she wanted to fuck.

Autumn wasn't sure how she felt about Bowie, but that wasn't the only complication. She'd had to remind herself more than once that Bowie was just as much Bluebell's brother as Marley was. She'd need permission from her friend before she let anything happen. And Autumn was adamant, no matter how intense her growing attraction to him — no matter how lovely and attentive she found him or how comfortable he made her feel — they should not sleep together tonight. It was too complicated.

Still, that rationalisation had not stopped Autumn imagining what Bowie would be like in bed. Though she hadn't fully registered it when she first met him — especially when comparing him to a twin who carried himself as though he was ten times better-looking — Bowie was sexy in his own right. There was something about how good he was that made her want to coax him into badness, and she wanted to know what he looked like when he was lost to ecstasy. She was enthralled by this sudden desire for a man whose shyness masked his looks and had made her feel at first and second glance that he wasn't as physically appealing as his brother because of his lack of confidence. Bowie was quiet and shy, humble and reserved, and those were attributes that typically turned her off, but she could no longer deny that her attraction to him was inexplicably visceral. With hair that was shorter round the sides and untidy on the top, a long face and large features, Bowie was stereotypically good-looking, but it was almost certainly his lips and his use of them over the course of the evening that had done something to her. He didn't say anything at first and she dared to hope for a second that he might be too well-behaved to accept her invitation. She held her breath and willed him to get them out of the mess she had put them in, but he didn't.

Instead he blushed, mumbled something, and agreed to go home with her.

CHAPTER 3

Autumn's tiny top-floor apartment had actually been the attic of the flat below, but her landlord, Walter, had knocked a hole in the ceiling forty years ago and put in a wrought-iron spiral staircase. He'd been renting the space out, illegally, as far as she understood, ever since. The apartment was thirteen stories up, but the lift, when it worked, only went up as far as the sixth floor. It had been fixed for several weeks now and experience had taught her it was almost certainly due another breakdown soon.

Autumn and Bowie climbed the staircase in absolute silence. She really wished he would say something. She thought about trying to make conversation, but he looked breathless and consumed by something, so she went back to focusing on not falling over instead. It felt like the longest climb she'd ever done. She was relieved when they reached the door and she finally let them in. There was no hallway, the door opened straight into her very small, neat and tidy living room.

"This is lovely," Bowie said, smiling kindly.

"Make yourself at home." She tossed her bag onto her dressing table — irritatingly positioned in the living room because her bedroom was too small and there was nowhere else to put it — and headed to the kitchen to put on the kettle.

"What's your favourite movie?" he called from the living room.

"*Stand By Me*," she said immediately. He set about navigating her television set to a streaming service. She realised as she added soya milk to their teacups that she was smiling to herself. She forced her face straight before rejoining him in the living room.

"You've seen this, right?" she asked, handing him a mug of tea. He tutted a yes.

She sat down beside him and stared at the television. They were silent for the longest time, but she got the distinct impression he was not watching the movie. She wasn't, either. She was too busy feeling confused and a little bit ashamed of herself.

Seeing Bowie sitting on the sofa had imprisoned her self-control and restrained her capacity for rational thinking. She was stopping herself from kissing him now, not because he was Bluebell's brother but because she was not sure if he wanted her to. She felt reasonably guilty about that, but she liked him too much to hold back anymore.

She watched Bowie from the corner of her eye, wondering what he would do if she straddled him, or took off her tea dress, or hiked it up and touched herself. He moved, distracting her from her sexy thoughts by stretching his legs a little wider so that his knee was warm against hers. She didn't know if it was deliberate or not. She was not usually so confused about how men felt about her, but Bowie was different. He seemed like the type of man who might innocently accompany a woman to her home in the middle of the night. He caught her eye once or twice and smiled. For a while she felt something fizzing between them, but then he ran his hand through his straight, blonde hair, trying and failing to stifle a yawn. He was tired. He might be bored. He could be here without intention. She might make an idiot of herself.

She admired him from head to foot for what must have been the sixth or seventh time. He was tall, but apparently uncomfortable with it, because there was a little stoop in his neck when he walked. His demeanour was far from what she normally went for. She liked men who were much more confident. Men like Marley, who would have had her in the bedroom by now. They didn't have to be conventionally good-looking, but they were generally experienced. It wasn't unusual for them to have really bad attitudes, but that didn't faze her. She didn't want a boyfriend, she wanted good sex.

Yet men usually expected her to be better behaved. They could rarely believe she really wanted them to come home with her. One of her most recent conquests had asked her if she was secretly a serial killer.

"Why would a girl like you take a man home on the first night?" he asked her. "Don't you think you're worth a little more than that?"

Autumn slept with him once then never called him again. He left forty-two messages on her answering machine in three weeks. Autumn thought that spoke volumes about who was worth what.

She knew that there were people out there who might describe her as loose, but Autumn didn't care for one-dimensional descriptions of people based on something as trivial as who they slept with and how often. She especially didn't think the men who were benefitting from her love of sex had any right to judge her for anything. The double standard drove her mad with anger if she allowed herself time to dwell on it, but she rarely did. She was getting what she wanted from people she hardly cared about. What they thought of her afterwards was quite frankly none of her business. There were men out there who thought they could use her, but she didn't lose any sleep over that, either. As long as she was being satisfied, she saw no issue with men gaining pleasure from her too. She didn't think it was shameful and had no desire to worry about what they thought of her. She prided herself on being comfortable with what she liked and who she was.

But with Bowie, it was different. She cared how he felt about her. It was all very confusing and it was making her act weirdly. Typically unshakably confident, she did not feel like herself tonight.

Suddenly, he was speaking. "Tell me what you do?" he asked her. They'd spent hours talking earlier, but not, so far, about work. They'd had so many other more important things to say to each other. Small talk had been abandoned in favour of politics, economics, and social justice.

"I'm a writer." Autumn could still barely believe she got to say that about herself. She'd once been a social media manager for a charity, but had written a book three years before and seen some success when she'd published it online. Recently, it had been bought and released by a publishing house with a good reputation. It was all she'd ever wanted for herself, ever since she'd won a second-hand typewriter in a school tombola when she was eight years old.

"Ah, yes, Bluebell did mention that. What do you write?" he asked her.

"Everything." She beamed. She meant it. She wrote short stories, blogs, poetry and novels. Bowie laughed.

"OK, but what do you mainly write?"

"Novels," she said.

He looked impressed.

"Have you written anything I might have read?"

"Probably not. I wrote something online. It was picked up by a publisher and recently released."

"What's it about?"

"A pig called Beans—"

"*Beans: An Extraordinary Pig Tale*?"

"Yes!"

He smiled and turned his body excitedly to face her, spilling some of his tea on her sofa as he did so. He wiped absently at the cushion as he talked.

"Oh my God. I read your book. I read it last year. I thought it was amazing. I actually pre-ordered it from Amazon when I heard that they were releasing it in paperback because I wanted to give it to my dad. It hasn't turned up yet, though."

She leaned across her coffee table and moved a newspaper to pick up one of three copies she had kept for herself. She handed it to him and told him he could keep it for his father. Bowie held her work in his fingers and flicked through the pages. Autumn had never been prouder. It was her fourth attempt at having her work published and, although she had known it was a good story, she had been surprised by its success.

"I was tired of unrealistic portrayals of farm animals in children's stories. So, I wrote the truth, as I saw it, from a pig's perspective. I wanted meat-eaters to read it, but the vegan community has been carrying my sales. I'm not complaining. I'd be mad to. But I do hope it might reach the right people eventually."

"As soon as you said that you'd written a book about a pig, I knew it must be this. I can't believe I'm meeting you."

She eyed him sceptically.

"I am not bullshitting you, I really have read it. And I really do love it."

"I can't believe you've read it."

"I can't believe Bluebell never told me you wrote it," he said. "Actually, I don't talk to her much about what I'm reading. We have completely different tastes. And she might have told me, actually, a while back, one afternoon when I wasn't very well. Now that I think about it, it's ringing a bell. Wow! This is like fate or something. You were in our lives long before we knew you. Bluebell will love this. She's crazy about this stuff!"

Autumn stopped herself from rolling her eyes, turning her attention back to real life.

"She's the most unique person I have ever met," Autumn said.

"An amazing sister," he said. "Protective."

He gave Autumn a pointed look. She winced, feeling suddenly guilty. He was confirming her concerns, that being here without speaking to Bluebell first was inappropriate. An uncomfortable silence fell between them. Autumn gripped the top of her beer bottle in frustration.

"I think I should get going," he said, standing up quite suddenly and moving towards the door. Autumn was incredulous. Had she been reading this completely wrong? Sure, there was the Bluebell thing, but she'd still been sure they were seconds away from kissing. He liked her work and was attracted to her, or so she'd thought. He'd been ranting and raving about fate and serendipity thirty seconds before, for crying out loud. But Bowie, who she wanted more and more with every step he took away from her, was nodding with purpose.

"It's late and you have your big meeting in a few hours."

She'd told him that and now he was using it as an excuse. It disappointed her but she nodded, standing up to follow him to the door.

"You're right," she said.

"And my family will be wondering where I am. And Bluebell would just hate this."

"OK," she said. He opened the door and turned to face her, pulling her into a hug and then dropping her before she'd had a chance to hold him too close.

"It was really nice to meet you. I hope to see you again one day. Thanks for the tea. Bye, Autumn."

And then he was gone. Autumn stared at the door, listening for his footsteps on her rickety old staircase, but there wasn't a sound. He was still standing outside. She put their empty teacups on her dresser and stood a little longer. Silence. Enough men had come and gone from this apartment for her to know it was impossible for them to leave without making a noise. Why was he still standing there? She didn't know what to do now. She knew she should let him go, but she didn't want to. Clearly, he did not want to leave either.

Groaning at her lack of self-control, she marched to the door and opened it. Bowie was standing at the top of her staircase, his head in his hands. He peered at her from above his fingertips. In his eyes she saw embarrassment and relief.

"Whatever it is, stop thinking about it." She held out her hand, her eyes pleading.

With one stride of his lanky legs, he was before her. He lifted her up and kissed her.

* * *

He tried to carry her into the bathroom, but she grabbed the wall and guided him to her bedroom, hoping she'd moved her dirty washing off the floor. As they toppled onto the bed, he was hard against her. She moaned. Every move he made was fraught with desperation. This was going to be good, she could tell. She freed herself from his grasp, reached to pull his T-shirt over his head, but he stopped her, grabbing her hand and pinning it to the pillow.

"I have a scar," he said. He froze and closed his eyes, in obvious embarrassment. Autumn didn't know what to do, so she lay there, watching the part of his neck where his heartbeat was still expressing the extent of his desire, and waiting for him to elaborate.

"Excuse me?" she said, when he didn't say anything further.

"I have a scar. On my stomach. Quite a big one, so I normally don't take my T-shirt off when I have sex."

She had no idea what she should say. Would he want her to reassure him? Probably.

"That's fine. It's OK. You don't have to take it off."

It wasn't what she'd had in mind when she'd imagined them together, but her insides were aching for him and she'd take him half-dressed over not at all. He wet his lips, pressing them together. She panicked. Had she said the wrong thing? Did he think she'd be disgusted by his scar? She was quite sure she wouldn't be. Should she tell him that? What if she saw it and was disgusted by it? Autumn didn't think she had ever seen a real scar. Not a proper one.

"Or you can take your top off if you want to. I'm sure it will be fine. I don't think I'll find the scar disgusting or anything."

Autumn felt him tense. That had definitely been the wrong thing to say. She scolded herself for being the most inadvertently uncouth person in the whole world. This was why she normally said virtually nothing at all. She was much cooler when she was acting aloof. Bowie released her wrist, but did not vacate the space between her legs. They were silent. Autumn, who had once traded sex acts for a safe place to sleep, marvelled at how difficult it had been to coax this bashful man into bed with her. She watched him blink at her, his head hovering a little way above hers, his hips still pinning hers against her mattress, his T-shirt still raised half-mast, and felt a type of terror she'd never experienced before. She was frightened he might try to leave again.

Autumn had never been so frustrated. She'd never found herself so incapable of predicting an outcome. She had expected Bowie to cast himself upon her and burst like a volcano for two reasons. First, that's what men usually did. Second, there'd been sexual tension raging between the two of them for several hours. She was eager to begin the inevitable and he'd thrown himself at her as though he was, too. But now, this.

She tried again. "I'm sure they're fine. I don't mind. Or care. I bet I wouldn't have even noticed. If I had, I wouldn't have said anything. I mean, I might have, but nothing bad."

Bowie's mouth twitched. She implored herself to shut up, but her mouth was moving again.

"I—"

"Stop, Autumn." He laughed.

She was glad he found her conversational clumsiness funny. She relaxed a little, but he rolled off her and it made her feel empty. Bowie dragged the duvet over himself and sighed. She wanted to climb beneath it with him, but was afraid he was putting up a barrier between them and she didn't want to push him if he wasn't comfortable with what they were doing.

"Sorry," he said.

"It's OK."

"It's just that I don't do this very often. Not with women like you."

Women like her? She used her eyes to question him. He reached out to tuck a piece of her hair behind her ear.

"Look at you. You're incredible. I bet you don't have a single flaw."

Autumn didn't know what to say. She worked hard to look the way she did. She practised yoga and went to the gym. She was confident and comfortable with how she looked. She couldn't really identify with someone who wasn't and didn't want to pretend that she could. She took his hand in hers.

"We don't have to do this, Bowie."

What was happening to her? She was ashamed to admit she would typically be irritated by dramatics like these, but she felt concerned for Bowie and didn't want him to feel uncomfortable around her.

"Get into bed with me?" he asked.

She nodded, thought about taking her clothes off, remembered she didn't want to pressure him, then slipped beneath her flowery bedspread fully clothed, shuffling as close to him as she could get. They lay side by side, wrapped in her floral duvet, staring at each other.

"Everything you do is so sexy," he said. It didn't seem like the kind of thing he would normally say, but she could tell he was being sincere. She smiled shyly.

"I don't do it on purpose."

"Yes, you do." He called her out. She giggled, then blushed. Despite her confidence, she wasn't used to people looking her in the face for so long.

"I like your freckles," he said.

"I like your eyes," she replied.

"I like your nose," he said.

"I like your mouth," she replied.

"I like your hair," he said.

"I like *your* hair," she replied.

They were silent for a minute or so, his fingertips drifting seductively over the bare skin of her neck.

"This is so stupid," he whispered. He was staring at her as though she was the best thing he'd ever seen.

"I know," she said. She wasn't quite sure which bit of 'this' he was referring to: his shyness, the intensity of what they were feeling, or a familiarity neither could explain. To her, all of it was stupid. They should be having sex by now.

He shuffled closer and kissed her with a level of tenderness she was not expecting. She resisted the urge to press her mouth more firmly into his. Autumn had never desired a man like this before. She knew she needed to move slowly. Bowie was nervous and needed to lead this. Her patience paid off as a few moments later, he moved himself on top of her and back between her legs, but he didn't try to take her clothes off. Instead he wrapped his arms around her back, so that every part of him was touching every part of her, and kissed her mouth for the longest time, then her neck, then her collarbone, so gently she wasn't sure if it was his lips or his breath she was feeling against her skin. For someone who did not do this very often, Bowie knew what he was doing. She shuddered in anticipation and felt him smile in response.

"Tease," she said. He laughed and it broke the ice. Until then she'd been frozen rigid, afraid anything she did might scare him away. Now, she let her hands wander across his chest and torso. When he did not object, she pushed him up onto his knees and pulled his T-shirt up over his head. His arms moved across his torso to protect her gaze from the scar he was so obviously self-conscious about, a scar she had forgotten existed until now. It was large. She didn't know anything about operations, but she knew a scar like that didn't come from insignificant situations. She guessed there had been an accident. Perhaps even a transplant. She could see now why it made him feel self-conscious. She bet there'd been women who'd lost interest in him because of it. She was ashamed to admit to herself that, had Bowie been any other man, she might have been one of them.

Pained by his uncertainty, she sat up.

"Don't do that, Bowie," she whispered, touching her fingertips to his cheek. "You're beautiful."

When he didn't move, she took hold of his wrists and pulled them gently away from his stomach. He resisted at first, then relaxed. She pulled him back on top of her and ran her hands to the button on his jeans, gently rocking herself against the weight of him and moaning when his erection hit her knickers.

There was no stopping him then. He ripped the rest of their clothes off, with no further hint of shame. She was about to stop him charging into her body to talk about protection when he took it upon himself.

"Tell me you have a condom," he said.

"In the drawer beside the bed."

He nodded, moving to retrieve one. Whilst he did what he needed to do, Autumn found herself inexplicably reassured by the fact he clearly didn't have one himself. Perhaps he was telling her the truth, maybe he really didn't do this very often. That felt important to her not because she would ever judge anyone for having sex often, but because it suddenly felt really important to her he hadn't lied about it. She wasn't sure why.

She was so busy ruminating that she missed him putting it on, and he was suddenly inside her. He was big and it took her by surprise. Autumn whimpered with pleasure. He lifted his head from the pillow beside her head.

"Are you OK?" he whispered. He sounded alarmed by her reaction. "I mean . . . I'm sorry, is this OK?"

She was breathless in her reply.

"Yes."

This first time was quick and ugly. They bit and scratched one another, until she came and he followed. The second time was sweeter and gentler. He stroked her hair and kissed her, no teeth this time. By the third time, they were sleepy and satisfied, but thoroughly relaxed with one another. The sex was slow and punctuated with conversation. It ended with her orgasm but without his when he said he could no longer keep his eyes open. He held her to him and quickly fell asleep.

Autumn lay beside him, staring at his sleeping face with an earnestness that might alarm him if he caught her. She felt like she might be in trouble.

* * *

She must have been dozing because suddenly her alarm was screaming at her. She'd last looked at her clock less than two hours before. Autumn loved sleep, but she didn't feel tired today. She was thrilled to find Bowie beside her and as excited to see her as she was to see him.

Still, she hurried their fourth tryst along. There was nothing for it. She really had to make it to her morning meeting and it was important that she looked presentable when she did. On no sleep, that was going to take some effort, and as an irregular user of public transport she still hadn't completely worked out how to navigate the complicated New York subway system, so she needed plenty of time to get there. Six months in this city had taught her she could not rely on online time estimations to accurately predict how long a journey would take. Anything could happen: a burst water pipe, a public emergency, a flash mob, a parade or protest. She thought Bowie understood, but he followed her into the shower and she realised his earlier passion had been prompted by his own lust rather than an understanding that she was in a rush.

Bowie was insatiable. Less than half an hour later, as she sat at her dressing table trying to put on her underwear, he knelt pointedly before her, running his hands up her smooth legs and eyeing her suggestively. She sighed. Oh, God, how she pined. Still, she pushed him playfully away.

"I have to get ready."

"I'm helping." He grinned, rolling her knickers vaguely in the right direction.

"You are not helping." She pushed him again, reluctantly raising her shoulders to stop him from nuzzling into her neck. He sighed and stood up, throwing himself dramatically onto her sofa.

"Love-hoarder," he mumbled sulkily. She laughed and cocked her head, desperate to lock away a memory of him until she could see him again. It was no good — she would forget what he looked like the moment he left. She was imaginative, but he was perfect to her now, like the sunset or a budding rose, and she knew her mind's eye could never do him justice. He was unimaginable — a dream — and he'd be nothing except a jumbled mess of frustratingly pretty features whenever she thought of him. She wondered if he was on social media. Bluebell was not as she didn't like it, and Autumn knew, somehow, that Bowie would feel the same.

"What's your last name?" she asked. Bowie blinked at her.

"Your best friend is my sister and you don't know our second name?"

"It never came up."

"It's Whittle," he said. "But don't try to find me on Facebook. I'm not on it."

"There's still Google," she said. He laughed a little nervously.

"What's yours?"

"You've read my book and you don't know my second name?" She mimicked him and he laughed. "Are you going to google me?" she asked.

"Maybe."

"It's Black."

"Any middle names?"

She didn't want to tell him. The reaction was always the same.

"Rain."

He laughed.

"Your name is Bowie and your sister is called Bluebell — you're in no position to laugh about names."

"That's *why* I get to laugh," he said.

"Don't you have a job to get to too?" she said teasingly. "Bills to pay? Bread to put on tables?"

He scrunched up his face. "You really don't know anything about our family, huh?"

She felt her mood deflate. No, she didn't. Both Bluebell and Bowie had managed to make her feel as though she had known them for ever without really telling her anything about themselves at all. He sensed her apprehension.

"I do have a job, but I don't need to get to it."

"What do you do?"

"I'm a songwriter and musical director. I'm in the theatre."

She smiled, turning back to her mirror.

"What?" He sounded a little defensive.

"Of course you are." She smirked sarcastically, watching him in her mirror.

"Don't be like that. I bet it annoys you to death when people snicker at you being a writer, and look at you. You're wildly successful."

She looked pointedly around her tiny flat. It had four rooms: a living room she had struggled to squeeze a sofa, a television, a coffee table and a dressing table into, a bedroom with just enough floor space for two people to slip past one another if they needed to, a functional kitchen and a teeny tiny bathroom. Autumn could walk across the entire apartment in ten strides. Bowie could probably do it in five. Still, she'd done her best with it. She'd ripped the shoddy carpets up and painted the floors white to lighten up the rooms, adorning each of them with pale pink rugs that matched her curtains. There were blankets and cushions everywhere, and attractive antique furnishings. She had made it the best it could be.

She scoffed. "*Wildly successful?* Sure I am."

"You live in Manhattan," he said.

"I can only afford to do that because I flirted with my landlord, Walter, until he asked me what I could afford to pay." She was worried about how he might react to her admission, but he laughed.

"Doesn't he want anything in return?"

"He's about a hundred and two years old," Autumn said, exaggerating. Bowie laughed again. "He doesn't need the money. He just wanted a tenant who wouldn't cause him any trouble."

"Well, you look like all sorts of trouble to me."

"I'm not the kind of trouble he's afraid of," she said. "I bring him food and cigarettes. Sometimes I clean his apartment for him. I'm undisruptive and quiet."

"That's not my experience of you." Bowie smirked. She blushed and he smiled. "Well, you can afford to live in New York. That's impressive. And success isn't measured by the things you own, it's measured by how happy your heart is."

He stood up and walked towards her, leaning down to bring his face close to hers. It was an incredibly intimate gesture.

"Is your heart happy, Autumn?"

She kissed him. She thought it might be the first time she had ever moved in to kiss a man first. She pulled away before they got too caught up in each other.

"What are you doing to me, Bowie?"

"Magic," he said, standing up. He looked thoroughly pleased with himself. He reached out and gestured for her to join him on his feet, cupping her face in his hands. "Can I see you tonight?"

"Yes," she said.

"Good. I don't have a mobile phone, but write your number on my hand and I'll call you later."

"From a payphone?" she asked.

"Probably."

She shook her head as she wrote.

"No mobile phone, no Facebook. You're the most bohemian person I've ever met."

He smiled, kissed her nose and turned on his heel. Hopeful and excited, Autumn watched from the door as he lumbered, ungracefully but with absolute purpose, down the stairs and across the hall, swinging his arms to a tune and whistling a song as he went.

***

How sure she had been before she'd met Bowie that instant connections were the invention of romantic minds. How adamantly she had believed that real love did not exist. Autumn revisited their first evening together many times in the years that followed. She could never figure out what it was he had done differently to everybody else. She'd compared him to the dozens of other men she'd slept with in the run-up to their meeting, analysing their conversations, desperately searching for something he might have said or done to forge the connection that had formed between them the second their eyes met. Why had her heart chosen this man? Plenty of perfectly adequate potential partners had presented themselves over the years, some more impressive than Bowie at first glance, and Autumn had never been interested in any of them.

She searched, but there was nothing there out of the ordinary. No perfect storm, no algorithm, no rhyme or reason, no explanation. It just was. Their love for each other had been instant and impossible to ignore.

Celestial, even.

CHAPTER 4

He possessed her every thought that morning. Her entire body felt invaded by him. Everywhere she went, despite the stench of petrol fumes and food, Autumn could smell Bowie on her skin. It was incredibly distracting and she could think of hardly anything else except when she would see him again. It made her mad. She needed to be sensible. She had not been exaggerating the importance of this meeting. The UK branch of her publishers was in love with her, but the American branch might not be so easily influenced. She needed to focus.

The coffee shop they'd agreed to meet in was swanky, not at all like the places she usually frequented. She was relieved when a man arrived. She was much calmer negotiating with men than with women. They were typically easier for her to charm through flirty smiles and a strategic flick of her hair.

His name was Jim. He was tall, with dark hair and a pretty smile.

"I'm pleased to note your strong Instagram following and that you take advantage of social trends," he said, replying to a text message as he spoke. Autumn tried to tell him her writing was not about taking advantage of anyone, but she could tell he didn't care, so she stopped talking. He was paying her to write and putting it out there. That was all that mattered.

When she finally had Jim's full attention, she told him the details of her next project, which he'd asked to see before she showed it to any other publishers. He was a little disheartened to learn it was about chickens and not the stray dog story she had pitched to his assistant on the telephone, but she told him the plight of egg-laying hens was a more pressing issue for vegans, and would likely be better received by fans of her work. Since they were her biggest supporters, it made sense to make them happy. He listened intently, but ordered an egg sandwich to take away with him for lunch. He agreed Autumn should write about what inspired her and gave her permission to submit a first draft. She was thrilled to negotiate a significant advance should her manuscript be accepted, which would give her plenty of time to write her book without worrying about eating too far into her savings. She felt proud of herself. She was powerful.

She checked her phone the second Jim said goodbye, certain she'd have a voicemail from Bowie. There was nothing. Her heart sank. She chided herself. It had only been half a day. Tired, she moved to cross the road to take the subway home, where she planned on snatching a few hours of sleep.

"How did it go?" someone asked from behind her. She recognised Bluebell's voice. Bluebell, sister of her lover, who had been on her mind, dancing in the periphery, all day. Guilt and shame coursed through her body. She fought hard to hide them from her features as she turned to face her friend. Bluebell looked flustered. She was fishing through her purse. It gave Autumn the ten seconds or so she needed to hide her jitters. "Sorry I'm late," Bluebell added.

"What are you doing here?" Autumn asked. She was sick with shock. Bluebell, who was still faffing with her bank cards, replied absentmindedly.

"I said I'd meet you here," she said. "Don't you remember?"

Autumn shook her head. She urged herself to act naturally — to hug her friend and express her delight at her presence like she usually would — but she felt too guilty to manage it. Plus, she was quite sure Bluebell would not want Autumn's grubby sex hands all over her. She felt awful. In the light and sensibleness of the morning, she was now even more certain that Bluebell would definitely not be OK with her doing what she had done with Bowie, the brother her friend adored, five times in just less than seven hours. She swallowed audibly. Bluebell heard it. She tossed her purse back into her bag, pouting.

"You're mad at me, aren't you?" she said.

Autumn focused very carefully on the inflection in her answer.

"Why would I be mad at you?"

"Because I forced you to come out last night then bailed on you for Adam?"

Autumn had completely forgotten.

"No." She shook her head. "I'm not mad."

Bluebell had actually done her a favour, although she didn't know it yet.

"Well, I'm sorry." Bluebell sighed. "It was a shitty thing to do."

"Don't worry about it." Autumn shook her head again. Bluebell smiled sweetly and stepped forward, taking Autumn's hand and swaying playfully from side to side.

"Well, I feel bad," she said. "Let me buy you a coffee to apologise? You can tell me about your meeting and I can tell you how annoying Adam is."

Without waiting for an answer, Bluebell gracefully turned their handholding to arm-linking, leading Autumn in an unfamiliar direction.

"And thank you for understanding," she added. "I knew you would. You really are a truly great friend."

* * *

Bluebell was still regaling Autumn with tales of the evening before when their coffee arrived twenty minutes later.

"So, basically, we're exactly where we were before. I want to sleep with him, but I don't want him to be my boyfriend, but he only wants to be with me, so he says he won't sleep with me again until I agree not to sleep with anyone else, which is ridiculous, because I really couldn't care less who he puts his dick in, and I don't see why he cares so much about who puts their dick in me, do you know what I mean?"

Autumn did know what she meant, so she nodded. She didn't mind Bluebell's rambling. It was a welcome distraction from her own torturous thoughts. Bluebell continued.

"We had amazing sex, then a massive fight, then amazing sex again. I don't know why he won't just do what I want him to do. Men are so frustrating."

Autumn checked her phone. Still nothing.

"How was Marley?" Bluebell asked.

Autumn snapped to attention. "Marley?"

Bluebell's eyes went wide and she gasped.

"He didn't hit on you, did he? Was he pestering you? He swore that he sat in the front seat of the cab and you sat in the back."

Bluebell stopped suddenly and stared straight at Autumn.

"But I know he had a girl home last night," she continued in a foreboding tone. "I heard him ushering her out this morning. It wasn't you, was it?"

Autumn was quick to reassure her. "No, it wasn't me. Marley was a perfect gentleman."

She felt bad for withholding the truth, but guessed it was imperative she play along with whatever Marley had told Bluebell. Bowie must have asked his brother to lie about how she'd gotten home and who she'd gone with, which meant he wasn't ready for Bluebell to know about them yet. She was relieved to have an excuse to be secretive besides her own cowardice.

"Oh, good!" Bluebell looked relieved. Autumn tried, unsuccessfully, to push rude images of Bluebell's other brother out of her mind. "I was worried there for a minute. We're not supposed to sleep with each other's friends anymore. Marley screwed every one of my school friends when we were younger and it caused no end of drama. And Bowie, actually, though he was a little bit better behaved. Marginally."

"You're sleeping with Adam," Autumn said pointedly.

"Yeah, exactly," Bluebell said. "We fight about it all the time. They aren't really friends, they're just in the same band, but when it's convenient for Marley he says they're best mates, so you would be fair game as far as he was concerned. You're just his type, too."

In the interest of acting normal, Autumn forced herself to laugh. It took great effort. She checked her phone. Nothing.

"Did you meet Bowie last night?" Bluebell asked. "Mum said he went in the end."

Autumn nodded.

"He's lovely, isn't he?" Bluebell asked.

Autumn agreed. "Quite lovely."

"He's one hundred per cent my favourite brother." Bluebell grinned. "Don't tell the others."

Autumn forced herself to smile. To her relief, Bluebell changed the subject.

* * *

Autumn was angrier with herself than she had ever been with anybody else ever. She seethed as she swigged from a bottle of the beer she'd bought for them to share, glaring at the clock on her mantelpiece. It was midnight. It felt much later, but it was still late enough.

Until ten minutes ago, she had been hoping Bowie might still turn up. She'd finally realised he wasn't coming. Not only that, he hadn't even bothered to call and tell her he couldn't make it. She felt pathetic. If he had been any other man she'd have given up hours ago. She'd have gone out in search of someone else to have fun with, or stayed in to catch up on the sleep she'd lost the night before. For Bowie, Autumn had wasted time sitting at home and stewing. It made her exceedingly angry. Not with Bowie, but with herself.

There was nobody to talk to about it. Bluebell, for obvious reasons, couldn't know, and any friends she had in England — and there weren't many — would think it was hilarious if she called to ask them for advice about a man. Her friends had learned at an early age that Autumn was drastically less than sympathetic when they discussed concerns of the heart. She had never been able to empathise with people who caught feelings and felt hurt when somebody rejected them. She'd suggest they find someone who wanted them and move on. She'd been so thoroughly unsupportive that they'd stopped coming to her with their romantic woes. She annoyed them. She didn't understand because she couldn't, they concluded. *It must be so nice to be Autumn*, they'd said. *How easy it must be to attract and keep a man when you're so beautiful.* Autumn would blush and lie, telling them her prettiness had nothing to do with it. They would tut, and tell her to stay away from their boyfriends. The last thing they needed was Autumn batting her big green eyes at men they were trying to keep.

They had warned her, too. One day it would happen to her, then she would know how they felt. Well, here she was. Admitting to them that a man she barely knew had made her feel this way was not something her pride would ever let her do. She did, however, resolve to be more understanding if they ever came to her to share their heartache again, though she knew they wouldn't. They hadn't come to her for sympathy for years. In fact, she hadn't heard from either of them in quite a while. She wasn't even sure they were friends anymore.

As her mind ran wild through the witching hour, Autumn realised she was actually embarrassed. She'd told this man he was beautiful. She'd kissed his scar and chased him when he'd tried to leave. She was becoming increasingly suspicious he had taken her to bed to irritate Bluebell. The thought had been torturing her since her friend's words at lunchtime.

Also, Bluebell had very suddenly abandoned their coffee date. She'd stepped outside to speak to Marley on the telephone and when she'd returned, she'd told Autumn she had to go. She'd been shaking and frantic, but was gone before Autumn could ask what was wrong. Autumn had texted her a couple of times since to check if she was all right and hadn't had a response.

Oh, God!

Bluebell definitely knew. Autumn could think of no other reason her friend would ignore her messages. The twins must have told her.

Autumn gave in to her tears. She'd lost the only friend who understood her. The only woman who'd ever treated her like a sister instead of competition. Unlike the friends Autumn had somehow acquired in childhood, Bluebell had never made her feel like she had to tone herself down. In fact, Bluebell encouraged her to be her very best self. She was a staunch advocate of women supporting women. Autumn had known and loved that about her since the day they had met.

"Why do men expect us to pretend we don't know we're beautiful?" she'd asked Autumn that very morning. Autumn had laughed, not sure what to say. "You're watching a movie and the leading lady is beautiful. I mean, jaw-droppingly stunning. Incredible to levels that are completely unattainable by most mere mortal women. That's why she's an actress, right? She's beaten millions of other wannabe actresses to win the part because she's vaguely-to-incredibly talented and also immensely attractive. Then they get her on camera and ask her to play a woman who everyone else in the world can clearly see is perfect, but she's not supposed to know it herself. It's such a hackneyed narrative in movies and songs. Everyone wants a beautiful girl who doesn't know she's beautiful. It's all about male insecurity. Men don't want their beautiful woman to know that she's beautiful because then she might leave. They want her to be thoroughly humble, grateful and surprised every time they tell her that they think she looks nice. It's fucking bullshit and I got sick of playing the game years ago. If someone tells me they think I'm beautiful, I tell them that I think so too. You'd be surprised by how many men that enrages. It cuts through all their bullshit, though. Because it is fucking bullshit. Women can't even own their own beauty these days. The world is fucked. And what about all the average-looking actresses? Or the not-so-good-looking ones? Those women are glorious and the pretty women are stealing their parts because of the patriarchy and its insistence that even women who don't meet traditional beauty standards must be secretly beautiful. Oh, I could go on about this for ages."

And she would have, Autumn was sure of it, if she hadn't had to rush off.

Autumn and Bluebell had spent so much time together Autumn had come to take this pro-woman outlook for granted. She knew there were other girls like Bluebell out there, but they were few and far between. Autumn might never have another friend like her again and she had thrown her away over a man.

They'd only ever argued once and it had been for good reason. Bluebell had tried to encourage Autumn to have group sex on a date she'd arranged spontaneously with some men they'd met in a nightclub. Autumn hadn't wanted to participate and Bluebell had drunkenly assumed it was because she'd thought it was slutty. Autumn had been hurt by her assumption. She'd believed that her new friend knew the kind of person that she was by then, and judgemental — about this kind of thing at least — Autumn was not. Thankfully, Bluebell had realised almost immediately that she was being unreasonable and had graciously admitted she was wrong.

"I'm being a bitch, aren't I? You know your own mind. I know you do. I'm sorry, Autumn. You don't have to come with us if you don't want to."

And that was that. Argument over. Bluebell left to take part in 'the best orgy ever' and Autumn had happily gone home on her own and eaten Chinese food in bed by herself. She was glad she had. She could barely begin to imagine how complicated this situation with Bowie would be if she'd ever had sex with Bluebell.

She sighed, tired of herself. She had hoped it might transpire that she was more upset at her surprising reaction to Bowie's absence than the absence itself — that would be easier to deal with — but her thoughts betrayed her and it didn't seem to be the case. Autumn shook her head and scolded herself, trying to eradicate thoughts of him from her mind.

"Stop it. You loser."

She forced herself to go to bed.

* * *

Autumn barely slept and, without sexual endorphins to wake her up, getting out of bed was a real effort. She felt groggy and disgusting. She wasn't sure what time she'd eventually fallen asleep, but she knew she'd spent several hours crying into her pillow before eventually succumbing. She was embarrassed about that, but trying, with real effort, to give herself a break. She had always been honest with herself about the way she was feeling and didn't think she should be exceptionally cruel to herself because of the silly way her heart had behaved and how it had left her reeling. She should let herself cry if she needed to. It wasn't as though she was being unnecessarily dramatic. She had good cause to be upset — she felt utterly alone. She'd thought those days were over. She wanted a hug, which was most unusual. It was almost torturous enough a feeling to wish she had never opened up in the first place, to Bluebell or to Bowie. Before she had known either of them existed, she'd been fine. Now, it seemed she was the same as most other people — her happiness relied at least a little bit on the way people treated her.

She pulled on a pair of jeans, a white T-shirt and a pair of pumps. She hadn't had chance to eat much since the piece of cake she'd shared with Bowie and she was starving. She decided to head to a café, grab herself a coffee and a sandwich, and sit on a window seat and write. Today was about self-care and this was her favourite thing to do. She knew it would make her feel better.

Getting there took every ounce of energy she had and felt like an extreme effort, but she was feeling much better by lunchtime. She'd spent several hours consumed by writing her second book. Intricate sentences flowed freely from her fingertips and she hardly thought of anything except the world she was creating, seemingly from nowhere. She paused only to marvel at the gift she had been given and how much it had done to help her. She'd been using it to escape reality since she had been a child, creating the most wonderful friends for herself, and, as she did, forgetting the pain that came with living in the real world. It had helped her ignore how little she was loved. It had helped her pretend she was not alone.

She paused in the early afternoon to write a poem, something she had not done in a while. Writing novels came easily to Autumn, no matter what mood she was in, but poems were different. She had to be feeling very strongly about something to pull words together in a way that made sense as poetry. She switched from writing on her laptop to a trusty pen and paper and, without much thought, wrote down the way she was feeling. She re-read it, crossed a few things out, then re-read it again.

> *You'll never be mine outside of my mind and that's all right with me.*
> *I long too strongly to own your gaze.*
>
> *I'm quite sure that you're sweeter than a spring blue sky, but skies split sometimes,*
> *and I already know I couldn't weather the thunder.*
>
> *If you were to love me with any less strength than that of a raging sea, it would destroy me.*
>
> *So stay in my head, where I'm safe from your wide-eyed indifference.*
>
> *Live in my imagination.*
> *Save me the bitterness of your disinterest.*

*And I'll plead with a star,
to keep the wonder of your universe,
far from me.*

*My perfect friend, my fanciful lover, may we never meet again
beyond fantasy.*

It needed work, but she was quite happy with what she had written. Apparently she was as inspired by heartbreak as everybody else seemed to be.

She didn't think to check her phone in the morning or early afternoon, but glanced at it at around three o'clock. There was still nothing from Bluebell. This was the longest she'd gone without speaking to her friend. She felt her stomach twist with worry and stared, despondently, around the café. She could try to ignore it, but the real world was there: big, empty and waiting for her.

She felt, very suddenly, as though she needed sleep.

***

Autumn was so distracted by exhaustion she almost missed the note tied to the railing at the bottom of her staircase. She was on the third step when she spotted it, fluttering hopefully in the ever-present hallway draught. As she was untying it, her neighbour and landlord, Walter, emerged from his flat. He feigned surprise to see her but had, quite obviously, been waiting for her.

"A young man knocked on my door earlier and asked me for a pen," he said.

"Oh," Autumn said. "Thanks."

She untied the note and guarded it with her hand, stepping pointedly up onto the first step. Walter was nosy enough to ask her what it said if she read it in front of him. It had to be from Bowie. Anyone else would have texted her. She started to climb.

"I've read it." Walter blurted out the words.

She stopped, turned, and stared at him.

"I'm sorry." He grinned. "I couldn't help myself. I don't know why he didn't put it under your door."

She was horrified.

"Don't ever read my post again, Walter."

She was also amused and he could tell. He laughed.

"He was a nice boy," he said. "Better than those other boys you bring back here sometimes. He talked to me for ages. Mainly about you. I told him stuff."

"Oh God." Autumn whined, rubbing her free hand over her face.

"Only good stuff. He likes you — I can tell. He wanted to know all about you."

Walter would have plenty to tell him, too. He and Autumn had spent a lot of time together since she had arrived. Despite his blabbermouth and how often he moaned about the news, she couldn't bring herself to dislike him. Walter was good-natured and funny. He'd spent thirty years of his life working as a security guard and then inherited a fortune from his late cousin. He had never been married, but spent thirty-five years taking care of his best friend's widow, Margaret. She'd passed away only eighteen months before. Walter had waited until then to admit to himself that he had always loved her. Now, he spent his days regretting the things he'd never said. Autumn wanted to write that story one day. She was waiting for the right time to ask his permission.

Though she had moved away from her little town to live in London, Autumn had been entirely unprepared for how big New York City was. She had not realised just how tiny she would feel when surrounded by permanent crowding and the tallest buildings she had ever seen. There were barely any streets that didn't hum with activity all through the day and night. No matter where she was, she always felt crammed in, the way one might feel even in the quietest corner of a busy nightclub. She had been hugely overwhelmed by it at first, but was slowly getting used to the atmosphere here.

Still, she knew this was not her forever home. She'd been longing for a cottage with a vegetable patch for as long as she could remember. City life was necessary for her right now, but she planned to settle down somewhere with less grey and more green one day.

Walter, who was still loitering, had been born and bred in New York. He loved it here and didn't understand why anyone would want to leave. Despite an issue with his leg that made it difficult for him to climb the stairs to his apartment, he refused to move. Autumn expressed her concerns about his health and safety pretty much every time she saw him — if there was a fire he'd have absolutely no chance of making it out of the building — but he'd insisted he would never leave his home, no matter how difficult or dangerous things became. He would starve and die up there first, he'd said. She'd argued with him a lot about it at first, but eventually realised there was no point. Walter's opinions were as strong as his American accent. He would not be moved.

They'd had many heated debates, mainly about veganism, but Autumn continued to visit Walter, even if only for a few minutes, most afternoons. They settled eventually into talking about things they agreed on, like the state of immigration, the national healthcare tragedy and the obesity epidemic. He had been good company as she'd settled in. For a while, he had been her only friend for thousands of miles. Like most friends, they agreed to disagree on a lot for the sake of keeping the peace. Still, despite several conversations about veganism, he was obsessed with offering her ham sandwiches, sometimes leaving them on the stairs for her tea, then pretending he didn't understand what he had done wrong when she redelivered them to him. He put it down to his age, and, most of the time, she couldn't be bothered to argue. Autumn knew he was trying to be kind. He did not accept a world in which being vegan was healthy and blamed her skinniness on her diet.

She admired him now, his eyes sparkling with nosiness, and resolved to forgive him. He lived through her experiences.

"Thanks, Walter," she said.

"Be nice to him, Autumn."

He turned and went back inside. If only it were that simple, she thought, as she opened the note on the staircase.

I'll come back later. I can explain. Bowie.

Her body flooded with the kind of anxiety-inducing dread she'd felt often in England, but hadn't experienced since she'd moved to New York. Her heart quickened, her chest hurt and she felt like she couldn't suck in enough oxygen. She didn't want to see him. Sleeping with him had been the wrong thing to do. She might have lost a friend over it. Perhaps if she just never saw him again, she could go back to life before him. When she and Bluebell had been firm friends, in constant contact, when she had known who she was and what she wanted, and all had been right with the world. She had no desire to be around a man who made her feel so vulnerable. She'd never allowed anyone to have such control over her.

Panicking a little bit, she let herself in, tossed Bowie's note in the bin and picked up the phone to call a man she'd been ignoring for a fortnight. They'd met in a bookshop and exchanged numbers, but she had been too busy having fun with Bluebell and meeting other people to return his calls. She asked him to dinner. Despite the short notice, he agreed to meet her in an hour.

Autumn didn't feel remotely like going out, but she didn't know how else to avoid Bowie. She thought about replacing the note he'd left her with another asking him to leave her alone, but suspected he'd ignore it. If he started banging on the door, Walter would come out and tell him she was inside. She couldn't be bothered with the drama. It was a better idea to make sure she was unavailable until he got the hint and left her alone. She'd need a distraction in the form of a man to pull that off. She hoped that this one was handsome. She couldn't remember what he looked like and when she tried, she only saw Bowie.

She put on a flowery mini-dress and blazer, brogues, and oversized earrings. Just before she left, she kicked the brogues off, slipping her feet into a pair of plain black heels, instead. She very rarely wore them, but they made her feel sexier, and she really wanted to feel good.

She had just set off down the first set of steps when she ran into Bowie. He was almost at the top, and looked rather dramatically breathless. They froze, each with one foot in front of the other, so that it might look to anyone who saw them as though they were intending to collide into one mass. He planted his gaze on hers.

"Autumn," he said.

He said her name as though he could still taste her on his tongue. Her attraction to him overwhelmed her. In a conscious effort to put a barrier between them, she clutched her bag to her chest.

"I'm going out," she said. Bowie made no effort to hide his disappointment. He stared at the carpet for a moment, then tentatively raised his gaze to look at her again. She knew he'd taken those few seconds to work through all possibilities, and willed him not to ask her to elaborate.

"Date?" he asked her cautiously. She nodded. She was acting much colder than she'd meant to. She heard his breath catch in his throat and willed herself to give him nothing but stiff posture and an expressionless face, but her pride was getting in the way. She waited for him to say something, but he was silent.

"I couldn't let you know because I don't have your number and you didn't call when you said you would," she said, a little snippily. He opened his mouth to speak, then closed it again. His shoulders slumped low and he sighed. He had given up. Disheartened by his lack of fight, she started down the stairs again.

She hoped he might follow her, but he didn't.

* * *

Autumn spent the next few hours trying to focus on what the handsome man in front of her was saying, but she couldn't.

It wasn't because he wasn't interesting — he was a humanitarian aid worker and had spent most of their evening together telling her about the most dangerous parts of the world. Autumn, who was not well-travelled, would usually be enthralled, but tonight she was too consumed by her lingering feelings for Bowie to care even a little bit about what Anthony had to say.

Seeing Bowie again had reminded Autumn that he wore his heart on his sleeve. He was not the type of person to hide how he felt about a person or a situation — his sister was the same. There was probably a perfectly valid reason he couldn't see her last night, but Autumn had overreacted and made herself look like a fool. Her head had shoved her heart aside. She had been spiteful to him and that didn't sit well with her at all. She was unpleasant to men only when they deserved it, but Bowie didn't, he was kind and good. She was ashamed of herself.

She knew that the right thing to do was to be honest about everything. She should tell this lovely man her mind was on someone else. She should leave the restaurant, call Bluebell, explain what had happened, apologise for breaking their unspoken code of friendship, and ask for a way to contact her brother, but she hadn't been able to bring herself to do that yet because she was afraid. Everything had gone too far. Bluebell adored Bowie, and Autumn would be in trouble not only for sleeping with him, but for upsetting him afterwards, too.

When the waitress asked them if they wanted coffee or desserts, Autumn politely declined. A coffee forfeit on a date like this would ordinarily occur in order to fast-track the inevitable: coffee and sex at her place. If it wasn't for Bowie and the way she felt about him, she'd have taken Anthony home with her. He was well-dressed, intelligent and articulate. He had beautiful brown eyes and greying hair. There was a protective quality about him she liked. But she couldn't wait to get away and she certainly couldn't bear the thought of his hands on her.

"I have to go, actually," she said. He seemed disappointed.

"Oh. OK. We'll pay, then, please."

The waitress smiled sweetly and nodded. She had been batting her eyelashes at Anthony all evening. Autumn couldn't say she blamed her. He really was exceptionally handsome. In spite of her own lack of interest, she felt lucky to have had his attention, and a little sad she wasn't in the right frame of mind to receive it.

"I'm sorry," she said. "I have a really early meeting tomorrow, and—"

"It's fine." Anthony smiled. "You're not into it. Don't worry. It happens."

His gentle words made Autumn feel guilty, but when Anthony hugged her goodbye a few moments later, he held on to her for longer than was necessary, and his hand was a little too close to her backside.

Perhaps he was not such a nice guy after all.

* * *

Autumn insisted she could flag her own taxi, waved goodbye to Anthony, then sheltered in the restaurant doorway to think seriously about what she should do next. She absently pulled out her mobile phone, contemplating calling Bluebell to come clean. She wanted to speak to Bowie and that was the only way she could get hold of him. She pressed the button that lit up the screen and recoiled in surprise. She had six missed calls from her friend. Autumn panicked. Bluebell never did this. She hated talking on the telephone and would absolutely choose to send a text message unless she had no choice. Something was wrong. With shaking hands, Autumn called her back, willing her to pick up. When she did, she didn't even say hello.

"Where are you?"

Bluebell sounded frustrated.

"I've been out for dinner. Is everything OK?"

"I'm at your apartment with Bowie. Can you come straight here?"

CHAPTER 5

Autumn didn't need to ask how they'd gotten in. Bluebell knew Walter had a spare key because Autumn was always locking herself out. Her neighbour loved Bluebell because she flirted with him and told him he was handsome, and he'd have given her the key the second she asked for it.

They were sitting on her sofa. Bowie was holding his head in his hands and Bluebell was sitting beside him, holding a bowl of cooked plain pasta. It looked like she was trying to feed it to him. They stared up at her when she opened the door, their fretful features as foreboding as she felt. They were about to drop a bomb on her life — she could see it in their body language. She fought the urge to turn around and leave them there.

"What the hell is going on?" she asked.

"I'm going to give you some space," Bluebell said, taking a forkful of pasta for herself and picking up a coffee she'd obviously helped herself to. She moved into the bedroom. She would still hear everything — the walls were like paper — but Autumn was more alarmed to realise that Bluebell must know she and Bowie had slept together, and yet she hadn't mentioned it. Not even to tease Autumn. Something was seriously wrong. She found herself annoyed at them both. She'd always hated drama. It was the main reason she didn't get properly involved with anyone. Now, thanks to the first friend she'd let into her life in years and the first man she had ever liked, it looked like she was knee-deep in it. In that moment — sick of their flightiness, their unpredictability and their self-centredness — Autumn wished she'd never met either of them. She no longer liked the way they made her feel, as though she was the most important person in the world to them one minute, then absolutely nothing to them a moment later. She tried not to glare at Bowie, but she couldn't help it. He was staring at the floor.

She prompted him. "Bowie?"

His eyes met hers.

"Can you sit down, please?" he asked.

"Do I need to?"

"Yes." He swallowed. "I think you do."

Autumn threw her bag on the floor and sat down opposite him on her dressing-table stool. She didn't want to sit beside him. She was afraid to. She could smell his alluring aroma from across the room and she didn't trust herself not to forgive him instantly on the basis he smelled so appealing to her. He watched her, saying nothing. Autumn braced herself.

"Go on." She urged him to speak.

"I'm really ill," he said.

Autumn frowned. She hadn't been expecting that. She'd been sure he'd been about to admit to having a girlfriend or offer her a feeble excuse of some sort. She felt relieved, until he continued. "Not just ill," he said. "Really, properly ill. I have a diagnosis, I mean. I should have told you before but everything was so perfect, and then yesterday, after I left you, I got so tired I couldn't get out of bed. I couldn't get Marley on his own to ask him to call you and the only other person I could get to let you know was Bluebell, but I didn't know how she would react . . ."

Bowie was becoming hysterical. Autumn suspected he was going to cry and she wasn't sure how she'd feel if he did.

Where she was from, men didn't show their emotions so readily. Without thinking too much about it, she crossed the room to comfort him. He opened his arms and pulled her down onto the sofa, clutching her to him.

"Mum forced me into the shower," he said. "And it washed your number off my hand. I came over as soon as I could, but you didn't come home and I had to find somewhere to rest, so I put the note on your stairs and went to a hotel around the corner to sleep. I came back the second I'd woken up, but walking up and down stairs is really hard for me sometimes, I'm really tired and my back hurts. After I saw you on the stairs and you left for your date, I needed to stop for a rest, so I finished the climb and sat down on your landing, but I was in so much pain. I knew I couldn't handle walking back down on my own, I was stuck at the bottom of your fucking spiral staircase, on the landing outside your neighbour's apartment. I couldn't just stay here. If you'd come back with that guy, Autumn . . . I was terrified about how that would make me feel. I had to knock on your neighbour's door so I could call someone from his phone. Marley wasn't answering, so it had to be Bluebell because hers is the only other phone number I know off by heart. I obviously had to tell her everything when she got here, though she had pretty much guessed it all by then."

Autumn couldn't quite believe what she was hearing. She felt upset with herself. If only she had given him a chance to explain earlier.

"I'm so sorry, Bowie," she said. "I had no idea."

"Please don't apologise. How could you know? It's my own stupid fault. I should have told you. I shouldn't have let the other night go as far as I did without telling you what I'm going through, but it was perfect and it was so good to be around someone who doesn't treat me like a china doll for once."

"What's wrong with you?" she asked. It felt like a really harsh way to ask the question, but she couldn't think of any other way to word it.

"I have lymphoma. Do you know what that is?"

"Cancer?" she asked.

Bowie nodded. "It's cancer of the lymphatic system, a type of blood cancer. I was diagnosed when I was twenty-one with what's referred to as low-grade advanced stage non-Hodgkin lymphoma. It was slow-growing but diagnosis took so long there was a lot of it, so I had chemotherapy and a treatment called rituximab. It put me into remission for a while, but it's come back several times since then, most recently a year ago. It makes me so tired, I can't begin to explain how fatigued I feel some days. I shouldn't have promised you I'd come back because I didn't know I'd be able to. Some days I'm OK, like I was the other night. That was a good day for me, my pain was manageable and my fatigue was almost non-existent. That's why I turned up to the show to watch Marley. I haven't been able to do anything like that for ages, this cancer has stolen so much of my life. But yesterday, once I'd left here, I just felt worse and worse. I was so tired I could hardly keep my eyes open. I barely had the energy to get myself home. I got into bed and I couldn't get out again."

"That sounds terrible," she said sympathetically.

"I knew five minutes after we sat down in that café together that I wanted more from you than a one-night stand and I should have told you what you were getting yourself into. I'm really mad at myself."

"It's OK." She lied. He was right, he should have told her. Probably before they'd slept together, most certainly before the morning after. But she didn't think it was as big a deal as he was making it out to be. Now that she knew, they could handle it together. She could encourage him to sleep and excuse him if he wasn't feeling well. She moved in to kiss him, but he shook his head, swallowed, and said,

"I'm going to die, Autumn."

Autumn felt her body go rigid with shock. She searched his face for any hint of over-dramatisation, desperate for something, anything, but there was nothing. She no longer knew exactly what her own features were doing, but the ball in her throat told her she might cry, so she turned away from him, trying to hide her disbelief. Bowie let her absorb his words for a moment, then reached out to take each of her hands in his. She knew instinctively he'd done it because he needed her to listen to what he was saying, so she forced herself to look at him.

"My cancer has always been incurable. I've always known it was something I'd have to live with for the rest of my life. But it was low-grade, so slow-growing. I'd go into remission for years at a time, then it would come back, we'd monitor it and I'd manage the pain until it was time for treatment, then we'd go through the whole thing again, chemo, radiotherapy and other treatments, sometimes months at a time in hospital, the hair loss, the weight loss, the weakness, the sickness and the pain . . . pain I can't even describe, Autumn, just hoping I'd get more cancer-free time this time, that I'd be one of the many people who live to a ripe old age fighting this off whenever it shows up. But the last time a lump appeared and I was tested, I was told it was transforming into high grade non-Hodgkin's lymphoma. That means it grows quickly. It'll respond better to treatment, but there's a higher chance it will come straight back. And the treatment is . . . intense. I can't go through it again. These treatments, they're life-altering. They have a lasting impact on your body. They cause other issues, long-term side effects I don't want to deal with, not when I know it's going to get me eventually. So many people fight this disease successfully, but I've known for a while I'm not going to be one of them."

"Oh my God."

"I should have told you. There is no excuse."

She agreed with him. He absolutely should have told her. Not before the first time they had slept together, but as they'd talked over tea and cake. He should have told her then.

"Jesus Christ," she said, putting her head in her hands.

"Bluebell is furious with me," he said, lowering his voice. "And with you, for sleeping with me."

"Yes. Yes, I am."

They turned to look at Bluebell, standing in the bedroom doorway. Autumn wasn't sure how long she'd been there. She stared between them, then stalked across the room until she was in front of them, swinging her coffee cup in her hand. Autumn let go of Bowie.

"So, first you fuck my brother . . ." She was counting Autumn's transgressions on her fingers. "Then you meet me for lunch the next day and you don't think to mention it?"

Bowie opened his mouth to speak, but Bluebell gestured at him with her mug.

"Don't even get me started on you." Autumn thought she heard Bowie catch a laugh, but his sister either didn't notice or chose to ignore it, turning her attention back to Autumn, instead.

"I-I thought you'd be angry," Autumn said.

"I *am* fucking angry." Bluebell gesticulated wildly. "What on earth were you thinking?"

"I wasn't thinking."

"Come on, pal." Bluebell eyed her sceptically. "This is *me* you're talking to." She threw herself dramatically onto the stool beside Autumn's dressing table, slouching despondently.

"I know how much you love me," she continued. "You want me to believe you didn't give me a single thought in any of this?"

Autumn shook her head. "At first I did, but, then, no, I didn't. Not really. Not until the next day. I forgot he was your brother for most of the night."

Bluebell tried to hide her smirk, but couldn't. "I should fucking hope so, too," she mumbled.

Autumn was hit by a wave of relief. Once Bluebell's humour barrier had been broken down, Autumn knew she found it very difficult to return to an angry state. She was too light-hearted.

"Seriously though," Bluebell continued, deadpan. "I am worried, Autumn. I know what you can be like with men."

Autumn stiffened and felt Bowie tense beside her.

"No judgement, I'm exactly the same. You're my best friend, but that's my brother, Autumn." Bluebell shrugged. "That's all I'm saying."

"What *are* you like with men?" Bowie enquired. Autumn could tell from his tone that he was teasing her. She smiled sarcastically at Bluebell, then turned to Bowie. She impulsively reached for his hand again, and was relieved when he took hers gently in his. Their eyes met and they each blushed.

Bluebell sighed and stood up, turning to pick up her jacket.

"Well, this is a car crash waiting to happen. But you're adults, so what the hell has it got to do with me? Bowie, I'm going to leave you here. Please do not disappear again. I'll tell Mum you're feeling much better and staying out with Marley. I'll also tell Marley to lie to her if she asks and to pretend to be you when she calls to check on you later."

She paused, momentarily lost in thought. "He's a lying little shitbag as well, isn't he? Marley? He told me you shared a cab home the other night, Autumn, when he quite clearly had no idea where either of you were at the time."

"It's a twin thing," Bowie said.

Bluebell leaned down to hug him. She held him close, murmuring lovingly into his ear. "Can you take it easy? Actually get some sleep tonight? And tone down the marathon shagging sessions, will you? I don't know who you think you are."

Bowie laughed, pushing her away. "You're gross. Get out."

Bluebell skipped across the floor to the door, turning back to look at them when she reached it. Her eyes flicked from one to the other. She eyed their clasped hands with fondness. Autumn felt shy in front of her friend for the first time since the day they'd met. This was a new kind of vulnerability. She wasn't used to anyone seeing her act this intimately with someone, never mind a friend, and most certainly not Bluebell, who thought monogamy was against human nature and that it was stupid. It was just one of the many things they had agreed on until now. Bluebell would never say anything, but she would almost certainly be perturbed that Autumn was feeling a little differently since meeting her brother.

"I'm serious, guys. Please be careful. I mean, I personally don't think there's a much better way to go than in the middle of an orgasm, but I think Mum and Dad would quite like the six months or so they were promised."

Autumn reeled. *Six months?* That was no time at all. She tried to cover up her shock, but her reaction had been noticed by Bowie and Bluebell. They stopped conversing and looked at her. She tried to straighten her face, but she couldn't. *Six months?* But he was so sweet and lovely and . . .

"I'm going to let you two talk," Bluebell said. She looked a little teary. Bowie nodded, smiling lovingly at his sister. Bluebell blew him a kiss and then left.

* * *

Bowie threw up the second Bluebell had gone, into the coffee cup she'd left on the mantelpiece.

"I am so sorry," he said. "That happens quite a lot."

Autumn took it from him to wash. When she came back, he was sitting down again. She sat beside him, her hands clasped pointedly before her. She was afraid to touch him.

"Why do you vomit?" she asked.

"It's just stress. At least, I think it is. There could be a mass in my stomach. I've no idea where it's spread to. I'm just sort of . . . rolling with it."

She nodded, fixating on the stain he'd left on her sofa when he'd spilled his tea in an expression of excitement the night before last before. She had been tossing up the pros and cons of seducing him then, and things had seemed so complicated. She'd had no idea just how complex they really were. She didn't know what to say now. She was stunned by his revelation, and couldn't hide it. She was sad that he was suffering, and overwhelmed by this sudden impediment.

He spoke quietly to her.

"Whatever you're thinking is OK."

She didn't answer.

"Meeting you wasn't part of my plan," he added.

Before she could stop herself, Autumn started to cry. She couldn't help it. She felt so despondent. She'd seen a change in herself she had liked and felt as though the option to explore it had been ripped away from her. In the very best-case scenario, this would be difficult. She wasn't experienced at this relationship stuff even when it was easy. She figured she'd be useless at it if it was as tricky as Bowie and Bluebell were implying. On top of that, she felt so unbelievably sad for Bowie and for his family. Embarrassed, she covered her eyes with her hands.

"Oh, Autumn." Bowie sighed. "Please don't cry."

He shuffled towards her and she let herself fall against his chest. She liked it there; it made her feel safe. He held her tightly, whispering nonsense into her ear until she began to calm down.

"Maybe I need to just make this decision for you?" he said. Autumn wiped her eyes and pulled away.

"What decision?"

His face fell.

"For us to end this now."

She swallowed hard and nodded, wiping her tears and moving away from him. She felt a sudden need to protect herself. Bowie winced at the space she'd put between them.

"It's not what I want, Autumn. I—"

"It's because of what Bluebell said, isn't it? About the way I am with men."

Autumn let herself jump to the vilest conclusion: that he had found his excuse to cut her off. She knew most men wouldn't be comfortable with the number of sexual dalliances she'd had, even if they were self-proclaimed feminists. Judgement, especially from men, was something she and Bluebell had discussed a lot. Adam, the man Bluebell was sleeping with, had been quite nasty about Bluebell's attitude to sex on a number of occasions. It was born of insecurity, they both knew that, but it didn't make it any easier to navigate, nor was it any less disappointing when it happened.

Bowie stared at her and then laughed. She was taken aback. She tried to look away, but he put his finger beneath her chin, gently tilted her face to look at him, and fixed his eyes on hers, a disbelieving smile on his face. His gaze bewitched her.

"I don't care if you've slept with half of New York City. Your worth is not determined by how many men you've slept with. Not by me. Do you understand?"

She nodded.

"I only care that you're happy and about the way you treat me. OK?"

She nodded again, swallowing the lump in her throat.

"Do you want to do this?" he asked her.

She didn't need to ask him what he meant by 'this'. He was about to ask her if she wanted to be with him. Autumn felt shock and a curious urge to blurt yes all at once. She tried to give herself a silent talking to. She needed to think properly about this. This was a big responsibility. Starting a relationship would be complicated if Bowie being Bluebell's brother was the only tricky part of this, but they wouldn't only have to navigate Bluebell's feelings, they were dealing with a serious disease and all its symptoms. She knew nothing about lymphoma except what he'd told her very briefly, but it sounded terrible. Autumn had never been in a relationship before. Could she, a woman so inexperienced when it came to taking care of anyone except herself, really be the type of woman a man as lovely as Bowie needed right now? What if she wasn't up to it? She might hurt him. Perhaps she would disappoint Bluebell and lose her, too. And she barely knew Bowie. It didn't feel like it, but they'd met for the first time just a few days ago. That felt crazy to acknowledge, but it was true. A week ago, she'd have warned any woman who was thinking of getting involved in a situation like this to think very carefully about it, yet here she was, ready to say yes without giving it much thought at all. There was so much at stake here. His question shouldn't feel straightforward to answer, but it did. Autumn couldn't explain it. She couldn't imagine saying anything except yes. Still, she listened to Bowie elaborate. She knew he felt like he needed to do it and was grateful he wanted to make sure she knew what she was signing up for.

"You and me? Properly, I mean? I don't have time for games. If you are interested in me, we have to do this now. My whole family is fighting over the time I have left. We can't date or mess around. If you want me, we do this, but you'll have to be sure. It'll be fucking hard. I'll get sick. You'll see me cry. I'll be in pain. I'll throw up and moan and whinge. I'll get snappy. Some days I won't be able to do anything at all. There'll be times I won't even know what day it is because all I'll do is sleep. I'll let you down. I'll do and say things that make you disappointed in me. Cancer is like that. It makes you crazy. I'll lose my sex drive. I'll lose my energy. I'll lose my will to live. And then, some day, somehow, six months or so from now . . . I *am* going to die."

***

They had sex once that evening, right there on the sofa. She told him she wanted to be with him and he asked again if she was sure. She assured him she was and he kissed her. The moment his lips touched hers, Autumn knew her decision had been the right one.

"Are you well enough for this?" she asked him.

"Yes." He pushed her back onto the sofa, pulling her legs around his waist.

"I don't want to hurt you," she said.

"You're really *not* hurting me," he whispered into her neck, grinding his erection provocatively against her.

"Will you tell me if I do?"

He pulled away to scold her.

"Autumn, stop it."

From then on, she did. Their lovemaking had elements of their previous sleepy encounter and all of the urgency of their first time. They were lost in each other. Bowie's body told Autumn a tale of relief and hope and coming home, and she let go in a way she never had before, forgetting about the way she looked, and if her appreciative moans were attractive and delicate enough, and pulling him greedily into her whenever he left her body, without any second thought or sense of shame.

He came so violently and collapsed so hard against her she worried for a second their sex had killed him.

"Bowie?" she whispered.

"That was amazing," he said.

Afterwards, they lay wrapped in one another on the sofa. He tickled the skin of her arm with his fingers and played with the hair at the nape of her neck.

"Come and meet my family tomorrow?" he asked her sleepily.

"Tomorrow?"

"Yeah, like tomorrow-tomorrow."

She laughed. "How many tomorrows are there?"

"Not many for me. That's the whole point."

She leaned up on her elbow and stroked his chest. He could barely keep his eyes open.

"Rule number one . . ." she murmured.

"There are rules?" He groaned softly.

"Yes . . ." She hesitated. "Relationship rules."

The word 'relationship' sounded strange to Autumn coming out of her own mouth. Bowie whimpered theatrically, then smiled.

"Rule number one," she repeated. "You are not allowed to remind me all the time that you're dying. I won't be able to do this if you do."

He nodded in agreement. His eyes had closed now. He sounded drunk when he spoke.

"My turn. Rule number two. You're not allowed to treat me as though I'm dying all the time. That includes asking me if I'm well enough to do things I like to do. Like have sex."

He grinned lasciviously.

She smiled and draped her body over his. He wrapped himself around her. She kissed his jawline and tugged gently on his ear with her fingers, hoping it might soothe him into slumber. She knew he needed it. He moaned at her touch and spoke again, although Autumn could tell that he was somewhere between asleep and awake.

"Rule number three. Sleep is always a good thing."

"That's not a rule."

"My mother would disagree with you," he said.

CHAPTER 6

They were woken by a knock on the door. It was light outside. Autumn jumped up from the sofa and ran to the bedroom to get her dressing gown. She was too tired to ponder who it might be. She hurried clumsily across the living room. Bowie had barely moved. She checked him over and was relieved to note that he was still breathing.

She yanked the door open and did a double take. She had forgotten just how similar Bowie and Marley were.

"Hi." Marley waved awkwardly. She pulled her dressing gown further around herself.

"Hi. Shit. Hi."

"Sorry to burst in on you like this but I told Mum Bowie and I would be home for lunch in an hour. If I don't take him with me, she'll have a nervous breakdown."

"Come in," Autumn said, stepping away from the door to reveal his brother. Bowie was covered in a blanket but he was clearly naked underneath it. Marley grinned.

"Big fan of sofa sex," he said.

Autumn cringed. She and her sister, Lilly, may have talked about sex a little bit when they were much younger but she couldn't imagine being so open with her about it now. Still, she didn't get the impression that he was trying to make her feel uncomfortable. If Marley was anything like Bluebell, and Autumn suspected from the ease with which he teased her that he must be, then he wouldn't feel sex was something to be embarrassed about. He nudged his brother's leg with his foot.

"Bowie, get up."

Bowie opened his eyes and sat up, leaning on his elbows.

"What the fuck are you doing here?"

"It's midday. We have to go home. Mum called last night to talk to you and was ranting and raving about your appetite, so I agreed, on your behalf, that you'd let her feed you lunch today."

"I hate it when you do that."

"Well, if you would get a mobile phone like a normal human being, then you could refuse or accept her force-feeding parties yourself. Autumn, it's lovely to see you again."

Marley reached out to shake her hand.

"Bluebell tells me you're all up to date on the shitshow that is our lives."

She didn't know what to say. She nodded earnestly.

"It's going to be a real adventure," he said, blinking steadily at her. Although he was smiling, she thought she felt his fingers tremble a little as he spoke. In that moment, Autumn realised she hadn't properly thought as to how Bowie's terminal diagnosis would impact his family, but she saw all she needed to know there in that moment, reflected in Marley's eyes. It was a depiction of fear like she had never seen.

Marley nodded and let her hand fall, turning back to his brother, who was still lying motionless on her sofa.

"Mate, seriously, move!"

***

Autumn went by taxi with the brothers to a side of the city she had not yet visited. The bigger the houses became, the more apprehensive she felt.

When the elevator opened into the hallway of the penthouse apartment Bluebell, Bowie and Marley were currently sharing with their visiting family, a middle-aged blonde woman was posing comically in the doorway in an obvious attempt to make them laugh. It worked.

"My boys, my boys, my boys!" They stepped forward, arms outstretched, and she stood on her tiptoes to rest her chin where their shoulders met. They wrapped their arms around her and each other, creating a circle of love that made Autumn smile. Their mother closed her eyes, as though she was really drinking them in. Autumn wondered how long it had been since they'd seen each other.

"Oh! Now, who have we here?" She gently nudged her sons aside. She looked exactly like the type of woman who would name her children Bowie, Marley and Bluebell. She was wearing a baggy, burnt-orange jumpsuit, large hooped earrings, and had a leopard-print scarf braided through her wavy, shoulder-length hair. Autumn had seen Bluebell wearing the same scarf in exactly the same way.

"Mum, this is Autumn," Bowie said.

She took Autumn's hand in hers. She had given her children the deep, dangerous blue of her eyes. There was a playfulness to the way her gaze danced over Autumn, as though she was looking for ways to cause mischief. Autumn was unalarmed. Bowie, Marley and Bluebell had all admired her with the same unabashed gaiety more than once. They looked very much like their mother and Autumn could see their confidence reflected in her demeanour.

"I'm Emma," she said, expertly turning their handshake into an affectionate handhold. Autumn warmed to her immediately. She was naturally comforting. "What a beautifully unusual name," Emma added.

"Thank you."

"You're a friend of Bluebell's, am I right?" Emma asked.

"And a friend of mine," Bowie said pointedly. Emma's smile turned immediately rigid. Whatever warmth had been there before was suddenly gone. Her eyes searched her sons' faces and she cleared her throat as though to speak, but Bowie stared meaningfully at his mother. Autumn watched his gaze — hard and sharp— reset his mother's expression.

Eventually, after what felt like an age, Emma turned without a word and led the way along a marble-tiled corridor and into a large kitchen. She encouraged them to sit at the table, which was piled high with vegetables. There were pans simmering on the hob and the smell of something sweet baking in the oven. She asked them what they'd like to drink, lectured them on their caffeine consumption when they all asked for coffee, then made them a pot nevertheless. Her eyes never strayed from her sons for very long — she touched them tenderly each time she passed them, radiating love as she went. Any awkwardness inspired by Bowie's revelation about the nature of his relationship with Autumn had apparently dissipated.

"I don't suppose you know where your little brother is?" She handed Bowie and Marley a mug each, sighing when they shook their heads. "Can you call him?" she asked.

"Nope." They answered simultaneously.

"Why not?"

"Because he's a grown man and he can stay out all night if he wants to," Bowie said. Marley nodded in agreement. Autumn wondered if they ever disagreed on anything. Emma sighed.

"Bluebell was out all night as well. I'm not sure why we needed so much space if none of you are going to live here anyway."

The door swung open and an extremely stylish young woman wandered breezily into the room. Autumn had not been aware there was anyone else in the apartment. Though the young woman looked nothing like Bowie, Marley, Bluebell or Emma, there was a relaxed quality to the way she walked that Autumn realised was a Whittle trait. This must be Maddie, Bluebell's only sister. She was wearing a floral dress with a dotted headscarf. Autumn had always been impressed by people who could wear clashing patterns with style.

"I live here, Mum."

"I know you do, my darling." Emma kissed the back of her hand affectionately. Autumn watched Maddie and her mother with intrigue. They were total opposites. Maddie's eyes were brown, her hair was dark and her skin was creamy and tanned.

"Golden child," Bowie muttered. Maddie glared at him playfully.

"Says Bowie, who we moved halfway across the world for. I'm Maddie, by the way. Younger sister." She held out her hand for Autumn to shake.

"Autumn."

"She's here with Bowie," Emma said meaningfully, chopping a carrot rather viciously. Autumn winced. Apparently their revelation hadn't been entirely forgotten. Maddie raised her eyebrows in surprise. She made Autumn feel nervous and she didn't know why. She seemed sweet and polite, but Autumn could sense a sisterly protectiveness that made her feel shaky already. Bowie nudged Autumn supportively with his elbow. Marley locked his gaze on his brother and winked when their eyes met. Though she hadn't been aware he was tense, Autumn felt Bowie relax a little beside her and wondered what it felt like to have consistent, unwavering support.

"Nice to meet you, Autumn," Maddie said. "Cool name, by the way."

Their sister picked up a knife and busied herself cutting up cucumbers beside their mother. The room was silent, the atmosphere claggy and uncomfortable. Autumn stared at her drink. She felt on edge and wished someone would do something to change the mood in the room.

"So, how many of you are there altogether?" Autumn asked, when she could no longer stand the silence. She already knew, of course, but she just wanted someone to say something.

"Five," they all replied together.

"And two parents," Emma added.

Autumn nodded. "So, there's Bowie and Marley, Maddie and Bluebell . . ."

"And Pip," Marley and Bowie said in unison.

"Our lovely surprise child," Emma said.

"He's the cutest thing ever," Maddie added.

"He's a little shit." Marley shook his head.

Bowie concurred. "He has these girls wrapped around his little finger."

Emma laughed, rolling her eyes.

"He's wonderful, Autumn," she said. "You'll love him. These two are just jealous."

"We are." Bowie nodded. "And that's because Pip is Mum's favourite."

"I don't have a favourite," Emma said. "I love you all. Very much. In different ways, but in equal amounts."

"Lies." Bowie and Marley chimed in together. Their words were equally fervent. Autumn laughed. Maddie smiled knowingly at her.

"They do that all the time. You'll stop noticing it after a while."

The women went back to chopping veggies, and Bowie and Marley lost themselves in thought. Autumn felt her anxiety returning, but, before they'd fully descended into awkward silence, she was startled out of her dread by a bell in the hallway.

"That's the elevator intercom," Bowie murmured to her, squeezing her knee affectionately. Marley was watching them. He smiled.

"Is that my invisible boys I hear?" a gruff voice called from the hallway. The twins answered with a loud, identical laugh. Autumn heard the removal of shoes, and then a middle-aged man entered the room. His thick brown hair was shoulder-length and his eyes were a lovely shade of golden brown. It was abundantly clear who Maddie resembled. He hugged his wife and his daughter, then greeted Bowie and Marley with a kiss on the cheek. Autumn thought it was sweet. Her own father was against kissing anyone, never mind other men. Bowie made the introductions this time.

"This is our dad, Ben."

He took her hand to shake, watching Bowie expectantly.

"Dad, this is Autumn."

"Lovely to meet you, flower. You're a friend of Bluebell's, right?"

Autumn smiled and nodded. She found herself wishing Bluebell had not discussed their friendship with her family quite so much. She waited for Bowie to correct him.

"And mine too," he said.

"Oh!" Ben said, raising his eyebrows. He sat beside his daughter and nodded at Bowie, pointedly ignoring Emma, who was fishing for his eye across the island. Marley smirked.

"Well, my love," said Ben. "Welcome to the family."

***

The fact that Bowie and Bluebell were brother and sister, that his parents were also her parents, felt odd to Autumn. When Bluebell arrived around an hour later, Autumn found herself feeling distinctly uncomfortable. Despite her friend's customary warm greeting, Autumn felt a little as though she were being introduced to her for the first time. She bet the Whittles didn't know Bluebell like she did, her proclivity for orgies and all.

Bluebell kissed everyone except Marley, whom she smacked around the side of the head instead.

"What the fuck was that for?" Marley asked, and Emma scolded him.

"Language, Marley."

"You lied to me the other day about taking Autumn home in a taxi!" Bluebell said accusingly.

"I was lying for Bowie."

Bowie braced himself for his sister's assault, but Bluebell's stance softened.

"Well, I can't hit Bow, can I?"

Bowie relaxed with a grin.

"You shouldn't lie for Bowie anyway," Emma said.

Marley was rubbing his head.

"Then tell him to stop *asking* me to lie for him."

"Bowie, stop asking your brother to lie for you," Ben said.

"Well, if you tell my parents to stop being so ridiculously overprotective, then I will."

***

Emma made more coffee, and they talked about things they had seen on the news. In the middle of a debate about how to save the UK economy, the youngest Whittle arrived. Emma had been right. Autumn loved Pip instantly. He was young, perhaps eighteen, but had the bearing of a much older man.

"Bluebell's friend, right?" he asked as he released her from his embrace.

"And mine," Bowie added again.

"Yeah, I heard," he said. He wrapped his arms lovingly around Maddie's shoulders, pulling her back into his chest and rocking her from side to side. She reciprocated his affection with a loving smile.

"We were out together last night," Bluebell explained. "But then I lost him."

"Where did you go?" Bowie asked.

Marley grinned. "Did you meet a handsome man?"

"Actually, I did." He glanced meaningfully between their parents. "I'll tell you about it later."

"Here I was, thinking my children could talk to me about anything." Ben sighed with mock sadness.

Marley shook his head. "Not sex, Dad. That'd be gross."

"Then I suggest you adjust your volume when you bring women home with you, Marley," Ben said with a wink. Everyone laughed except Emma, who shook her head in dismay.

"Can we not have these kinds of conversations when we have a guest?" she said.

"We're not going to pretend to be something we're not." Marley shrugged.

"That's not what you taught us," Pip added.

Bluebell chipped in. "Autumn already knows who we are."

They were warm and kind and welcoming. The most unique and interesting collective Autumn had ever met. She'd known from the very beginning that Bluebell was eccentric. Bowie had seemed somewhat more conventional, but only somewhat. Meeting their family made everything clear to her. The Whittles were on a spectrum of strange. They clearly adored one another and that made her like them even more. Autumn wondered if Emma and Ben knew what a wonderful family unit they had created. One in which their children were able to really be themselves. To express themselves fully. She wondered if it had been intentional.

On cue, Emma threw her hands up in surrender.

"Oh, you're right, you're right, you're right. Autumn, I apologise in advance if we do or say anything that makes you feel uncomfortable. We're all very close and extremely open. Not everyone is OK with that. If we get too much for you, do feel free to shut us up. We won't be offended."

"I fucking will be." Bluebell announced this loudly.

Emma glared.

* * *

An hour or so later, they moved from the kitchen into a dining room that was twice as expansive and equally as impressive. They carried trays of roasted vegetables, tabbouleh, hummus and root vegetable stew to the table. Emma spoke quietly to Autumn, despite the hustle and bustle, telling her Bowie barely ate anymore, so she always made lots of little dishes in the hope something might take his fancy. It was the first time anyone had addressed his cancer with her directly.

They sat, served up, then settled into chit-chat. The large round table made conversation easy.

"So, how did you two meet?" Emma looked to Bowie and Autumn. Autumn had helped herself to a small plate of hummus and some vegetables. She was eating slowly so she didn't finish before everyone else, but in a way that made it look like she'd eaten a fair amount. She'd become a talented illusionist over the years.

"We met at a Marley show," Bowie said. His portion was even smaller than hers, but he didn't seem to be eating any of it. Every now and then, he raised a forkful of vegetables to his lips, but mostly returned it to his plate.

"Ah, so you've witnessed how talented our son is?" Ben rubbed Marley's shoulder affectionately.

"I have. He's great." Autumn smiled at Marley.

"Thank you," Marley said shyly. Autumn was surprised. He didn't seem the type to be bashful. He was working his way through the mountain of food as though someone was about to steal it from him.

"And what about Bowie? Have you heard any of his music?" Emma asked. Bowie blushed.

"Mum, can we not turn this lunch into a showcase of our achievements?"

"I'm not showcasing you. I don't need to. She seems pretty smitten with you as it is."

Autumn confirmed his mother's observation by squeezing Bowie's knee under the table. He was all she really wanted to talk about. It made her feel warm inside. She had been a little worried that she might spend the entire afternoon longing to be alone with him, but, now, despite the initial awkward silences, she was very much enjoying spending time with his family. He lit up when he was around them and she was learning more about him. So far, everything Autumn had heard made her like him even more.

"I haven't heard any. We haven't really had a chance yet," she said.

Ben and Emma glanced at one another, and Bowie tensed beside her. Autumn knew she'd said the wrong thing. Her eyes darted to Bluebell. Her friend winked at her, then put down her knife and fork and eyed her mother warily. Emma shot her daughter a warning glance.

"When did you two meet?" Ben asked. His voice was saturated with concern. Autumn looked to Bowie to respond.

"Just the other night," he said.

"Oh, Bowie." Emma put her head in her hands.

"Don't do this, Mum," Bowie said warningly.

The room fell into awkward silence. Marley and Pip focused on their food, their eyes meeting meaningfully every now and again. The rest of the family had stopped eating. Autumn stared at the table. Out of the corner of her eye, she could see Bowie maintaining eye contact with his father. They were locked in wordless communication. Autumn had never felt as though she'd known anybody well enough to do that. When Ben spoke, it was to her.

"Autumn, we don't mean to be rude. Please don't take this personally, but Bowie is at a uniquely difficult point in his life, and it's inevitable we would be concerned about him becoming involved with someone at this time."

"In actual fact, I'm at the end of my life, Dad, so I'd appreciate it if you'd let me be happy." Bowie pushed his plate away. Marley put down his cutlery and placed his hand supportively on his brother's shoulder. Autumn could see pain and frustration etched on Bowie's face, but she felt him relax a little at Marley's touch. Maddie glanced sympathetically at Autumn and then she spoke, too.

"This isn't just about you, Bowie. This is about Autumn, too. The next few months are going to be awful. It isn't the right time to be dragging someone else into it."

"Autumn knows what she's getting herself into," Marley said.

Maddie scowled. "Marley, we don't need your biased twin-sibling defence mechanism to kick in right now, OK? Thanks."

Marley bristled. "What the fuck do you know about it?"

"Don't start!" Emma held a hand up to each of them. They ignored her and braced for battle, squaring their shoulders towards each other.

"Get over yourself." Maddie glared at Marley. "Just because you shared a womb at the same time you think Bowie can do no wrong?"

Bowie tried to interject. "Maddie—"

"You have no idea what we're going through." Marley shook his head at their sister.

Bowie tried again. "Marley—"

"This isn't happening to *you*." Maddie stood. Marley followed.

"Exactly." He threw his hands in the air. "It's happening to Bowie. So shut up and let him live his life."

"You think you're the only one who loves him," Maddie said, incredulous.

"I love him more than you do."

"What a load of shit—"

"Stop it right now!" Ben stood, glaring between his children.

Autumn had covered her mouth with her hand. Her eyes searched for Bluebell's. Her friend smiled sadly at her and Autumn knew then that these kinds of arguments over Bowie and what was best for him were common in the Whittle household.

Bluebell addressed her mum and dad.

"As much as it pains me to ever agree with Marley, I'm going to stick up for the twins. Bowie has been miserable for such a long time. Autumn could make him happy. She's strong and smart, and she knows that this isn't going to be easy. She isn't someone who will go along with anything she isn't comfortable with. If it gets too much, she'll be the first to say, won't you, Autumn? If she can give Bowie some happiness, isn't that all that should matter?"

Pip began to applaud his sister, but stopped abruptly when Ben and Emma glared in his direction. His eyes darted purposefully and comedically left and right. Bowie and Marley smirked at each other, and the tension was broken. Autumn had to fight hard to stop herself laughing out loud. Composing herself, she asked if she could speak. Emma nodded, smiling weakly. She was already defeated, and she knew it.

"I don't want to be rude, but Bowie and I are both adults. We've made this decision together and, to be honest, I can't see why it should involve any of you."

Whatever it was they'd expected her to say, it clearly hadn't been that. Autumn had surprised herself, in fact. She'd intended to make a declaration of her commitment to Bowie, even though she couldn't quite see the point. She wanted to be with him, and he with her. A family fallout about it was a waste of time that they didn't have the luxury of. She hoped that they would find her audacity endearing. Ben certainly seemed to. He raised an eyebrow at Bowie, a smile twitching at the corners of his lips. Emma cleared her throat, turning to Autumn.

"Well, young lady. It has been a long time since my children brought an individual with your dauntlessness to meet us. You're right. You're fully grown adults. There is nothing I can do to stop you if you want to be with my son and he wants to be with you. But, I warn you, the next few months are going to be horrendous. We've fought for years to keep Bowie alive. It's incomprehensible to us that he isn't going to survive this."

Emma stopped talking and grabbed Ben's hand. Maddie's eyes filled with tears. She excused herself to Autumn, brushing away the comforting hands of Bluebell and Pip as she left the room, wiping tears from her face as she went. Marley watched her go, his face fraught with guilt. So far they'd seemed to be coping so well, but their heartbreak was palpable now. Autumn moved to speak, to apologise, but Bowie shook his head. Eventually, Emma continued, her voice cracking.

"I don't imagine anyone you love has ever asked you to kill them, have they, Autumn?"

Autumn murmured a no. Bowie rubbed his hand nervously across his face.

"We sat around Bowie's bed three weeks ago during a particularly bad pain episode and argued about fulfilling his wish and putting him out of his misery. That's what we're dealing with. If you want to be with him while we face this, we'll need you to be part of those conversations without feeling like there's a stranger in the room. You are going to need to throw yourself wholeheartedly into this family as though you've always been here. You'll need to be honest with us about your feelings and your thoughts, even when you know we won't want to hear what you have to say. That's the only way we'll be able to include you in what we're facing. If you think you can do that, I'll accept you as one of our own, because if you are going to go through this with us, that's how we'll need it to be."

Bowie held her hand tighter beneath the table. Autumn knew he was unafraid to hear her answer. Her feelings for him were entirely beyond her control. There was no way that she could conceive of him — or Bluebell — facing this without her.

"I'm not going anywhere," she said.

* * *

They accepted her words and, at Bowie's request, moved the conversation on. Marley left the table to find Maddie and came back into the room a moment later holding her hand. She mouthed an apology to Autumn across the table. Autumn waved it away. Nobody managed to finish their lunch, but Emma made sure they knew they'd find it in the fridge when they got peckish later on.

"And you will be eating later," she told Bowie sternly.

The living room, with its ivory gold wallpaper and hardwood floors, took Autumn's breath away. Colourful throws, textured rugs and soft cushions were scattered artfully and invitingly, and the floor-to-ceiling window overlooked the city from a breathtaking height.

"Your home is beautiful," Autumn told Emma.

"Thank you. We don't like it so much, actually. It's so impersonal. It belongs to a friend of ours. We're just staying here while we're in New York. We prefer our own home."

"Even though it's just as pointlessly huge," Bluebell quipped.

"But so much homelier," Emma said.

"And much, much colder," Bowie added.

Ben opened the drinks cabinet and poured himself a whisky.

"You ungrateful little shits. Do you know what some people would give to have the home we made for you?"

Bowie and Bluebell smirked at one other. Emma chuckled, shaking her head.

"They are grateful, Autumn, they just like winding Ben up."

Autumn chose to sit next to Ben on the smallest cream sofa. She was inexplicably intrigued by her lover's father. He was warm and kind, and it drew her to him. She could already see so much of Bowie in him.

"What do you do, Ben?" she asked as they settled in.

"Nothing now. I did own a content-writing company but I sold it last year when Bowie became seriously ill. I mentor other writers now."

"I'm a writer too," she said. She was thrilled to find they had something in common. He turned to give her his full attention.

"Oh, really? What do you write?"

"Everything," Bowie answered for her, his face exploding into a grin. He said it with the same expression of wide-eyed wonderment she'd used when she'd said the same thing to him three evenings before. He winked at her. She laughed.

"He's right. Everything. Mainly novels. Poetry, although it doesn't pay. Articles, sometimes. And my blog."

"Autumn wrote that book that I was telling you about, Dad," Bowie said. "About the factory farm."

"Ah, yes." Ben nodded. He looked impressed. Autumn felt proud.

"She gave me a copy. I'll give it to you later," Bowie said.

"Is it having the desired effect?" Ben asked. "I'm guessing you wrote it to encourage people to consider changing their eating habits?"

"That's not really happening because it's mostly vegans who are buying it."

"People are afraid of change, especially such a big one. It will come. Give it time."

Something in the way he said it told her he really believed it. His tone was friendly and comforting, and she felt like he had faith in her. She hadn't had much experience with dads, but she didn't feel uneasy or uncomfortable around Ben. He engaged her in effortless conversation for over an hour, displaying the same impressive intellect and genuine interest that had attracted her to Bowie, and talking mainly of his children and their ambitions.

"If my parents had let me do what I loved, I'd have been a musician. That's why Emma and I have always encouraged our children to do whatever makes their souls sing. We have the money to allow them to chase their dreams and that's what they've done, with some real success along the way."

She found him so warm, friendly and charming, like the dads she'd read about in books and seen on TV. There was something comforting about his presence. Autumn knew if she wasn't careful she'd commandeer his attention all night. She felt as though she should mingle a little more, perhaps pay some attention to Bowie, his mother and his siblings, but they were entertaining themselves and Ben was so easy to talk to.

"Tell me more about Bowie?" she asked. His face filled with pride.

"Autumn, he's a wonderful person. Of course, I'm his father, I would say that, but everyone who meets him tells me how lovely he is. He's sweet and kind and caring, and he works hard. He's always worked hard at everything, ever since he was a little boy. He's funny, and would do anything to help anyone. He has such a passion for adventure. He's never been afraid of anything."

Ben's final words caught in his throat. He tossed back his whisky, swallowing hard.

"I'm immensely proud to call him my son. That's why you must excuse what happened earlier. If things go the way we expect, we don't have long left with him. We want him for ourselves."

Autumn nodded. She hadn't thought about that. To his family, she would be an extra demand on Bowie's time. They wanted to spend every minute with him and she might keep him away from them. She resolved to make sure that didn't happen.

"Tell me about his music." She liked to hear Ben talk about his son. She let herself wonder if her own father ever spoke of her in this way. She doubted it. To her parents and her sister, Autumn had always been 'the weird one'. She knew they told people that she wrote, but they were embarrassed about her vegan literature and her blog was too liberal to warrant their support. Autumn knew that because of her name and her personality, most people would assume she was from a very different background. They would think she had a family who'd showered her with affection and lovingly pruned her character, who'd consciously raised a confident, independent and determined woman. Privileged people like the Whittles would almost definitely fall into this trap, but Autumn, and people like her, knew better. She was willing to bet her mother had given more thought to naming her than she had to absolutely anything concerning her welfare since. She was sure the Whittles would never believe her and could guarantee she would never feel comfortable talking to them about it. She'd tried that before with people, the conversation always ending with their eyebrows pitched high by scepticism. She'd learned her lesson. Ben beamed.

"Oh, he makes the most beautiful music. He really is very impressive. It kind of happened by accident for Bowie. He wrote some songs when he was younger for an amateur theatre group we performed with and fell in love with the process, but he can be a little shy. He never would have put himself out there if we hadn't been behind him. We joke that he and Marley are the same, but they're not. Marley absolutely loves attention — he's a real extrovert — but Bowie would rather stay in the background and watch someone else showcase his work. Whenever he's written a piece he wanted to post online or send to a director or whatever, Marley has performed it for him."

"They adore each other, huh?" Autumn smiled. Ben nodded, continuing.

"Hopelessly. Marley, in particular, would do absolutely anything for Bowie. I suspect there were times he even pretended to be him. Bowie doesn't see how special he is. He thinks Marley is the talented one and he's the one who just got lucky. I suspect you'll never get to see him commanding a stage full of performers and an orchestra the way he used to, but I'm sure we have a video of it somewhere. I'll try to dig it out for you. He lives and breathes what he does. He really comes alive."

"I'd like that. Thank you."

"Any excuse to show off my boy. He has great talent. He writes love songs — that's where he really flies. He has a romantic heart. He's been waiting for a very long time for someone to give it to. He'll hate that I've told you that."

Autumn smiled. "Your family is very creative." Ben chuckled.

"It ends there, actually. Maddie is a carer and she loves it. She adores her job — all she ever really wanted to do was help people. There isn't much room for creativity in care, sadly. She used to sing, but not so much anymore. Pip is studying politics, but spends most of his time getting drunk with animal-rights activists and LGBTQ campaigners. Whenever we ask him what he wants to do, he tells us he's going to be prime minister."

Autumn laughed.

"Emma taught drama."

"All noble professions."

"And Bluebell, as you well know, makes a career of doing nothing."

He didn't sound bitter. More like he found it amusing.

"Why doesn't she work?" Autumn asked. If Autumn had been given the position of privilege Bluebell had, she'd have been writing full time at the earliest opportunity. Her circumstances had left her with little choice but to pursue a pay packet wherever she had been able to, while writing in her spare time. Bluebell didn't have to. She could craft a career in whatever she wanted to and yet she chose to do nothing instead.

"She hasn't found anything that makes her heart happy," Ben said. Autumn smiled. Bowie had used those words once: 'Success isn't measured in the things you have; it's measured by how happy your heart is.' His father had obviously been a great influence on the man he had become.

Autumn looked over at Bluebell. She was sitting with her head on Marley's shoulder. They were laughing heartily at something Pip had said. She always seemed so full of joy. Perhaps doing nothing was enough for her. Ben continued.

"To be honest, they'll argue about it, but I think what's happening to Bowie has hit her hardest of all of us. Except for Marley, of course."

Autumn hadn't been given the impression Bluebell and Bowie were particularly close. She wondered if Ben was making excuses for her behaviour. It had been Maddie who had been unable to sit at the table when they'd been talking about his lymphoma and it was Marley who seemed to defend Bowie no matter what.

"She was studying drama in sixth form when Bowie was first diagnosed and she was completely devastated. Bluebell always treated Bowie's cancer as though it were a death sentence, from the very beginning, even when the doctors were reassuring us about it. It's as if she's always known it would take him from us. She had so many dreams and aspirations as a young woman, but she dropped everything to spend her time with him. When Marley wanted to move over here to try to break into acting, it went without saying Bowie and Bluebell would follow. Bowie can work here and Bluebell follows Bowie wherever he goes. She has for fourteen years."

Her friend was obviously in more distress than Autumn had registered. That realisation made her feel guilty.

"How's Marley handling it all?" she asked. Ben winced.

"He isn't, really. Twin relationships are usually special, but those two are inseparable. I could count on one hand the number of times they've been apart for more than twenty-four hours. They adore each other, Autumn. They don't know how to live without each other. Marley tells us all the time that he wishes this was happening to him instead of Bowie. He can't stand the thought of living without his twin. Of course, Bowie would tell you he would take this disease any day over the idea that he might have to live without Marley. If they could, they would literally fight over who got to be the one to die, just so that they didn't have to be the one left behind."

Autumn's eyes filled with tears. The idea Bowie might feel like the lucky one because he wouldn't be the one left living made her heart break. Ben rested his hand affectionately on her arm and asked her if she was OK. She nodded.

"For those two," he said, "dying feels easier than living without each other and I'm quite sure Marley won't ever get over it."

Autumn watched the two of them together. They were sitting side by side on the sofa. Marley had his arm around Bowie's shoulders and was massaging his head with his fingers. He was staring, lost in thought, into his glass of rum. Bowie was asleep.

"Will Marley be OK?" Autumn asked. Ben paused for a moment and Autumn knew, somehow, it was not because he didn't know what to say, but rather he did not know how to say it.

"No. I don't think he will be OK, my love. And there's only one thing more terrifying for Emma and I than the fear of losing one child, and that's the idea that we might lose two."

***

Suddenly it was late and Emma was reasoning that they should all stay in. Bluebell, Marley and Pip had been vehemently insisting since the early evening that they were going out to a bar, and Autumn, who feared she had overstayed her welcome, had been trying to leave for hours by then. Autumn suspected Emma believed Bowie would go with her if she went home and she wanted her children close at all times. She hadn't said it outright, but she was heavily hinting Autumn should spend the night. There was no way Autumn would feel comfortable doing that if Bowie's siblings went out, and Emma probably knew that, so she'd focused her attention on persuading them to drop their plans, and this was a woman who knew how to bribe her children. "I'll make you breakfast in bed," she said. Maddie rolled her eyes.

"Don't do that, Mum. They should want to stay in of their own free will."

"I'll stay in if there's more rum." Marley knocked back his drink.

"There's always more rum." Ben took a bottle from the cabinet, filling his son's tumbler and moving to refill Autumn's empty glass. He raised his eyebrows questioningly. She looked to Bowie for guidance, but he was still sleeping on the sofa. Marley took the bottle from Ben and poured it into her glass.

"He's not going anywhere tonight, so you might as well stay here and party with us," he said. Autumn turned to Emma.

"Are you sure that's all right, Emma?" she asked. There had been rules in her family home about love interests spending the night. It had been forbidden. Autumn had tried to argue that their male cousins on her mother's side were allowed girls in their bedrooms, and had pointed out that she had allowed those cousins and their girlfriends to stay in their home and in the same bed, but her mother had said it was different for girls. Autumn had accepted it at the time, sneaking boys in through her bedroom window, but, as an adult, she objected to such unequal treatment. Her mother was entitled to have rules under her own roof, but Autumn was against those rules being different for boys and girls. It was highly unlikely they'd ever have the argument, since Autumn didn't plan on staying at her mother's house ever again.

She had gathered, by now, that the Whittles were a little more open-minded when it came to sex. The topic had come up more than once tonight. They talked openly about it, accepting it as a normal part of adult life. Their conversations were free of smut and embarrassment, so Autumn knew that staying the night would be OK with Bowie's parents, but she thought it was polite to check. Emma smiled warmly.

"Of course it is. Although I think you might be disappointed if you're hoping for a night of passion."

Emma ran her hand affectionately across Bowie's face. He murmured and opened his eyes a little, but went straight back to sleep. Autumn blushed. Marley laughed.

"Cigarette?" he asked her. She nodded, clambering up from the floor. Autumn hardly ever bought cigarettes of her own accord to smoke alone, but she did smoke socially occasionally, purchasing a pack or two here and there to repay people when she felt she'd accepted a few too many. She hated the habit, but couldn't help herself. She'd seen Marley duck out onto the balcony several hours earlier and had followed him shyly to ask if she could have one. He'd obliged, then invited her to join him every time he'd gone out since. Autumn was surprised Marley smoked given his brother had cancer, but wasn't bold enough to ask him how he reconciled it in his mind. She knew she probably shouldn't smoke either, but it hadn't stopped her tonight.

"I wish you wouldn't do that, Marley," Emma said.

He put a cigarette between his lips and batted her comment away nonchalantly as he handed one to Autumn. He was unsteady on his feet and Autumn was not surprised. He'd drunk almost an entire bottle of rum to himself. She was mildly impressed that he hadn't thrown up yet. If she'd tried to put away even half of what he'd had, she'd already be in bed.

Emma persisted. "You're killing yourself." Marley bristled. His eyes darted to his sleeping brother. He shrugged again.

"And?"

"Don't you dare start that again." Maddie spoke up from her armchair in the corner.

"Start what? Telling the truth? I don't care if I die—"

Emma opened her mouth as if to shout a retort, but Ben stepped between his son and the rest of the family, pushing him playfully towards the balcony.

"Get out. Get out, you drunk. Go and have your cigarette."

Marley laughed, allowing his father to shove him through the doors. It was an expertly engineered tension breaker, but Autumn was dismayed to see real terror in Emma's eyes when she turned to send her an apologetic smile. Emma forced the fear from her face, gesticulating her permission for Autumn to follow Marley outside.

It was so very cold. Autumn picked up a blanket from the wicker garden chair and wrapped it around her shoulders. Marley did likewise.

"They're crazy, aren't they?" he asked her. He'd used the same conversation starter every time they'd stepped outside. Apparently, he was not as talented a talker as his brother and father.

"Yeah. Crazy. But lovely."

He nodded, puffing his cigarette to life.

"Yeah. They're the best."

They stood in silence for a minute. She felt comfortable in his company. She watched him, admiring the way he smoked. His movements were graceful and well-rehearsed.

"I know he's my twin and I'm biased, but Bowie is the greatest."

"I don't think you are biased, actually," she said. Marley smiled, blowing smoke dramatically towards the sky.

"He's been waiting for someone like you for ages. Someone he can share the things he cares about with. Someone who can think deeply about things the way he can."

"I know how he feels." Autumn had always been aware that most people thought she was strange. She had always been told that she cared about things a little too much. Things that didn't matter to most people, like seabird welfare, the

UK social-care crisis, or men who bullied women off the equipment in the gym. Being called weird had bothered her when she was young, but now she viewed it as a compliment. She wanted to care. She had a strong sense of justice, that was all, and no interest in being like everybody else, even though it made finding people who understood her extremely difficult. Marley smiled knowingly.

"Me too," he said.

They smoked in silence for a while. The roar of the city below bounced off the canopy above their heads. The cool breeze made Autumn shiver. Marley took the blanket from his shoulders and offered it to her. She shook her head, but her teeth were still chattering.

"Take it," he said, wrapping it around her shoulders so that she didn't have to untangle her arms from the warmth of her own blanket.

"Marley, you've no proper clothes on," she said. He was wearing just a pair of jeans and a plain grey T-shirt. He shrugged his shoulders as high as they would go and wrapped his arms around his chest to shield himself from the wind. He was clearly freezing, but it was pointless trying to get him to take the blanket back. Autumn knew that men like the Whittle men were never anything but chivalrous.

They smoked their cigarettes down to their stubs in silence. Despite the snap in the air, Marley seemed in no hurry to head back into the warm. She felt compelled to stay with him for a while longer, so when he offered her another cigarette, though she wasn't really a chain-smoker, she accepted it with good grace.

"We had a fight tonight. Bowie and I," he said.

"What about?" she asked.

"Because he's supposed to be leaving for England next week and now he's saying he doesn't want to go anymore."

Autumn blinked in the darkness and said nothing. She tried to ignore the knot of fear in her stomach. Marley was staring out across the city.

"The plan was that we would all go home and spend the next few months together. I've quit my band. We have our tickets. Everything is all set, but now he's saying he doesn't want to leave you."

He paused to take another drag. She could tell he was struggling to say whatever it was that he needed to say next. "We all want to be at home when . . ."

He stopped and blew smoke out until it surrounded them both. Autumn tried to communicate her understanding wordlessly. She didn't want him to feel like he had to speak words that were torturing him. She watched his face, and realised he had been frowning since she'd first opened her apartment door to him that morning. This man was in serious pain.

"But Bowie wants to be wherever you are," he said. His eyes pleaded with her. She knew what he was asking her to do. She smoked her cigarette, thinking carefully. Autumn hated living in England. As soon as she'd been able to, she'd left her home country. Her mum and her sister had pretended to cry when they'd dropped her off at university like all the other families, but nobody called her for a week after that, and even then it was only so they could ask her if she had space in her uni dorm to store some boxes because they wanted to turn her bedroom into a gym. She'd made one real friend during her time there, but they had lost touch not long after graduation. Becca had married a man they'd met in a grubby bar in freshers' week almost right away. Autumn had been a bridesmaid at her wedding, but now she could barely remember Becca's husband's name. Was it Jonathan or James? It definitely began with a J.

Autumn had worked as a journalist for a small newspaper in Manchester after her studies, then as a charity worker in Brighton. She'd moved to London for a role as a copywriter when she was twenty-five. Fortnightly phone calls with her mother had drifted into awkward chats once a month and then every other, and now she barely heard from them at all. Family just wasn't Autumn's thing. That was fine by her. She hadn't chosen them and they weren't the type of people that she liked. Still, she had often wondered why she struggled to make friends.

On the best day of her life, the day someone called to say they wanted to publish her book, she'd had absolutely nobody to talk to about it. Autumn didn't feel as though she'd had enough casual conversation with her mother in the weeks beforehand to ring her up and announce her success. It would have been profoundly uncomfortable for both of them. Her mum and her sister would feel awkward about congratulating her and probably think she was bragging. At the very least, they would be confused about why she was choosing to tell them. They were under the impression she had a vibrant social life and plenty of friends, so they might ask why she wasn't celebrating her success with them instead of ringing up to boast.

Autumn couldn't stand the idea that they might realise that she didn't really have anyone. Plus, they wouldn't be able to give her what she wanted anyway. They wouldn't appreciate the commitment she'd needed to work full time while simultaneously writing and publishing her book, nor the hours spent poring over paragraphs to make her story right, or the courage needed to face the many, many rejection letters she'd received. They wouldn't recognise that her blood, sweat and tears were on every single page, or what a big deal it was to Autumn herself. She hadn't dared to believe that she wrote well for a very long time. She'd kept her words to herself, avoiding her dreams being dashed, inevitably as she saw it, throughout her teenage years and her twenties, because if she didn't have writing she didn't have anything.

Being published was the greatest thing that had ever happened to her. It was confirmation she was actually good at the thing she loved to do most. Still, to her surprise, it had saddened her to have no one to share her joy with. Those had been her happiest days and also her saddest. Instead of marking her success, she'd found herself crippled with loneliness, so when her publishers suggested she participate in a book tour and Autumn had visited and enjoyed New York, she'd set about figuring out how she could move here. The city provided the perfect new backdrop for her relentless social media posting, which had so far been the key to her success. Autumn was quiet and private in her everyday life, but she'd cultivated a quirky and confident internet persona, a heavily edited and outgoing version of herself, who ranted and raved about animal rights, writing and the joys of eating vegan. Her timing had been accidentally impeccable, she'd started her page when building an audience online had been possible if you were brave enough to try it and at the very start of a surge of people adopting a vegan lifestyle. She'd built a moderate following of dedicated activists, who had followed her writing journey and — eager to push her message — bought her book in bulk to leave in public places as part of their activism. By the time she was considering moving to New York, Autumn felt invincible. She was ready to try surviving somewhere new. It had been the best decision she'd ever made. She had found her home, then Walter, then Bluebell had come along, and now there was Bowie. Despite the new and scary things happening around her, she hadn't felt as happy as she had that afternoon, doing nothing really except relax with the Whittles, in a very long time.

Autumn knew Marley was studying her while she mused. They leaned back against the railings, aware that the lights in the lounge meant nobody could see them looking in on them. Bowie was still sleeping, his family gathered around him. Autumn watched Bluebell, who was sitting on the floor supporting Bowie's head, staring into his face and stroking his hair with her fingers. Autumn shook her head bitterly. Bluebell was flighty, but she was an extraordinary friend. When Autumn had admitted recently that she'd had nobody to celebrate with when she'd won her book deal for *Beans: An Extraordinary Pig Tale*, Bluebell had recoiled in horror, insisting they celebrate together immediately. She'd listened to her talk about her writing for hours on end, held her hair back over the toilet when she was sick, and cooked for her when she had been too busy with her writing to remember to eat. Bluebell was the only person in the whole world who knew how lonely Autumn had been, and that she still cried when she watched movies about parents who loved their kids. She even knew that once, just once, Autumn had thought seriously about jumping off a balcony as high as the one she was standing on now. All this time, she had not realised just how much pain Bluebell had been in and, since Bowie had told her what he was facing, she was ashamed to recognise that she'd not looked at how Bluebell might be coping with it all. Perhaps it was because she had no real relationship with her own sister, but that was no excuse. She had believed herself a better person than that.

And Bowie. He'd smashed his way into her life with more enthusiasm than anyone ever. He had, somehow, driven his way into her heart, and there was no removing him now. The Whittles felt like her people. The tribe she had been looking for. Her happiness seemed to be wherever they were. Although England didn't mean home to her, she understood completely why they wanted to be there together for the end of Bowie's life.

"We can buy you a ticket . . ." Marley said.

Autumn shook her head. She knew what she had to do. Bowie's family wanted to take him home and there was no real reason to argue. There was no other way.

She turned to Marley, her phone poised.

"I can buy my own ticket. When do we leave?" she asked.

CHAPTER 7

The New York apartment Ben and Emma rented from their friend was huge, but it was still an apartment. Unlike the first night, when Bowie had been carried to bed by his brothers in a deep slumber and barely moved until the following morning — it seemed now that Autumn and Bowie could not keep their hands off each other. She felt as though everyone could hear absolutely everything they got up to.

Adamant Bowie should be close to his family in case his health deteriorated suddenly, Autumn struggled through silent sex every night, working hard in the daylight hours to honour the promise she had made to herself. She would not take Bowie from his family. She insisted he be with them while they prepared to move, refusing to allow him time on his own with her aside from in the evenings, when she reasoned he would ordinarily be in bed anyway. He complained, of course, and she felt guilty, but she remained determined she would not get in the way of their time together. Autumn could tell his mother and father were grateful, but it was torturous for her, too. She wanted him all to herself more than anything.

"You realise he just sleeps all day anyway." Bluebell was teasing her over lunch in Manhattan one Friday. "He's exhausted from whatever it is he's doing with you all night."

"Sorry." Autumn grimaced. She felt the need to defend herself. They also talked, often into the early hours. Autumn wanted to know everything there was to know about Bowie and there was so much to take in. They'd talked about silly things, the background stuff it took some couples years to mention, like whether their grandparents had fought in the war, and the names of the children who'd bullied them when they were young. She'd told him her biggest fear was failure and he'd admitted his was death. Bowie had told her he didn't believe in an afterlife and he had accepted he would 'just be . . . gone'. They'd talked about how unfair it all was. He'd told her he was jealous of everyone who would survive him. He couldn't quite believe that the world would just carry on without him, as though he had never existed. Their conversations were important to her and Autumn was unhappy that his family might think all they did when they were alone was have sex.

"Stop overthinking it!" Bluebell said. "We don't give a shit about what you do. As long as he's happy, we're happy. And my God, is he happy!"

Autumn was happy, too. Bowie personified everything she loved about people, from his sincere desire to help others, to his ability to make people laugh, to the unashamed love he had for his parents and siblings.

"My family loves you, Autumn. We like having you around, so please don't feel as though you can't be with us whenever you want to be. Bring your work over here. Stay with us and eat breakfast. Move the fuck in, if you want to. No one will mind. You want to be with Bowie, so *be with Bowie*."

Autumn felt herself relax a little. Bluebell was right. Before she could concur, her friend launched into a dramatic rant about Marley's friend, the trumpet player she was sleeping with whenever she felt like it.

"So, Adam and I! He found out I slept with someone else and now he's refusing to talk to me. He says it's over. It's handy, really, because we're going back to England anyway and I absolutely cannot stand goodbyes, but I felt a little bit sad when he said it. He's good in bed. I wouldn't have minded an angry shag or two more before we went home. Never mind."

That afternoon, Autumn dutifully followed her friend through the bustling, busy streets of a city so big it still overwhelmed her. They found Emma and Maddie at home with Bowie, who was asleep on the sofa. His mother pulled Autumn into a hug.

"I'm glad she's made you see sense," she said, with real warmth.

"She always does," Autumn said.

Bowie opened his eyes at the sound of her voice.

"Hey," he said softly.

"Hello." She gestured for him to move over so she could sit beside him. He settled his head on her lap. She stroked his hair back from his face, working really hard to keep concern from creeping across her expression. He looked pale. Autumn could barely believe there had ever been a time when she'd not known that Bowie was ill. He had hidden it well early on, but he wasn't so good at it anymore. Bowie was in almost constant pain. He'd confided in her that he strongly suspected his lymphoma had spread to his bones. He had chronic pain in his back, pelvis and legs, but he was most worried about headaches he'd been experiencing and an infrequent pain in his skull. Bowie's biggest fear was skull metastasis. He was afraid of the confusion, seizures and personality changes that sometimes came with it. He was scared of the impact it might have on his sight and the feeling in his face and what that might mean for his quality of life. He didn't want to tell his family of his concerns because he knew they were already terrified, but he found it very difficult to hide it when he was worried, so instead he'd become visibly withdrawn, curling up on the sofa under a blanket and pretending to be asleep. But these were the good days, he'd say. She would soon see the bad, he promised, because they never stayed away for long.

She knew he didn't like to talk about it if he could help it, so Autumn had been doing her own research about lymphoma, often on her phone while he was sleeping beside her, as well as asking his family for more information about his personal journey whenever she could. When he'd first revealed his diagnosis to her, he'd told her many people lived to normal life expectancy with low-grade non-Hodgkins lymphoma, and her Google searching confirmed this. Some people went into remission and never needed treatment ever again. He had been extremely unlucky, and that was why he was so concerned about bone metastasis, which was extremely rare. She learned lymphoma was one of the most common cancer types for teens and people in their early twenties. The first sign of Bowie's cancer had been a painless swollen lymph node in his neck. The doctors had dismissed his symptoms for months. By the time he'd been diagnosed, the cancer had spread and he'd need a combination of treatments to save his life. Since then, Bowie's cancer had returned a further three times. Since some treatments couldn't be recycled because they'd stop working and potentially permanently damage the body, there had been periods when Bowie had been living with the knowledge his cancer was spreading for several months at a time, waiting until he could no longer manage the pain and discomfort to begin a new course of treatment. That, he said, was incredibly difficult to navigate. He worried during those times he was leaving it too late, but he was also gravely concerned about requesting treatment too early, which could mean it didn't work properly and then it could never be used again. When the cancer had returned the third time when Bowie was in his late twenties, it had presented as a large tumour in his spleen, which is where the scar on his stomach had come from. The last time, he'd suspected it had returned in his abdomen because he'd lost his appetite. He'd been sent for a PET scan, where he'd been injected with a radioactive liquid that was absorbed by the lymphoma and, though he and his oncologist had already prophesied he was very sick, they had both been surprised by just how far the cancer had spread. That had led to the discovery some of his cancer had transformed into high grade lymphoma, and Bowie's decision to stop treatment. They could work to prolong his life, but his chance of survival was incredibly slim. He was tired. He didn't want to do it anymore.

She'd gathered quite a lot of information in dribs and drabs given the Whittles hardly ever talked about it. That being said, everything they did was done with the end of Bowie's life in mind. Maddie had given up work to spend more time with the family, Pip was studying from home and Marley spent every single moment he could with his twin.

After Autumn had succumbed to his pleas for her to accompany them to England, Marley had hugged Autumn so hard and for so long that she'd wondered if he'd been crying. When he'd eventually pulled away, he'd turned away from her with unnatural speed, before she'd seen any hint of a tear. She'd followed him warily into the lounge and found him perfectly composed and addressing his family.

"Autumn's coming back to England with us." He'd poured himself another drink.

Autumn was worried about the family's reaction, but it soon became clear that Marley's suggestion was a collective one. There was a sudden and unmistakable sense of relief in the room.

"Bowie isn't going to like this," Maddie warned.

"Well, Bowie doesn't always know what's best for himself," Ben said. Bluebell objected.

"He does, it's just that he'd rather we did whatever is best for everybody else."

Bluebell hit the nail on the head, Autumn realised. Bowie was selfless. He put the well-being of those he cared for above his own needs, often at his own expense, and she realised it was very likely he wanted to stay in New York only because she did.

Once his anger about Marley's ambush of Autumn subsided, Bowie conceded that he did long for his family home in Hertfordshire, but he didn't want her to feel bullied into joining them. Bowie didn't know all the details of her miserable upbringing in England, but did know about her desperation to get away. She never spoke about her family and he was sensitive enough to know something wasn't right about her life back home, so never asked her to go with them.

Autumn thought long and hard about what she should do about her apartment in New York. In the end, she decided to continue paying rent, telling herself she could move back there when this was all over. She never let herself dwell on what that would mean for Bowie. The more time she spent with him, the more difficult it became for her to imagine a time when he wouldn't be there, so her forethought went only as far as keeping her home options open.

A few days before she was due to leave, Autumn returned to her apartment to pack. She visited Walter one last time, promising she'd be back. As sorry as he was to see her leave, he was happy she would be settling down with the nice young man he had given a pen to, despite the tragedy of his situation.

"Will you be coming home after he dies?" he asked, rather bluntly. The question took Autumn's breath away, but she nodded, unable to speak.

"Good. It's been nice having someone so lovely living upstairs. Will you call me every week from England while you're gone?"

Nodding again, Autumn pulled Walter into a hug.

"Don't worry about your rent, girl. You go focus on that young man of yours. I don't need money, not really. Now, you listen to me. I want you to know how grateful I am for the kindness you've shown me since you got here. I'm going to hold this place for you, but don't you rush. Take your time. Don't protest. Just promise me you'll take care of yourself?"

Autumn tried, through tears of appreciation, to give him money to cover the rent on her apartment for the next six months, but he refused her. She clutched it to her heavy heart and assured him she could afford to pay what she owed, but he wouldn't hear of it. His compassion overwhelmed her and Autumn cried so violently into her cardigan sleeve on her way back to the Whittles' place that the taxi driver cautiously asked her if she was OK.

"I'm fine," she said through sobs, knowing she sounded ridiculous. How could someone so hysterically sad be fine?

"Is there anyone waiting inside for you?" he asked, pulling up onto the kerb. Autumn smiled weakly, nodding a yes.

"And they're people who will understand," she added with glee. That was the part she was trying hard to remember. She was doing this for her best friend, for the man she was falling in love with, and for their family, who were showing her what real compassion looked like.

"Good for you," said the driver, with an awkward little nod of his head.

Autumn wailed her way through the lobby, where she ran into Marley and Pip. They were dressed up for a night out.

"Autumn, what the fuck?" Pip pulled her into his arms.

She laughed pathetically, trying to explain as they guided her upstairs to the apartment, listening all the way. She told them how sad she was for Walter and how guilty she felt for leaving him, how mad it made her that she felt relieved this would only be for a few months, and how unfair it was that she could somehow feel so happy and yet so sad all at the same time. Marley carried the bags she had brought with her and Pip never took his arm from around her shoulders. Whatever they had been going out to do, they abandoned their plans for her. Although she felt a little bit ridiculous, Autumn was strangely relieved they had witnessed a dramatic reaction like this from her now. She tended to do this when something upset her, so it wouldn't be the last time they were privy to it. Better to get it out of the way. Still, she said sorry after almost every sentence, while Pip sat patiently beside her, holding her hand and brushing away her apologies. "Say sorry again, Autumn," Marley said, handing her a cup of tea and playfully shaking his head. "How dare you be so kind and attached to the old man who lives next door. The audacity! Disgusting behaviour."

She laughed at his teasing, feeling, for the first time in her life, proud of her sensitivity and pleased someone had interpreted it as kind.

"You're just like Bowie, you know," Pip said. "He does this, too. Feels guilty about things that aren't his responsibility to sort out."

She'd asked them not to tell their brother but they had, of course. Later, Bowie told her he was proud of her for caring so deeply, but reminded her Walter had been OK before she'd arrived and would be OK again when she was gone. She knew he was right, but that didn't make it any easier. Walter had come to rely on her for company and now she was leaving him all alone.

She returned to give Walter one last hug the day before her flight, suddenly concerned he might pass away before she saw him again. She promised herself that no matter what happened, she would never forget him.

She never did.

* * *

The Whittle family home was built in ageing grey stone and centred in a garden that wrapped all the way around it. It took a full five minutes to walk from the end of the driveway to the porch. A forest ran along one side of the property. She'd never seen privilege like it in real life before and it made her a little uncomfortable.

Ben, Emma and Bluebell waited for Autumn at the airport for three hours after their own flight had landed and watched her with an element of pride as her jet-lagged brain tried to absorb the grandeur of her new home from the back seat of their four-wheel drive. Autumn, eager to please, 'ooh-ed' and 'aah-ed' in the right places. Bluebell, who knew Autumn would feel uncomfortable about the number of times she'd condemned wealthy people out loud, sat silently beside her, restraining a small smirk at the edge of her lips.

As they clambered out of the car, Emma told Autumn that they kept three sheep, Dolly, Nellie and Jessica, as well as four feisty chickens called Carrie, Charlotte, Miranda and Samantha. The animals had been under the care of a neighbour whilst they'd been away.

"Stupid names," Emma muttered. "You know, Autumn, I didn't realise for a long time that the kids named my chickens after improper TV characters."

"They're not improper, thank you, they're sex-loving women and they're awesome," Bluebell said.

"How is being sex loving relevant to chickens?" Emma asked. "They're not known for being particularly amorous, are they? Unless there's a cockerel around, which there isn't."

"It's not that deep, Mum, and what did you want us to name them? Breast? Or Nugget? Or Thigh? Or . . ." Bluebell paused, deep in thought. "I can't think of a fourth."

"Thank God." Emma winced.

"Feet?" Autumn suggested helpfully. "People eat chicken feet, don't they?"

"Good shout," Bluebell said. "Or skin, because people eat that."

"Kiev," Autumn added.

"Girls," Ben said warningly.

Autumn and Bluebell giggled.

"I was thinking something more like Lady Featherington or Henny Penny. Henrietta or something like that."

"Mum, Marley wanted to name one Hennifer Aniston and you were having none of it," Bluebell said.

"Oh, because that's stupid." Emma sighed. She wanted them to think she was irritated, but Autumn could tell she was actually mildly amused.

The house was gothically beautiful. Its tall, wooden front door was rusting at the hinges and its stonework chipped and crumbling, but it was still breathtaking. Exhausted, they took their time climbing the steps up to the door, dragging their luggage behind them.

"Listen to that." Emma held her hands out to quiet their heavy breathing. Bluebell and Autumn stood still, looking at each other. Autumn held her breath.

"Nature's silence." Emma sighed happily. Bluebell rolled her eyes.

Prompted by Emma, Autumn made an effort to take in her new surroundings while they waited for Ben to open the door. It had been months since her ears had been free from the sound of wheels whirring and horns blaring. Here, there was no shouting, no buzz of electricity, no unnatural noise. Autumn let herself breathe in tranquillity. She had never been anywhere like this her whole life. It was far from the town she had grown up in, and even further from New York.

The door opened into a double-height living room, with three large sofas and two squashy armchairs arranged around a television sitting on a coffee table upon an enormous, patterned rug. Off to the left was an open-plan kitchen, and a wide staircase to the right led to a second floor, with a mezzanine level that looked down into the lounge. There were framed photographs on every wall, mostly of the children all together, many of them wearing various costumes. Autumn could not tell the difference between Bowie and Marley when they were young. Emma explained that the family had been appearing in amateur dramatics productions since they'd been old enough to walk. She had many more pictures of them performing and she would show her later, she promised. Bowie and Marley, who had taken a taxi straight home from the airport so that Bowie could rest, groaned in unison from the sofa. Emma laughed, leading Autumn through the living room and into a bedroom on the ground floor. It ran almost the entire length of the house.

"This used to be a dining room but we turned it into a bedroom for the twins because they used to stay up all night laughing together," Emma said.

Ben laughed. "They still do that now! Looking back, Autumn saw Marley nudge Bowie affectionately, and the twins grinned at each other.

"True," Emma said. "Anyway, we moved them down here, out of the way, so they don't disturb anyone."

The room had soft green walls and wooden floors, white linen, several ornate, expensive-looking lamps, and blankets and cushions that complemented the décor. There were two double beds with matching nightstands, a dressing table, and a desk sitting between two floor-to-ceiling windows that looked out across the garden at the back of the house. Autumn felt as though she was in a hotel. She turned on the spot, trying to take everything in. When she arrived back at her starting position, Marley was standing before her, holding the luggage she'd abandoned in the living room.

"I'm going to bunk in with Pip." He set Autumn's cases down in the middle of the floor.

Autumn protested. "You don't have to do that."

"As if I want to be in here with you two lovebirds," he said jokingly.

"I meant . . ."

"I know what you meant." He batted her comment away, checking to make sure they weren't being listened to before he continued. "It's fine, Autumn. Stop being so nice all the time. Settle in. This is your home now."

She appreciated the sentiment because she *was* feeling really nervous and was touched he had noticed. She thanked him with a smile and he nodded reassuringly at her, his eyes crinkling at the corners under the weight of genuine warmth.

Her developing friendship with Marley had taken her by surprise. Bluebell had not been lying when she'd told her Bowie would need a lot of sleep and, so, in her final days in New York, Autumn had spent a lot of her time sitting and writing with Marley. He wrote songs while she wrote notes for her new project. He hadn't been anything like she had expected. He had seemed cocky and arrogant that first night in the theatre — aloof and dismissive — but that wasn't how Autumn saw him now. He was open, attentive and empathetic. He cared about things the way Bowie did but, unlike his brother, stopped just short of allowing his heart to rule his head. He was incredibly intelligent, quick-witted and opinionated. She felt comfortable around him, which was just as well, because he wanted to be with Bowie *all the time*. Autumn didn't mind — the twins were the same, yet different. She enjoyed being with them, both individually and together. They brought out the best in each other and it was entertaining to be around them.

Marley broke their moment to take the duvet and pillows from one of the beds.

"Really, Marley," she said. "Thank you."

"Don't mention it," he said, heading for the door. He kicked Bowie playfully, joking as he passed. "I'll think of some way for you two to repay me. It'll probably be washing-up. Or laundry."

Bowie. They had only been apart a matter of hours, but Autumn had missed him terribly.

"Where's my girl?" he called to her.

She marched from the bedroom and cast herself into his arms.

***

"Imagine if I'd told you three weeks ago this is where you'd be right now," Bowie murmured later that night. The house was colder in the evening. They'd made love and then he'd wrapped himself around her to keep her warm. She wanted another blanket, but Autumn couldn't face the cold wooden floors beneath her feet. Concerned for his wellbeing, she had swaddled the spare one they had around Bowie, but she knew he would try to give it back to her if he felt her shiver. Emma and Ben did everything they could to keep the house warm, but Bowie's father had warned her that the heat seeped through the old stone like water through a sieve.

"I wouldn't have imagined I'd be back in England, let alone here, in this beautiful house, with my best friend and her big brother. It's wild," she said. She shuffled unconsciously closer still and he held her tighter to him.

"Cold?" he asked. She nodded. "I have a way to warm you up," he said. He hooked his leg over hers and turned her to face him, kissing her neck suggestively.

"Bowie . . ." There was an edge of warning in her tone.

"Rule Number Two."

"I think you need to take it a little easier than that."

He rolled insistently on top of her in reply. She was powerless to resist this man. She let him kiss her, but her mind was elsewhere.

"I'm scared, Bowie," she whispered. He'd been doubled up and crying out because of pain in his back for hours and had confessed he was having heart palpitations all evening. In the kitchen over coffee, while Emma and Ben combed the house for painkillers, Maddie had told Autumn that Bowie's lymphoma caused him anaemia, which meant his body had to work harder than was typical to get oxygen, and that's where she suspected his heart palpitations came from. The consequences of this anaemia were likely to get worse and lead to further complications. Still, ever grateful and optimistic, Bowie had told Autumn he could handle anything this disease threw at him as long as it didn't attack his central nervous system.

He persisted now. "Rule Number Two."

She sighed. "I'm not treating you as though you're dying."

"Yes, you are. If I weren't dying, you'd let me do what we both want me to do."

He kissed her deeply and she responded with great enthusiasm this time. Bowie moved his mouth to her breast and she found herself unable to focus on her argument.

"Those rules are stupid," she said breathlessly. She felt his smile against her skin, wrapped his hair around her hands and marvelled at how obsessed she had become with him. He was much more than a lover. He was an obsession. An addiction.

And that, though glorious, was the foundation of all of her fears.

**

They slept well afterwards, despite the cold, but Bowie was not done with having her to himself. He promised her he felt well enough to take her out for the day. Though Autumn was frightened he might be overdoing it, he whined until she gave in. When Emma and Ben tried to object, he beat them down with whinging, too. They were persuaded by the revelation that he was craving pizza. It was so rare for Bowie to fancy anything to eat because the side effects of his medication left him feeling nauseous all the time. Emma was on a one-woman mission to force-feed him at every available opportunity and she was thrilled to hear that he might entertain the idea of eating willingly.

They decided to go to the cinema first. They were jet-lagged and tired, but the atmosphere between them was joyous and playful. At the sweet stand, they stuffed the largest paper bag they could find with more gelatine-free fizzy cola bottles, sherbet lemons, gummy lips and mini gems than was sensible, taking it in turns to hold the seams together, and guessing, with giddiness, how much their haul would cost while they waited in line. The man behind the counter found their folly amusing, telling them, with a grin, that they owed him sixty-two pounds for the sweets and the tickets. It felt so good to be one half of the cute couple people laughed at.

"How long is this going to take us to eat?" she asked, confident that she could polish it all off, with his help, within a couple of days.

"That depends," he said. "Are we getting popcorn or no?"

"Obviously."

"Two hours then," he said. She laughed and he smiled.

The movie was rubbish, but it had never really been about seeing a great film. Autumn leaned as far across her seat as she could, resting her head on his shoulder and wedging the armrest so painfully between her ribcage and armpit she knew that she'd be left with a bruise. She didn't care. Bowie fed her a mixture of sweets and popcorn, and they sat happily together in the semi-darkness for two hours, just like a normal couple would. It was almost as though one of them was not dying. Autumn managed not to think about it. She thought about her work, her parents, his parents, about how his hand felt in hers, how long and slender his fingers were, everything except how crap the movie was and how soon days like this would be impossible.

As they left, Bowie rubbed his hands together.

"Pizza, then?" he said.

"I thought you were making that up so Emma would let you come," Autumn said.

"I was. But now I want pizza."

She clutched her stomach, full to the brim with sugar and popcorn.

"I can't eat another thing, Bowie—"

"You promised me pizza!" He pouted, folding his arms petulantly across his chest. Autumn laughed, her stomach fluttering at the sight of him. She could hardly believe if she'd come across Bowie for the first time in any other situation than the circumstances in which they'd met, she'd have almost certainly looked straight through him. Now that she knew him, his wide blue eyes and floppy blonde hair made her heart melt. She loved his height and his trademark awkwardness and his ridiculously large feet. She relished the fact his nose was too big for his face. She liked his lips, the little freckle on his cheek, and even how pasty his skin was. Occasionally, Autumn thought back to the other men she'd slept with and those she hadn't deemed attractive enough to even consider. How many of them could she have learned to love in the way she loved Bowie if she'd only gotten to know them? Maybe none of them. The storyteller inside her liked to believe what she had with Bowie was special, although she also knew that that was probably naive.

When Bowie's pizza came, Autumn found she couldn't help herself. Eating was becoming ever easier for her now that she was happy. Being around Bowie and his family was doing her good, she knew. Autumn felt strange admitting that to herself, she was here because Bowie was ill, after all. But it was true. The simplicity of their family life calmed her nerves and helped her focus on small joys in a way she never had before. Glimmers, Bluebell called them. Little things that made her smile or gave her peace. The more she did that, the less she felt she needed to control things, including what she ate. She took her time chewing her way through a slice. Bowie ploughed through the rest like a lion on a carcass. It was good to see him enjoying his food.

"Are you ever going to tell me about your family?" he asked her, with no warning. Autumn looked down at the table, shaking her head. "Why not?"

She knew he wasn't trying to make her feel as though she was obliged to talk, but his request still made her bristle. Bowie's family were completely in love with each other. She wasn't quite sure he knew how rare that was. Like most people, he was a reflection of his parents: he was liberal and open-minded, non-violent and loving. For him to even begin to understand her family, Autumn would need to reveal a side of herself she wasn't very proud of. She would never take any man she met to her hometown. She didn't want to talk about her parents and sibling at all. She was ashamed of who they were and of who she had been, and had worked hard over the years to erase the girl she had been in her past.

"I don't want to," she said. She knew this would be explanation enough. Bowie would never force her to talk about anything she was uncomfortable discussing.

"Will you be going to visit them?" he asked. She wished he would leave it alone.

"No." She shook her head.

"Do they even know that you're home?"

"No."

Nodding and eyeing her cautiously, he threw her a dopey smile. She forgave him his curiosity and he changed the subject.

* * *

There wasn't much else to do in a provincial town on a Wednesday night, but Bowie and Autumn were not ready to go home to everyone else. They wished they'd gone to London straight from the cinema, but Bowie was too tired now for a big night out. In the end they found a bar nearby. Autumn bought a bottle of wine and a packet of cigarettes, and they sat outside beside a fire pit.

"This is all Marley's fault." Bowie watched her light up.

"No, it isn't." She shook her head, making sure to blow her smoke away from him. "I've always smoked socially."

"I'd say that what you two are doing at the moment is more than social smoking," he said. He was right, she conceded. She and Marley had smoked their way through hundreds of cigarettes since that night on the balcony. She hardly thought about smoking when he wasn't there, but when he offered her one she was powerless to resist. He *was* a bad influence, but she wasn't about to admit that to Bowie. He, understandably, wanted them both to quit.

"I'll stop soon," she said.

"Life is too fragile, too short, to mess about with this shit," he said, pointedly tapping the packet.

Autumn flicked her cigarette snippily. "He says, though he's no longer accepting treatment that could extend his life."

"Please don't," he warned her. His voice was soft, but his expression was stern. Autumn sighed. She'd never once yet suggested he deviate from his chosen course of action, but the more she got to know him the harder she found it hard to accept he no longer wanted to fight.

He swallowed hard. "Maddie is the best person to speak to about this. She's a great believer in letting people do what they want. We had a whole conversation once about suicide and she basically believes that if someone really wants to kill themselves, they should be allowed to."

Autumn raised her eyebrows.

"I mean, within certain limits, obviously. But, basically, her reasoning is that those who are crying for help should be signposted to the right support, but someone who really wants to end it should have the freedom to choose for themselves. Even helped, in some situations."

"What situations?" Autumn asked, wishing, instantly, that she hadn't.

"Mine, I guess," Bowie said.

Autumn considered his words before responding.

"I support euthanasia for the terminally ill, but what about people with manic depression? I don't think you can ever really know that someone wouldn't recover with the right support."

"I'd like the opportunity to decide when I've had enough. I hate begging people to kill me. It's very undignified."

She winced. She'd spent a lot of time dreading the day Bowie might ask her to do the unthinkable, ever since Emma had mentioned it on the night she'd met his family for the first time. She'd found out later that had happened because Bowie had been experiencing extremely bad bone pain for several days and — in an exhausted, confused and dehydrated state — had convinced himself cancer had spread to his brain and had panicked. He seemed to sense her concern.

"If I asked her to, I know Maddie would help me," he said.

Autumn reeled. "She could get in serious trouble for that."

"I'd have to be one hundred percent sure that wouldn't happen before I'd allow it," he said.

Autumn didn't have to ask about expensive clinics in Switzerland. The Whittles would never give him their blessing to go and he would never cause them the pain that would come with sneaking away, or put them through the inevitable desperation they would feel to chase and stop him.

"What about Marley?" Autumn asked, instead. "Will Maddie help him kill himself when you're gone?"

Bowie dragged sadly from his cigarette and sighed. Despite lengthy conversations about trivial things and existential matters, she and Bowie had never spoken about Marley's intention to take his own life. The entire family seemed to think ignoring the issue was the best way to deal with it. Autumn felt like someone should be talking to Marley about it, but every time she mentioned it to any of the others they politely shrugged her off, and she didn't feel she knew Marley well enough to broach the topic directly with him herself.

"Probably. I don't know. I think these things are easy to say but, when it comes to it, I think it would be harder than she imagines. Helping me is different. I'm dying anyway. But Marley . . ."

Autumn was irritated by his flippancy. She wanted him to be distraught. She cut him off. "Marley will get over you," she said.

Bowie shook his head.

"He *will*, Bowie. Things won't ever be the same for him, I know. But given the right time and the right support, Marley will get through it."

"*I* would never, ever get over it, if Marley died. Never. I can't imagine my life without him. There is no life without him."

"You would," Autumn said insistently. He stared at her.

"Marley is more than just my brother and my best friend, he's the other half of me. Long before I was diagnosed with cancer, when we were kids, we used to talk about what we would do if anything happened to either of us all the time, because we were absolutely terrified about one of us dying and leaving the other. We've never wanted to live without each other."

"But he has so much to live for."

"It doesn't matter what he has." Bowie shook his head. "You know how much I love the rest of my family, but how I feel about them doesn't even come close to how I feel about

Marley. I would sacrifice any one of them to protect my brother. That might be an ugly thing to say, but it's true. I can't explain it. I could cope with anything, absolutely anything life has to throw at me, but not losing Marley."

"That's ridiculous." Autumn shook her head, exasperated. "I don't know how you can . . ."

"You don't know because you're not us." She was stung by his suddenly harsh tone, but he did have a point. She had no real right to tell him what he and Marley could and couldn't cope with. She watched his face flood with remorse. "I'm sorry." He sighed.

"It's all right," she said.

"No, it's not." He shook his head. "The others don't bother anymore because they already know all of this, but you don't. How could you? You're brand new here. It feels like I've known you so long that I forget that sometimes."

She knew he was trying to end the conversation. She knew he expected her to stop. But she couldn't. Words were Autumn's way of working out the world and she needed to know more.

"What if Bluebell told you she was going to kill herself when you were gone?" she asked.

"I'd get on my knees and beg her not to do it."

"Have you done the same to Marley?"

"It's different," he said. "He'd call me a hypocrite. And he'd be right."

It was so tragic Autumn could hardly stand it. The more time they'd spent together writing, smoking and talking, the fonder she was becoming of Marley. He was talented, funny and sweet. She felt desperate to stop all of this from happening, but she didn't know what she could do except hope against hope that when it came to it, Marley would discover — as she had once for herself — thinking about and acting on that feeling of hopelessness were two entirely different matters.

"Do you really think he could do it?" she asked. She had once felt exactly as Marley did now — certain she was going to take her own life, waiting for the right moment to do it. Climbing over the railings had been easy for her, but letting go and stepping out had been harder than she'd expected. Her potential non-existence had frozen her rigid. No matter how hard her frantic mind had tried to convince her that was what she'd wanted, in the end she'd found herself frightened she might slip. She'd been sober enough to realise that that must have meant she hadn't really wanted to die. The entire episode had transformed the way Autumn felt about suicide. As far as she was concerned, someone had to be unimaginably distressed and immeasurably brave to take that step. Sure, Marley was threatening suicide, but would he actually find himself able to do it when the time came?

"I know he will," Bowie said. "We've never wanted to live without each other. This is exactly what Maddie is talking about. She would argue Marley should be allowed to make his own choice when the time comes because he knows what he wants."

"I bet your mum and dad love that," Autumn said.

"Nobody talks about it because we know it'll turn into a fight. Marley won't discuss it with anyone. Sometimes he starts when he's drunk, but Dad is pretty good at shutting him up."

"Losing you both will destroy your family."

"Yeah, we know that."

"Well, can't Marley consider how they will feel?"

It sounded selfish; she didn't really know why. She didn't want Marley to die. How could that be wrong? She closed her eyes and sighed. Bowie reached for her hand.

"I can't set myself on fire to light the path for you," he said.

It was a line from her favourite piece of poetry, a piece by a woman called Pippa Benjamin. She'd recited it to him on the evening they'd met. The context he was using wasn't quite right — it was actually about someone taking the blame for her lover's poor behaviour. She considered defensively telling him he'd interpreted the poem wrong, but Autumn knew what he was trying to say. Marley could not live his life for the sake of others who depended on him for their happiness. And that was the point of poetry, wasn't it? To take the bits that had meaning for you and use them when your own words failed you.

Autumn lit another cigarette.

"That's an odd defence for a man who'd snuff out his own life because he loves you so much," she said. "And I think we both know Marley would do absolutely anything to make life easier for you. He dotes on you. You live for him and him for you. I'd hazard a guess he would, in fact, set himself alight to light the path if he was doing it for you, he just wouldn't do it for anybody else."

"The rules don't apply when it comes to each other."

"You've made surviving without each other impossible," Autumn said.

Bowie shrugged. Autumn continued.

"He's spent thirty-four years living for you, existing because you do. It's up to you to convince him there's life out there beyond the two of you growing old together. Other people to live for. Joy and happiness that exist without you. You're the only one who can do it."

Bowie stared at her.

"I get it now," she said. "Nobody is talking to Marley because everyone thinks it's pointless. You've convinced yourselves there's no life unless you both have one and everyone who loves you knows it. They think Marley's suicide is inevitable. This course of action was decided by you both when you were children who didn't know any better and now Marley won't listen to anyone. He thinks it's the only way forward for him, because he can't imagine living without you, and because *you're* certain *you* would kill yourself if things were the other way around. But you *could* convince him otherwise."

Bowie swallowed, shifting his gaze to the floor.

"You could at least try," she said.

"I have," he whispered, fixing his eyes on hers again. He was fighting back tears. "I promise, I have. In private, so he doesn't feel ganged up on by everyone. He shouts me down, Autumn. He asks me what I would do and I can't lie, not to him, he can spot it in a second, so he calls me a hypocrite. He turns on me, tells me I don't know what he's going through. Sometimes he cries. I can't stand it, so I give in. He wants to know at least one person understands and how can that be anyone but me?"

She switched seats so they were sitting closer together, wrapping her arm supportively around his shoulders. Bowie closed his eyes and cried.

"I'm haunted by visions of the things he might do to himself. By the idea that he'll be all alone, scared and unsupported. It's there, in my head, all the time. I'm the only person who can put myself in his shoes. I'm the only person who gets it. He knows everyone else thinks he's mad. Every time I try to argue with him about it, it pushes him further away from me and into himself. I can't keep arguing with him, Autumn. Every time I do, I'm telling him he's on his own."

Bowie sobbed and Autumn held him close to her, lost in thought. She'd been forever changed by this conversation.

They really were all alone. All of them. No matter who you had around you and how much they loved you, you were battling through life by yourself, free to decide what was too much for you to live with. Or without, as the case might be. When it was your time to die, you'd be doing it on your own, whether people were sitting at your bedside holding your hand or you were alone in your flat with a noose-shaped rope.

Still, it mattered. She knew that now.

CHAPTER 8

It was 7 a.m. on a Thursday morning and Bowie was staring despondently at a stranger at the front door.

"I've been calling your home number but nobody ever answers."

"And you didn't take the hint?" Bowie asked, stepping back to invite him in. He sounded amused, if not a little irritated. Bowie led the way to the kitchen, his fluffy blue dressing gown floating dramatically behind him like a cape.

Autumn, who had come to investigate, could barely manage a friendly smile. She, Marley and Bluebell had shared an entire bottle of rum and a whole bottle of vodka between the three of them the night before. Her head felt like someone had taken a chainsaw to it. Bowie put the kettle on, inviting the man to sit down.

"Autumn, this is Larry Ross. Larry Ross, this is my girlfriend, Autumn."

"Nice to meet you." He reached out to shake her hand. Autumn took it and shook it, but could not summon interest in Larry Ross or whatever it was he wanted. She wished she hadn't left their bed to answer the door with Bowie and wondered if it would be rude to bid them goodbye and slither back into their bedroom. She was about to do it when she noticed Bowie had taken three mugs from the cupboard, one for each of them. She sat down, dejected. Larry was making small talk. She focused her attention on his bony cheeks, hollow green eyes and pointy, middle-aged nose.

"I didn't know you had a girlfriend, Bowie. How long have you two been together?"

"A couple of months. We met right before I came home."

Autumn saw judgement flicker across Larry's face. She scowled at the kitchen counter. Who was this stupid Larry Ross, with his stupid opinions and his stupid, expressive face? She was not in the mood for this.

"Nice," he said.

"What do you want, Larry?" Bowie asked stiffly, handing him a mug of coffee. Larry took a sip and set it down. He clasped his hands in front of his face and blinked theatrically. Bowie rolled his eyes.

"I need you, Bowie," he said. Bowie shook his head.

"I'm retired."

"I know that, but I need you."

"I know that, but I'm retired," Bowie repeated shirtily.

"How much do I need to pay you?"

"I have enough money."

"Then what do I need to do?"

"There's nothing you can do. I don't want to work."

Larry guffawed dramatically, quietening himself with a hand across his mouth. His laugh echoed throughout the house. He mouthed a silent sorry at each of them in turn, hiding a smirk behind his fingertips. His playful manner succeeded in making Autumn smile. If she hadn't been seriously considering the possibility she might have alcohol-induced kidney failure, she imagined she might even like him. Bowie glared at him.

"If my mother comes down those stairs and finds you here, she's going to kill us both," he said warningly.

"I know. I'm sorry. But, seriously, Bowie, everybody who knows you knows that your work is your life."

Larry Ross had a stupid face, but he was right about that. Bowie was still working constantly, no matter what he said.

Emma disapproved, but he often hid himself away to scribble down melodies or play compositions on his piano. He and Marley would sit for hours with their guitars in the garden. They talked and wrote and sang together, while the other Whittles enjoyed the sunshine and Autumn tried to focus on writing her own work. Emma, always desperate for attention from her sons, whined incessantly about it.

"Nobody ever wishes they'd spent more time at work when they're on their deathbed." She would remind them of this at least once a day and Marley would argue back every single time.

"That saying only applies to people who hate their job."

"Do something you love and you'll never work a day in your life," Bowie might add, depending on if he had the energy.

Autumn knew Bowie loved his job as much as she loved hers. He'd been far too ill to do it now for several months. The theatre needed reliable people and Bowie's unpredictable fatigue meant he couldn't be relied upon. One evening, as they'd lain side by side on the sofa, she'd asked him if he missed being able to work and he'd almost burst into tears.

"Yes. More than anything. I have stuff in my head that I want to write down all the time, but it's so painful to work on ideas I know I'll never be here to see."

"You should do it," Autumn said encouragingly. "It's your art and art should be expressed. Let other people feel it. Imagine if Freddie Mercury hadn't written 'Bohemian Rhapsody' because he had AIDS."

That made him smile.

"Freddie Mercury wrote 'Bohemian Rhapsody' in 1975 and wasn't diagnosed with AIDS until 1987."

"That is ridiculously pointless knowledge!" she said. He laughed. "You know what I mean. How many people are there like you, stopping themselves from being creative for one reason or another? How many songs like 'Bohemian Rhapsody' have we missed out on because people were too afraid to write stuff down?"

"You think about things differently," he said, kissing her on the tip of her nose. "I love that."

"Not everyone is capable of creating things. If you have something magic inside of you then you owe it to the world to set it free."

He pondered her words for a minute.

"I wish you'd say this to Marley. He's wasting so much potential, lying around here singing with me. He's wasting his talent. He should be setting up a future for himself. Perhaps if he was, things would be different . . ."

She couldn't disagree. Autumn had seen something special in Marley the night she'd watched him play — the night she'd met Bowie. She'd bet her life hardly anyone in that room had taken their eyes off him for more than a minute all evening. He rarely actually performed anymore, preferring to spend his time writing with Bowie. The songs they wrote together were catchy, creative and conscientiously crafted. Autumn was always impressed by how quickly they could take a melody or a lyric and turn it into something that sounded exceptional. They sometimes wrote two or three songs a day.

Like his brother, Autumn knew Marley was struggling to cope with a lack of purpose. He'd seen little success with his band — they'd performed at small venues and weddings mostly — but his bandmates had kept him busy and he'd confessed to her over a cigarette one evening that he was finding it tough to stay strong without some sort of distraction.

"When I was in New York with the band, I could forget all of this shit. I could focus on the music. Now, I have nothing to do but think about what's happening to Bowie. It's driving me mad."

He was compelled to write almost all day, every day. He took his guitar wherever he went. The songs he wrote were haunting and beautiful. Bowie and Autumn often implored him to upload them onto music-sharing platforms but he always refused. Every piece he produced was written from a place of pain. Strangers hearing them was absolutely not what he wanted.

Autumn understood how he felt. She'd split her time that summer between writing her manuscript and penning poetry, something that did not typically come naturally to her. The bedroom she shared with Bowie was littered with pieces of paper she'd made him promise he would never pick up and read. She didn't know what was happening to her, why she felt so suddenly inspired. She'd never been able to pull words together in this way. Inspiration flowed through her brain and out of her fingertips at all hours of the day and night. She never read anything she wrote twice. One day, probably long after Bowie was gone, she would throw the scraps of paper away, but for now she was using them as therapy and it offered her a little bit of relief to be around people who understood how it felt to be utterly overwhelmed and frustrated by the constant urge to be creative. At least the three of them were facing that unusual form of torture together.

Lifting her head from her reverie, Autumn heard Bowie lie to Larry.

"Work used to be my life," he said.

Larry sighed. He looked defeated.

"I have two days until previews and I cannot get my finale to work."

"Where's your musical director?"

"He's there. But he's no Bowie Whittle."

Autumn was surprised to see Bowie's chest swell, almost imperceptibly. Bowie was not typically the type to take comfort in compliments but his reputation as a musical director meant a lot to him, she knew. Larry clearly knew it too. She suspected this wasn't the first time he'd used flattery to manipulate Bowie.

"I need you to have a look at it and tell us what to do with it," he said. Bowie paused to think. He shook his head again.

"I can't. I've already said goodbye to it all."

Larry gripped his coffee cup and stood up to reach across the kitchen counter. He touched Bowie's hand. It was an incredibly intimate thing to do. Bowie had never mentioned Larry to her, but the two were obviously friends.

"Bowie, don't make me beg you. Please. Please. We need you. You're the only one who can help us. Most of the cast is asking for you. Why else would I come all the way out here? It's going to go to shit unless you sort it out. Think of it as—"

"If you say the words 'lasting legacy', you dickhead, I'm going to throw this coffee in your face."

Larry made a show of rolling his lips tight shut and clasped his hands together, shaking them towards Bowie in a pleading motion that made them both smile. Bowie was beginning to waver, Autumn could tell. She silently willed him to agree to do it. He'd been feeling well recently and he quite clearly missed his life in the theatre.

"Please?" Larry whispered when Bowie still said nothing. Bowie groaned, slamming his coffee cup into the sink. Larry's stupid face had won.

"There had better be an endless supply of soya cappuccinos there when I arrive," Bowie said.

* * *

"Bowie!"

There were no fewer than forty people up on the stage and they sang out his name like a chorus. Several of them ran down to greet him. He opened his arms to receive them in a group hug.

"Be careful with me," he said cautiously.

They were dressed in the most fabulous nineties costumes: oversized T-shirts, garish jumpers, pedal pushers, sequined crop tops and platform Union Jack boots she was sure she'd seen on the Spice Girls. Some of the women were wearing blue hair mascara and had glitter gel daubed on their faces. They were all wearing too much lip gloss. The stage was dressed as a nightclub, complete with disco ball and adequately dingy-looking carpet. There were streamers everywhere.

"The nineties are vintage now." Larry nudged Autumn and smiled. Now that her head was a little less tender, she'd decided she did like him after all. Larry was a big character: dramatic, exuberant and entertaining.

"When did we get so old?" Bowie asked, hugging everyone.

"How are you, hon?" asked a gorgeously tall man. He was wearing an impressively sparkly bodysuit and block-heeled sandals. Bowie embraced him a little harder than the others.

"I'm doing OK, Phil, thanks. This is Autumn, by the way."

Autumn waved shyly.

"We miss you," said a petite blonde girl. Her waist-length hair was slicked back in a perfectly tight high ponytail.

"I miss you all too."

"Lies!" Larry shot back. "If you missed us then you'd answer when we call."

"No, I do. It's just . . . hard." Bowie swallowed, turning to look at the stage. The cast exchanged sad smiles. Phil looked as though he might cry. Autumn had wondered what had happened to Bowie's friendships. He'd never spoken of any friends, or wanted to meet anyone, nor mentioned them in passing. She'd wondered if perhaps he'd been a bit of a loner like her, but now she knew the truth. Bowie had friends here, in the theatre, hordes of them, but he'd already chosen to let them go. His apprehension about helping Larry had never been about not wanting to work, he just didn't want to have to say goodbye to the people he loved all over again.

"One more time, eh?" Larry gripped Bowie's shoulders affectionately. Bowie slapped him playfully in the chest.

"Oh, go on then. It can be my bloody 'lasting legacy' can't it? Now get on the stage, you group of legends, and sing me this shitty finale, will you?"

***

On their way to the theatre, Larry had explained the premise of the musical to them.

"It's about a young devout Christian couple who get married at eighteen and then realise he's gay and that she's sexually inquisitive, too. He's Caribbean — Phil is the lead. You remember Phil? It's all jazz hands and love and passion and death and cheating and scandal and liberalism. All the things you adore, Bowie, basically. You're going to love it. But this fucking finale. This *fucking* finale! I just can't get it to work. It just doesn't have that zazz, you know?"

Autumn didn't know what zazz was but Bowie seemed to agree that the finale did not have it. He folded his arms across his chest two lines in and they stayed folded until the cast had sung the last notes, held their position for applause and collapsed in a heap of sweaty despair. Autumn watched him with keen interest. She had never seen Bowie so engaged in anything before. His eyes darted around the stage in every direction, taking in all that he saw. She was quite sure that there was not a single movement or facial expression in the entire eight-minute performance that Bowie did not absorb. Autumn clapped enthusiastically when they were done. She genuinely liked it. Larry and the cast thanked her graciously. Bowie did not applaud. He motioned for the cast to sit on the edge of the stage, unfolded his arms and leaned on the table in front of him.

"Do any of you like this song?" he asked. The cast remained still and silent. A few of them tittered uncomfortably. Bowie turned to Larry, who was hiding his face in his hands.

"Don't do this to me, Bowie," he said pleadingly.

"You need to rewrite the finale."

"I preview in *two days*!"

"You're not going to get what you want from them if your cast don't like the song."

"Fuck, fuck, fuckity, fuck, fuck!" Larry threw himself down into a chair. "Why didn't any of you tell me?"

"It isn't their job to tell you, it's your job to know." Larry peered sheepishly back at Bowie over his steepled fingertips.

"Can you do it?" he asked tentatively.

Bowie winced and hesitated. "Possibly. Probably. Yeah. If I have Marley."

Larry stiffened. His gaze moved to meet the eyes of the cast. He was taking his time to think about it. Autumn bristled. She found herself surprised by how fiercely offended she was on Marley's behalf, realising in that moment that she felt as close to him as she was to Bluebell. Their friendship had bloomed in the very same way, with speed and intensity. She couldn't stand a bad word said about him and had to force herself not to react audibly.

Larry sighed. He shook his head, defeated.

"OK, call him," he said.

***

Marley watched the finale with a sickly expression on his face, shaking his head unapologetically as it came to a close.

"It's shit," he said. Bowie nudged him. His brother could be far more direct than Bowie and Autumn knew this embarrassed him at times.

"I think we've already established that," Larry said irritably. "Can you rewrite it or not?"

Marley mused over the question. "You probably don't deserve me to. But, yeah, I think we can."

He handed Autumn the laptop she'd asked him to bring so she could work on her own stuff alongside them.

"I don't know who you're trying to kid," Marley muttered to her.

"What's that supposed to mean?" she replied indignantly.

"There's no way you're going to do anything except stare at Bowie all day." Marley enjoyed teasing the two of them about their romance in a way that was, she was assured by the others, entirely normal for siblings who were close.

"We can stare at him together." Phil hooted with laughter. "God, I've missed his face."

"What about my face?" Marley asked.

Phil grinned. "He's the better-looking one."

"I've always thought it." Marley nodded.

"I'd climb either of them like a tree given a shot." Phil nudged Autumn playfully.

"You had your chance," Marley said jokingly.

"Give me another one."

"I'd eat you for breakfast."

"Still banging strangers in public bathrooms?"

Marley guffawed. "You bet," he said.

"Dirty, dirty bastard." Phil laughed. Their frivolity made Autumn happy. Whatever was happening between Larry Ross and Marley, there was clearly no animosity between him and Phil.

While Bowie, Marley and Larry conferred in a corner, the cast regaled Autumn with tales of Bowie's theatre work, delighting in one particular story in which he'd been forced to perform because the lead actor and understudy had both fallen ill just before the curtain was about to go up on a performance.

"Half of us went down with it — it was the chicken kebabs they served at lunch, we think," Phil said. "But Bowie, the vegan, hadn't had any chicken. He was the only one who knew it off by heart and had the talent to perform it. He hated every fucking minute. Anyone who knew him well enough could see it written all over his face. He's so fucking fabulous, but he's so damn shy."

Phil was right. Autumn had no idea how Bowie had managed to become so successful in an industry that favoured extroverts and the unashamedly eccentric. Her lover was quiet and bashful — a private and contemplative man, even when around those he loved the most. When they ate together as a family, Marley, Bluebell, Pip and Emma dominated the conversation. Bowie, Ben and Maddie would listen attentively, involving themselves only if they were addressed directly.

"We still wind him up about it," said the blonde with the perfect high ponytail as she bit her nails. They were the first words she'd spoken to Autumn directly, and Autumn knew what that meant. This woman — Clara — seemed unnecessarily self-conscious, but curious, too. Experience and intuition told Autumn that Clara didn't know how to behave around her. She had almost certainly been involved with Bowie before. Autumn made an extra effort to be friendly towards her, laughing a little louder than she usually would. She couldn't care less if the woman had slept with her boyfriend some time in the past. It was over now. Autumn was invading *her* environment, if anything, and there was no need for Clara to feel awkward around her.

Hannah — a tall, pretty actress with a short dark bob — did not share Autumn's desire to avoid drama stoked by times gone by. Someone mentioned Marley next and Hannah burst into noisy tears.

"I can't believe he had the gall to turn up when he knew I'd be here," she said between sobs. Autumn eyeballed Phil for an explanation.

"He broke her heart three years ago." He turned to Hannah. "Are you sure he knew you were here?" he asked with kindness. Hannah nodded.

"We had phone sex three weeks ago and I told him I got the gig."

Phil rolled his eyes.

"She's a glutton for punishment," he muttered. "Marley isn't boyfriend material. He's told her. He's told her over and over again, but she won't listen. She thinks he'll change his mind. Look at her, she's stunning and Marley can't keep his dick in his pants. They go round in an endless circle of shit."

Autumn was not surprised. Marley had once told Autumn that he'd never found himself wanting anything from any woman except sexual gratification. Once that had been fulfilled, he tended to lose all interest.

It had been raining that evening and they'd been smoking together while watching the world darken, dangling their feet over the edge of the ledge and into the rain.

"I always tell them what it is I want," he'd said. "Or don't want, as the case may be. I tell them before anything happens. But sometimes they're adamant I might change my mind, then they blame me when I don't. It's almost enough to put you off sex all together."

She raised her eyebrows at him from her spot on the floor in the corner of the porch.

"Actually, that might be a bit extreme." He grinned stupidly, then knocked theatrically on the wooden floor in what Autumn knew was meant to be a superstitious physical retraction of his statement. "Why do women do this, though?"

"It's not just women. Remember Adam? Your mate from the band. He treated Bluebell the exact same way. This isn't a problem with women. It's a problem with everybody. They're obsessed with the notion of love. The harder it is to attain, the more they want it. It makes life difficult for folks like us, who generally don't want anything except casual sex."

Marley didn't know anything about Autumn's history with men, but he, like his brother and sister, was non-judgemental when she revealed herself to be a lover of one-night stands. They talked long into the evening that night, safe in the knowledge that Bowie was distracted by mother-son time Emma had insisted they have. When she looked back on it, years later, she wondered if that was the night Marley became one of her best friends.

***

Bowie and Marley wrote and performed a new version of the finale for the cast, then spent hours working with them alongside a clearly irritated orchestra and an angry-looking choreographer. Autumn watched them perform together, enthralled. She could see what Bowie had meant about Marley and his showmanship. His voice was deep and powerful; he threw every fibre of his being into performing the song they had written. Bowie looked awkward and uncomfortable, as though he would rather be doing absolutely anything else, but Marley, in contrast, was truly captivating, an absolute natural, and she could tell he really didn't know how good he was, he just loved it and it showed.

By the time the cast had confirmed they were happier with the piece, it was late and Bowie could barely keep his eyes open. He insisted they go home, but promised to return in the morning to fine-tune the dynamics. Marley opted to stay behind with the orchestra and help them write up the changes to the music. Marley's ex-lover, Hannah, said she would stay too. They'd been looking anywhere but at each other all day, but Autumn saw them smile shyly at each other now.

Bowie climbed sulkily into a taxi. Autumn knew the extreme fatigue his lymphoma brought with it frustrated him more than any of his other symptoms because he so desperately wanted to be active. He wanted to stay with Marley and finish the job, but it was impossible, and she knew his mood would plummet as a result. Still, she thought she might know a way to cushion his disappointment.

"Don't fall asleep." She pinched his thigh flirtatiously. His whole body flinched and she knew he had been dozing. He groaned, rubbing his hand over his face.

"Am I on a promise?" he asked, shuffling closer to her. She laughed and kissed his hand, running her fingers up the inside of his thigh and nibbling playfully on his earlobe in an attempt to thwart his exhaustion.

"Yes, you are." She kissed him deeply. The initial urgency they'd once felt to make love had worn off a little, though neither took much persuading if the mood took the other. Still, these days they were in agreement that an evening spent eating snacks and watching movies in bed was an equally intimate use of their time. But not tonight. Autumn had always been incredibly aroused by talent, and watching Bowie when he was so wanted, so needed for his unique abilities, had driven her to distraction all afternoon. She'd watched his loping frame bound around the room and desired him so deeply she'd had to talk herself out of following him into the toilet to beg him to take her in a cubicle.

They kissed the whole way home and were relieved to find everyone was either in bed or out of the house when they got back. Bowie pulled her straight into the bedroom and kicked the door shut, slamming her back against the nearest wall. She hitched her leg around his waist and he hoisted her up, holding her hands above her head and biting gently at her neck.

"You're so sexy, Bowie," she whispered. He groaned and carried her to the bed. They undressed each other frantically. She hadn't wanted him this badly for a while.

"Autumn . . ." She gripped his back with one hand in anticipation, but nothing happened. He hovered above her, his face twisted and awkward. "I need a little more time," he said softly.

She realised she was grappling with him and stopped, embarrassed. He opened his mouth as though to say something, but nothing came out. She didn't know what to do. She'd never encountered this before. They watched each other for a moment. She willed herself to do something. Bowie was blushing and she didn't like his unease.

"Should I . . . touch myself, or something?" he asked.

"Here." She pushed him away from her, gesturing for him to lie on his back on the bed. Ignoring the concern in his eyes, she straddled him, hovering a few inches above him and leaning down to kiss him hard on the mouth. He moaned. His hands gripped her hips, driving her down into his groin. His skin was burning. He wanted her, she could feel it in every move he made, hear it in every sound that rose from his throat, but there was no response where they needed it. He muttered something. Autumn didn't catch the words, but she did hear frustration and concern. Desperate, she took him in her hands.

"Autumn—"

She shushed him and kept trying. He fell silent and she could tell he was waiting for her to stop. After a few minutes, she sat up beside him, defeated.

"I'm sorry." He reached out to tuck a piece of hair behind her ear. She shook her head, then took up residence in her usual spot, wrapped in his arms with her head on the dip in his chest, her favourite part of him.

"It's OK," she said.

They lay still for a minute.

"It isn't you," he said.

"I know." She kissed his bare skin.

They were silent again.

"We can still do . . . other things?" Bowie said. She looked up at his face in the moonlight, trying to ignore the burning desire his impotence had left between her legs. He was making himself a martyr to her needs. Any action he could not participate in fully would torture him, she knew, so she lied to Bowie for the first time ever.

"I think the moment might have passed for me too," she said.

* * *

Autumn slipped into the shower beside Bowie the next morning, hoping his body's reaction had been due to tiredness and stress, but they kissed passionately for close to ten minutes and nothing happened. This time, Bowie forgot his graciousness, slamming his fist so hard into the tiles above Autumn's head that Emma ran to the bathroom door to check on him.

"I'm fine," he said.

"OK, love. Be careful in there," his mum said.

They stood motionless in the shower. The water — so erotic to Autumn just moments before — battered her unpleasantly in the face. The senior Whittles' only house rule was that nobody had sex outside of their bedroom, out of respect for the rest of the household and to avoid any embarrassment. Emma would not be happy if she caught them in the shower together, so Autumn had no choice but to cling to Bowie until they were sure his mother had gone. Even then, she surprised herself. She didn't move. She was frozen rigid.

"I'm sorry," Bowie whispered. "I didn't mean to scare you."

Scared was an understatement. She hadn't been this frightened in years. Her heart was racing in a way it once had, a way long forgotten to her until now. She realised she'd let down a guard she hadn't known she'd had up until now, and that was because she had never expected such aggression from Bowie. He attempted to hug her, but gave up when he realised she was not responding, and tried to explain.

"I'm frustrated, but not with you." Those were not the words she needed to hear. The idea they may have shared their last ever tryst was torturous for her too — he didn't need to explain that. That wasn't the problem. The problem was the way he had reacted. She couldn't tell him it was OK, because it wasn't.

"I know." She peeled him off her and stepped out of the shower. Feeling vulnerable, she covered herself immediately with a towel. Mercifully, Bowie stayed where he was. He let her leave the bathroom and left her alone to get dressed. She yanked on a pair of jeans and one of his T-shirts, loading her fingers and neck with costume jewellery and popping a leopard-print headband on her head. She was tying the loose ends when he appeared. Her heart had slowed by then, but the surprise was still there, pouring through her veins and flushing her face an irritated red. Bowie was dry and she knew he'd been waiting in the bathroom to give her some space. He loitered in the doorway in his dressing gown.

"I'm sorry," he said. "That was a disgusting thing for me to do."

She turned to face him. She didn't know what to say.

"I didn't mean to scare you," he added.

"Well, you did," she told him. He flinched and looked down at his feet.

"I know. I'm so sorry. If anyone threw that kind of weight around my sisters, for any reason, I would punch them through a fucking wall."

Autumn turned back to the mirror. She wasn't done being mad at him yet. She stared at their reflections — hers pink with upset and his white with sorrow — and acknowledged her anger at his violence was more complicated than she'd realised. Autumn's stepfather had thrown his fists around as easily as that. After a year or two, her mother had become his punchbag of choice, and eventually Autumn had made it onto his list of things it was OK to hit. Her sister hadn't been immune, either. Any time anyone had done anything he hadn't liked, if he'd been in a bad mood or had just felt like hurting someone, he would beat them until they'd begged him to stop. When she was fifteen, Autumn had called her father and asked if she could live with him, but he'd said he thought it best that Autumn stayed with her mother. Autumn had always suspected her father didn't really care about her, but she hadn't expected him to turn her away when she'd explained what was happening to her at home.

It had been the first time she'd realised she'd had nowhere to run. Autumn had learned to deal with the punches over time, bracing her body to make sure that her bruises had been in places people couldn't see, but she had never forgiven her mother for staying with her stepfather, nor her father for turning her away when she'd needed him so desperately. Eventually, her stepfather had left her mother for another woman. Katherine had been heartbroken for weeks. Autumn had promised herself she would never again allow any man to act so violently around her, and she hadn't. Bowie had been the last man she'd expected to find herself so disappointed in.

She could feel him staring at her now. She'd never told him any of her story, but her reaction to his outburst, although appropriate, was undoubtedly uncharacteristically raw, and Bowie had recognised that instantly. She'd seen a sense of realisation flicker across his face, followed by a look of fear and then a deep remorse. She hated the potential for pity that came with being a victim. She'd never used what had happened to her as an excuse for anything. Ever. Now, because of Bowie, she'd behaved in a way that made her vulnerability obvious and she hated the fact she'd been forced to confront her demons, and to do so in front of him. She was madder at him for that than she was the act of violence in itself. She watched him now, still standing in the doorway.

The softer part of her, the bit he had awakened when he'd burst into her life, wanted to soothe his concern, but the old version of Autumn wouldn't let her. She wondered if this was what being comfortably in the middle felt like. Open, but not completely.

"I'm not one of them, Autumn," he whispered.

"Every violent man I've ever known has insisted he 'wasn't one of them'," she said.

"I know." He swallowed.

"Don't ever do that to me again."

"I won't." He shook his head.

She watched him in the mirror for a minute. Eventually, she turned and held her hand out to him. He padded across the room and scooped her up in his arms. She held on to him tightly. The teenage Autumn inside her — the tough girl from the council estate — felt cheated by her adult self and her readiness to forgive, but Autumn pushed that part of herself aside. She would not make excuses for him, but she wanted to acquit him.

"Do you want to tell me about it?" he asked, and she realised she was crying. She held him tighter and closed her eyes.

"Can you take me for breakfast first?"

He laughed and nodded. Autumn's appetite had been growing at the same rate as her happiness. The Whittles presented her with delicious vegan food alongside a healthy dose of appetite daily, and Autumn found it difficult to restrict her eating anymore. She knew now that there was something psychological there — something about control and insecurity — but she wasn't ready to psychoanalyse it yet. Instead she ate more intuitively and exercised with Bluebell and Maddie in the garden almost every day, mainly yoga, but sometimes they'd do laps of the house.

There were many healthy rituals and one of those was breakfast with Bowie in a local café on Friday mornings. Despite their commitment to return to the theatre that day, they'd been showering early so as to stick to their routine. Autumn had been looking forward to it. It was one of her favourite things they did together, probably her favourite now it seemed they could no longer have sex, and she didn't want to miss a single one. If she'd known their last time together would be their last time, perhaps she'd have taken it slower. Savoured it more. Done it more often. She had taken that part of their lives for granted and she didn't want to do that with this.

They walked to the coffee shop, placed their order and waited for their breakfast to arrive: the full vegan works for Autumn and vegan pancakes for Bowie. She knew he would barely eat any of it. He'd writhed with stomach pain all through the night. His anxiety about the musical was not helping. They chatted about it while they waited. Bowie wanted to do his absolute best for Larry, and Autumn was certain he was managing it.

They came to a natural pause in their conversation as their food arrived and Bowie eyed her anxiously across the table. She knew what he wanted to ask. Autumn smiled sadly at him.

"I don't need to tell you about it. It won't help me if I do. And whether or not what happened to me happened to me, what you did this morning was wrong."

"I know that," he said. "I'm not trying to make myself feel better about it. I just want to be there for you if you need me."

Autumn sighed.

"I hate the narrative that goes with it." She almost spat the words. "It's so frustrating. Women are *not* these delicate little flowers, you know? But almost half of the human population of the planet could kill us any time they wanted to if the mood took them. That must be a really difficult position to put yourself in, as a man. I think it's something that most women subconsciously recognise but don't really think about until something happens to them. Something like what happened this morning."

He reached sheepishly for her hand. She let him hold it gently in his.

"I'm so sorry."

"I know you are, Bowie."

He took a sip of his coffee, his pancakes virtually untouched. He looked sad in a way she hadn't seen him before.

"I know it was a mistake. I don't think you'd ever hit me. You just surprised me and I reacted."

"I surprised myself, too. It's just . . ." He hesitated.

"Go on."

"No. It'll sound like I'm making excuses and there really are none. I shouldn't have done it; it's as simple as that."

She was glad to hear him acknowledge that his sudden impotence and the way he'd reacted in the shower were two entirely separate problems. She knew why he'd done what he did — he was overwhelmingly frustrated and afraid of letting her down — but that didn't excuse it. She understood — sex had always been their thing. Even when Bowie had been feeling unwell, they'd always found ways to be intimate with each other. It was inevitable this would challenge his sense of who he was and the way their relationship worked, and — although it was not unexpected — it was premature. Neither of them had counted on it happening while he was still as physically capable as he seemed to be at the moment. It made her wonder.

"Can we talk about your penis now?" she asked.

He laughed, spitting out coffee into his saucer. She smiled.

"Sure," he said. "Why the hell not."

"Do you think it could be related to your medication?"

A person in Bowie's condition would ordinarily be in the early stages of a palliative care plan, but Bowie had made it clear he didn't want any of that. Easily embarrassed and frustratingly private, he'd checked his family were happy to nurse him until he succumbed, then rejected his GP's offer to arrange for community nurses to come to the house and help him manage his pain. He had a professional carer at home in the form of his sister. Maddie could look after him just as well as anyone else. His GP had reluctantly agreed to honour his wishes, prescribing him a cocktail of drugs to ingest every day to help him manage his symptoms.

He shrugged. "I don't know. I'm not sure what's going on."

"Is there anything on your mind?"

"No." He shook his head. She had no real reason not to believe him. She felt sure he knew that he could talk to her about literally anything. Still, something had been bothering her since the day before — their day at the theatre — and she felt she needed to ask him about it.

"This isn't because of Clara, is it?"

She knew he'd been surprised, and he was. His head snapped up at the mention of her name. Autumn's heart sank. Her gut rarely lied to her when it came to reading people, but she realised she'd been hoping her suspicions about the two of them would be wrong.

"You have had sex with her, haven't you?" she asked his questioning expression. He took his hand from hers and rubbed it across his face.

"How on earth did you work that out?" he asked.

"Female intuition. She avoided me at all costs and then became my very best friend, all in one afternoon. Women tend not to do that unless they've slept with your boyfriend."

"I'm sorry," he said. "I should have told you."

"I don't care if you've slept with half of London," she said, mimicking the words he'd said back in New York. "I only care that you're happy and about the way you treat me."

"Nice circle back." He smiled. "You should be a writer."

"So, if it's not her, what *is* going on, then?" she asked again.

"It isn't anything to do with her. I really hope you'll believe me. We were together for a little while, three or four years ago, then Marley wanted to move to New York and I wanted to go with him. She wanted to stay here and I didn't ask her to come anyway. She's nice, we got on well, but she wasn't what I was looking for. I think she felt the same about me. Clara is great. I can only assume she avoided you to begin with because she didn't know how to handle the situation, then acted like your best friend because she wanted to make up for her weird behaviour."

Autumn could tell Bowie was being honest. She hated the fact she'd felt the need to ask him about it, but she felt better for hearing his answer. She'd lain awake for hours pondering Bowie's sudden inability to perform and arrived at the conclusion Clara must have something to do with it in the very depths of the night, when thinking rationally was always most challenging. Now, she felt a sudden urge to spill her darkest fears to him.

"I believe you, Bowie. Can I ask you something else?"

"Sure."

"Do you promise not to think I'm neurotic?"

"Promise."

"When we first met, you told me you'd never slept with a woman like me before. You said I was flawless or something like that. I really liked you, so I don't think I've ever felt so good about myself in all my life. Now I've met Clara, it feels as though you lied to me. She's perfect. Stunningly beautiful. Suddenly, I don't feel so confident that I'm the most beautiful woman you've ever been with. That would have been fine if you'd never implied it, but you did. I'm afraid that you flattered me to get me into bed."

Autumn became suddenly tearful. Bowie looked close to tears himself. He moved his chair alongside hers and put his arm around her shoulders. She waited for him to answer, but he didn't. She knew he was thinking carefully about whatever it was he wanted to say to her, but she couldn't bear the silence.

"I know that this all sounds ridiculous and I hate myself for feeling this way, but you're the most amazing thing that has ever happened to me, Bowie. You were this wonderful surprise. I never expected it. But we haven't known each other for very long. For all I know, you could really be the type of man who punches walls and talks shit to get women to sleep with you. It frightens me."

"That isn't who I am, Autumn." He rested his forehead against hers. He was panicking, she could tell. Every feeling she'd associated with Bowie until now had been warm and fuzzy. Bowie liked that. He loved that she loved the type of man he was. She knew he'd be afraid his reputation with her might be in jeopardy, but she had to get it off her chest. She wanted to know he really was who he said he was. He stared straight into her face.

"When I said I'd never slept with a woman like you before, I didn't only mean that you were the most beautiful woman I had ever seen — which you are, by the way — but that I'd never been with anyone like you in any way. I'd never been with anyone with a mind that works like yours, or who makes me laugh the way you do, or any of the other countless things I loved about you that night. And still love about you. You were smart and funny and kind and curious in bed, and totally in control of yourself. I was totally overwhelmed by your appearance in my life and the consequences of your timing. You marched into my world and blew it up completely. I was afraid to do or say anything that might make you go away. That's why I stopped to tell you about my scar. I was telling you the truth about that too, by the way. I usually do keep my top on when I have sex. You can ask Clara if you like, although she may think it's a little weird. But with you, I felt completely at ease. Like we'd done that before, or something. Like you wouldn't be frightened away by them because you'd already seen them, I guess. Like you were already a part of me, of this. I'm not as good with spoken words as you are — I can't describe it properly. I'm sorry if I gave you the impression I was inexperienced. I'm a straight man who works in theatre. There's no shortage of attractive women looking for men like me. I like sex, that's the ugly truth of it. I've slept with lots of women, enough of them to know you're the only one I've ever been able to reveal myself to completely, physically and emotionally."

She was ashamed she'd chalked the depth of his comment that night down to her appearance only. She felt like she should apologise, but didn't know how to apologise in the middle of an apology.

"I think you're pretty good with words," she said instead.

He tilted her chin up to look at him and wiped away her tears with his thumb. She smiled and saw his features flood with relief. He stared deep into her eyes.

"I could tell you I'm in love with you," he murmured. "But I've never said that to anyone before and I certainly didn't want to say it to you for the first time as the crescendo to a conversation like this. I had other plans. More romantic ones. But I do. I love you. So, can I say it, then can we pretend this isn't the first time I've told you? Save the real declaration for a happier day?"

She smiled, nodding her head.

"I love you, Autumn," he said.

She kissed him.

"I love you, too," she said.

CHAPTER 9

The theatre was empty when they arrived. Autumn dialled Marley's number, but his mobile phone rang out from underneath their seats. He'd obviously dropped it the evening before. They picked it up. He had thirteen text messages, mostly from women in his contact list. When he finally arrived, he was with Hannah. She was holding his hand. Bowie rolled his eyes, but waited until Hannah excused herself to go to the toilet before he scolded his brother.

"You're a fucking idiot," he said.

"Why?" Marley asked defensively. "She knows there's no strings."

"You told her that before."

"She knows this time," Marley said.

The cast and crew piled in shortly afterwards. Autumn was thrilled when both Phil and Clara greeted her with warm hugs. She liked them. They were open and friendly, and they really cared about Bowie. They were constantly asking him if he needed a break or if they could get anything for him. Autumn was glad to know he had people out there besides his family keen to take care of him.

She offered to pick up coffee and pastries so they could get started straight away. Bowie was anxious, and she figured satiating the cast and therefore hurrying the process was the best thing she could do to help. She knew why he was nervous. He and Marley had written new parts for almost every cast member, and some of the actors were looking more enthusiastic about learning the number than others. Bowie tried to encourage them with gentle and inspiring words. He sat front and centre on the stage, watching closely to see what wasn't working so well and making corrections with good-natured encouragement. Marley moved from seat to seat around the theatre, watching each performance from the perspective of the audience. For quite some time, the whole thing was in total disarray. By mid-afternoon, the twins were almost hoarse from shouting.

"Sing the right fucking words!" Marley yelled, over and over again.

At times, it was painful to watch. There was a very obvious difference in the level of enthusiasm being shown by the members of the cast who were throwing themselves into it wholeheartedly and those that weren't. Bowie and Marley pleaded repeatedly with three unenthused actors to give it all they had, but they did not want to get on board. At first, Autumn couldn't work out why, but their attitudes towards Marley made it obvious eventually. They didn't like him. Marley seemed to know.

"Maybe they'll pull together when Marley isn't here?" Larry said to Bowie.

"Sack them," Marley hissed. "They're supposed to be professionals, here to do a job. They're dragging everyone down."

"I preview tomorrow," Larry said.

"You only need to replace the ringleader." Marley pointed at a tall man with curly hair.

"Find me someone else with the talent and time to fill in at short notice and I'll do it." Larry shrugged.

Bowie spoke up. "Marley could."

Larry shook his head. "No."

"Oh, come on, Larry, it was years ago," Bowie said.

"I don't have a choice." Larry held his hand up. "I put him on stage, I'm finished. You both know it."

Autumn had no idea what they were talking about, but she saw Marley clench his fists and jaw. Bowie and Larry winced at each other.

"You three!" Marley shouted at the offenders.

Bowie sighed. "Marley—"

"You're ruining the whole fucking thing for everybody. For Larry, for the audience, for your fellow cast members, who are working their backsides off to put on a good show. Get down here and watch them, and if you don't think you can join in like the professionals you're supposed to be, piss off somewhere else."

The rest of the ensemble ran through the closing number again. Marley filled in for the curly-haired man. He did a good job of hiding his hurt. His performance was captivating, but Autumn could see from the stillness in his eyes that there was something lurking just beneath the surface. Bowie saw it, too. Every time his eyes landed on his brother he flinched.

Autumn wasn't sure if it was public humiliation or a desperate need to prove they could do it better than Marley, but the three under-achievers upped their game after that. Bowie had been promising the cast they would know when they'd nailed it. It was late in the evening before that happened. They launched themselves into each other's arms in congratulations. Autumn stood up to applaud them. She was genuinely impressed. She had never seen so much talent in one place. Solos and duets were layered with intricate harmonies and combined with rhythmic melodies and acapella sections. Performers ran on stage and then off again, dancing and singing their hearts out to a song it was obvious they loved. Even the choreographer with anger issues seemed appeased. Bowie and Marley embraced, and the cast swarmed around them. Autumn had never felt pride like it. Their difficult morning was long forgotten, though the words Bowie had said to her had not been far from her mind all day. He loved her. This wonderfully talented, passionate man was in love with her.

Despite their utter exhaustion, Larry persuaded them to stay for a drink. Someone offered to pick up beers and snacks, and they moved backstage into an enormous dressing room. Autumn sat cross-legged on the floor between Phil and Clara, away from Bowie. She wanted to give him a chance to catch up with his friends. Sipping contentedly from her bottle of beer, she talked about how they'd met, her love of writing, and what it was like to live with the Whittles.

"They're the most gloriously eccentric family I've ever met," Clara said. "I loved them. Their mother is such a doll and their dad is just the sweetest man."

Autumn couldn't agree more. In the weeks she'd been living in the family home, she'd bonded with Bowie's parents in a way that secretly rather alarmed her. True to their word, they'd treated her as one of their own. Autumn cooked and shopped and watched trashy television shows with Emma. Some evenings — usually when Autumn was feeling a little down — she offered to brush her hair for her. Soon, Autumn was dismayed to find she was craving this kind of attention from Emma constantly. It made her feel safe. Bowie's mother was a sweet-natured and demonstrative woman, quick to hug and kiss, and her love for her children knew no bounds at all. She existed for them all, and Autumn felt lucky to be part of it.

Ben was even more adorable. He had brazenly become like a father to her. There was no discernible difference between the way he treated Bluebell and Maddie and the way he was with Autumn. She'd found they had so much in common. They both read widely, wrote for pleasure and loved to discuss the news, from politics to economics. He gave her his favourite reads when he'd finished them, told her off when she was being unreasonable, and put his arms around her when he knew she needed to be comforted. At first he had been reluctant to express his affection for her physically, but following a frank and open discussion about it one evening over a bottle of gin, Ben now hugged and kissed Autumn without hesitation, just as he did his daughters. She'd once accidentally called him Dad, and he had been visibly thrilled; he had encouraged her to continue to do so, if she wanted to.

Autumn had politely declined, citing her respect for his children. She was sure that her slip of the tongue, while lovely, had come as a consequence of the fact that five of the eight people living in the house called him Dad. She didn't tell Ben that, though. He enjoyed feeling like a father to her. Like the rest of the family, he knew nothing of her troubled background, only that Autumn never mentioned her family, and that they were not aware that she was back in England.

The long and short of it was, Autumn knew Bowie's parents cared for her very much. He'd told her once that they were concerned about what she might do once he'd gone.

"There's no pressure, Autumn. You can stay here or you can go wherever you need to go. Do whatever you need to do," Bowie had said in bed one morning. "But you should know that they love you and they'd be very happy for you to stay."

Autumn hadn't answered. She hadn't been able to. Not only because she was completely overwhelmed by the idea that they cared for her so deeply but also because she'd managed to block out of her mind the fact that Bowie would be gone soon, and his candour had taken her breath away. She didn't know what she was going to do. She had no idea what a loss so monumental would do to her and didn't want to commit herself to anything.

She would think about it only when she needed to.

* * *

One post-rehearsal beer became two, followed by three, four and five. By the time she stepped outside at midnight for a cigarette with Marley, Autumn was drunk. She was completely intoxicated by the atmosphere backstage and she really didn't want to go home, but she could sense that the frivolity was drawing to a close. The cast and crew had a show to open the very next night, and Bowie was obviously completely exhausted. She was distracted enough that she didn't want a cigarette, but this was important. Despite her excitement about the spontaneity of their gathering, Autumn had taken time out between conversations to check on Marley and had spotted a sombre expression across his face more than once that evening. This was the first opportunity she'd had to ask him about it. She forced the tipsy grin off her face.

"You OK?" she asked him, nudging him affectionately.

"I'm fine," he said.

She let him wallow in silence for a few seconds. Marley had a habit of saying he was fine at first but, if she let him stew for long enough, he usually revealed the truth without further prodding.

Eventually, he sighed. "I fucking love the stage."

"Well, yeah, that's pretty obvious," she said warily, conscious that Marley was already fragile. "Do you want to talk about this?"

He took a long drag on his cigarette, staring at her intently as he did so. He seemed to be searching for her understanding.

"I want to talk to you about it," he said. "But I can't fully explain it to you because it isn't actually my story to tell."

Autumn stayed silent. She nodded, acknowledging his predicament, and waited.

"I totally lived for it when I was younger. It's the only thing I ever really loved to do. The band was OK. At least it gave me the chance to make music and play. But performing on stage was taken away from me. Today, doing this, I've somehow managed to forget about the fact Bowie will be gone one day, and it's allowed me to focus on the only other thing I really love."

Autumn squeezed his arm. He offered her another cigarette. Autumn knew by now that this probably meant that he had more to say. She took one and lit it, leaning back against the cold brick wall.

"Larry's hosting his annual summer ball in a few weeks' time. He's trying to get us to sing a tribute to Bowie at it," he said.

"'Us' as in 'the family'?" Autumn asked.

"No, 'us' as in me . . . and you," he said nonchalantly.

To say she was surprised was an understatement. She didn't sing, not really. Larry had no idea if she could sing. True, she'd been cast in a couple of musical productions at school when she was younger, but she'd never done anything like it since. Nor did she plan to. She liked music, but it wasn't in her to perform the way she'd seen the cast perform today.

"I was listening to your voice when we all sang the finale together. You can hold a tune. You can handle what I'm planning."

"I-I'm not sure . . ." Autumn stammered.

"There'll only be a couple of hundred people there. It's a medley of the songs Bowie's written for the stage. It would mean so much to him if we did it together and he definitely wouldn't be expecting you to be a part of it, so it would make it a massive surprise for him. I don't think you'd need more than three or four rehearsals and . . ."

"A *couple of hundred* people?"

She felt sick at the very thought of so many people looking at her. Marley put one hand on each of her shoulders, smiling down at her with affection.

"I'm not going to force you, but, please, think about it, Autumn. He would fucking love to see us up there together — I know he would."

Autumn couldn't argue with that. Bowie loved that Autumn and Marley got on so well. He was often pointing out their similarities and the qualities they shared, despite the fact it was already obvious to everybody. They were both largely unashamed of anything they said or did, unquenchably curious, stubbornly impatient and frustratingly provocative. Bowie was grateful they were able to find so much common ground. He was the first to say how important it was to him that his two best friends liked each other so much.

"I'll think about it," she said.

There was one last drunken rendition of the finale in the green room before Autumn, Bowie and Marley jumped into a taxi together with Hannah, who had barely left Marley's side all afternoon. She wasn't the first woman Marley had taken home with him this week, but that wasn't unusual. Autumn and Bowie would often hear him throw Pip out of the bedroom they shared to sleep on the sofa, and then they'd try valiantly to ignore everything they could hear through the ceiling. Sometimes, if it went on for hours, they'd laugh together, making jokes about his stamina and how shameless Marley was when it came to sex. The women had usually left by the time she and Bowie got up in the morning. If anyone else heard it, and Autumn suspected that they did, nobody seemed to confront Marley about it.

Still, Autumn knew Bowie suspected there was a more disturbing aspect to Marley's sexual libertinism. His brother had always enjoyed the company of women, but his seemingly obsessive need for sex had increased as Bowie's cancer had progressed.

"He's a man, he likes sex, of course he does. It's just that he's never chased it in the way he seems to now. I think it's a way of trying to forget how he feels about losing me. It all seems a bit empty to me. Like, he's not actually enjoying what he's doing, beyond the obvious need for physical release. It's as though he's just trying to find some way to escape the mess we're all in for a while."

Autumn was not concerned about sleeping through Marley and Hannah's lovemaking tonight. Bowie slept all the way home in the car — despite an animated debate between Autumn, Marley, Hannah and their taxi driver about whether or not the Beatles were overrated — and nobody slept like Autumn slept when she'd had a few too many. It had been a long and busy day, and she couldn't wait to crawl into bed beside the man who'd told her he loved her.

Bowie was so exhausted he was barely able to walk unaided, so she and Marley drunkenly helped him into the house and undressed him. Once he was nestled comfortably beneath the duvet, she shooed Marley out of their bedroom into the arms of Hannah, who was waiting for him in the hallway. Autumn climbed into bed and kissed Bowie on the cheek. He groaned in his sleep, clasping her hand.

"I love you," she whispered drunkenly into the dark.

***

Autumn woke up with a start. She never woke in the night, especially not when she'd been drinking. Something felt wrong.

Bowie was gone.

She sat up, her eyes searching the darkness, but she could tell the room was empty. The door to the hallway was ajar. Autumn panicked. Bowie never left the room during the night without rousing her to tell her where he was going. He didn't want her to worry. She leaped out of bed and raced into the living room, hoping she might find him dozing on the sofa, but there was no one there. Autumn's heart fluttered with panic.

She ran to the nearest bathroom, the one next to the kitchen. They'd had a lot of gin so perhaps he'd had a sudden urge to be sick and not had time to tell her. Even as she was thinking it, she knew she was wrong. Bowie always shook her awake. Always. She grabbed the doorknob and tried to twist it, but it was locked. The knot in her stomach dissolved into panic and she heard herself make a noise, something between a scream and a shout. She banged her fist on the door, yelling Bowie's name as loud as she could, knowing it would wake the others.

"Bowie!"

There was no answer. She rattled the handle as hard as she could, hitting the door again and again when it didn't budge.

Marley reached her first. He launched himself at the door with a power that would have impressed her if she hadn't been so terrified. The wooden door cracked a little, but didn't break open. He threw himself at it again. Ben was suddenly behind him, pulling Marley away.

"Move!"

He rammed a knife he was holding into the lock.

"What's happening?" Emma's hands were in her hair. Bluebell, Maddie and Pip were close behind her, the two girls clinging to each other desperately. They stood watching Ben struggle with the handle. Autumn was hoping against hope she'd made a stupid mistake. That her lover might appear, drowsy and confused, from somewhere.

It took Ben's shaking hands three attempts to swing the lock back and get the door to open. When he did, he revealed Bowie lying motionless in the middle of the bathroom floor, his legs and arms splayed out in a manner that told them that he had collapsed. His lips were blue. Autumn stepped back, shaking her head from side to side. No. This could not be happening now.

Emma started screaming, a high-pitched, frantic scream that Autumn knew would be lodged in her memory forever more. She rushed towards her son, but Ben and Marley were already there, and Autumn knew Bowie's mother could be of no help in the state she was in. She held Emma back. It took every ounce of strength she had.

"Take your mum with you and go and call an ambulance!" she yelled at Bluebell, wrestling them both in the direction of the kitchen. Bluebell dragged Emma away, still shrieking.

"You do this at work." Pip was shouting at Maddie. "Do something."

Relief flooded through Autumn. Maddie was a care worker. She was trained in resuscitation. She could step in and save her brother. She could tell them what to do to bring Bowie back to life. Autumn urged Maddie forward with her hands on her back. Pip — on the other side of his sister — was pushing her towards Bowie, too.

"I can't." Maddie put her head in her hands, turning her face away from where her brother was lying, dead the worst case and dying in the best. Autumn caught sight of the scene before her, gave up on Maddie, and watched. Ben was holding Bowie's head and trying, through sobs, to breathe air into his son's mouth. Marley was pressing his entire weight against Bowie's ribcage, hysterically begging him not to die. Autumn could hear Bowie's ribs cracking beneath Marley's desperate palms, but he was not responding. Bowie's head flopped limply from side to side with each compression.

Autumn had never felt more useless.

"Can I do anything, Ben?" Her voice came out in a wail. She didn't expect him to answer. Autumn couldn't watch any longer. She dropped to the floor, hugging her knees to her chest and covering her face. She concentrated on listening for sirens, trying in vain to hear anything above Emma's hair-raising screams from the kitchen and Pip's hysterical sobbing from where he sat beside her on the cold tiles. He kept repeatedly asking if Bowie was dead. Autumn was certain he was. She didn't tell Pip that, though. To do so would make it real.

When she heard sirens close by, Autumn stood up and bolted, barefoot, out of the front door and down the gravel driveway as quickly as terror could carry her. She punched the button to release the gates and raced alongside the ambulance to the house, screeching at the paramedics.

"Hurry up! Hurry the fuck up!" She yanked the driver's door open as they braked by the porch. Ignoring her stream of profanities, the paramedics jogged after her, along the hallway and into the bathroom.

"Get away from him, please, guys." The paramedics moved through the doorway. Both Ben and Marley fell back against the bathroom wall, weeping.

"He doesn't want to be resuscitated," Maddie shouted at them.

"Shut up, Maddie," Pip cried.

"Dad, don't do this." Maddie addressed her father.

One of the paramedics turned to Ben.

"Go ahead. Please. I'm his father. He wanted to live. He just wasn't sure."

"He WAS sure!" Maddie was becoming hysterical. Autumn moved to take hold of her, but she was inconsolable, pacing the floor of the corridor manically and shaking her head violently when she heard them mention a defibrillator.

It took three attempts to restart Bowie's heart, then they moved him rapidly onto a stretcher and carried him out to the ambulance. Bluebell had released Emma from her grip so she could go with them, but Emma had changed her mind about wanting to be beside her son, paralysed by the idea this might be the end. Ben had to lift her into the back of the ambulance.

The paramedic barked the name of a hospital at Maddie, and then they were gone.

Barefoot — and in various states of undress — Autumn, Maddie, Bluebell and Pip piled into Maddie's estate car, leaving Marley's lover sitting by the front door.

"I'm so sorry," she said to Autumn as she passed. Autumn told her to get a taxi home. She promised she would give her the money next time she saw her, but Hannah shook her head.

"Are you sure you're going to be OK to drive?" Autumn asked, plugging in her seat belt. They couldn't hear the sirens anymore. They were going to have to move fast to catch up with the ambulance. Maddie nodded agitatedly, turning the key in the ignition and stalling the car. Autumn reached out to grab her wrist. Her hands were shaking violently. "Bowie wouldn't want us to kill ourselves trying to get to him," she said.

Haste was not worth risking their lives for. Bowie was on his way to getting the care he needed and they would get there soon. They sat for a few minutes in silence. Autumn didn't know what the others were thinking, but she was working hard on pulling herself together. She knew shock was debilitating, and that wasn't what Bowie needed from her now. She had to find strength from somewhere and she spent those few minutes scratching around in her soul for the strongest parts of herself.

"Is he dead?" Pip asked into the silence.

"I don't know." Maddie shook her head.

"He's fucking dead." Bluebell wailed, sobbing into her hands.

Nobody said anything. Autumn started to cry.

Maddie waited a few more seconds, then turned the key in the ignition. This time, the car roared to life.

* * *

When she woke, Autumn didn't know where she was. It was light outside. She saw white sheets and Bowie's clammy hand in hers, and it all came flooding back. She wished she was still asleep.

Emma was sitting across from her, holding Bowie's other hand lovingly to her face. The others were all there: Ben, sitting with his back against the wall beside Pip, who was asleep on his father's shoulder. Maddie, who was staring out of the window, and Bluebell, who was dozing in the foetal position on an ugly blue sofa. Marley was sitting at the end of the bed. Autumn was sure he hadn't taken his eyes off Bowie since they'd all been allowed into his room a few hours earlier. The medical team had stabilised his condition but — with no idea how long he'd been lying on the bathroom floor — they couldn't be sure when he would wake up, or what sort of state he might be in when he did.

Autumn reached across the bed to touch Emma's wrist. She was crying quietly, her tears dripping onto the palm of Bowie's hand.

"He squeezed my hand earlier," she said.

At the sound of their mother's voice, Bluebell and Pip opened their eyes. They searched Autumn's face for any hint of a change in Bowie's condition. Marley answered for her with a shake of his head. There had been none. Despite Emma's insistence that her son had moved, Bowie was still unconscious. He was covered in deep purple bruises and was being closely monitored for signs of internal bleeding, a significant risk for someone with non-Hodgkins lymphoma. The CPR he had been given in an attempt to save him could in fact kill him. It was an instance of irony Autumn did not want to consider too carefully.

"You need to get some sleep, Mum," Bluebell said. Autumn looked at the clock. It was midday.

"I'm not going anywhere until he wakes up," Emma retorted.

"*If* he wakes up," Maddie muttered.

Emma's gaze was suddenly steely. She homed in on her daughter. "Maddie, Bowie doesn't need your negative attitude. What he needs is positivity and love from us now."

"He needs us all to do what he asked us to do," Maddie said, her voice cracking under the weight of Emma's glare.

Marley stood up, stepping in between them.

"What do you want us to do, Maddie? Rip his fucking breathing tube out?"

Maddie's eyes darted to her poorly brother. She started to cry.

"Now isn't the time, sweetheart." Ben pulled her into a hug. She sobbed into his chest.

"I love him just as much as you do," she said. "But what you've done here is wrong."

"So why are you here," Marley hissed. "If you want him to die?"

"I don't want him to fucking die." Maddie raged at her brother. "I want you to respect his wishes as a human being who knows his own mind."

Emma's eyes were back on Bowie.

"Stop it. You'll upset him."

"He's *dead*, Mum." Maddie sobbed.

Pip raised his hands to his ears to block out his sister's words. "Shut up, Maddie, for fuck's sake!"

"You need to come to terms with it . . ."

Marley moved in his sister's direction in such a way Autumn felt compelled to hold him back. She wasn't sure what he was going to do, but the last thing they needed was to be kicked out of the hospital. Bowie would be frightened if he woke up on his own. If he woke up at all. Autumn watched Maddie for a moment. She was already mourning him, Autumn knew.

"Calm down," she whispered to Marley. She felt him soften beneath her grip. He was still staring at his sister.

Maddie tore her gaze from his and spoke again.

"This is uncomfortable for everyone, but he's been in pain for years. He's tired of it all. And I haven't said this to him, or to any of you, but I do think the lymphoma is spreading to his brain. I'm sorry, but I do. His head is getting more and more fuzzy. His headaches are getting worse, he's forgetting words. If he wakes up, you've confined him to an existence he never wanted for himself."

"Stop." Marley pleaded with his sister. "I can't stand it, Maddie. I'll jump out of the fucking window, I swear."

Bluebell stood up and left the room. There was no sense of urgency. She opened the door and walked out without a word, as though she were getting up off the sofa at home to get a drink from the kitchen. She looked almost catatonic. Autumn thought about following her, but couldn't bear to leave Bowie.

"I can't just let him die," Emma whispered, placing the palm of his hand on her cheek again, as though he were cupping her face the way he sometimes did. She closed her eyes and laid her head on Bowie's shoulder, crying silent tears.

***

When Bowie woke up two days later, Autumn saw the exact moment he realised — to his horror — he was still alive. She saw the pain in his eyes when he registered his family had gone against his wishes. She didn't know whether to be devastated for him or relieved his reaction was an encouraging sign of his cognitive function. He accused his family — one by one — with his stony gaze. When he met his mother's watchful eyes, a tear ran down his face. Emma brushed it away.

"It'll be OK," she said.

"Everywhere hurts, Mum," he whispered.

"It'll get better," she said.

"You don't know that." He started sobbing, wincing through the pain his own anguish exacerbated.

"I do." She wiped away his tears with her sleeve.

Bowie cried and cried. He was full of rage and wouldn't talk to anybody. Autumn knew he wasn't angry with her. She'd had no idea what his full wishes had been. That felt wrong to her now, but this was not the time to ask why nobody, not even Bowie, had bothered to tell her what he wanted.

Autumn didn't want to talk to his family either, not now Maddie had told her the whole story. Bowie had made it clear six months before — after he'd been warned by his oncologist that anthracycline-based chemotherapy treatment could have damaged his heart and that could be why he was experiencing chest pains — that he did not want to be resuscitated should he collapse. He didn't think he'd have the physical strength he'd need to recover. Overwhelmed and petrified by the enormity of the thought that he might be debilitated until the end of his days, Bowie had told them, expressly, that if this happened they were to allow him to die, trusting them not to ignore his wishes. Autumn couldn't begin to imagine why he hadn't told her. Perhaps he hadn't wanted to upset her, or maybe he had really believed his family would honour his request the way they should have, so there would be no need for her to know. He certainly hadn't expected something like this to happen so soon, she knew that, so it was entirely possible he'd been building up to telling her.

Autumn did have some sympathy with his family's decision. She knew why they couldn't let him go. They loved him. Still, she wanted to believe she'd have had the courage to stand in the way of Ben and Marley and stop them from trying to save Bowie if she'd known what he wanted. Letting him die would have been the hardest thing she'd ever had to do, but she would have done it if he'd told her to.

Autumn had growing admiration for Maddie, the only one who'd even tried to uphold his request. That must have been an incredibly difficult thing to do, especially when everyone you loved was against it.

"If we get some say in the way we die, I believe that should be respected," she'd said.

Autumn would never say it, but she was beyond relieved Bowie had survived. She hadn't yet had the six months with him she'd been promised and she wasn't ready to lose him. She needed more time and was glad to have it.

She'd never dare tell him that, though.

* * *

"Rule Number Four."

The first time they were left alone, Bowie spoke. Autumn smiled, leaning into him and running her fingers through his hair.

"If that happens again, make sure that they let me die."

Autumn had been holding it together pretty well, but she let herself break down now. Bowie had barely said a word in the four days since he'd regained consciousness. It was good to hear his voice again.

"I'm so sorry," she whispered.

"Why are you saying sorry?" He wiped her tears away with his fingers. "You didn't know. You haven't done anything wrong."

She shook her head sadly. "I'm sorry you're in so much pain. And that they didn't listen. I'm sorry I didn't hear you get out of bed and that you were all alone in that bathroom. I'm just so sorry for all of it."

He hushed her gently, stroking her hair this time. She leaned her cheek against the palm of his hand.

"You're so beautiful," he said.

"Thanks." She sniffed uncouthly to make him laugh. It worked. "Maddie tried to stop them," she added.

"I knew she would," he said. "What about the others?"

"Bluebell didn't really do anything wrong. She called the ambulance, but only because I told her she should. I think she thought you were already dead. Pip just screamed at everyone."

"And Marley?"

Autumn didn't want to cause trouble between the twins. As far as she was concerned, Marley could be excused. Nobody could ever expect him to let Bowie die. The very concept of losing his brother was enough for him to threaten suicide. How could he be expected to control himself? Autumn shuddered at the memory of Marley pounding on Bowie's chest. She wasn't sure that she would ever forget it.

Bowie shook his head in response to her silence. She felt defensiveness rise up inside her. He hadn't witnessed the extent of Marley's distress that night.

"Go easy on him, Bowie," she said.

"No! He promised to let me go when the time came. I *knew* he'd back out."

"He loves you," Autumn said.

"So does Maddie," Bowie said belligerently. Autumn couldn't argue with that. Perhaps there was even an argument that Maddie might love him more. She was the only one to try to respect his wishes and would be no less devastated by his death than any of the others.

"I know they love me," Bowie said. "That's never been something I have to worry about. And I know how lucky I am to have people who care so much. I just wish they loved me enough to let me make my own decisions. But they're not thinking about me. They're thinking about themselves."

CHAPTER 10

When they brought Bowie home from hospital, everything was different, both physically and emotionally. The moments of high energy and happiness he'd enjoyed before had gone and he was barely able to walk across the room. Marley had broken a couple of his brother's ribs in his effort to save him, but that was the least of Bowie's issues. His entire body was swollen and bruised, his backache was ten times worse than it had been and his headaches had increased in severity. His pain was no longer sporadic, it was constant and unbearable. Bowie made it very clear that he held them all responsible. Every time he writhed in agony, he glared at whoever was nearest to him. He barely spoke to anyone except to snap at them all. Even Autumn and Maddie, the only people he permitted to touch him, were not immune to his rage. He had warned Autumn once that he was ungracious when he was ill. She knew now what he'd meant. At times he was so rude, ungrateful and selfish that she didn't like him very much at all. He took every twinge out on the people around him and the Whittles retreated into themselves in a way Autumn hadn't thought they would ever do. She found herself wishing he'd accepted the palliative care he'd been offered by the doctor. They were out of their depths here — drowning in a sea of despair — but when she dared broach the subject with him, he snapped at her. He didn't want strangers in his home. He didn't want anyone he didn't know to see him like this.

Maddie feigned strength in Bowie's presence but, when he wasn't in the room, she sat alone and cried. Sometimes Ben tried to comfort her, but she would push him away. She was almost as angry as Bowie at their parents for going against his wishes, and even angrier that they still — despite the state of him — couldn't see that what they had done had been wrong.

Everyone else was different too. Bluebell barely acknowledged anyone. She stayed close to Bowie and tried to help him as best she could but, mostly, he ignored her. Eventually, she took the hint and stopped trying altogether. Still, she spent her days close by, usually staring at the television screen and watching him out of the corner of her eye.

Marley barely came out of his bedroom. He'd tried, earnestly, early on, to get his brother to talk to him but Bowie constantly ordered him to leave him alone. Pip and Marley were sharing a bed, because Marley cried so violently in the night that Pip was afraid that he might get up and attempt to take his own life.

Autumn was greatly concerned for her friends and their mental states, but she didn't have any time or energy to attempt to help them. She was far too busy trying to lift Bowie's spirits all by herself.

He was awake all night almost every night. He'd curl into a ball in their bed and clutch his chest or grab his head in his hands, trying to concentrate his way through waves of pain. One night, a violent spasm took him so much by surprise that he bit through his lip until it bled everywhere. Autumn did everything she could think of to help him. She stroked him wherever he hurt, tried to distract him with stories or aimless chatter, let him squeeze her hand a little too hard when he needed to. His mood swung unpredictably between desperately frightened and terribly sad. When she wasn't there, he called for her constantly, shooing away anyone else when they tried to tend to him instead. He never said it, but she knew he had grown afraid of being alone. Even when they were sleeping next to one another, Bowie would wake her up as soon as he was conscious, just so that he wouldn't be by himself. There was nothing Autumn could do to help him, but she would rush to be beside him whenever he called. It was terrifying. His cancer was taking him out piece by piece. His body would either survive it or it wouldn't. All they could do was wait.

When things got really bad, Bowie would ask Autumn to kill him. Those were the worst times. It was always during the night, when she was feeling at her most fragile, and nobody was around to stop her if she gave in to him. He would hold her body close to his and beg her, sometimes for hours at a time, to end his suffering for him.

"I can feel it, it's in my head. Please find a way to help me die, Autumn. Please."

Autumn would largely ignore his requests, hushing and soothing him with meaningless words. She felt so terribly sad for him, so unbelievably sickened by it all, that some nights she would start to think about it. On those occasions, Bowie would sense her self-doubt and latch on to it.

"You could smother me," he'd say. "Just knock me out with alcohol and smother me in my sleep."

"I'd get caught," she would reply. "Do you want me to spend the rest of my life in prison?"

"Then buy me some strong painkillers. Leave them by the bed and I'll take them myself."

"No."

"Autumn—"

"No, Bowie!"

For the first few days after Bowie was discharged, she felt as though she was managing quite well, but — after a fortnight — when Autumn realised she hadn't showered for four days, eaten in twenty-four hours or slept for any period longer than an hour for almost a week, she started crying in the shower one afternoon and found she couldn't stop. She tried everything, but every time she quelled her sobs for more than a few seconds, they returned more obvious and violent than ever.

In the end she gave in, resolving that the family would have to see her cry today. It would be the first time since Bowie's heart attack that she'd let any of them see her being emotional. She'd pretended to everyone, thus far, that she was coping just fine.

She wrapped her hair in a towel and pulled on a dressing gown, preparing herself for concerned conversations about the state she was in. As she padded down the corridor, relieved to feel at least clean at last, she heard Bowie calling for her from the bedroom and froze, realising she wasn't going to be able to go to him. She couldn't take another day of it. She was sick of the same four walls, of the endless cups of tea, of the crying and sobbing and screaming. Autumn willed her legs to take her into their bedroom, but she felt paralysed.

Her reluctant feet turned left into the living room instead of right towards their bedroom. Emma and Ben were sitting, still and silent, on the sofa. Autumn marched past them and out of the front door. She tore her towel turban from her head and threw it down on the grass. She didn't know where she was going, she only knew that she needed to be out of there and on her own.

She tore barefoot and shivering across the garden and into the shrubbery that surrounded it. Distraught, she sat against the trunk of an oak tree in a wooded area at the front of the house, as far away from the bedroom she shared with Bowie as she could get without leaving the grounds. She pulled her dressing gown around herself, put her head in her hands, and wailed. For the first time in a very long time, although she knew she could completely surround herself with people if she wanted to, she felt totally on her own. She stayed there for hours, well aware that Bowie would be upset by her disappearance. He would be forced to accept help from people he was angry at for their betrayal. But she couldn't bring herself to go back to him.

It was dark when Marley came looking for her. He headed straight to where she was sitting. Autumn fathomed there were security cameras somewhere she didn't know about. She bet they had been watching her. She didn't care. Maybe it would do them good to see what they were doing to her.

He sat down next to her, saying nothing. Autumn hid her head in her hands, feigning indifference. They stayed that way for almost an hour. He listened to her crying without a word and she felt supported by the heat of his body beside her. Eventually, she collapsed in on herself and sought his comfort. Marley wrapped his arms around her, kissing the top of her head.

"I'm sorry, Autumn," he whispered.

His voice was kind and his arms protective and strong. She realised nobody had held her in weeks. Marley smelt and felt the same way Bowie did, so she wound her hand in his jumper and closed her eyes, pretending it was Bowie's chest she was nestled into instead. Marley rested his chin on her head, the way Bowie sometimes did in bed. He let her hold on to him until she stopped crying. She wondered, guiltily, if he knew she was pretending he was his brother. If he did, he didn't say. He let her rest against him until she'd stopped crying, then encouraged her to look up into his eyes by cupping her face in his hand.

"Done?" he asked softly. She nodded. "OK, then. The family wants to talk to you. When you're ready."

Autumn was gripped by sudden fear. She remembered their very early conversations in the apartment in New York, when Emma had warned her that she'd need to act like part of the family — she'd need to put her own feelings to one side and let them focus on Bowie's care — or else she wouldn't be welcome to stay with them. She knew Bowie would never let them make her leave, but she was still worried she'd lose their blessing to be here, and now, though she'd wanted nothing more than space all day, she wanted nothing except to be back in the arms of their family as night approached.

"Are you going to send me home?" she asked Marley.

"Autumn . . ." He laughed gently, shaking his head. "You already are home."

* * *

For the first time since Bowie had left the hospital, the Whittles were all sitting together in the living room. Autumn searched for Bowie, who was propped up in an armchair in the corner. He held his arms out to her when he saw her and pulled her down onto his knee. She protested at first — she knew Bowie's hips and back were causing him great pain even without the weight of her pushing them out of position — but he was insistent. He held her tightly to him.

"I'm sorry," he murmured into her neck. She returned his embrace and he winced. She wasn't sure if that was because he was hurting physically or because she didn't tell him it was OK.

Marley perched on the arm of the sofa beside his mother, who patted his leg affectionately. Ben poured Autumn a glass of wine, winking away the apology she tried to offer as he did so. They were all making eye contact with one another again, and Autumn knew that they'd been talking through their issues while she'd been in the garden. The air felt lighter already.

"Right . . ." Emma began, clapping her hands together gently.

"Mum, I don't think you're the best person to lead this," Pip said. Emma clamped her mouth shut, a dejected expression on her face, but she didn't object.

"This is Bowie's meeting really." Marley gestured towards his brother. Their gazes lingered on one another and Autumn knew they were communicating love and hurt, apology, concern and betrayal all at once. Bowie turned away first, leaving a wounded-looking Marley bereft.

Bowie sighed, rubbing his free hand across his face. He looked so tired. Autumn wanted to wrap him in a blanket and cradle him to her chest. He was frail and she noticed with a start just how much this disease had taken a toll on his appearance. He'd lost weight, and his hair looked dull and unhealthily coarse. His skin was pasty and clammy. There were new lines on his brow, formed by constant frowning. The sparkle in his eyes was still there, though. Overcome with love, Autumn kissed him lightly on the cheek. He turned to smile at her, leaning in to peck her gently on the lips. For a moment it was just the two of them there in consciousness, and they were happy and problem-free. A moment later, Bowie cleared his throat, turning to his family.

"Dad and I called this family meeting because we want to sort things out. I don't think any of us have been enjoying the way things have been lately. I love you all . . ."

His eyes met Marley's once more and his words stuck in his throat. Bowie buried his head in Autumn's shoulder, taking a minute or so to compose himself. When he spoke again, he was breathless with rage.

"I love you all, but I'm so fucking angry. Every time I feel a twinge of pain I feel furious with all of you. I shouldn't be here, I shouldn't be feeling this, and—"

Emma tried to interject, but he snapped at her.

"I know why," he hissed in her direction.

"Bowie . . ." Ben said warningly.

Instantly contrite, Bowie took a deep breath and held his hands up. "I'm sorry, Mum."

It was the first hint of restraint Autumn had seen in him for weeks. Bowie had spat much harsher words at his mother in the days following his resuscitation. Autumn smiled subtly and knowingly at Ben, who nodded poignantly in reply. Ben hated it when any of his children insulted their mother. He'd allowed Bowie a grace period for his anger, but that was over now. There was no way he would let his son speak to Emma like that any longer. She was their mother, she had created them and was their most ardent supporter. Her unwavering love for them demanded their respect as far as Ben was concerned and Bowie would obey his father because he valued Ben's opinion probably more than he valued anyone else's.

Emma smiled meekly and apologised for interrupting Bowie. He took another deep breath and continued.

"I can't put myself in your position. If I were losing any of you, I know I'd probably be exactly the same. But I do need you to put yourselves in my position because I'm the one who's going through this. I know you all have visions of me slipping away peacefully while you sit around my bed and hold my hand, but it might not be like that. It might be as ugly as what happened a fortnight ago. You're still going to have to let me go."

"I will, Bowie," Pip blurted. Emma glared accusingly at her youngest son, but he ignored her. "I'll throw myself on top of you to stop them next time if I have to."

Bowie nodded sadly at his little brother and Pip looked relieved. Autumn relaxed a little bit. Pip and his feelings were often overlooked because Marley and Emma were so expressive about losing Bowie and how it made them feel, but the youngest Whittle had confided in her several days before that Bowie's anger at him was destroying him and he was too afraid to apologise in case Bowie refused to listen. His brother rejecting him would break Pip's sensitive heart.

"So will I," Marley said. His voice sounded strangely strangled, as though he was physically squeezing the words out past his vocal cords. "You know I don't want you to die, bro, but I don't want to see you like this either. What we did was wrong. If you collapse like that again, I, for one, am prepared to let you go."

Bowie raised his eyes to meet his twin's.

"I promise," Marley added. Autumn felt the tension seep from the room. Bowie nodded.

Ben spoke next.

"We are sorry, Bowie. We weren't as strong as you needed us to be. You're right, it wasn't how we'd imagined the end.

We couldn't cope with how it was happening. We were wrong, son."

Bowie closed his eyes for a moment and then opened them to look at Bluebell.

"What about you?"

She was hugging her knees to her chest and rocking backwards and forwards on the floor. Her eyes darted uncomfortably between them all.

"I'll do the same thing I did last time. Nothing. Don't ask me to do anything more, Bowie. I'm not strong enough to do anything to help you die, but I won't try to stop it if it happens."

Autumn had not yet acknowledged that Bluebell's lack of involvement that evening had not been panic or frozen trauma, but an attempt to protect Bowie's wishes. Suddenly she knew why her friend had been unable to sit in his hospital room and listen to their family berate her sister for trying to do what Bowie had asked of them by letting him die. The words they'd hurled at Maddie might as well have been meant for Bluebell, too. Bowie nodded again, then looked at his mother. She was trying hard not to meet anyone's eye.

"Mum?" She folded and unfolded her arms, swallowing anxiously and nervously shaking her head. Bowie sighed. "I need you to say it, Mum. I can't stand the idea that they'll be wrestling you off me. You have to accept that this is what I want. Please. Let me go."

He stopped and stared up at the ceiling. He was blinking back frustrated tears. "I can't believe we're having this conversation again. I thought you were better than this."

"Why can't you just fight a little longer for us?" Emma whispered.

Bowie spoke through gritted teeth. "Because I don't want to. And it's my choice."

"Bowie . . ." Ben said. Bowie waved his father's warning away irritably, but relaxed his jaw.

"You have Autumn now," Emma said. "Why can't you fight for more time with her?"

Before Autumn could react, before she could tell them that Bowie in pain for longer on her behalf wasn't what she wanted, Bowie protectively pulled her closer to him.

"That has nothing to do with anything," he said. "I've had enough, Mum. I woke up in the night, knew what was coming, and locked myself in that bathroom, away from Autumn and everyone else, because I wanted to die. You must have known that, when you had to break down the door? I'm sick of being in pain. I'm tired of waiting for the next horrible thing I have to go through. Do you know what that's like? Can you imagine how it feels to be constantly waiting for something traumatic to happen to you? You know it's coming but you don't know when, and there's nothing you can do but hope it isn't that really awful terrible thing you'd been dreading, that it's something else instead. I was lying on that floor for what felt like hours and I was hurting everywhere but I was still relieved. I thought it was all about to be over. Now, because of you, I'm going to have to go through something horrendous again. I'm terrified all the time. I'm all on my own in this. None of you can go through it with me. At the end of the day, every time something happens, I'm the only one who really feels it. I don't want to do it anymore."

Emma lowered her head into her hands and sobbed. Marley and Ben wrapped their arms around her. Bowie gave them a minute for her to calm down. He let his head fall against Autumn, closing his eyes. Autumn thought he might fall asleep, but he rested there until he heard his mother's cries quieten, and then he spoke again. This time, his voice was much softer.

"I want us to go back to the way things were between us when I thought you all knew how I feel and would do what I want when the time comes. I can only do that if I know everyone understands this time." He opened his eyes and looked directly at Marley. "I need you to really, actually, understand — not just try to make me feel better."

Marley nodded gravely. Autumn's heart broke. She still felt as though Marley should be excused. His love for Bowie ran deeper than an ordinary sibling bond. Standing by and watching Bowie die would always be too much for him to cope with. It was too much to ask of him and she knew he would never be able to control himself when it came to Bowie. Autumn could tell that he truly believed it when he said he would let Bowie go, but she didn't think it was true. Not for a second.

"OK," Emma whispered, looking Bowie right in the eye. Tears were running off her jaw and into her lap, but she ignored them, her full attention on her oldest son. "Next time something happens, I swear, I'll let you go, Bowie. I'll let you go."

* * *

Unlike other families, when the Whittles agreed to put something behind them, they really did put it behind them. The atmosphere got better almost immediately. Ben poured more wine for those who wanted it and the living room erupted into conversation. Marley and Emma moved to sit with Bowie, perching themselves on an arm each of his chair. Autumn got up to give them the space they needed. They both kissed him and stroked their hands over him as though they hadn't seen him in months.

Autumn stepped out of the front door by herself, leaving him to his family. It was July and warm enough — even at nighttime — that she didn't need to put on shoes or a jacket. She took herself to sit on the double swing at the bottom of the garden and rocked back and forth for close to an hour, staring absently at the discarded towel she'd thrown on the lawn earlier. She felt cool, but her skin was hot to the touch, anxiety bubbling beneath the surface. She was still a nervous wreck.

She heard the door open and shut and recognised Bluebell's delicate form on the porch, her pretty eyes peering out into the dark, searching for her. Autumn waved.

"I bet you regret the day you ever met me," Bluebell said, sitting down beside her. Autumn laughed. She would have said the same if she were her.

"Nothing could be further from the truth," she said. It was all so hard, but so worth it. Bluebell held her hand out to Autumn, and the two friends, so different than they had been just a few months ago, worlds away from the party girls who had fallen into platonic love, interlaced their fingers, resting their foreheads together. They had barely spoken for weeks. Autumn had missed her.

"You're my family," she murmured.

"We are." Bluebell smiled. "I don't know how you're doing this. I don't even know how we're doing it and we're tied to him."

"I love him," Autumn said.

"Naw, now that's a loser thing to say," Bluebell said teasingly. Autumn laughed again. It felt good to admit her feelings to her friend. She and Bowie had not said those words to one another since the first time over breakfast in the café, but how Autumn felt about him had not changed. If anything, they'd become even closer throughout his ordeal. She loved him more now than ever. Bowie was her darling, her sweetheart, her whole heart, he was everything to her. She stopped short of revealing quite that much detail to Bluebell, though. There were some things a sister didn't need to know. A comfortable silence fell between the two of them. They rocked the swing together. Apart from the tiny squeak it made each time it reached the top, the garden was silent. Autumn felt the sweet call of slumber and nodded off for a moment.

"You don't hate my mum, do you?" Bluebell asked Autumn, shattering her peace and making her gasp.

"Why on earth would you ever think that?"

"I don't. She does. Mum's worried that you're upset because of what they did to Bowie."

Autumn pondered. She was upset with them all, but that didn't mean she couldn't see why they'd done what they had. She certainly didn't hate them for it. Perhaps she'd been a little preoccupied and detached from them these past couple of weeks. She could see how that might look.

"I have been cold, haven't I?" she asked. Bluebell nodded. "I'm sorry. I'll make it right."

"It's difficult, isn't it?" Bluebell said. "Because what they actually did was save his life. That's usually a good thing."

"Apart from the fact that he doesn't want to live anymore," Autumn said. Her words sounded sterner than she'd meant them to, and she realised she was disappointed that Bluebell was defending their parents. She had hoped they agreed on this. It had given her relief.

"Well, yes," Bluebell said. "But he could live longer, if he wanted to. If we keep saving him the way we have been, who's to say he wouldn't have another twenty years before it actually got him? That's what Mum and Dad struggle with. If it were me, I would want them to keep resuscitating me and treating me until they couldn't do it anymore."

"You don't know that. Look at the pain he's in, Bluebell. Not only physically, but mentally, too. We can't know what he's going through," Autumn said.

"He was happy though, Autumn," Bluebell said. "Before the heart attack. We'd never seen him so happy. He has to recover now, but he could get back to that again. You two could have more time together."

"It's his decision, Bluebell . . ."

"I know that," Bluebell said. "And I'd never go against what he wants. That doesn't mean I have to agree with him, though. And I don't."

There wasn't anything Autumn could say to that. Nobody could force Bluebell to support Bowie's decision and Autumn couldn't criticise her so long as she was conceding to let him decide for himself. Still, she was surprised. Bowie could do nothing wrong in Bluebell's eyes usually. Autumn had expected his sister to find it within herself to agree with him completely.

"We thought he might change his mind when he met you," Bluebell went on. "About not having treatment. We thought you may have given him enough reason to try to go on living."

The words stabbed at Autumn. Not only did they make her feel as though she had failed at something she'd never signed up for, they revealed a harsh truth, one that made her feel uncomfortable. Apart from their initial attempt to intervene in her relationship with Bowie when she'd first met them, the Whittles had been surprisingly and extraordinarily supportive of Autumn being in a relationship with their terminally ill son. They had accepted Autumn for everything she was and welcomed her into their family. They'd promised her a home with them for ever, if she wanted it. She'd be lying if she said she hadn't wondered why. It all made sense to her now. They'd believed she might be Bowie's saviour. She wondered if everything they'd ever done for her had been based on that. She guessed she would find out when he was gone. For now, she would continue to fight for Bowie and his rights.

"Bluebell, doesn't that tell you all you need to know?" she said. "He's so happy, but he still doesn't want to live like this anymore. Imagine the pain he must be in."

Bluebell swallowed, nodding. Autumn could tell that she'd changed Bluebell's perspective, if only by a fraction. They held on to one another a little tighter and fell silent, their inertia driven by the weight of their bodies, the swing rocking them backwards and forwards until they'd almost fallen asleep. They rose when they grew cold and wandered dizzily, hand in hand, back to the house. All was quiet. Everyone else had gone to bed.

Autumn hugged Bluebell goodnight and opened her bedroom door, expecting to find Bowie lying anxiously awake and waiting for her. Instead, she found him sleeping in their bed beside Marley. They faced each other on top of the duvet, fully dressed and holding forearms. Sleep, it seemed, had caught them unawares. She stood in the doorway, watching them for a while. They looked so sweet together. So peaceful. Autumn hadn't seen Bowie look so restful in the entire time she'd known him. She realised in that moment that Bowie never felt totally complete when he wasn't with Marley. He was fidgety when his brother wasn't there. Anxious. His sleep was frequently disturbed, something she'd put down to pain until now. They were two halves of one whole. The missing piece of each other. They were never really happy if they were without the other. A lesser partner might have been jealous, but Autumn understood. She couldn't begin to comprehend the bond they shared, she knew that. Perhaps it was the kind of love that only came with growing in a womb together. No wonder they couldn't see life without one another. She watched them sigh simultaneously and shuffle closer together. Her heart ached.

She thought about covering them with a blanket, but was worried Marley might wake up and feel as though he had to leave. They'd missed out on so many precious hours together these last few weeks. It was important for them to have this time together, she knew, so she tiptoed back into the hallway, closing the door softly behind her.

She knocked gently on Pip's bedroom door and — in an attempt to avoid worrying him — entered the dark room without waiting for a response. It didn't work. Pip jumped out of bed and bolted towards her in a panic. Autumn held her hands out to calm him.

"Autumn, what's happened!"

"It's OK," she whispered, holding him by his shaking arms. "Marley's fallen asleep in our bed with Bowie. Can I sleep in here with you?"

Pip sighed with relief, nodding. He stumbled back to bed. Autumn let him settle in, then slipped beneath Marley's duvet and wrapped herself in it contentedly. She knew she'd fall asleep quickly for the first time in weeks. All felt right with the world again, plus it had been a while since she'd had a bed to herself and she was really comfortable. Her heart fluttered happily. She hoped they might all leave her to sleep for as long as she needed to tomorrow. She definitely had some catching up to do.

She drew in a deep breath, turning her nose to the pillow to chase the faint smell of tea tree oil, and instead catching the unmistakable scent of Marley.

She allowed it to comfort her.

CHAPTER 11

"I can't believe we're still doing this." Three days after Autumn's mammoth meltdown and subsequent lay-in, Marley was marching her through a cool and persistent drizzle across a neighbouring field towards a sheltered corner of evergreens. It was the second day in a row he'd dragged her out here to rehearse the stupid tribute medley they'd promised Larry Ross they would perform at his annual summer ball. Despite the promise of a storm in the air — and much to Autumn's amusement — the chickens flapped inquisitively after them, as they had the day before. It was the only part of this fiasco she was managing to take any pleasure in.

"Bowie wants to go to the ball and we promised Larry we would do this," Marley said. "When did you become so whiny?"

Autumn was self-aware enough to know she *was* being whiny — she'd been this way for a while — but she couldn't stop.

"I don't know. Probably at some point after the love of my life had a *heart attack*." Marley rolled his eyes, searching on his phone for the backing track he'd recorded.

"Oh, did Bowie, my twin brother, have a heart attack? You should have mentioned it." It was somewhere between a joke and a goad, and it took her by surprise — he'd been entirely patient with her up until now. She was annoyed. She'd never been through anything like this before and she didn't think she deserved Marley's ratty remark. She told him so.

"I'm joking, Autumn, for fuck's sake," he said, propping his phone up on a clump of dry grass. They stopped bickering to listen to the track. It sounded higher than it had the day before. Faster? Autumn felt panic swell in her abdomen. She had no idea how she was going to do this. Marley had completely overestimated her vocal ability when he'd pulled together a selection of Bowie's songs and woven them into a medley. She didn't think she could manage to sing it to a standard acceptable even to her own ears, let alone the ears of two hundred strangers. Standing beside Marley and his melodic tone, Autumn knew that she sounded like a schoolgirl singing with Johnny Cash. She was beginning to hate him for making her do it. She was already embarrassed and nobody had heard her yet besides Marley.

"It's easy, see?" he said, as they came to the end of the song.

"For you, maybe," she retorted. "When all this is over, I'm going to ask you to write an eighty-thousand-word novel and send it to a publisher, then we'll see what's easy."

***

"From the top!" he called out, resetting the track to the opening bars. Autumn closed her eyes and sang as best she could. There was no denying that the arrangement was beautiful. It began with some joyously upbeat lyrics about two people finding one another against all odds, moved into a piece about everything turning out fine if families stuck together through whatever they had to face, and the finale was a soulful ballad about how it felt when you had to say goodbye. It was this last song that scared Autumn the most, not just because it was difficult to sing, but also because she was worried how

Bowie might react to hearing it. He was always going to be grateful, surprised and overwhelmed by their efforts, but she had grave concerns he might well become upset. These songs were written from his heart. The lyrical goodbyes in the last number were deeply distressing. The Whittle men had been raised in a way that was at odds with social norms. They were shamelessly emotional. Bowie would cry. Autumn didn't think reducing him to tears in such a public situation for the sake of nostalgia was fair to him.

"You're not really trying," Marley said when they were done.

"Fuck off," she replied curtly.

"You're not, Autumn!"

"I'm not a singer, remember? I am doing the best that I can."

"No, you aren't," he said. "You sang better than that just sitting in the dressing room that night we were all together."

"The night you signed me up for this without my permission?" she said . Marley sighed.

Petulantly, Autumn plonked herself down on the pine needles on the ground. A deliberate act of defiance. He'd already asked her to stay standing when they'd rehearsed the day before, insisting she needed her full lung capacity to be able to sing properly. Well, Autumn didn't want to sing. She was on strike. The ground was wet and uncomfortable, but she was too stubborn to let him see her get back up. That would be admitting defeat. Marley watched her for a moment, then leaned against a tree trunk.

"Ryan Gosling and Emma Stone weren't professional singers when they were cast in *La La Land*," he said. "And they won Oscars."

"Good for them." Autumn picked up a stick and snapped it, launching one half of it at the ground. The chickens thought it was something they could eat and ran towards it, pecking at it eagerly and clucking irritably when they realised it wasn't appetising. "Bowie isn't going to be able to go to this stupid ball anyway."

"Oh, yeah, that's the spirit," Marley said sarcastically, folding his legs beneath him and joining her on the ground. They sat in silence. The sky was elephant grey and Autumn could hear thunder rumbling away somewhere in the distance and could see heavy rain falling on the horizon. It wouldn't be long before it reached them.

"Don't worry, Autumn," Marley said, defeated. "I can just sing it for him by myself."

Autumn was wrong-footed. That wasn't what she wanted. She'd thought it was, but now she felt suddenly sad. Marley was cutting her out of Bowie's lovely surprise, just like that. It wasn't fair. She wanted to take it all back. She didn't know how to tell him what she was feeling without sounding as though she was losing her mind. She'd been a nightmare to live with for three days now. On the morning after they'd all resolved their differences, she'd woken up in a terrible mood and hadn't been able to shake it off. She'd tried everything to lift her spirits but they were still all over the place. No one was being spared her irritation but, for some reason, her inner monster had settled mainly on taking it all out on Marley. She'd been incredibly rude to him, snapping at him whenever he spoke, ignoring him when he asked her for her help with anything, and sneering when he was talking to the others. She'd been so vicious to him over dinner the evening before, Bowie had torn into her about it when they had gone to bed. She'd promised him she would try her best to stop, but had admitted that, at the moment, for some unknown reason, Marley's presence alone was enough to piss her off.

Autumn looked up and sighed at the sky above them. She was fizzing with rage. Although she knew, deep down, that Marley was only trying to give her what she wanted, she felt as though he was trying to take her part in Bowie's surprise away from her. She wondered if she was subconsciously resentful of the night Marley had spent with Bowie, which meant one less *she* got to spend with him. Or perhaps, subconsciously, she was upset with Bowie, but taking it out on his physically fit twin instead.

Whatever it was, she was way too tired to try to figure out what was wrong with her. She lay back and closed her eyes. Marley let her sleep.

When the rain reached them, they got to their feet in moody silence and made their way back to the house.

* * *

"There are only three chickens out there today," Emma said the following morning. She was clutching a mug of coffee and looking at the coop out of the kitchen window. Autumn, Bowie and Marley joined her. She was right. They were scratching around at the ground in the same way they did every morning, but there were only three of them.

"There were four yesterday," Marley said. The chickens had followed them obediently home. Autumn remembered because she'd almost fallen over one as they'd clambered over the perimeter fence and into the Whittles' garden.

"Definitely?" Emma asked Marley cautiously, so as not to alert Bowie to the time they had spent together. He'd been sleeping when they'd left and with Pip when they'd returned. Autumn thought about it. She knew for certain that at least two chickens had followed them home, but she couldn't be sure there had been four. They'd run almost the entire way back. She'd headed straight for the house, Marley had followed her to the porch, realised he needed to lock up the chicken coop, then run back out into the rain to do it. She'd presumed he'd checked all chickens were present, but she could tell from the worried expression on his face he hadn't. Marley eyed his mother.

"Yes, I'm pretty sure there were four."

"Oh God, what if Miranda's been out all night?" Emma said, putting down her coffee cup and picking up her scarf, her brow lined with worry. Autumn winced. Emma had saved the chickens from slaughter and was so incredibly fond of them. The storm had rumbled overhead for hours in the night and the rain hadn't eased. If the chicken was lost, it was likely that she'd gotten into some sort of trouble. Marley handed his mother's coffee cup back to her, unwinding the scarf from around her neck and wrapping it around his own.

"I'll go, Mum," he said lovingly.

"Are you sure, baby?" she asked. Marley nodded. She stood on her tiptoes and kissed the tip of his nose.

"I'll come too," Autumn said, feeling guilty. If Miranda had got lost, it was their fault.

"No, don't worry," Marley said, pulling on his duffle coat. "This is all my fault. I locked up the coop, I should have checked. And there's no point in us both getting wet."

"I don't mind." Autumn took a yellow raincoat down from the peg. "We can cover more ground between us. Can I wear this, please?"

"Of course," Emma replied.

"Be careful," Bowie called as they left.

The rain was still practically apocalyptic. They hesitated on the porch, hoping Miranda might appear. She didn't. They eyed one another apprehensively, heading for the coop. It was warm, but the morning was dark. Raindrops pelted the ground, bouncing several inches up into the air before they settled into puddles that were flooding the garden. Thick, black clouds swirled threateningly above their heads. If the chicken was alive, she must be hiding somewhere. Autumn prayed the whole way that they would find Miranda, but the coop was empty. They'd have to look further afield.

"Ready?" Marley asked her. She nodded through her discomfort. The rain pounded against her head so hard it took her breath away. Marley headed straight towards where they'd been rehearsing. It suddenly seemed a long way away. Autumn wanted to go back inside, but couldn't bear to leave Emma's precious hen to fend for herself, so she followed Marley, pushing the tall, wet grass aside with her hands as they walked, wishing she was wearing something on her feet other than pumps. They checked everywhere they thought a chicken might hide as they went, but she was nowhere to be found.

"Maybe she's at the back of the garden," Marley shouted. Autumn could barely hear him. In the ten minutes or so they'd been searching, the rain had grown even heavier. It was belting down through the leaves of the trees and smashing against the muddy ground.

They scoured the entire garden in their search for Miranda, but there was no sign of her anywhere. Autumn was starting to panic. If they'd left her out in the field all night, she could be anywhere by now. She might slowly starve to death. She could have wandered for miles, feeling lost, scared and alone. She might have been eaten by a fox. Autumn felt sick.

The Whittles' chickens were the first chickens Autumn had ever known personally, and she had grown to care for them. They'd come into her life at exactly the right time. She'd been writing her new book all wrong, depicting her chicken characters in a way that was flat and monotonous. Now, she could see that chickens were bursting with personality. They were funny and sweet. She especially liked it when Emma scrambled their eggs and crushed up their eggshells to feed back to them, something Autumn had learned gave them nourishment. They'd smell the eggs cooking and peck eagerly at the front door, clucking noisily and jostling one another out of the best spot. She'd once helped Ben chase them around the garden after they'd stolen a bunch of grapes from the fruit bowl on the kitchen windowsill. Whenever anyone sat on the swing in the garden, the chickens jumped up next to them, fluffing up their feathers expectantly and cawing gently if they were stroked. Emma was pleased to hear Autumn's second book was focused on the plight of caged hens, as it was a cause very close to her heart. She would never keep pets, she insisted, it wasn't vegan to do so, but she would rescue animals who had nowhere else to go. She told Autumn these four had very sadly had a tough start in life.

"Pip and I sometimes visit the slaughterhouses nearby and join protests against them. One day, we managed to sneak a few of the chickens out of the lorry on their way in. It's one of the hardest things I've ever had to do, because I could only grab hold of a few and I had to leave so many others behind. We managed to bring six home between us, but two passed away pretty quickly. They had no feathers and were terrified of us. When we put them on the grass for the first time, they obviously hadn't seen anything like it before."

The Whittles as a collective couldn't bear the idea any living creature might suffer because of them. Emma had been vegan since she was a teenager, and her children had never eaten meat or dairy except by accident. Autumn had asked Bowie once if he'd ever felt as though he was missing out and he'd shaken his head in a defiant no.

"Mum was always honest with us about what has to happen for us to eat meat, so we've never had any interest in it," he'd said. "We don't eat our friends, that's what she used to say. And why would we, when there is so much amazing vegan food out there to eat?"

Autumn's stomach had rumbled at the thought. She had eaten some of the best food she'd had in her life while living with the Whittles, lots of it cooked by Ben, Bowie, Marley, and Pip. Emma, who objected to gender stereotyping of any kind, had armed her sons with skills in the kitchen.

"I've always been adamant that any partner of my children would never have cause to complain to Ben and I that a Whittle baby didn't know how to cook," she'd said.

As far as Autumn was concerned, Emma was a goddess. A hero. She'd once spent almost an hour out in the rain removing slugs from the driveway so that she didn't drive over them on her way out. She'd parked out on the road on her return, mortified by the idea she might kill one. To her, there was no difference between running over an insect or hitting a dog. The chickens had become like family to her. If Miranda was dead, she would be devastated. Autumn knew Emma would blame herself for not double checking when Marley had insisted he'd locked up the chickens the night before and they were safe. She wanted so desperately to find Miranda and put Emma's mind at rest.

"One more look around the field, do you think?" Marley asked. They'd been out for almost an hour now and Autumn was beginning to feel a bit off-colour, but she caught sight of Emma, watching them from the kitchen window, and nodded.

She knew less than a minute later she'd made a mistake. There was something wrong with her chest. The borrowed raincoat was sticking to it and she could barely breathe. She tried to pull it away from herself as she walked, but she couldn't close her hands around it. Her strength had gone. She was dying.

Marley reached their rehearsal spot a few seconds before she did, and she was planning on telling him as soon as she reached him that she felt lightheaded, unsteady on her feet and might be dying, but when she saw him search an area of undergrowth and then pick up a lifeless lump of feathers, she felt like she might lose her mind first, instead. She started to screech.

"No, no, no, no, no!"

"I'm sorry, Autumn," he said gently.

"This is all your fault!" She screamed the words at him. "You and your fucking tribute. You said you'd locked them up and they were safe. This is all your fault, Marley."

"I know, Autumn. Calm down."

"Don't tell me to calm down." She put her head in her hands and walked in a circle. Where had all the oxygen gone? There was no oxygen anywhere. Through her fingers, she saw Marley lay the chicken on the ground and come towards her, and felt her body flood with sudden and overwhelming panic. Irrational fear washed over her and she shoved him away.

"Autumn! Stop!" he cried.

"Don't put her on the floor!" She pushed him again.

"Autumn, it's going to be all right. Come here."

"Leave me alone, Marley!" She hit out at his outstretched hands, stepping back away from him. She felt as though her chest might burst. She tore off Emma's raincoat and threw it onto the ground, doubling over in an attempt to stop her lungs exploding. Her face felt red raw, her neck as though it might tear open. No matter how hard Autumn tried, she couldn't drag enough air into her lungs to make herself feel better. She was terrified.

"Autumn, you're going to be OK," Marley said. She saw him take a step towards her.

"Fuck off!" She held out her arms to protect herself from him. She wanted to be left alone until whatever was happening to her had passed her by or killed her. She didn't have it in her to care which.

"Autumn, listen to me." Marley was suddenly kneeling on the floor in her eyeline, his hands held out towards her, palms up. "You're having a panic attack," he said.

"Pick the chicken up!" As she shrieked at Marley, still doubled over, she could see Miranda's frail, soggy body, her feathers waterlogged with rain. How dare he leave her like that when she was dead and he was to blame?

"Autumn—"

"Fucking pick her up!" Marley got to his feet and, taking Miranda's tiny body in one arm, went to stand beneath the trees. He held out his free hand to Autumn.

"Come out of the rain."

Feeling a little better now he had the chicken in his arms, she wanted to be near him. She was too scared to stand, convinced she would have a heart attack if she did, but she moved towards him in the only way she felt able, still bent double, and with her hands on her knees. She knew she must look utterly ridiculous, but was too freaked out to care. When she was close enough that he could reach her, Marley asked for her permission to touch her. She nodded and he grabbed her by the top of her arm, dragging her towards him, and pulling her in close. She fell against him and burst into tears.

"It's OK, Autumn," he said. "You're going to be OK, I promise."

"I think I might be dying." She gasped, gripping his duffle coat with both of her hands. She buried her head in the soggy fabric, desperately seeking the heat of his body. She could feel no warmth at all through his coat, so her fingertips searched out his neck. She lay her hands against his bare skin.

"You're not going to die." He held her tighter. "It's going to pass in a minute, I promise. Take deep breaths."

He stood holding her — and the chicken — beneath the trees, murmuring reassuring words. Autumn felt her heart-rate return to normal. The pain in her chest eased. She could breathe again. Eventually, she felt safe enough to stand, but not strong enough to hold her own weight. She peeled herself away from him and sat down on the grass. Marley lay the chicken gently on a tree stump, took off his coat, wrapped it around Autumn's shoulders, and then sat down beside her. She stared at the discarded bird.

"Would you rather I held her?" Marley asked. Autumn nodded. He picked up the hen's body and sat beside Autumn, cradling Miranda in his arms. He watched her, concern written all over his face.

"I'm so sorry," she said. The anger she'd felt towards him had evaporated.

"Don't apologise," he said. "It isn't your fault. It's mine. This is all my fault."

"I've never had a panic attack before," she said.

"Well, you looked like a pro," he said jokingly.

She laughed and he winked at her, nudging her affectionately with his elbow.

"I have them all the time," he said. "Eventually you learn to see them coming."

"How?" she asked. She didn't really care — she never planned on having one again — but his voice was a distraction from the humiliation she knew she'd soon come to feel. Had she put her hands on his neck? She cringed.

"I turn into a complete bitch." He sighed. "Ring any bells?"

"I'm so sorry," she said again. She'd been truly terrible to him these past few days. She was lucky he was still speaking to her at all.

"It's OK," he said. "When it happens to me, I take all my frustration out on Bowie. How bad is that? As if he doesn't have enough to deal with."

Autumn winced, feeling guilty.

"*You* have enough to deal with, too," she said. "Without your brother's girlfriend treating you like crap."

"My brother's girlfriend?" He feigned indignation. "We've spent a beautiful summer together and that's all you think you are to me now."

"You know what I mean."

"Is that all I am to you?" he asked. "Your boyfriend's brother?"

"No." She shook her head. "You're my friend, too."

"Good," he said. "Case closed, then."

She supposed he was right. Friends forgave one another.

"Be honest—" he interrupted what she thought might be a moment of comfortable silence — "do you think it's because of the tribute?"

She nodded. It was definitely that.

"I'm sorry," he said. "I didn't mean to put pressure on you like that."

Autumn shrugged. He hadn't meant to do her any harm, she knew that. She wished she had the energy to tell him properly that it was all right, but she felt battered. She watched the raindrops fall, instead. Rain had always been her favourite weather. There was something incredibly magical about it. A wall of raindrops could make you feel as though you were all that existed in the entire world. She had always been able to see why rainstorms were the backdrop to so many kisses in books and movies. There was something inexplicably lovely about the idea of two people caught out in the rain.

All of a sudden, things felt inappropriate. She wasn't sure what had changed, but something had. Being close to Marley had never made her feel this way before. She was disappointed, but the feeling was undeniable, so she pulled her coat tighter around herself and shuffled a little way away from him. He watched her.

"There are cigarettes in my coat pocket," he said. Grateful for the distraction, she took out the packet and a lighter, passing them to him. He lit them a cigarette each, inhaling sharply from his own. The silence between them had become uncomfortable. She willed him to speak.

"You know, for someone with so much confidence, you don't actually have much at all," he said eventually.

"What does that mean?" she asked.

"Nothing bad, Autumn, I promise. Just, back when Bowie first met you, he told me you were the most confident woman he'd ever met, but I don't see that in you. You're happy doing things you know you're good at, you know, like writing brilliant stuff, but if you have to do anything you're not used to excelling in, you're terrible at hiding how much you hate it."

He stopped to tap his cigarette. Autumn did the same, holding her breath.

"Like with Bowie," he continued. "You love him so much that it makes you feel uncomfortable."

Autumn didn't respond. He was right thus far. She *did* find being in love with Bowie difficult at times. She found the monotony of their lives challenging to cope with and some days she was driven half mad with boredom. She missed her freedom and longed for the simplicity of not caring, that synonymous ease that came with her capacity to shut her heart down and shunt her attention onto something else — or someone else — when anything caused her pain. Her silence was tacit confirmation of Marley's words, she knew.

"I know how much you love him," he told her again. "But you've found each other at such a bizarre time. If I'm honest, I think it's only working because you know it isn't going to be for ever."

"That isn't true," she said. He was pushing this too far. She couldn't let him say something like that without objecting. She had never felt for anyone what she felt for Bowie. She was sure that they would be together whether he was ill or not. Her restlessness was driven only by boredom. If things were different, they would be back in New York, surrounded by the bright lights and excitement of the city she'd made her home, instead of spending their days and nights on a sleepy country estate. Her struggles had nothing at all to do with how she felt about Bowie. She was about to say that, but Marley was shaking his head.

"If he hadn't been ill, you'd have tired of him by now."

"I would not!"

"You'd have eaten him for breakfast and moved on to lunch, Autumn."

"You're wrong!" She raised her voice. He held his hands up in mock surrender, but didn't apologise or take back his words. To stop herself from punching him in his self-righteous face, Autumn looked away again, taking her rage out on the butt of her cigarette by stubbing it viciously into the ground.

"I don't mean to offend you," he said. "I'm just telling you what I see."

"Yes, well, you're being awfully judgemental for someone who has never held on to a relationship of their own," she said.

"Maybe that's how I know—" he shrugged — "because we're the same."

She stubbornly shook her head, but she knew he was right. The more they'd got to know each other, the more apparent it had become how similar the two of them really were. Before Bowie, Autumn's whole life had been about having what Emma called 'frowned-upon fun'. It filled a hole she seemed to have that other people didn't. It woke something up in her. When she wasn't 'up to no good', she felt dead. For a while she'd suspected Bluebell slept around for the same reason, but they'd talked about it and it wasn't the case she just liked it. But with Marley, it was. They had never talked about it, but there was something missing within him, too. Bowie, who was never judgemental, had admitted that he couldn't understand them. She had so much in common with her lover intellectually and they were crazy about each other, but he would never know how it felt to be frenzied for the power that came with holding someone's heart in the palm of your hand and knowing you would crush it later. He didn't desire it the way Marley did. The way Autumn had, before Bowie. She wasn't even sure that Bowie knew the extent of how empty she had been before she'd met him. How empty she was starting to feel once again. But Marley could see it and she was desperately worried that he would think it was because she didn't love his brother, which wasn't true, it was just that the hole was still there and there was no way to fill it when you were living in Hertfordshire with a terminally ill boyfriend. What was wrong with her?

Marley gave her time to calm down before speaking again.

"You know what's funny about this? Bluebell sent you backstage at my gig that night to meet me. She knew she was going to end up with Adam and she thought I might take you to the after-party. That we might have sex, I suppose, though she'll never admit it. She would never have chosen to set you up with Bowie because I don't think she thought you could give him what he wanted. I don't think you thought it, either. But it worked itself out. You and I would've fucked the way we do — the way I do and you did — and then frightened each other away, and Bowie would still be miserable. You're the only reason he's still here. I know that. He'd have given up weeks ago if it wasn't for you. Despite everything he's going through, he's having the time of his life. He loves you so much. I know now that you can't save him, but it was still the best thing that ever happened to any of us, Bowie finding you. You've given us all more time. And if you weren't who you are, Autumn, someone who has never been worried about owning a lover for ever, then you wouldn't be able to cope with any of this. You'd have run away as soon as you found out Bowie came without a lifetime guarantee. You've temporarily become someone else because you do love him and because he needs you, I know that, but you don't have to be ashamed to admit that you're someone who struggles with this type of monotony. Not to me. I won't think you love Bowie any less. You're an excellent girlfriend, for the record, though I know it doesn't come naturally to you. You're better at some things than you know. And it's fine to feel a little lost, especially when you're being forced to live a life you wouldn't choose. I feel it, too."

Marley finished his cigarette and immediately took two more from the pack. He lit one and held it out for her. She eyeballed him as she took it.

"I wouldn't have fucked you," she said. "You're not my type."

He guffawed and she smiled, then they returned to watching the rain.

"What are we going to do about the chicken?" she asked.

"When they die we leave them in the forest for the foxes," he said. Autumn recoiled. "Hear me out. It means the foxes get a meal without having to hunt for another living creature. Some poor soul gets to live another day. She's dead. She doesn't need her body anymore."

Autumn relaxed a little bit. That actually made sense to her.

"I'm glad we found her," she said.

He nodded. "Me too. Mum would've hated it if we hadn't. At least now she knows the poor thing wasn't killed by a fox or anything."

"What do you think happened?"

"Dunno." He shrugged. "Hard to tell. It's almost certainly my fault, though, for leaving her out all night."

"This is why I'll never have pets," she said. "I could only cope if I could lock them up and keep them safe, and that doesn't seem very vegan. If they were my chickens, I wouldn't want to let them out of the coop."

"We used to think like that," he said. "Mum wouldn't let us have pets for years. We only have the chickens and the sheep because they're rescues. Mum knows letting them wander means they might get into trouble. We've been lucky up to now, we haven't lost a single one."

"Poor Miranda," Autumn sighed.

Marley gently stroked the chicken's wing. "Poor Miranda," he repeated. "This is all my fault. I just took for granted she'd be in the coop. Mum checks and double checks. I reassured her. I talked her out of going out in the rain. I'm an idiot."

Autumn didn't want to disagree with him. To do so would feel like an insult to Miranda, who'd had her own likes and dislikes, her own personality, her own sense of self. Her life had been important — that was a fundamental vegan belief — and there was no justification for his carelessness. They sat in silence for a moment and then he groaned. "Mum's going to be devastated," he said.

"She is," Autumn agreed, picking anxiously at her fingernails. She wanted to talk to Marley about something important — something she was aware he would not want to discuss with her — and she knew this might be the only opportunity she'd get. The weight of that conversation and the responsibility that came with it was making her fidget. Marley noticed.

"What's happening?" he gestured to her restless legs. "Why are you nervous all of a sudden?"

This was it. It was now or never. She took a deep breath, then forced herself to say what was on her mind.

"How can you be this worried about how devastated your mum will be when she finds out Miranda is dead when you know you're planning to kill yourself?" She was babbling. "Surely you must know what that will do to her, Marley? The pain you'll cause her, it'll be a thousand times worse than this! You're worried your neglect last night will hurt her when she finds out Miranda is gone, but you're planning on . . ."

"Stop it," he cut her off. He was surprised, she could tell. They'd never spoken about the plans he had to end his own life. Perhaps he'd come to believe she would never confront him about it.

"I don't want you to do it," she said. It seemed like a stupid declaration, but it felt like the right thing to say. Marley winced, but didn't reply. He was still holding the chicken's body in his hands, gently stroking the feathers on her neck with his thumb. For someone who was so intent on ending it all, he had an exceptionally attractive attitude towards all living beings. She'd once laughed long and hard when she'd caught him talking to a spider in the kitchen using the exact same tone he used to talk to other humans. Autumn had never seen anything like it, but Marley had not been at all embarrassed. The memory made her sad now. He was special. His death would be a great loss to all creatures great and small.

"I've always known I would never want to live life without Bowie," he said. "My decision was made long before he got ill."

"There is no denying that it's going to be shit," she said. "But there are other things for you to live for."

"I don't care about anything except him," he said. "Not really."

"That's not true," she said. "You have your family. Your career. Friends and the people who love you."

He shook his head, pursing his lips. She knew it was no use. Marley and Bowie could not comprehend a life in which the other did not exist. She'd always thought it was tragic, but in that moment she realised that she would also miss him so very much. He was her friend. Losing him as well as Bowie seemed incomprehensible. She wished that she could tell him, but she didn't have enough energy to force him to talk and she didn't want to fall out with him again. Reluctantly, she reminded herself that Marley was not hers to save. She would have to try to prepare herself for losing them both. She had no fucking idea how she was supposed to manage that. Maybe she wouldn't. Maybe she'd just forget all about it until it smacked her in the face.

"She's at peace now, at least," he said eventually, looking down at the chicken in his arms. Autumn shivered. She realised they had somehow huddled close to one another, so she stood up to put some space between them, retying her soggy laces and changing the subject as naturally as she could.

"What do you want to do about the song?" she asked.

"What do you want to do about it?" He was good at answering her questions with a question.

"I'd like to try it again," she said. "Now I've calmed down a bit."

"I don't have the music with me," he said.

"We could just sing it through without?"

He nodded, stubbing out his cigarette. "OK. I'll start. You can join in when you feel ready."

His smooth, low voice rolled out across the field, backed by the rain and the rustling of the trees overhead. Autumn found herself so captivated by him that she almost forgot to come in when she was meant to. She closed her eyes and followed his lead, harmonising with him the way he had taught her. She remembered what he'd said earlier, about being better at things than she thought she was, and mentally heaved her self-doubt out of her mind. She faltered a little as they transitioned into the second song, but he encouraged her to continue with an enthusiastic grin and an affectionate nudge in the ribs. She was so excited by how good it sounded that she dared to open her eyes for the third song. She caught Marley peeping out from beneath his eyelids. He opened his eyes properly and gave her a delighted thumbs-up. They watched each other as they sang to the end of the song. Autumn marvelled. When had this man become her biggest supporter? She acknowledged with a jolt that the sicker Bowie had become and the less energy he had to talk or to play with her the way he used to, the more reliant she had become on Marley. He was struggling with the absence of his brother's playful nature too, and was always there, willing to entertain her and help her if she needed anything. She appreciated him. Loved him, even. Not the way she loved Bowie, but the way she loved Bluebell. She didn't tell him. He would be embarrassed, she knew.

"Didn't I say you could fucking do it?" he said, handing her another cigarette in celebration. Autumn beamed. She could fucking do it. She had fucking done it. She was no professional, not by any stretch, but she knew that their voices had sounded lovely together.

"Emma Stone and Ryan Geeseling, eat your mother-fucking hearts out!" She punched at the sky, lighting her cigarette.

"It's Gosling." Marley laughed. "But OK."

CHAPTER 12

The day before Larry Ross's summer ball, Emma insisted on taking Maddie, Bluebell and Autumn dress shopping. They protested, but she was adamant that they needed some frivolity. It would do them good to get out of the house and away from the men, she argued. Her decision had been driven by one too many arguments over Monopoly, which they'd taken to playing on the kitchen table in their pyjamas. Bowie and Marley were incorrigible cheats, and Pip was a terrible loser. More often than not, the game descended into chaos.

Emma had told them her plan two days before, but Autumn had hoped she might forget about it. She had always hated going shopping with other women, preferring to look for clothes by herself when she had to, and not at all if she could help it. She had some dresses she'd had since she was a teenager.

"I'm really not into this," she told them snippily once they were inside the shopping centre. She knew she should have said so earlier, but Emma would have told her she didn't have to come even though they really wanted her to, and Autumn would've spent the whole day feeling guilty. Still, they might as well know that she was not in the mood. "I have something I can wear."

"You brought a ballgown back to England with you?" asked Emma, fluttering her eyelashes in a way that made it clear she already knew the answer. Autumn blinked vacantly. She definitely hadn't. She didn't even own a ballgown. She'd had no cause for one in her entire life.

"I have to wear a ballgown?"

"To a summer ball?" Emma raised her eyebrows and smiled, placing a loving hand on her shoulder. "Yes, my love. Yes, you do."

Autumn agreed to try on some dresses so long as Emma promised not to try to stage any kind of fashion show.

"But that's the best part about having daughters," she said, a whiny note in her voice. "And we haven't done it for so long. We haven't ever done it with you, Autumn. I know you're a modern 'screw-the-patriarchy', 'feminism-for-all' type woman, but does that mean we can't have a bit of fun when we shop?"

Emma was right. Autumn, Bluebell and Maddie were in agreement when it came to the issues facing women and girls, believing it impossible to achieve the kind of standards society expected of them and even harder to maintain them. They were of the opinion that life was generally harder for women. Autumn wasn't sure where trying on clothes for your would-be mother-in-law fit in in terms of feminist principles, but it didn't sit well with her anyway. If she thought hard enough, she could probably think of a legitimate reason why.

"It's not about that, Mum," Bluebell said, leading them into an expensive-looking boutique. "It's just that we'd rather pick out what we want as quickly as possible and then go for a beer."

Emma rolled her eyes, drilling ferociously through the hangers on the first clothes rail she came to.

"I'm not happy about how much alcohol you're drinking at the moment, but I'll take you for lunch and buy you bloody beer if you'll just parade yourselves around a little bit for my entertainment. Humour me, would you?"

"That's bribery," Autumn said pointedly, but she agreed to Emma's terms nevertheless. Maybe Emma was right and wearing a beautiful dress would be good for her. She had barely been out of her pyjamas for longer than a couple of hours at a time in weeks. Perhaps getting dressed up to go to a ball could even be a little bit exciting.

"How's the song coming along?" Emma asked nonchalantly. They only ever talked about the medley when they were out of the house. There would be a Marley-induced mutiny if Bowie found out about it in advance.

"It's going all right," she told Emma. They'd been rehearsing for a few hours almost every day for a week. They'd stomped back and forth through the field so many times that they'd forged their own little pathway through the grass. The three remaining chickens still accompanied them every day. They were careful now to make sure they brought them all back to the garden.

Autumn had turned a corner with her performance and was actually quite looking forward to showing everyone what she and Marley had been able to put together. The more they rehearsed, the better they sounded. She was not as hesitant as she had once been. She had faith in her ability to deliver now and she had Marley to thank for that. He was an excellent teacher and a fabulous cheerleader.

"I don't know why I'm not more afraid of it," she added.

"Neither do I," Maddie said musingly. "You do know there'll be over two hundred people there, don't you?"

"Thanks for that," Autumn said.

"They'll all be professional performers too," Bluebell added. "Like, the kind of people who actually get paid to do what you're going to do for free."

Autumn shuddered. "Now I'm terrified," she said. "Thanks, guys."

They laughed.

"I just keep reminding myself that it's not about any of that," Autumn said. "It's about Bowie and what it will mean to him. Marley's brazen talent doesn't help, though. Your boy has nerves of steel."

"Well, he lives for the stage," Emma said. "And he's looking forward to performing in public again."

As she looked up from the clothes rail, Autumn caught a wordless exchange between Emma and each of her daughters. She hated it when this happened. It was the only time she remembered she was not genuinely a part of their family. There were things she didn't know. A past she hadn't been privy to.

"Has he told you his plan for the evening?" Emma deftly changed the subject. Autumn worked hard to free her face of confusion, and nodded. Marley was going to tell Bowie he had to fly to New York on Saturday evening to play with his band on Sunday because they had nobody else to do it. In fact, Marley would actually be waiting backstage for Autumn at the ball. She would need to listen for a prompt and then tell Bowie she needed the toilet. Someone would meet her in the ladies' loo and bring her through to Marley backstage. "He'll realise something's going on," she'd said, anxiously chewing on her cheek — "when I'm gone so long . . ." Autumn really wanted this to work. She was looking forward to giving Bowie such a sentimental gift.

"Maybe, but by the time he does we'll only be a few seconds from starting to sing," he'd reassured her. "It will still be a surprise."

Now that they were looking for something suitable to wear, Autumn could barely wait. She was eager to get to the beers and the dancing, singing and performing. It was the adventure she needed. Plus, she'd get to see Bowie in a suit. She'd always liked snazzy men.

"Autumn, I think I found your dress." Bluebell called from across the shop. She was holding up a black, strapless gown with a raised hem at the front, a train at the back, and peacock feathers embroidered intricately on both the skirt and the bodice. From a distance, the feathers looked like tiny, indistinguishable splashes of extraordinary blues and greens. It was made all the more special when it became apparent what they actually were. Bluebell knew her too well — it was beautiful and Autumn loved it.

"And I found mine." Bluebell held up a floor-length dress with full sheer sleeves. It had a fitted bodice covered in tiny silver sequins and the skirt was floaty and paisley-patterned, with an almost waist-high slit up one side. With its beaded, multicoloured belt sewn into the waistline, it was the most boho formal gown Autumn had ever seen. Maddie eyed it enviously.

"I could never pull off anything like that," she said, looking downhearted. Bluebell and Autumn exchanged knowing glances. Maddie did this sometimes. She didn't mean to, but she had a habit of making them both feel guilty about the self-confidence they shared. They loved her, so they'd never taken her to task over it, but she was the only woman they would take that from.

"You have your own thing going on," Autumn said. She'd told Maddie with sincerity many times that she was envious of the ease with which she managed to wear clashing patterns, funky headscarves with fat, hooped earrings, and costume rings on her fingers to dress up jeans and baggy T-shirts with style, but Maddie usually brushed off her compliments. She couldn't see anything good about her appearance and dressed the way she did to distract attention from her figure, which she believed inadequate.

Maddie was shorter than her brothers and sisters, and not so perfectly in proportion, but her curves were exactly where most women wanted them, and she had the most amazing hair and smile — she just wasn't able to see it herself. She'd been bullied at school by girls who'd called her 'fat'. She still couldn't see past the fact that she wasn't a size ten. She openly lusted after features and traits her siblings had: Pip's perfect little nose, Bluebell's wavy blonde hair, Marley's unabashed sexiness and Bowie's charismatic awkwardness. Autumn had tried to tell her that the way she thought about herself was wrong, but Maddie had insisted that *she* was the normal one; her brothers and sister were the weird ones. She was quite sure it wasn't normal to fancy yourself as much as they all did.

"They've always loved themselves," she'd said. "Not in an ugly way . . . They just know how much they have to offer and they've always been happy to admit it. I've never felt that way about myself."

Autumn would never understand how Ben and Emma had managed to produce four unabashedly confident children alongside a middle child who couldn't stand to look at herself in the mirror. She set about searching for a dress that might make her friend feel as fabulous as Autumn thought she looked.

"What about this?" she asked, picking up a floor-length, pleated, canary-yellow gown. It would skim and accentuate Maddie's frame in all the right places.

"Oh, that's gorgeous," Emma said, hoisting the pile of dresses she was carrying onto her hip to finger the fabric.

"I'm not sure." Maddie reached out to feel it too. "It has a halter neck. I hate my shoulders. I'm not sure about the yellow either. And the pleats might make my hips look too wide."

"You're wrong." Bluebell snatched up the dress and nudged her sister into the dressing room. Maddie sighed and gave in. Autumn and Emma followed. Emma was struggling under the weight of an armful of garments.

"Why do you have so many?" Autumn asked her, afraid she may have been selecting dresses for all of them to try. She had at least seven.

"I like to try on a few different ones," she said.

"Mum! What a fucking waste of time." Bluebell watched her mother arranging her dresses in order. The emerald-green one they already knew she would buy was settled strategically at the back, to be tried on last. Green was definitely Emma's colour and the dress, which was velvet and gothic in style, would suit her perfectly.

"You girls don't know how to do this properly anymore," she said. "In the olden days, before we had Facebook, this was all we did with our Saturdays. You have to try on a load of different things. Otherwise, how will you know when you've found the right one?"

"That's exactly how I feel about lovers." Bluebell grinned.

"I just hope you're careful." Emma winced, pulling her changing room curtain across dramatically.

"I've never once heard you say those words to Marley," Bluebell said accusingly to her mother through the fabric.

"I tell him to wrap it up, all the bloody time," Emma called. This was true because Autumn had heard her.

Smiling at their tomfoolery, Autumn stepped into a cubicle and took her time getting changed. They'd be waiting for Emma for a while yet, she reasoned. As she pulled up the zip on the very first ballgown she'd ever had a reason to put on, she was thrilled to feel the fabric hugging her form exactly as it should. It fitted perfectly. She allowed her eyes to roam over her reflection. She looked older. Exhausted. She'd never looked this worn out even when she and Bowie had been up all night every night having sex. She wished she'd bothered to wear make-up for this; it might have made her feel better, though she supposed she would still know what was lurking underneath.

A dramatic swoosh from the cubicle next to hers followed by Bluebell's dejected whine interrupted her thoughts.

"Nobody was here for my grand reveal."

Autumn plastered a smile across her face and pulled back her own curtain. "Is it the one?"

"Of course it is," Bluebell said, turning from the mirror she'd been admiring herself in to twirl. Her friend looked sensational. Autumn nodded her approval.

"You look amazing," she said.

"So do you," Bluebell replied.

"Let me see." Emma poked her head out from behind the cubicle curtain. "Oh, girls, you look fab."

"Show us yours, Mum," Bluebell said. "And I want to see some vogue from you."

Emma drew the curtain back to reveal an unflattering black lace number. She did not pose. Autumn shook her head.

"Again, please. This time with feeling."

"Oh, for God's sake." Emma whipped the curtain closed, then opened it again, raising her arms theatrically like the good sport that she was. Autumn and Bluebell laughed. Emma's eyes crinkled up too.

"I thought I was the one forcing you into a fashion show?" She smiled.

"Be careful what you wish for," Bluebell said. "Now, take it off and put the green one on so that we can all go for a beer."

Autumn giggled.

"Don't you like this one?" Emma asked, stepping out to survey herself in the full-length mirror.

"Do you?" Bluebell asked.

"No," Emma replied.

"Good, because it's utterly hideous. Put the green one on."

"I want to try the purple one first." Emma closed her curtain again. Bluebell sighed, plonking herself down onto a beanbag with no attempt at grace.

"I'm having a really good time," Autumn said, a little surprised.

"Me too." Bluebell smiled. They stared happily at one another for a few seconds, before Bluebell looked guiltily away. She always did that these days, whenever she enjoyed herself for more than a moment. Autumn watched anxiety creep slowly across her friend's face. She knew the same thing was happening to her. Every tiny twinge of pleasure she felt was always accompanied by an unhealthy hangover of guilt. They were only together and enjoying this moment for one reason: Bowie was dying. They never discussed it, not ever, but they were haunted by the same shadows.

Bluebell called out to Emma, and Autumn knew that she was shattering the moment intentionally. "I'm not even going to comment on any of the others."

"Oh, why not?" Emma shouted back.

"It's a waste of my breath."

"Many of the things you say are a waste of your breath, my darling girl."

Bluebell ignored her, calling out to check on her sister, instead.

"Maddie, how are you doing in there?"

Maddie had been so quiet Autumn had almost forgotten she was there, but, then, suddenly, there she was, standing awkwardly before them, dazzling them in the bright yellow dress she had seemed so sure would not suit her. Her shoulders were hunched and her hands were positioned awkwardly in front of her chest but, nonetheless, she was breathtakingly well-suited to the gown she was wearing. Bluebell stood up. She and Autumn stared at her together.

Maddie frowned. "Don't be weird. We're not those girls. Let's not pretend we are."

"Oh my God," Bluebell said.

"Have you seen yourself?" Autumn blinked wildly at her, reaching to pull her out of the cubicle and positioning her in front of the full-length mirror. Bluebell stood at the other side of her. "You look amazing."

"I can already see our Instagram selfies taking shape." Bluebell pouted ridiculously, posing for an invisible camera. Autumn followed suit and the two of them burst out laughing. Maddie tried to hide her amusement.

"I'm so glad there are two of you now." She rolled her eyes.

"Maddie, just look at yourself," Bluebell said. Maddie was still avoiding her reflection.

"I've seen myself already," Maddie said. "I think I look OK."

They groaned. If Maddie couldn't see how incredible she looked in *this* dress there was no hope for her. Autumn didn't say that, though. Truthfully, she was still a little wary of Bowie's youngest sister. Despite her insecurities about her appearance, Maddie was a strong character and was unafraid to call anyone out for the entitled and unreasonable behaviour they were all guilty of at times. She'd even snapped at Bowie on a couple of occasions. She could silence Autumn's whining with a severe warning glance from across a room.

Still, Autumn loved her. She would have willingly shared some of her own self-confidence with her if she could.

"You're everything I hate," Bluebell said.

Maddie shook her head. "I'm not fishing. I genuinely think I just look OK."

Autumn sighed sadly, wrapping her arms around her friend's shoulders. "Well, that's a shame, sis, because you look like a snack."

Bluebell guffawed, clutching her hand to her mouth. When she removed it, her expression had become oddly serious. Suddenly, she lunged — quite desperately — to hug her sister from behind. Maddie gasped, grabbing Bluebell's forearms to steady herself. Before she knew what she was doing, Autumn had thrown her arms around them both. Although she protested at first, Maddie leaned into them eventually, and, when she did, Autumn felt Bluebell trembling. She tightened her arms around them further, and felt like she might cry. She didn't want to, but the only way to stop herself from sobbing would be to let go of the women she was holding, and she couldn't bear to do that either. She felt like they were holding each other together. Like they were clinging on to normality the way Bowie was holding desperately on to life, and they could no longer manage unless they literally pushed each other's broken bits back together. She couldn't say for sure how the other two women were feeling, but that was how she felt. She was sure there were variations of the same sentiment running through the minds of her friends. Maddie was half right — they may not have been gushy, overly sentimental women, but it still felt good to embrace one another, all three of them, in a way they'd never done before. They stood there — a circle of supportive sisterhood.

Autumn didn't hear Emma step out of her cubicle, but she was suddenly there. She was gentle but purposeful as she approached them without a word, eager to foster the moment they were having. Perhaps that had been her intention all along. She was wearing the green dress.

They pulled her into their group hug and stood in comfortable silence together for what felt like an age.

Autumn let herself cry when she realised that the women surrounding her already were.

* * *

"Bowie and Marley are doing my fucking head in," Bluebell said later that afternoon. They'd bought their dresses — Emma had purchased the green one they'd all known she would choose — and she'd taken them for lunch as promised. They'd decided to drink wine instead of beer and had been sinking glass after glass for over an hour, perched around a tall, circular table in a restaurant they knew served great vegan burgers. Nobody had ordered food, nor had they talked about their hug, which had ended when a teenaged girl had appeared in the fitting room. They'd broken apart with sad smiles, collecting their things and leaving without a word to one another. They'd been in Cassie's American Diner — Bluebell's recommendation — ever since. So far, Ben and Bowie had both called Emma more than once to ask when they were coming home. She'd told them both rather curtly that the women were having fun without them and would probably be back much later. She'd asked that they respectfully leave them to their 'girl time' unless there was an absolute emergency. They could entertain themselves for an afternoon, she'd insisted.

Autumn was surprised it had taken so long for the twins to come up in the conversation. So far, they'd spent most of their time talking about how frustrating it was trying to get Bowie to eat anything, the difficulties they had keeping the chickens safe whilst still allowing them a good quality of life, veganism, and how wonderful Autumn thought it was that Ben was so affectionate with his children. Two evenings before, he'd offered to spend the night with Bowie, who'd been struggling with exceptionally uncomfortable neck pain for the third night in a row. He'd sent Autumn upstairs to Bluebell's room to get some sleep. In the morning, she'd found Ben laying on his back on the sofa, cradling Bowie who'd slept peacefully on his chest. He'd told her, in a whisper, that it was the only position his son had been able to find comfort in. Autumn had almost burst into tears. She'd never seen a father hold a son of Bowie's age so tenderly.

There had been so many beautiful moments, but that didn't mean living together didn't come with its issues. Bowie and Marley were also doing Autumn's head in, but she didn't feel like it was her place to express her frustration to their mother. She was glad Bluebell had done it, instead.

"I know they're annoying, my darling." Emma reached across the table now to stroke Bluebell's cheek. "You just have to try to ignore them."

"How can I ignore them? They're there, doing my fucking head in, all the time."

The Whittles loved each other deeply, but they were not used to spending quite so much time together. When they'd first returned to the UK, everyone had come and gone as usual, but the sicker Bowie became, the less they socialised with anyone except each other. It was so intense that Autumn and Bowie now had to ask for time alone when they wanted it. She hadn't told anybody that they couldn't have sex anymore, not even Bluebell, and neither had he, so their request for time to themselves usually came with a certain amount of teasing. Far from being embarrassed enough to correct them, Autumn was happy to let the family continue to believe that they were still sexually active because it stopped them bursting into the bedroom unannounced whenever they felt like it, meaning that Autumn and Bowie could spend time talking and hugging and sleeping without interruption. Sometimes she read him poems or short stories aloud, or they watched a movie together. For a while he'd helped her to satisfy her own desires but, in the end, they'd come to the conclusion that it was too frustrating for them both. Although Bowie could not perform, he still had a sexual appetite, and her writhing around in front of him felt unfair. She made love to herself most mornings in the shower now instead.

Marley wasn't having sex either. He had stopped inviting women back to the house and never really went out anymore. There was still a stream of women's names clogging up his social media pages and bombarding his mobile phone with messages, but he'd quite suddenly lost all interest in any of their attention, spending all of his time with his family instead. Although Autumn continued to enjoy having him around, she hadn't realised quite how overwhelming he and Bowie could be to live with until she'd seen what they could be like when they were together all the time. When tensions ran high in the house, which they often did now with so many strong characters around, they tended to make it worse. Marley could be incredibly argumentative and Bowie would defend him beyond all reason, even when he was in the wrong. When Bowie's family challenged him about how much he'd eaten or if he'd taken his painkillers or whether he was well enough to be out of bed, Autumn would watch him actively seek Marley's support. The raised voice of one twin was like a distress signal to the other and winning an argument with them became impossible. They were extremely intelligent, quick-witted and relentlessly combative, and would take on anyone or anything together.

Bluebell struggled with them the most because she and Marley disagreed a lot, and he knew that Bluebell found arguing with Bowie distressing. He would call on his brother to add weight to his argument when he wanted to have the last word. He was shameless about doing it, too. Bluebell had privately begged him to stop, but he wouldn't. The twins continued to present a united front, calling Bluebell out every time she and Marley were at odds. Their poor sister was so terrified that any disagreement she had with Bowie might be their last conversation that she would give in and agree with his point of view. Autumn felt sorry for her. It must be so frustrating. She pouted in empathy with her friend and gave her shoulder an affectionate squeeze.

"And Pip," Maddie said, resting her elbows on the table, her chin in her hands. Her cheeks were flushed red from the wine they had been drinking and there was a ruby tinge to her lips. "When did he turn into a world-class binge-drinking sass-machine?"

Pip had always been spoiled by everyone. Now, it seemed he absolutely had to have his own way at all times. Pip was the only one who could get Bowie and Marley to do whatever he wanted, and with the weight of the twins behind him he was invincible. Autumn would go as far as to say that he was running the entire household with his tantrums. When he wasn't spending time with Bowie, he spent most of his days arguing for LGBTQ rights on social media sites and ranting relentlessly to his family. He was a whole lot of passion, but Autumn appreciated hearing Pip's perspective nonetheless. She'd had no idea of the issues gay people continued to face. Blinded by straight privilege, she was ashamed to admit she'd thought that things were getting much better for the LGBTQ community. Pip was always quick to enlighten her.

"You think I can just hold hands with someone in the street? Or kiss them?" he'd asked her one afternoon. "I can pretty much guarantee that you know at least one person who would feel uncomfortable with me doing that, just because I'm gay."

They whiled away their days with lots of important conversations, some silly ones, board games, arguments and lots of food. Everybody knew what was really going on, but nobody wanted to talk about it. Bowie did not have long left to live. Though he was in good spirits and his pain had lessened a little, he had never fully recovered from his heart attack — and they knew, deep down, that he never would. Nobody dared to go out any more in case Bowie wasn't there when they came back.

Despite her deep concern over the Whittles' denial in the beginning, Autumn found herself no better at accepting the reality than any of the others. While Bowie could be spoiled and grumpy and stubborn, he was also funny and mischievous, clever, caring and compelling. He was smart, creative and talented. He cared unapologetically about the things that really mattered and was curious to learn like no one Autumn had ever known before. He treated every conversation as if it was an adventure and he was, in so many ways, so full of life. To acknowledge that Bowie was dying was to begin to comprehend the hole he would leave behind in Autumn's heart and she couldn't bring herself to even try to imagine it. She was completely in love with him and with his sincere attempts to make her happy. He took pride and pleasure in making her laugh and complimented her constantly, sometimes until she blushed beetroot-pink. He still hadn't told her he loved her again, but he made sure she knew it. It was there, in everything he said and did, every day.

They were a happy little group most of the time, but, every now and then, somebody would become suddenly swept up in the realisation of what they were facing. It was usually Emma. She'd stop and stare at Bowie, her face frozen in an expression of abject terror, or stand up without warning and leave the room to cry. Sometimes it was Autumn. She once collapsed in tears in the kitchen, because Ben had suggested they take a family trip in the springtime — his favourite season — and she'd seen Bowie crumple inside, his head bowed and his face subdued, as he humbly let them plan for a time when he would no longer exist.

She knew Marley struggled with it, too. In the depths of the night, Autumn would hear him crying in his bedroom above theirs. Sometimes she would text him to come downstairs and they would sit on the porch together, smoking and drinking rum until they fell asleep. They always woke up at first light and went back to bed. They never talked about the time they'd spent together, with each other or to anyone else. In fact, it had been left unsaid for so long now it felt wrong they were even doing it in the first place.

"Pip has always been this way." Emma's voice distracted Autumn from her thoughts. They each nodded, lifting their glasses and sipping their wine. Autumn browsed the menu for vegan snacks, her stomach rumbling unhappily. "But he's still so young," Emma continued. "He's had us all to himself until now. You all moved out and weren't there to experience how challenging he can be at times."

"He's been ruined." Bluebell pointed an accusing finger at Emma.

Emma laughed. "You've all been ruined. But Pip had less competition for our attention, so he can be even more bratty than the rest of you. He's just got some growing up to do, that's all."

"I don't know about that," Maddie said. "It's not as if Marley has grown out of it. He's still so entitled."

Autumn was about to nod. Maddie was right. Marley could be a real brat. His parents had been subsidising his lifestyle for years so that he could pursue a career in music. Emma and Ben were OK with it, but Autumn knew it made Maddie feel uncomfortable. Until recently, Marley had spent every penny on wild nights out, alcohol and new guitars. By contrast, Maddie was saving the allowance her parents insisted on giving her to buy a house some day.

"Marley is not entitled." Emma's voice bounced around the restaurant. Several diners stopped eating to look at them. Autumn had been about to laugh, but managed to stop herself just in time. Emma's tone had taken her by surprise. She had never heard her defend Marley like that before. She took a gulp of her wine. Nobody spoke for a while and Autumn's thoughts returned to the plight of her lover's brother.

They were all growing increasingly concerned about Marley and his mental state. The sicker Bowie became, the more openly Marley would discuss his own suicide. Earlier that week, he and Bluebell had had a blazing row, because she'd heard him ask Maddie how he could kill himself without causing himself any pain or making a mess for his family to find. A few days before that, Autumn had caught him looking up information on his phone about how many painkillers a man of his weight would need to take to end his life. The songs Marley wrote almost always contained references to suicide now. There was no longer any room for doubt or hope — Marley wanted to cease to exist once Bowie had gone.

Autumn didn't feel able to talk to Maddie about it because she found her attitude to suicide frustrating. Maddie's belief was that if Marley was of sound mind when he made his decision, he should be allowed to choose for himself. Although Autumn might have agreed with her in principle, she could not force her head to overrule her heart — she wanted Marley to live. She couldn't talk to Bowie about it. He would just reiterate that he'd be doing the same if their roles were reversed. Emma and Ben would not discuss it with her either, so Autumn found herself chewing over her concerns with Bluebell and Pip whenever they were alone. Individually, they had all spoken to Marley and they all felt the same way as a result — that nothing could be done to convince him that he would have a life worth living without Bowie by his side. He wasn't interested in a career anymore, and couldn't see the point of marriage or children, nor was Marley able to take any pleasure from ideas of travel, art, poetry or even music, if Bowie wasn't there to share them with him.

Bluebell's voice brought Autumn's attention back to the conversation. She was glad to notice that the nosy diners had gone back to focusing on their food.

"We could all have done with a bit of a kick up the backside, to be honest, Mum," Bluebell said ruefully. Autumn was impressed by her friend's honesty. Emma laughed lightly and the atmosphere lifted a little.

"I can't bloody win, can I?" she asked incredulously. "I gave you everything you could ever want and now it's my fault you're all spoiled?"

Emma's five children often talked among themselves about how ridiculously extravagant their lives had been. As Emma had just said, they'd always had everything they could ever want. Their home was perfectly picturesque, with space to run and play, and their bedrooms had been full to the brim with toys, books and clothes. They'd been educated privately and their university tuition fees were paid for by their parents. In essence, they'd never wanted for anything. As adults, they were able to recognise how lucky they'd been growing up. Autumn knew Bowie was sometimes ashamed of their absurdly good fortune.

"I won the privilege lottery," he'd said one afternoon across the Monopoly board. "I'm eternally grateful for it, but I'll never be sure how many of my achievements have been due to my own tenacity and how much of it is down to the luck I've had being born into such a wonderful family. I'm straight, I'm white, I'm a man. I'm not ashamed to admit that life has been easier for me than it has been for every other demographic."

Autumn winced at his words. She could cut in here and tell them exactly what it was like to be born on an estate that chewed up its children and spat them out, but that would mean revealing a part of herself to them she knew they would be fascinated by. She was quite sure she was a long way from being ready to address the questions she knew would follow her admission.

"There is something truly special about paving your own way to success when you started out with nothing, I think," Bowie continued. "Still, I wouldn't exchange the upbringing you gave us for anything. Thanks, Mum; thanks, Dad."

Autumn didn't point out that his desire for less privilege because he wanted talent validation was one of the most privileged things he could say.

"You, of all people, don't get to say that you're lucky," Emma said. "Not given your situation."

Bowie frowned. "Yes, I do. Because if it wasn't for my privilege, I'd have been dead long ago."

He argued, persuasively, that white men were taken more seriously than any other group when seeking a diagnosis for symptoms like those he had experienced, a view that Maddie corroborated. That his family, whom he did not take for granted, were willing not only to fund his care when necessary, but also to look after him, while thousands of other people died in under-resourced hospitals because nobody could afford to make the sacrifices needed to be there for them.

Bluebell nodded. "We are pretty privileged." She rolled the dice and handed Marley the fifty-dollar Monopoly note she owed him for landing on a house he owned. "I mean, we could house half a council estate in these grounds and none of us even live here anymore. Not technically. Our homes are all over the world now. You two could make do with a townhouse with one bedroom and give this space to people who need it more."

Ben and Emma laughed, shaking their heads and accusing their children of having no idea just how hard they'd worked to be able to buy them all the things they had, or what it was really like to have no space.

"Where would you all sleep on Christmas Eve? On the living room floor?" Emma asked them.

"You're hoarding space so that we have somewhere to sleep on Christmas Eve?" Marley laughed.

"No. We're hoarding space because we paid for it," Emma said, moving her shoe token three spaces around the board and then to the 'jail' square as instructed. Bowie handed her the money she needed for freedom from his own pile of cash, which Autumn knew was against the rules. There was no point in mentioning it they made up their own rules most of the time. Still, she glared at him.

"She's my mother." He shrugged.

Playing with them was so frustrating.

"I'm fine with sleeping on a floor," Maddie said.

"Me too," said Pip.

That evening, they made a point of dragging their duvets and pillows into a corner of the lounge to prove they meant it. At around three in the morning, disturbed by their children's raucous laughter, Emma and Ben joined them. Nobody slept. They stayed up talking until dawn broke and then went to bed and slept until noon.

"Maddie isn't spoiled," Autumn said now, putting her menu down and gesturing to the sweeter of the two Whittle sisters. Maddie acknowledged her remark with a grateful nod in her direction. Autumn, in turn, was glad to see that she was able to accept compliments now and then. She meant what she'd said. Maddie was one of the humblest, most honourable people Autumn had ever met. Having to accept her parents' financial support was driving Maddie mad. She'd had nothing set aside when she'd handed in her notice to spend more time with Bowie because her salary would not allow her to save money as well as cover her costs of living. Autumn knew it was causing Maddie great discomfort to rely on Emma and Ben, and the allowance that they gave her. Most of it she kept set aside in a jar, swearing she would use it for something meaningful and life-changing instead of frittering it away like Marley and Bluebell did.

"I know how lucky I am," she'd told Autumn one evening over a glass of wine. "Both in terms of the money we have but also how much our parents love us. Just because they *could* make it possible for us not to work and spend time with Bowie, it doesn't mean they *had to*. Do you know how many people die on their own in hospital because the people who love them can't get time off work?"

Now, Maddie called the waitress over to them and ordered two portions of fries and another bottle of wine in an attempt to deflect attention away from herself.

"It's true. Maddie is perfect." Bluebell nodded, without the slightest hint of sarcasm. Bluebell and Maddie were about as different as sisters could be, but they loved each other very much.

"Nobody's perfect." Maddie blushed.

"You are," Autumn said. "Perfect daughter. Perfect sister. Perfect friend." Bowie, Autumn knew, had a special place for Maddie in his heart and was eternally thankful to have her. He was aware there weren't many people who would do for him what she had tried to do the night he'd almost died. He often said she was the bravest and most selfless person in the Whittle family, and perhaps the most valiant person he'd ever met.

"Well, I think you're all pretty impressive, to be honest." Emma rescued her embarrassed daughter. "Autumn, the way you've loved my son these last few months has been really quite extraordinary."

"I can't help it." Autumn poured herself more wine and avoided looking at any of them, blushing nonetheless. Aside from that night on the swing with Bluebell, Autumn and Bowie had never revealed verbally to any of them their love for one another, but it was pretty clear that the whole family knew how they felt and it made Autumn feel happy and uncomfortable all at once.

"He's incredible." She smiled shyly.

"Don't do that." Bluebell shook her head. "Don't deflect from yourself. Mum is absolutely right. I can't imagine how we would've got through this if you hadn't been here for Bowie. And for us. You've made these last few months worth living for him."

"It was a consequence of falling in love with him," Autumn said, revealing her feelings only because she felt it was the only way to stop them insisting she'd done something special. "I'm not being a martyr."

"That's what makes it so incredible though," Maddie said. "I don't think I've ever met anyone who would have allowed themselves to fall in love with someone facing what Bowie's facing."

Autumn shrugged off their words. She felt uncomfortable being the focus of their admiration but knew that the best way to get them to stop was to silently accept it. Protesting would only make them more insistent.

"And, Bluebell—" Emma reached out to touch her eldest daughter, but Bluebell snatched her hand away and shook her head.

"Don't, Mum."

Her words were defensive and thick with warning. There was suddenly an atmosphere again.

"No, I need to. We need to, darling, I'm sorry," Emma said. Out of the corner of her eye, Autumn saw Maddie wince.

"I knew this was why you were doing all of this." Bluebell put her head in her hands.

Emma sighed. "We can't let Autumn go to that ball on Saturday night without telling her."

"Do you really think Bowie is going to let anyone near her?" Bluebell spoke through her fingers. "He'd kill them first."

"Bowie's ill," Emma replied.

"Marley isn't, though," Bluebell said hopefully. "He's just as protective of her."

Autumn switched her gaze back and forth between the two of them as they argued, willing Maddie to join forces with Bluebell and tell Emma it really wasn't necessary for them to reveal to her whatever it was they were hiding, but Maddie stayed quiet and that told Autumn everything she needed to know. Whatever it was, it was clearly important Autumn heard it, so she reached for her friend's hand and squeezed. Bluebell stared down at the table, but her face softened a little at Autumn's touch. She nodded slowly, then looked back up at her mum.

"Do you want me to do the talking?" Emma asked.

"Yes," Bluebell said. Her voice sounded meek and afraid, and Autumn could feel Bluebell's hands shaking in hers.

"OK, then," Emma said gravely. She readied herself by smoothing her jumper with both hands and wore an expression that told Autumn she was about to share something it required her whole strength to say. Autumn had learned to feel afraid at the sight of this expression. It only ever came out when Bowie's condition worsened, when her children argued and, most recently, when they'd told her that Miranda the chicken had died. Autumn braced herself for what was to come.

"Autumn, my love, our Bluebell is a survivor of sexual assault and grooming."

It took everything Autumn had not to react instantly. She sat still, her eyes wide, and waited for Emma to continue to explain. She was unbearably enraged, but she knew

Bluebell was crying beside her and that her anger wouldn't be helpful.

"It was a man we all trusted," Emma said. "A man who'll be at the ball on Saturday night."

Autumn looked at her. "I'm not going then."

"Yes, you damn well are," Bluebell said defiantly.

"I'm not." Autumn shook her head. She couldn't believe any of them were even thinking of going.

"Listen first," Maddie said gently. "And then tell us you won't go."

Autumn nodded. Emma paused for a moment, watching her daughter closely. Bluebell gestured for her to continue.

"He was a family friend, a member of the theatre group we sent the children to. They all went, almost from the second they were old enough to walk, so he'd known Bluebell since she was a baby. His kids played with our kids, and he and his family would come to our house for dinner. We even went on holiday with them—"

"OK, I get it." Autumn's words sounded harsher than she'd intended. "Sorry, Emma. I just can't bear the focus of this conversation being on him."

"You're right." Emma paused. When she spoke again, her words came out in a rush, as if she had to get them out of her as fast as she possibly could. Autumn wasn't sure if it was for Bluebell's sake or her own. "Vincent began abusing our daughter when she was thirteen but, with hindsight, he'd been grooming her for years before that. By the time we found out, four years later, he was woven intrinsically into our lives, an investor in Ben's business who'd convinced Bowie to drop out of university and helped him get a scholarship at the music school where he was a patron. Bluebell and Marley had both been given lead roles in his latest production. And when our son walked into a dressing room and found that monster having sex with his seventeen-year-old sister, I think the arrogant bastard really didn't expect Marley to try to kill him."

Autumn closed her eyes, sure she knew instinctively where this was going and that it was going to break her heart.

"Marley made a real mess of him. He was lucky to survive, to be honest. Marley was arrested and charged with assault. He'd been blowing away audiences night after night with his performances all season and he really was the next big thing, but he lost his part in the play and no one would even consider hiring him after that. Even those who knew him, who knew that Marley would never have hurt anyone without cause, wouldn't defend him, because they were too afraid that getting involved would jeopardise their own careers. Marley was twenty and his reputation was already utterly destroyed. His dreams had been ripped to pieces."

"What happened to that man?" Autumn asked, fearing she already knew the answer.

"Nothing. He was arrested and released without charge. He told the police that their 'relationship' hadn't begun until Bluebell was old enough to legally consent and she loved him so much at that time that she told the police he was telling the truth."

Bluebell sobbed, dropping Autumn's hand to cover her face, and Autumn started to cry, too. She had always been aware of an unspoken tension between Bluebell and Marley, and it made so much more sense to her now. Bluebell's lies had ended his career and he had never felt fully able to forgive her. It seemed she had yet to forgive herself.

"I thought he loved me," Bluebell said. "And I thought I loved him. I was devastated when Marley attacked him and I swore to Marley, like a fool, that I'd never forgive him for it. It's such a fucking cliché. I was just a child and I was utterly manipulated."

"That's why Marley moved to New York." Emma passed her daughter a napkin to dab her eyes with. "He wanted to start again. Bowie went with him, of course, and Bluebell followed them almost straight away. Bowie found work right away and he hoped that, after a while, he might be able to use his influence on the casting directors he was working with to get auditions for Marley, but the theatre world is tight-knit and Marley's reputation had followed him. He gave up trying completely three or four years ago."

"I can't believe it," Autumn said.

"Larry Ross loves Bowie enough that he's prepared to risk his reputation. He's the first person to allow Marley onto a professional stage in thirteen years," Emma said. Autumn closed her eyes and sighed. There was no way she could refuse to go to the ball now.

"Marley has always lived for two things," Maddie added. "Bowie, and the stage."

She knew what they were trying to tell her. This might be Marley's only shot. It could be the only thing keeping him from following through on the drunken promises he'd made to end his own life. If he had even a glimmer of hope in his heart that he might be allowed back into the world of theatre, this might just give him something to live for.

"I need you there, Autumn," Bluebell added. "And so will Marley."

"OK, OK." Autumn held up her hands. "I'll be there."

Emma smiled gratefully across the table. Autumn could not bring herself to smile back at her. She felt like she might never smile again.

"There's something else," Emma said, looking sheepish. "I fear you're going to be furious about it but there was no other way, I'm afraid."

"What is it?" Autumn asked. She wasn't sure she could bear much more.

"You don't have to tell her," Bluebell said, cautioning her mother.

Maddie spoke up. "Yes, we do. Everyone else knows except Autumn and Marley, and there's no reason not to tell Autumn now. It isn't fair to her, Bluebell."

"What do you all know?" Autumn asked again, impatiently.

"Bowie knows, Autumn," Emma said. "About the medley."

"What? How?" Disappointment flooded through her. They had done everything they possibly could to keep it from him. She had been so looking forward to surprising him.

"It was his idea, babe," Bluebell said. "When Larry asked him to rescue his finale, Bowie told him he would only do it if Larry let Marley perform at the ball. But Bowie knew that Marley wouldn't just agree to do it because he's never forgiven Larry or any of the other big theatre bosses for turning their back on him and driving him out of the industry. There had to be an incentive. That incentive was to surprise Bowie with a tribute."

"Larry agreed to it, but warned Bowie that Vincent had already been invited to the ball and he was absolutely not prepared to uninvite him, no matter what," Emma added.

"Does Marley know Vincent is going to be there?" Autumn asked. The Whittle women all shook their heads.

"Shit," Autumn said. "Why didn't you tell me?"

"No offence, Autumn," Emma said. "But we have such a lot riding on this. Maybe even Marley's life. We just couldn't risk anything going wrong. Still, it wouldn't be fair or responsible of us to let any woman go without knowing that a sexual predator will be there, too. We could never see you walk into a situation like that. Saturday night will be profoundly difficult for Bluebell. Bowie told her not to come, but she's adamant she wants to and it will help her if you are there. We're also extremely worried about what might happen when Marley realises that he's in the same room as that man again. For a while, you're going to be the only one backstage with him. I'd be very surprised if Vincent doesn't try to approach at least one of us at some point. His arrogance really does know no bounds. If it's Marley, we'll need you to stop the inevitable from happening."

"How am I supposed to do that?" Autumn asked. She was terrified. They didn't need to tell her that another fight between the two of them would, one way or another, mean the end for Marley. She wasn't sure she could cope with the pressure that came with them expecting her to prevent it.

"Marley loves you," Maddie said. Autumn found the way she said it a little uncomfortable. "You can talk him round, Autumn. You can calm him down."

Autumn nodded, defeated.

"Tell me what he looks like," she said. "I'll do everything in my power to stop it if I can, I promise."

* * *

Autumn confronted Bowie the second she got home.

"I can't believe you let me think you didn't know about the tribute."

He peeped warily at her from beneath the duvet. She was standing in their bedroom doorway, her hands planted on her hips.

"I'm sorry," he said, reaching his hand out for her to take. She raised her eyebrows playfully. He smiled sweetly, wiggling his fingers in a little wave. She didn't make a move.

"Do you have any idea how hard we've worked, Bowie?"

"Yes, I do." He nodded. "I can't tell you how lovely I think you are. Or how grateful I am. Come here."

She sighed and walked towards him, stamping a little petulantly. When she was near enough for him to reach her, he snaked his hand around her waist and pulled her onto the bed. She let him wrap himself around her. He smelled like sleep. He nuzzled into her neck and she lost herself in him.

"I'm still really excited about seeing you up there," he said.

"Well, we were excited about surprising you," she said sulkily.

He squeezed her tighter to him. "I'm sorry."

Autumn did not answer, but she tickled the back of his hand with her fingertips to show him she wasn't upset. She was restless. Staying still was an effort. Earlier, before she'd come to confront Bowie, Bluebell had pulled her to one side.

"Are you OK?" she'd asked. Autumn had nodded.

"Why wouldn't I be?"

"I saw your face when Mum told you about that monster and what he did to me. I've always felt something like that might have happened to you too. Do you mind me asking?"

Autumn had never told anybody anything about the scary way her stepfather treated her, but it didn't surprise her that Bluebell had deciphered the secrets of her past from her reaction to various things. Talking about sexual abuse stoked a rage in Autumn that she found hard to hide. There was nothing to be gained from lying this time. She nodded.

"Do you want to talk about it?" Bluebell asked.

"It was a long time ago. My stepfather. It only happened once and it wasn't rape. He kissed me. Grabbed at me when we were alone. I screamed and ran away. I tried to move in with my father, but, well, he didn't have room for me, so I spent my teens trying to avoid what I knew was inevitable if he ever got the chance. It's not really the same situation. I can't pretend it is."

"Yes, it is." Bluebell said. "Sexual assault is sexual assault. Does Bowie know?"

"God, no!" Autumn said. "He has enough to deal with. Please don't tell him. Or anyone else, Bluebell, please. I'd rather nobody ever knew."

Autumn couldn't sleep that night, fretting that Bluebell might not keep her promise. She knew that her revelation would be deeply distressing for Bowie and she really didn't want to put him through anything else. She'd hidden what had happened to her for her own benefit up until now, but — with people around her who really cared about her — she found herself becoming ever more secretive in her attempts to protect *them*, and that felt confusing for Autumn. Her stepfather's assault had not, outwardly at least, impacted her beyond her development into a staunch women's rights advocate and her conviction that she should not be affected by or treated any differently because of the misfortune of falling prey to a predator. She recoiled at the prospect of the pity she might receive. She would rather push her experience away, along with the rest of her past, into a part of her mind she rarely unlocked. She reasoned it did her no good to dwell on it.

She was still awake when Bowie jolted upright just after midnight, holding his chest and gasping for breath. He stumbled out of the bed. Autumn rushed after him.

"Bowie?" She reached for him.

"Fuck," he whispered, staggering towards the door. "It hurts."

"Stop! Bowie, please. Stop."

He crumpled to the floor in the doorway, clutching his heart. Autumn threw herself down beside him and held his face in her hands. Her palms shook violently against his cheeks.

"What's happening?" she asked. "Bowie? Are you having another heart attack?"

He leaned back against the door and stared up at her. He looked afraid. Lost. She reached for his hand and held on tightly. She didn't know what to do. She started to cry.

"Don't." He shook his head. "Please don't."

She brushed her tears away, nodding. Bowie had never been able to cope with seeing her upset and it was the last thing he needed from her right now.

"What can I do?" she asked. "Shall I go and get Maddie?"

"No." He shook his head. "Please don't get any of them."

"Bowie, I have to." *This could be it.*

"They don't need to see this," he said. "Please don't leave me on my own, Autumn."

He groaned and fell against her chest. She held his head to her heart and stroked his hair, telling him, hysterically, over and over again that everything would be OK. His breathing was raspy and laboured. He wound his fist in her pyjama top every now and then, biting down on the fabric through a wave of pain. Autumn expected him to die every time, but his breath would catch again and he would cling inexplicably to life. They sat holding each other, willing the morning to come quickly. Things always felt less scary in daylight. Autumn watched the sun begin to rise through a gap in the curtains, following its rays as they crept across the bedroom floor towards their bare feet. She thought Bowie had fallen asleep until he spoke.

"It's so beautiful," he whispered. They were the first words he had spoken since he'd begged her not to leave him hours earlier.

"It is." She turned to kiss his forehead. His skin felt unhealthily clammy against her lips. At some point his breathing had steadied. She was sure now that the worst wasn't happening just yet, but reasonably confident he'd had another heart attack. Autumn thanked the universe silently for letting her keep him a little while longer, feeling selfish as she did so. Bowie was in pain. He wanted it to be over. She knew he'd probably hoped he would die in her arms.

"I love you, Autumn," he said into the silence.

"Now?" she asked him, shaking her head. "This is the moment you'd have chosen if we hadn't had our fight?"

He laughed softly, coughing and clutching at his chest.

"No," he said when he'd caught his breath. "I just realise how stupid I've been. Imagine if I'd died and never had the chance to say it to you ever again? I should have been telling you every minute of every day from the moment I first felt it."

She smiled and squeezed his hand. He squeezed back.

"I love you too, Bowie," she said. "You're too fucking romantic for your own good."

He sighed.

"Rule Number Five," he said. She giggled. They hadn't played this game in a while.

"Always tell people you love them when you feel it," she said.

CHAPTER 13

Once she felt it was safe for him to move, Autumn helped Bowie back into bed. It was ten in the morning and they could hear the house teeming with nervous energy. The Whittles were blissfully oblivious to the tragedy that had almost unfolded below them as they slept. Cautiously, Autumn asked Bowie how he wanted her to tell them that they would not be attending the ball that evening— clearly he was far too sick — but he shook his head vehemently in defiance.

"We're still going," he said. She blinked at him, blindsided.
"Bowie—"
"Don't fight with me," he said belligerently. "We're going."

She skulked from the bedroom to agonise over his decision in the shower. She was angry that he could speak to her so harshly, after all they'd been through together. She had a headache and was tired. She wanted to curl up in bed beside the sweet, loving version of her boyfriend, but his pain monster had hold of him and, even though she knew that it was not his fault, she felt furious with him for ruining their carefully laid out plans. It all made her feel rotten.

She tried to avoid everyone, calling a hasty hello into the kitchen as she shut the bathroom door behind her, only to run into Marley in the hallway on her way back to their bedroom.

"Not long now." He grinned.

"Yeah." She nodded, forcing herself to smile.

"Thanks so much for doing this with me, Autumn." He stooped to hug her.

"You're welcome," she murmured. He held her tightly for a few seconds before letting go, turning dramatically and flouncing like a prima donna in the direction of the kitchen. She knew that he was trying to make her laugh, so she forced out a half-hearted giggle. When she was sure he was gone, she leaned back against the hallway wall and sank to the floor.

"Fuck," she whispered into thin air. She'd concluded her shower adamant she would find a way to convince Bowie he shouldn't risk shortening his life for the sake of a ball, but she had just seen the very reason he wanted to do it with her own eyes. Marley was beside himself with excitement. Today, there was no sign of the permanently fixed frown he generally wore. Bowie wanted to see his brother back at his best, one more time. Nothing she could say would stop him from putting his life at risk to do it except potentially Bluebell declaring she was no longer comfortable, but that wasn't going to happen, either. Autumn knew Bluebell felt like she owed Marley a big break. Autumn would never be able to convince her otherwise.

"What happened?" Maddie asked her. The sound of her voice, full of concern, startled Autumn to her feet. Maddie was standing at the bottom of the stairs just a few feet away and had, no doubt, an unhindered view of Autumn for at least the last few seconds. Perhaps she'd even been there the whole time.

"Nothing," Autumn answered a little too quickly. "Everything's fine."

The words were barely out of her mouth before Maddie had hold of Autumn's hand and was dragging her back into the bathroom.

"Autumn, tell me," she said, slamming the door behind them and locking it. Autumn searched her mind for an alternative story to tell her but couldn't focus on anything except how desperately Maddie's eyes were boring holes into her own. She was tired and afraid and no longer knew what was the right thing to do. She could feel her panic rising.

"Autumn, you're not alone in this. Tell me what's happened and we can figure it out together."

"I think Bowie had another heart attack last night." She instantly felt relieved that she wasn't the only one who knew.

"Why didn't you come and get me?" Maddie asked, her breath catching as she spoke, her eyes filling with tears.

"He asked me not to." Maddie looked hurt. Autumn rushed on. "Only because he was worried one of you would try to stop him from going to the ball tonight."

Maddie's face softened and Autumn felt the tiniest bit proud of herself. She was usually a terrible liar but it seemed she could muster up untruths when it really mattered.

"There's no way he can go, Autumn." Maddie shook her head.

"Try telling him that." Autumn sighed.

"Because of Marley?" Maddie asked. Autumn nodded. They sat down together on the bathroom floor, hugging their knees to their chests. Autumn could hear Marley singing somewhere. She knew Bowie would be listening too. There was no way he'd change his mind. "It might be what kills him," Maddie added.

"Bowie would gladly die if it helped make Marley happy," Autumn said.

"Well, Marley is going to be devastated." Maddie ran her hands over her face.

Maddie was absolutely right. Marley would give anything for even one single minute with the brother he loved. "What do we do?" Autumn asked their sister. She felt utterly lost. Whatever they did, someone was going to get hurt.

"There's only one thing we can do," Maddie said, her voice thick with trepidation. "We can't mess around with Bowie's life, Autumn, but he isn't going to listen to us. We have to tell Marley."

* * *

They pulled him outside on the pretext of sharing a cigarette. Autumn started by telling him about Bowie's latest heart attack and they had to physically restrain him to stop him from running to his twin. They told him that Bowie knew about the medley. That he himself had engineered the whole performance to give Marley another chance. Then they asked him to talk some sense into Bowie. He didn't react the way they thought he would.

"We have to go," he said. Autumn and Maddie narrowed their eyes at him, and then at one another.

"Are you fucking kidding me?" Autumn asked.

"Did you hear what she said?" Maddie hissed. "Bowie had a heart attack."

"Yeah, I heard you." Marley winced.

He told them that he was touched that his brother had gone to so much trouble to come up with a last-ditch attempt at giving him some happiness. He said he knew Bowie was still clinging on to some semblance of hope that Marley might change his mind about taking his own life after Bowie had gone. He revealed that they'd taken to talking about it between the two of them, something they'd never felt able to do before. Bowie had pleaded with Marley not to commit suicide, even resorting to begging his brother, on his knees, to reconsider. Bowie was haunted by gory imaginings: Marley jumping from a building, Marley cutting his wrists and bleeding out, Marley hanging from a deserted staircase.

"He's torturing himself over what his death will do to me. If I perform for him and never mention suicide again, Bowie gets to believe he saved me," Marley said. "He might die quicker, but at least he'll die in peace."

Autumn thought it might be the most harrowing and beautiful expression of love and hope she'd ever heard.

* * *

"Marley knows about last night, doesn't he?" Bowie asked her later that day. "And that I arranged the tribute?"

Autumn was sitting at their dressing table, lazily swigging from a bottle of prosecco she was holding in one hand and applying foundation to her face with the other. She froze. She knew her silence would be confirmation of his suspicions.

It was all Marley's fault. He'd come to sit with Bowie in the afternoon and she'd seen the optimism drain from his eyes at the sight of his ailing brother. This latest heart attack, if that's what it had been, had possessed his features and lingered there still. Sleeping Bowie had looked as though he'd died. Marley had emitted a weird, choking, strangling sound, somewhere between a whimper and a sob, at the sight of him and Autumn had worried that he might faint. She'd stepped forward to catch him if he had and their gracelessness had woken Bowie up. Marley had tried in vain to talk with credibility about his fake flight to New York, but he hadn't fooled anyone. Bowie had let him stammer and had barely said a word, but Autumn had seen his eyes dart accusingly in her direction a number of times and she'd realised, there and then, that he'd known what she'd done.

"Yes," Autumn said now. "He knows, Bowie. I'm sorry."

Bowie nodded and stared down at his duvet.

"That was my last chance to save him," he said.

"It wasn't."

"Can you leave me alone?"

"Bowie—"

"Go away, Autumn."

His tone was heartless and it made her feel numb. She stood up and headed for the door, the bottle and foundation brush still in her hands. She stopped before she reached it. This was the first time he'd ever been truly angry with her and she found herself rooted to the spot by the same abject fear she knew Bluebell felt whenever they argued. What if he died and this was how they'd left things?

"Please don't do this . . ." she whispered to him. Bowie pulled their duvet over his head. He ignored her. She contemplated climbing into bed beside him but was worried he might tell her to get out again. She took a long swig from her bottle and stared bitterly at his still and silent form. She wanted to scream her pain straight into his face. She wondered how he might feel if she got into a car and drove away and never came back. She wished, for the first time, that she'd never met him, never become involved in any of this. What might she be doing now if this man and his family hadn't become her everything? Something less painful than this, she'd have been willing to bet.

"I love you," she said despondently. She gave him time to reply but was met with further silence, so she turned on her heel and left him alone as he'd asked. She took herself to Maddie's room, looking for the company of someone she did not have to explain herself to, but was disappointed to find Bluebell there as well. They had both, quite clearly, been crying.

"I told her about Bowie," Maddie said sheepishly. "Sorry, Autumn."

Autumn was annoyed, but didn't have the strength to argue.

"Bowie knows that Marley knows too," she said. The two sisters stared at her, their mouths agape.

"Turns out Marley isn't quite the performer we thought he was. Not when it comes to hiding how he feels about Bowie anyway."

"Is he mad about it?" Maddie asked. Autumn nodded.

"Seething," she said. She took another gulp of her wine. Bluebell licked her lips and reached out to take the bottle from Autumn's hand. Autumn fought the urge to tell her to go and get her own.

"But he still doesn't know that the two of you know," Autumn said. "He thinks I only told Marley, so please don't tell him. Or anyone else."

Autumn did not want to think about how much trouble she would be in with Bowie if he found out that his sisters knew about his not-so-secret heart attack, too.

"Give him some time," Maddie said. "He'll just be really disappointed, that's all."

Autumn felt disappointed, too. She was more upset than she cared to admit that the whole thing had been a set-up from the beginning, that Bowie was never going to be blown away by their performance in the way that she and Marley had dreamed he would be, and that she still had to sing the stupid tribute to him in public, knowing that everybody knew everything anyway. It all seemed like a massive waste of time and effort. She'd been stung by the venom she'd heard in Bowie's voice when he'd told her to go away, and she was hurt that Maddie had told Bluebell when she'd specifically asked her not to. She was angry that Marley's inability to hide his feelings from his twin had left her at odds with the man she loved. She was sick of them all. She was tired of the drama. She yearned for the sanctuary of her bed in New York. For some time on her own.

She sat down on the floor and they idly passed the bottle of prosecco between them until it was gone, talking through how they would handle things if Vincent approached anybody at the ball. Bluebell was adamant she would do nothing at all. She wouldn't look at him, she wouldn't run away, she would just continue whatever it was she was doing as though he did not exist and was not there. Autumn and Maddie agreed that was the best thing to do and promised to help her execute her plan should the situation arise. Soon, it was time to get ready. In her haste, Autumn had left her dress downstairs. Maddie offered to get it for her, but Autumn didn't want to risk Bowie asking his sister if she knew about his heart attack, too. She would not be able to lie to him and he was angry enough with Autumn as it was.

Bowie was asleep, or at least pretending to be, so Autumn crept across the room to retrieve her gown from where it was hanging in a dress bag by the window. She sighed and watched his sleeping form, remembering the way he had kissed her yesterday and how her heart had fluttered when he'd told her he couldn't wait to see her in it. She could never have considered that a heart attack between then and now would drive them so far apart. She hoped that he might still catch his breath when he saw her later. She stood and watched him sleeping for a while, hoping he might wake up and tell her he had forgiven her, that everything was going to be OK, that he knew that she had only betrayed him to protect him. When she rejoined his sisters upstairs, she found Bluebell pouring a massive wooden chest full of jewellery onto the bed and Maddie sorting through a mountain of shoes and bags.

"Oh my God!" She laughed when she saw them.

"We keep everything in this house," Bluebell said. "You never know when you might need blue velvet shoes."

She tossed a pair to Autumn. They would complete her outfit perfectly. She smiled, thanking her friend and pouring herself a glass of pinot grigio, their new drink of choice now that the prosecco had gone. She was shaking so violently that Bluebell had to hold the glass for her so that she didn't spill it everywhere. Autumn was grateful for the help. She took a sip, standing redundantly in the middle of the room, unsure where to start with sorting herself out. Getting ready felt like a monumental task and she was on the verge of falling to pieces. She didn't know how she was going to do it. She stared at the make-up and jewellery before her, completely overwhelmed.

Bluebell put on a nineties disco playlist and they sat Autumn in front of the mirror. She could tell that they'd been talking about how they might be able to do something to make her feel better. They were tender in their touch and gentle in their tone when they spoke to her. She was grateful for their love. Bluebell braided her hair, twisting it into a messy updo, while Maddie busied herself searching for the perfect eyeshadow to apply to Autumn's eyelids. She focused on watching them make her over in the mirror as she sipped her wine and sang along to the songs she knew. She realised, to her delight, that, together, Bluebell and Maddie were curing her of her fear of other women. They were her friends and they showed that they loved her. They knew, without asking, how to support her. They rooted for her in all she did, and cared about her wellbeing. It felt wonderful.

"Go easy on the alcohol, my friend," Bluebell suggested with a grin when they were done with her. They sat her on a beanbag in the corner to watch them getting ready themselves.

Autumn ruminated over her feelings and realised Bowie had made her feel like a little girl. Like a scolded child. This was the first time someone she really loved had been desperately disappointed in her. She'd hurt Bowie by ruining any opportunity he might have had to give his brother a reason to live. It didn't get much more serious than that. True, she'd done it with the best of intentions but Bowie had asked her not to and she'd still gone against his wishes. In failing to respect his decisions, she had let him down as badly as his parents had. She felt terrible.

"I'm going to go and help Bowie get dressed, OK?" Maddie said when she was ready. She had given her yellow ballgown a stylishly edgy twist by tying a golden scarf through her hair and adding a bold gold brooch shaped like a snake. She looked phenomenal. Autumn opened her mouth to object, wanting to help him herself if she could.

"I absolutely swear to you that I will not tell him I know about what happened last night." Maddie kissed Autumn's forehead and left.

Autumn distracted herself from her worry by watching Bluebell getting dressed. Her friend was wearing charcoal-grey eyeshadow with barely any other make-up and was meticulously curling her glossy blonde hair until it looked as though she'd given herself a perm. Tonight, she would catch the eye of every single person in the room. It wasn't like Bluebell to be so finicky about the way she looked. She was taking such care because this man, Vincent, would be there tonight. Autumn hoped that he would look at anything other than Bluebell, for Marley's sake as well as her own. The way she was feeling, Autumn might kill him herself if he didn't.

"Do you mind if I go and have a cigarette?" Autumn asked Bluebell. She wanted to sit on the porch and smoke for a bit. She'd numbed herself all afternoon with distraction and alcohol, and desperately needed some time to herself to think.

"Of course," Bluebell said. "Leave Bowie alone though, Autumn. He'll calm down in time. The last thing any of us need tonight is the two of you fighting."

Autumn nodded in agreement and stood cautiously, afraid that she might wobble under the influence of too much white wine. She felt sturdy, actually. Strong.

"Thank you for getting me ready," she said, slipping her dress on over her underwear before she left. "I feel lovely."

"You look beautiful, Autumn." Bluebell smiled. "Try to have a good night."

Bowie's family, minus Bluebell, were milling around in the hallway. They watched her as she came down the stairs. She heard someone murmur 'wow' from somewhere and bit her lip shyly, telling each of them, with sincerity, that they looked amazing. She looked for Bowie. He was sitting on his own at the kitchen table in a black tuxedo. He was staring at her, but didn't speak. She smiled meekly at him, but he turned his face away. With difficulty, Autumn swallowed the lump in her throat.

"Can I have a cigarette?" she asked Marley.

"Sure," he said. "I'll come with you. You look lovely, by the way."

"Thanks," she said, her eyes darting back to Bowie. He was still glaring at the kitchen table.

"Nice tux," she said, trying valiantly to engage him.

"Thanks," he muttered, scratching at the wood with his fingernail. She felt the gaze of the others upon her, knew their eyes were flitting between her and Bowie, and the room fell into a brief awkward silence, but no one said anything. She understood. They were desperately ready for an evening of fun and were, no doubt, assuming that an evening of frivolity would ease whatever tension there was between Autumn and Bowie. Autumn hoped they might be right. She followed Marley outside.

"Seriously, Autumn " he leaned against the porch fence and lit her a cigarette "you're beautiful."

She blushed, but didn't say anything. He smiled sadly at her. She knew he was trying to make up for the compliments she'd not received from the man she loved, and was grateful for his attempts to make things better for her.

"Are you feeling OK about the song?" he asked her.

The song. She had almost forgotten all about it. She instantly felt the weight of it pressing down on her chest and resentment for Bowie flooded through her. All at once, she knew she'd been naive to think loving him would be enough to carry her through whatever they might face before he died, and she was frightened by how blatantly she couldn't cope when he was angry with her. Just loving Bowie was not enough she needed him to get her through difficult times. She was upset he could abandon her like this and felt he was being unfair to her. She'd only been trying to help. She desperately wanted his forgiveness, but had no idea how to make him understand that. Now, she would have to stand on a stage in front of hundreds of people and sing for him, and he wouldn't even look at her. She stared at his brother in the porch light. Their similarity had never been so apparent. She had to fight everything inside her not to pull him into a hug. She wanted to beg him to pretend to be Bowie — just for a minute or two — and for him to throw his arms around her so she could bury her head in his chest.

"I think I'll be fine," she said. He eyed her suspiciously and opened his mouth to speak, but was interrupted by the sound of a ruckus from the house.

"Marley!" they heard Emma scream. They'd both heard her scream like that once before. Stubbing out their cigarettes, they turned and ran into the house.

* * *

Bowie sat at the kitchen table, bent over and holding his chest. He was calling for her, and for Marley. Autumn pulled Bluebell out of the way and knelt in front of him. She whispered his name, reaching out to wrap her fingers around his fists. He clutched her hand and looked up at her. The fear she'd spent hours trying to ease for him the night before was etched, once again, all over his face. He rested his forehead against hers.

Emma and Ben were talking about hospitals but Bluebell, Maddie and Pip had set themselves between them and their brother. They were holding their hands out to stop their parents approaching their son.

"We're going to the ball," Bowie choked out.

"No, we're not, Bow," Marley said. He was kneeling beside Autumn. He'd put his hands on top of hers, where they rested on Bowie's. She felt as though the three of them were holding his chest together.

"I'm OK," Bowie said. "It's just chest pain."

"We're not going," Marley said. "Bowie, I love you for what you've been trying to do for me, but no."

"He needs to go to the hospital, Marley," Emma said. "We need to take him to the hospital."

Marley ignored her and set about trying to comfort his brother. He asked him if he thought it was another heart attack, but Bowie was adamant he didn't think it was. Marley tried to stand him up to take him to bed, but Bowie sat straight back down again. They brought him a glass of water and some painkillers, then Marley pulled up a chair and sat beside him, a united front. Ben tried earnestly to break through the knot of his defiant children and Emma shouted with a shrillness that only intensified with every second that passed. Marley bore the brunt of her screams. How could he sit there and watch his brother die? Why couldn't he let her take Bowie to the hospital for a check-up? Why would he do this to his twin, she wanted to know. Eventually, he broke and bellowed at her, springing violently to his feet.

"Stop it, Mum. Stop it both of you. Nobody is taking Bowie anywhere this time. We promised him, remember?"

He left Bowie with Autumn and stood beside his siblings, forming a human wall of hurt and love and sheer force of will. He glared at his parents until they accepted that their fight was futile this time. When he was sure they had accepted his orders, Marley wrapped his arms around them both, collapsing into hysterical sobs himself. Autumn felt a surge of pride. Beside her, she felt Bowie force himself to look up at his brother. He was smiling.

***

"I'm still weirdly disappointed that we didn't get to confront Vincent," Bluebell admitted.

It was later that same evening and they were all sitting or lying on and around Bowie in his bed. They'd managed to move him and, at Maddie's suggestion, given him some cannabis to smoke. His pain had subsided so drastically as a result that he'd tried to convince everyone that they could leave him and go to the ball. No one wanted to, they assured him. They'd forced him into his room, protesting all the way, promising him they would stay with him instead. That's what they all wanted, more than anything. Time with him.

"He's going to think he's won when we don't turn up," Bluebell added, resting her chin on the side of Bowie's bed. Marley, who had only just been informed he'd narrowly avoided a run-in with his nemesis, smiled sadly at his sister.

"He's a child abuser," he said. "So he never gets to 'win'."

"He's still loved and adored and living in his gorgeous house with his lovely wife." Bluebell shrugged.

"And, yet, he's still a child abuser," Marley said again.

"Yeah, but not a convicted one." Bluebell sighed. Marley reached out to take her hand and squeezed it.

"He hasn't 'won' anything. You need to re-evaluate what it means to win."

"I really don't know anymore." Maddie joined their conversation. She was sitting beside Autumn on the dressing-table stool. "I always thought it was buying a house and having kids, but I don't think that stuff would be enough to make me feel like I'd won. Not really. It's just what's expected."

"Winning is knowing who you are," Bowie said sleepily. "And knowing it so unashamedly that it makes following everyone else and what they're doing completely impossible. It's living entirely for yourself and the things you love, no matter what anyone else tries to tell you is right, and finding other people who want to do that with you."

He moved to take a lazy drag from the joint, but Marley whipped it from his fingertips.

"I think you might have had enough of this."

The girls giggled. Emma sighed and rolled her eyes. She was still angry with them for stopping her getting to her son, but was too scared he might die to leave his side to sulk. She sat as close to him as it was possible to be, nestled into his chest with one arm beneath his torso and the other across his ailing heart, her eyes rarely deviating from his face.

"I don't think I've ever been a part of a posher hot-box," Pip said facetiously. Marley was wearing jeans and a T-shirt, and Bluebell had only half finished curling her hair, but everyone else looked like they'd just stepped off a red carpet.

Emma started to grumble. "You're turning my house into a drug den."

"It's just a plant," Marley said, drawing from the joint and then passing it to Autumn. She inhaled deeply, throwing Emma an apologetic smile.

"Where did it even come from?" she asked as she exhaled. Pip raised his hand proudly. Emma scowled.

"I also have a stash upstairs." Bluebell jumped to her brother's defence.

"So do I," Marley said. He stared pointedly at his father through the haze he'd created. "Anything you might want to add, Dad?"

Bowie laughed heartily. Autumn couldn't remember the last time she'd heard him do that. She smiled.

"Er, no?" Ben said. Emma glared from her son to her husband.

"No?" Marley nudged Ben with his toe.

"Nope." Ben shook his head. "Nothing at all."

One evening the previous month, shaking with anxiety and struggling to sleep, Ben had joined Autumn and Marley in the garden in the early hours of the morning and asked to share a joint with them. Autumn hadn't bothered asking how he'd known what they were doing, though she'd been absolutely convinced until that night that nobody knew they swapped cigarettes for weed every now and then. They'd accepted his company and his request without question. He'd admitted that he and Emma had enjoyed using recreational drugs quite regularly when they were younger, but that she had developed a raging hatred for anything of that sort when the twins became teenagers, claiming it was 'a slippery slope'. Autumn had not been surprised to hear it. From the way Emma dressed and the way she talked, to the names she and Ben had chosen for their children, Bowie's mum was a real hippy at heart.

Still, she had been furious when someone had produced a bud of weed for Bowie to try earlier that evening, and she'd told the others they were absolutely not to share it with him under any circumstances.

"I don't want to do it alone," Bowie had said. "It's a social thing."

"This isn't a festival," Emma said crossly.

"It doesn't need to be." He winced through a wave of pain and stared, wide-eyed, up at his mother. Relenting a little, Emma told him he could nominate one other person.

"OK." Bowie smirked. "I nominate you."

Emma rolled her eyes, slapped him playfully on the arm and said no more about it.

Now, they were halfway through their fourth reefer between them and she had returned to her sanctimonious stance.

"This is illegal, you do realise that?" she said.

"Well, it shouldn't be, not when people need it." Maddie gestured to her brother. "Look at him."

At this time of day, Bowie was usually curled up in a ball in bed with at least one hand placed protectively over his chest. Tonight, he was sprawled on his back, one hand behind his head and the other arm around his mum. Autumn had not seen him look so relaxed in weeks. He threw her a sheepish smile. He had forgiven her. She blew him a kiss.

"I'm so fucking stoned," Bluebell said stupidly.

Autumn nodded. "So am I.".

"Somebody go and get hummus and crisps?" Marley asked.

"No." Emma shook her head. "You'll get it everywhere."

They sat in quiet contemplation for a while. Ben, who had been resisting when a joint was passed to him until now, took the one in Autumn's hand and dragged from it with obvious prowess and pleasure. Emma watched him, saying nothing. Autumn broke the silence. Staring at Bowie and Marley, the drugs were loosening her lips.

"What's it like being a twin?" she asked. "You two only ever go on about the good parts. Aren't there any drawbacks?"

"No," Bowie and Marley said together.

"There must be," Bluebell said. "God, I'd hate it if there were two of me."

"We would hate that, too." Marley sighed. Bluebell hurled a pillow at him.

"What about fetishization?" Maddie asked. "Do people want to sleep with both of you?"

"It doesn't happen that much with male twins," Bowie said. "I mean, lots of women want threesomes, but I don't think women have 'sex with twin brothers' on their fantasy list as often as men have 'sex with twin sisters'."

"Straight men are fucking weird." Pip shook his head.

"That being said . . ." Marley grinned. Bowie laughed.

Emma sighed and put her head in her hands. Autumn knew why. This conversation would only get ruder. Bowie and Marley were on good form, and Autumn knew their mother hated conversations of this nature — where very personal details were discussed instead of their typical level of tomfoolery — because they made her feel uncomfortable.

Marley's eyes darted mischievously to each of his siblings and to Autumn. "We *know* that there *are* women out there . . ."

"Dare I ask how?" Maddie asked. Bowie threw Marley a warning glance.

"Let's just say we're not proud of everything we did together when we were younger." Bowie's eyes met Autumn's and he winked at her. She threw him a reassuring nod.

"Speak for yourself," Marley muttered. "I had a great time."

The twins guffawed. Their frivolity inspired the others and, eventually, everyone was laughing except for Emma.

"Who are these women who were sleeping with both of you?" Bluebell asked impudently.

"Fully grown and consenting adult women," Marley said defensively.

"I am familiar with how threesomes work," Bluebell quipped. Marley snorted, shaking his head. Autumn giggled at her friend's brazenness.

"Can you please stop this now?" Emma sounded flustered. The conversation was over. Autumn was a little disappointed, but respected their mother too much to push it.

They slipped back into comfortable silence. Pip rolled another joint, took a drag from it and passed it to Autumn. She'd had enough, but took it anyway. Pip was watching her.

"Why are you called Autumn if you weren't born in the autumn?" he asked.

"Why are you called Pip when you're a human and not a pip?" she replied. Bowie and Marley laughed. "It's just a name," she added.

"Fair play," Pip said.

Autumn moved to sit on the floor, drawing her knees up to her chest. She was too high. All she really wanted was to crawl into bed beside Bowie and drift off to sleep.

"Pip talks shit when he's stoned . . ." Marley said. Bowie grabbed urgently for his brother's hand. He looked as though he might be about to say something profound.

"But not as much shit as Bowie talks," Marley finished, turning his attention to his twin.

"Marley, do you like being called Marley?" Bowie asked. Autumn laughed at the simplicity of the question he'd seemed so eager to spout. She mused over how this little plant had the whole family focused on fun for once instead of Bowie's impending doom. Their postures were free from tension, their faces relaxed and beaming. Emma, by contrast, seemed still fraught with worry. Autumn wished that she would revoke her hatred of smoking and indulge, but knew that Emma felt as though that would be giving her children permission to smoke recreationally, something she did not, despite her own history, want any of them to do.

"Fuck, yeah, I do," Marley answered.

Emma cautioned her son. "Mind your language."

Marley whined. "Mum! 'Fuck' is the best word of all words."

"It's vulgar," Emma said. "And I don't like how flippantly you throw it around."

"It's so versatile," Marley continued. He mouthed it again, soundlessly.

"Marley . . ." Emma frowned.

"You can use it for everything. It's awesome." He gesticulated in the air. "Whether something's fucking shit or fucking brilliant, or someone's getting on your fucking nerves—"

"You mean, like you're getting on my fucking nerves," his mother said. They cheered and she could not hide her smile. Autumn loved it when Emma joined in with their horseplay, and she knew the others did, too. Marley changed the subject.

"Nice work on our names, Mum," Marley said. "I love having a name hardly anyone else has."

Autumn nodded her agreement. She'd once hated her name — kids at school had made fun of her for it — but she loved it now. She regarded it as one of the few things her mum got right, albeit she'd done it accidentally. Autumn was almost certain Katherine had chosen her name not because she wanted to give her daughter a special moniker, but because she wanted credit for picking a name that was different. Autumn knew that was the case because her mother hated everything that was unique about Autumn's personality. She'd wanted nothing more for Autumn than for her to fit in on their council estate and had regularly expressed her displeasure when her daughter had refused to conform. She hated the fact Autumn had grown into the type of woman who suited the name Autumn Rain. Emma, by contrast, adored her children's quirky personalities and was thrilled they'd grown into their names.

Emma gave Marley a hearty thumbs-up and then returned her hand to Bowie's chest. She was still clinging to him as though someone might drag him away from her. As the room fell again into contemplative silence, Emma touched her fingertips to Bowie's chin, staring into his tired face. Her smile was gone. Bowie met his mother's gaze. He squeezed her to him, swallowing hard. Marley was eyeing them with tears in his eyes. He got up from the floor beside Bowie, nudging his mum to move over so he could sit on the other side of her, sandwiching her between her twin boys. She moved to rest her head against his shoulder and wound her free hand up to stroke his hair. Autumn smiled to herself. Although Marley mocked his mother mercilessly, he always knew when he had taken it too far, and he'd leap to hold her in his arms or kiss her tenderly on her forehead. She would, of course, forgive him instantly.

"Why, Mum?" Bluebell was slurring, too stoned to make her question clearer.

"I was young when I had you," Emma said. "Only nineteen when the twins were born. At that time, music was everything to me. I loved Bob Dylan and Lenny Bruce too. I could have called them Bob and Lenny, I guess, but it didn't have enough fun factor for me back then as a teenage flower-child. It just wasn't me. Bluebell was named after my favourite flower. I may have grown up a little since then, but I've never regretted naming you as I did."

She patted Bowie and Marley on each of their heads.

"Pip's name came about for different reasons, of course," she said, turning to elaborate for Autumn. "We were in a car accident while I was pregnant with him. Not a really serious crash but it felt serious enough with four kids and an unborn baby in the car. It was the middle of the night and a young man stopped to help us. A very young man, only around eighteen. He drove us to the hospital. When Pip was born, we named him after him."

"That's lovely," Autumn said. "I didn't know that. Does he know?"

"No." Emma shook her head. "But that wasn't really what it was about."

"Imagine if he'd been called something normal," Marley said jokingly. "Like Steve."

Emma's nose wrinkled at the thought.

"I'm going to name my kids weird stuff when I have them," Bluebell said. "Like Astro. Or River."

"We wouldn't expect anything less," Ben said.

"I'm giving my kids totally normal names," Maddie said. "Weird names give bullies ammunition. You say you enjoy having an unusual name, Marley, but I think that's partly because you're so confident. Nobody ever bullied you, not really. If they had, and they'd been able to use your name to do it, you wouldn't be so grateful."

"I think we are going to need to agree on this, guys," Pip said. "We can't have half the family with weird names and the other half with normal ones."

"Imagine . . ." Marley laughed. "Astro, meet your new cousin, Keith."

Autumn tried to catch his eye, desperate to protect Bowie from flippant discussions about a hypothetical future he wouldn't witness, but he was laughing too hard to take any notice of anyone.

"I'm going to name my kid after Dad anyway," Marley continued. "If I ever have a son."

"Bless you, that's lovely, Marley," Emma said, scratching his head affectionately.

Autumn caught Bowie watching her. He smiled sadly.

Bowie had come to the realisation that he would never be a father or an uncle one evening when they'd been in bed together. It had been immensely painful for him even to admit it to himself. She shook her head, disappointed with their group insensitivity, but they didn't notice. Stoned or not, she couldn't believe how unfeeling they were being. It was only a matter of time before they realised how hurtful their idle chatter was. To stop them now would make things worse. She hoped her silence might alert them to their tactlessness. It did. In time, they each fell into a sheepish and mournful silence. Bluebell and Maddie covered their mouths with their hands. Emma hid her face in Bowie's chest.

"I can't believe we just did that, Bowie." Maddie shook her head gloomily. "I'm sorry."

"It's OK," Bowie said sorrowfully. Marley took his hand. They laced their fingers together. Bowie stared up at the ceiling. Autumn knew that he was blinking back tears. "Don't feel like you have to stop. I'm enjoying imagining it, to be honest."

"Oh, Bowie." Emma started sobbing. He turned to look at his mother, wiping her tears away with his fingertips.

"Please stop," he whispered, addressing them all. He let his tears begin to fall. "It sounds like it's going to be a lot of fun around here and that's all I've ever wanted for all of you. Live every minute of it for me and stop worrying about it. Please."

***

They stayed with him until he fell asleep. When they had all gone to bed, Autumn lay beside Bowie, studying his profile. She wanted to wake him and ask him if he was OK with her now, but he looked more peaceful than she had ever seen him. She listened to the sound of his breathing, then spread her fingers across his chest to feel the thudding of his heart. Eventually, restless and uncomfortable, she got up again. She knew she'd find Marley in the living room. He was sprawled across the sofa with a bottle of wine in his hand. He threw her a weak smile and made a move to sit up.

"It's OK," Autumn said. "I'll sit over here."

"Don't be stupid." He patted the cushion beside him. She sat herself down and he passed her the bottle of wine. She took a swig, spilling some of it clumsily across her chest and down her dress. He gestured for her to keep it when she tried to hand it back.

"Thanks," she said, tucking her legs under her. He was watching a music channel. She hadn't done that since she was a teenager. There was a pile of discarded beer bottles beside the sofa. "Having fun?"

"I'm having a great time," he said. "It's hard work sharing a room with your little brother. It's nice to have some time to myself."

"Want me to leave?" she asked.

"No, I didn't mean that," he said. "I'm just explaining why I'm out here drinking by myself."

"I don't think you need to explain that to me." She sighed. He turned to face her.

"Can we try something new? Can we not talk about Bowie and everything that's going on, please? Can we just be two friends on a sofa for once?"

She nodded and smiled. "Yeah, OK, let's try it."

"Good. More weed?" He produced a joint from the pocket of his pyjamas.

"In here?" she asked. Emma had been absolutely adamant that they were only to smoke it in Bowie's room.

"Mum will never know." He shrugged. "She might smell it, I suppose. We'll just say sorry afterwards."

"I think we should go out in the garden," she said, shaking her head. Autumn only ever defied Emma when flanked by a contingent of her unruly sons and daughters.

"Spoilsport," he said, but stood up and pulled her to her feet. He swayed a little and she suspected he'd indulged in at least one more joint on his own before she'd come in. They stood huddled together on the porch steps. It was freezing in the garden at this time of night, but going back inside for shoes and coats would be too much effort. She smoked quickly, shivering.

"Cold?" he asked her. Her teeth chattered in response. He put down his drink and started to take off his T-shirt.

"What are you doing, you crazy bastard?" She grabbed his hands to stop him. "It's freezing out here."

"It's OK," he said. "I don't mind."

He tried to lift his shirt over his head again, but she clutched it and pulled it back down, inadvertently brushing her hand against his groin as she did so. She saw a spark of excitement in his eyes, but he didn't say anything. He stared down at her with gentle curiosity and she wondered what had happened on her own face. She looked away.

"Let's just smoke and go back inside," she said. He nodded and relit the cigarette. She forced herself not to watch him. She had always enjoyed watching the way his lips moved when he exhaled. It felt more wrong tonight than ever before. He passed the cigarette to her and her insides responded reflexively to the way his fingers fluttered against hers. She raised it to her mouth and inhaled, allowing her eyes to glance up at him. He was watching her.

* * *

They finished their cigarette without saying another word and headed back to the lounge to get comfortable again on the sofa. In the early hours of the morning, Larry Ross called Marley to find out where they'd gotten to. He was worried something else had happened to Bowie.

"He's not well," Marley told him. "It was just too much for him."

"That's fair enough," Larry said. "Well, you were missed."

Marley scoffed. "By 'you' I suppose you mean Bowie. Nobody's missing me."

"No, actually, I don't just mean Bowie." Larry sounded a little sheepish. "We missed you too, Marley."

Marley was visibly surprised. He opened his mouth to say something, but Larry's expression of compassion had rendered him speechless. Autumn nudged him. The gesture snapped him out of it.

"Thanks," he mumbled.

"Don't be a stranger, OK?" Larry said. Marley frowned in confusion, watching Autumn as he spoke. Her heart broke for him in advance. He wanted to believe Larry's words more than anything — she could tell by the way he was struggling to string a sentence together — but she herself knew enough now to realise this wasn't as it seemed, and if she could tell and she barely knew Larry, then Marley almost certainly could, too.

"I know the performance was all some elaborate suicide-prevention plan," he told Larry. "So, you can drop the act."

Larry sighed. Autumn willed him to correct Marley's scepticism, but he didn't, and Autumn just knew Bowie, somehow, had put Larry up to this. He was still trying to give Marley hope for a future Marley didn't want unless Bowie was by his side.

"Don't worry." Marley answered Larry's silence. "I won't tell him how shit an actor you are. He can go believing you're the hero who helped save his brother. It might give him a little bit of peace."

Larry was silent, and Autumn was glad. There was nothing he could say. Marley lingered a moment then hung up the phone. She shuffled closer to him and they stared at the television, silent and sad. Frantic, Autumn searched her mind for something to say, but everything sounded too serious or too dispassionate. She was just reaching the conclusion she should wait for him to say something when he spoke.

"Favourite song ever?"

"'Summer of '69'," she said, with no hesitation.

"Nice," he said. "A little clichéd."

"What's yours?" she asked.

"Too many to choose from. 'You're My Best Friend' by Queen. 'Moon River' by Frank Sinatra. 'Common People' by Pulp. Our friends used to sing that at us when we were at university. The Verve. Oasis."

"Those are bands, not songs."

"Yeah, well. I like bands."

"How long were you with your band?" Autumn asked him.

"Two years."

He paused. The mood had suddenly and irrevocably shifted. It was the first time there'd been an uncomfortable break in their conversation.

"Are you OK?" she asked.

"They've replaced me," he said. "Adam called yesterday to tell me."

"I'm sorry." Autumn sighed in sympathy.

"They had someone filling in for me for a while, but they found somebody that was awesome and don't want to let him go in case I don't come back."

"I'm sure they'll let you play with them again when you're ready to." She'd worded her response with deliberate care. He gave her a knowing side-eye.

"Don't do that, Autumn."

"Don't do what?" she asked.

"Do that," he said. She turned so her back was resting against the arm of the chair and her legs were stretched straight out in his direction, drawing up her knees to her chest to avoid her toes coming into contact with his thigh. Touching tonight was not a good idea.

"Everyone else is carrying on as normal," he said. "It's easy to forget that sometimes."

"Are you really going to kill yourself?" She surprised herself and wrong-footed him all at once. He peered at her from behind the bottle of rum he'd been downing shots from for the last fifteen minutes. They'd run out of mixer but they were still, between them, succeeding in polishing off the entire contents of the drinks cabinet. He nodded, almost imperceptibly.

"Tonight you talked with your family about maybe having a son one day. About calling him Ben. Why would you say that if you're planning to end it all?" she asked.

"It was just a mistake," he said, taking another swig. "Like I said, sometimes it's easy to forget."

"Do you actually have, like, a plan and everything?" She felt her lips tremble. She didn't want to know the details, but she wanted to know how much he'd thought about this. He nodded, moving again to drink from the bottle. She held out her hand to stop him.

"Slow down a bit," she said. His gaze was steely when it met hers.

"Don't ask me not to do it, Autumn."

"I'm definitely going to ask you not to do it," she said.

"I thought we weren't doing this tonight? I thought we were just two friends on a sofa?"

"We are. And, as your friend, I'm asking you not to kill yourself."

"If you were my friend, you'd understand that I can't live without my brother." His voice cracked as he spoke.

"Yes, you can," she said. "It'll be hard, but you can. You won't be alone."

"What if I just don't want to live without him?" he asked.

She didn't have an answer. If he didn't want to live life without Bowie, there wasn't much she could say to that. He took another drink and she grabbed hold of his forearm. He watched her fingers gripping his skin.

"Please don't do it, Marley. I won't be able to cope with it all."

"Yes, you will." His eyes fixed on her fingers.

"Well, what if I don't want to cope with it?" The words were out of her mouth before she could stop them.

"Don't use your clever little word games with me." He shrugged her off. "You don't understand. You can't ever understand."

She wrapped her arms across her chest, hugging herself for comfort.

"Maybe you'll feel sad for a couple of months, but then you'll move on with your life," Marley said bitterly. She knew he believed what he was saying, and that hurt. She had a close bond with Marley now. He made her laugh and took care of her, he was funny, clever and talented. She had come to care deeply for him. If he weren't a part of her life, she would miss him terribly, and his loss would leave an awful hole in her heart. She wanted to tell him so, but was still sober enough to know that she shouldn't.

"Is that what you would do if I died?" She spoke carefully. "Move on with your life after a couple of months?"

"There's no point in talking like that because it isn't going to happen that way."

"Hypothetically, though?" Somehow, without revealing too much, she had to make him see how much he meant to her.

"Shut up, Autumn," he said from the neck of his bottle.

"Tell me. I want to know."

"How old are you? Fifteen?"

"If I just dropped dead, right here, right now—"

"Enough!" He gripped the bottle tightly in one hand and locked his gaze on hers, his eyes wide, his mouth set in a stern straight line. Autumn didn't have time to feel told off, his expression softened quickly and his anger and irritation dissipated, leaving sadness and resignation in their wake. He showcased so many emotions in such a short space of time that just witnessing them splattered across his face — jumbled and confused, like a sculptors first draft — left Autumn feeling exhausted and empty. Marley, she knew, was battling a secret complication. She wished she hadn't seen the evidence of it. She didn't want to know. But she didn't want to leave, either, so, for want of anything else to do, she took the bottle from him and drank from it. Marley balled his hands into fists and frowned down at his taut and whitening fingers. Autumn watched him, waiting patiently for him to calm down, and worrying about how inappropriate their conversation had become. They sat in silence for five minutes or more. When he spoke again, his voice was much softer. "Of course I would miss you if you died, Autumn. More than I can tell you."

She didn't know if that was because he couldn't find the words to express himself, or because he knew that he shouldn't. She didn't dare say anything else, so she nudged his leg with her toes instead. He held a hand out to her, his palm raised expectantly to meet hers. She stared at his long, slender fingers and the spot where his heartbeat pumped a rhythm through the veins in his wrist. She knew that it was wrong to indulge his gesture, but she really wanted to wrap her fingers around his. She eyed him with concern, but he seemed to be looking at the television, so she complied, telling herself that this meant nothing. That he was just being affectionate.

The touch of his skin felt comforting against her own.

* * *

She must have fallen asleep, because she was suddenly aware he was talking to her again. She had no idea how much time had passed.

"You know what's terrible?" he was asking her groggily. He was still holding her hand.

"The UK social-care crisis?" she murmured, in jest.

A gentle laugh escaped his lips. "No," he said. He smelled of red wine and cigarettes. "Well, I mean, yes, that too, but that wasn't what I was going to say."

She allowed her eyes to close again, stroking the back of his hand with her thumb. She hoped her gesture would encourage him to carry on talking. She liked the sound of his voice. It was soothing.

"I've thought a lot about what might've happened if I'd have met you first," he said. Her breath caught in her chest. "Isn't that awful?" he added.

His voice was riddled with guilt. She let go of his hand and opened her eyes. She wasn't sure how it had happened, but they had somehow snuggled close to one another again. She'd been resting her head on his shoulder. Their proximity felt very suddenly, entirely and obviously inappropriate.

"Yes," she said. "It is."

She'd meant for the words to come out more forcefully than they had. Marley's eyes bored defiantly into hers. He knew. He already knew what she hadn't known herself until just a few seconds before.

That she ached for him.

"I've thought about it too." She heard herself confess. She knew it was terrible, and had barely dared admit it, even to herself, before now. Life as Bowie's girlfriend had been far harder than she could have ever imagined. Every now and then, awake and alone in the depths of the night, Autumn's thoughts would wander to Marley, and what might have happened if it had been their paths that had crossed before she and Bowie had met. They'd have slept together that night, she was almost certain, but she had also pondered whether more might have come of it. Perhaps she'd have felt that same sense of familiarity she'd felt with Bowie. Perhaps it would have developed into something more than the one-night stands they were both so used to. Maybe she'd even have become his reason to live.

All at once, they were kissing. It was an unashamedly aggressive kiss, the kind they would not have been able to conceal if someone were to walk into the room. He pushed her back into the sofa cushions and Autumn freed him from his jeans, hitching her legs up around him, and pulling him down on top of her. He tugged frantically at her knickers, his tongue insistently exploring her mouth as he held her close and thrusted deep inside her, still fully clothed. Autumn groaned, lost in him.

"Shh." She looked up and into his terrified eyes. They were full of regret, but she knew he was beyond regaining control. She implored herself to stop him, but she couldn't. Instead, she tensed her arms beneath his hands where they were pinning her to the sofa. He held her there and drove himself into her again, stifling her unsatiated whimpering and his own lustful moaning by kissing her.

It was all over in less than three minutes, but it was the most intense sexual experience Autumn had ever had. They had been overwhelmed with lust, and frenzied in the way they had come together.

Immediately after, Marley was rolling off her and standing up. He sat down on the armchair across the room from her and stared at the floor. Autumn broke down into the kind of tears that would usually be accompanied by uncontrollable wailing, but she was too mortified by the idea that they might be discovered to allow herself to make any sound at all.

They stayed that way for hours.

* * *

Autumn crawled back into bed beside Bowie as the sun rose. She stared bitterly at the doorway. Twenty-four hours ago, she'd been sitting right there, her devastatingly sick boyfriend nestled against her neck, telling him, lovingly, that everything was going to be OK. That felt like months ago.

She and Marley had barely spoken before they'd parted. He'd insisted he would never tell anyone and had told her that she shouldn't either. She'd told him that they were horrible people and he'd agreed. Autumn had left the room then, leaving Marley still sitting in the chair in the corner. She'd gone to the bathroom, where she'd sat crying in the shower stall, scalding water raining down on her, for over an hour, trying to wash the smell of him off her skin. When she'd returned to the lounge, he had gone.

Despite her attempts not to disturb him, Bowie woke when he felt her creep into bed.

"Hey, you." He pulled her in towards him. Autumn turned her face away from his kiss.

"Hello," she said, feigning sleepiness and willing him to drift back into the slumber she'd pulled him from.

"Where've you been?" He yawned.

"With Marley," she said. His name tasted bitter on her tongue.

"Is he OK?" he murmured sleepily.

"He's fine," she said. She knew she wasn't answering him in the way she normally would and he would hear it, too. Her words were empty. Her voice didn't sound like hers. She was riddled with guilt. She needed him to stop talking to her because, in her exhausted, intoxicated state, she was incapable of hiding anything from him. The temptation to tell him was incapacitating. She couldn't focus on anything else. She could feel his eyes on her. She bit back her tears and lay perfectly still, hoping he would leave it alone. The atmosphere in the room felt suddenly heavy with suspicion. He moved to cup her face in his hand, but she winced and turned away. His hand hung redundantly in the air.

"It's OK, Autumn," he whispered, his words catching in his throat. "It's OK, I promise."

She broke down entirely then, curling into the foetal position and trembling all over. She knew that her actions were confirming his suspicions. He pulled her over to face him, dragging her in to hug him. She sobbed against his skin, marvelling at his capacity for mercy, for love. She couldn't believe how he was reacting when she knew that she was breaking his heart. Was it really possible that he had fully comprehended what had happened between her and Marley? Perhaps he thought they'd stopped at a kiss. Or a fondle. She wanted him to scream at her.

"Bowie, I love you so much," she said. She felt him tense. Words they'd been so happy to say to one another less than a day ago were causing him pain now, all because of what she'd done.

"I know you do," he said.

"I'm so sorry." He held her as she cried, soothing her until her sobbing abated. He took her head in his hands and looked lovingly at her, wiping her tears away with his thumbs.

"I don't want to know anything about it," he told her sadly. "I don't want to know what happened, how it came about, how many times—"

"It was only once, Bowie, I—"

"I don't want to know." He rolled across the bed and sat up. She thought he might leave, but he reached into his bedside table instead, producing a joint. He smoked it in silence. Autumn sat up, hugging her legs and crying into her kneecaps.

She wanted to reach out and touch him. With a jolt, she knew she might never get to touch him again. She searched desperately for a rational reason for what she had done, but could find none. No excuse would ever be good enough. Every reason, she knew, was as ugly as the next: she missed sex, she was selfish, Marley turned her on. The time they had spent together had been like extended foreplay. It had always been leading up to her quivering beneath him. She felt rotten to the core.

"I want to pretend it never happened," Bowie said eventually. She stopped crying and looked up at him. He was so beautiful in the light of the dawn.

"Why?" she whispered, her face swollen and red.

"Because I understand," he said. He held out his hand and motioned for her to join him. She couldn't move.

"How can we ever come back from this?" she asked. "If you won't even let me explain."

"I don't need you to explain." He shook his head. "I know why you did it. I know why you both did it."

Autumn doubted that.

"I'm not blind, Autumn," he said. She didn't understand. She searched his eyes for answers, but he was expressionless. "I know that you're falling in love with Marley, and that's OK."

She had to work hard to hold back a hysterical laugh. She knew that he had come to his conclusion to protect himself, to rationalise their behaviour, but it was so preposterous a notion that she would've found it comical if the circumstances were different. She wanted to tell him that it was in fact insatiable lust, not love, that had driven her to fuck his brother, but she didn't think that would make him feel any better.

"I'm not falling in love with him, Bowie." She shook her head.

"Perhaps you don't know it yet, but you are," he said. "And he's falling in love with you."

"You're wrong." Her voice sounded shrill. She was irritated, even though she knew she had no right to be. He eyed her sceptically, motioning again for her to come closer. He held her hands tenderly in his. "How can you even begin to forgive me?" she asked.

"Because I love you," he said. "And because I understand."

"But, Bowie, you don't understand," she said. He let his hands drop.

"I don't want to fight with you about it," he said. "I can't stand to fight with you about it."

He looked forlorn. Weak. Tired out. She drew him closer to her and urged him to put his arm around her. It felt uncomfortable, wrong, somehow, and she knew that she no longer felt as though she deserved him. She'd never deserve him again.

"If things were different, you'd have thrown me out." She shuddered.

"If things were different, you wouldn't have done it," he said.

* * *

They sat up talking until the sun had fully risen. Bowie only asked her one question about her transgression, and that was if his impotence had played any part in her infidelity. She lied and told him it hadn't. He didn't believe her, and he apologised. She begged him to stop. There was no cause at all for his apology, she said.

* * *

They were up before everyone else. Autumn hoped a cold shower might reduce the swelling in her face, but it didn't.

She'd have to come up with an excuse as to why she had quite clearly been crying.

"Tell them I was poorly all night?" Bowie suggested. He was eating cornflakes at the kitchen table and treating her as though nothing had happened, but she noticed that his eyes kept straying to the sofa. The carpet around it was still littered with the empty bottles of alcohol she and Marley had consumed between the two of them. It wasn't hard for him to guess where their betrayal had taken place. She shook her head, telling him she felt uncomfortable blaming him for anything, in any way.

Autumn had hoped that Marley might stay in bed, out of the way, until the rest of the family was up and about, but he was the first to appear. Bowie and Autumn had discussed what he might say to his brother, but not in any great depth.

"I'd rather he never found out that I knew," he'd said at the break of dawn. "He won't be able to live with himself."

"I don't think I can be around him and pretend we have this ugly secret when we don't." Autumn winced.

"You do what you have to do." He shrugged. "But you can tell him that if he comes to speak to me about it, I'm going to tell him exactly what I told you. I don't want to talk about it. I want to pretend it never happened."

Marley greeted Bowie with an affectionate pat on the back as he passed.

"Hey, bro," he said casually. Autumn saw Bowie's muscles tense.

"Bro," he replied, in an even tone of voice.

Marley put the kettle on and grabbed a bowl from beside the sink. He sat down at the table and poured himself some cereal. He looked everywhere but at Autumn.

She'd barely been able to recall any of their encounter, but now that she was looking at him, she could remember it all: the strength of his erection in her hand, the pressure of his mouth against hers, the great sense of overwhelming release she'd felt when he'd entered her. She could see his face hovering above hers, his lips slightly parted, his eyes wide with lust and fear. She remembered the texture of his hair and the urgency with which he had complied when she had grabbed it and begged him to take her harder. How his deliciously strong frame had pounded her slight hips against the sofa cushions. She could hear the sound of ecstasy he'd made as he'd come inside her. She remembered how panicked she'd felt by the potential consequences of their desperation. Heartbreak and pregnancy. She didn't know which was worse. She felt disgusted by the sight of him. She shut her eyes tight and focused on keeping her coffee down. Marley looked questioningly at them both, breaking the silence.

"So, what are your plans for the day?"

Marley's question was abrupt. Harsh. Unusual. If Bowie hadn't already known, it would certainly have alerted him to something.

"Nothing much," Bowie said. "I'm not feeling so good. I'll probably need to sleep."

"Oh." Marley nodded. His eyes crawled over his brother's face, then in Autumn's direction and away again just as quickly. "How about you, Autumn?" he asked.

It was a valiant attempt at normality and she was grateful to him for trying. She tried to speak, but no response came. She cleared her throat.

"Writing," she managed to say. It was a lie. There was no way she'd be able to focus on any work today. Luckily, she didn't have much to do. She'd spent so many hours writing her manuscript while Bowie had been sleeping away the summer months that it was almost ready for submission.

"Cool," he said, nodding and turning back to his breakfast. Bowie abandoned his cereal and excused himself to head back to bed. Autumn tried to follow but he asked her, gently, to leave him alone. As soon as he was gone, Marley dropped his spoon into his bowl with a clatter, hissing at her across the table.

"You're making it totally obvious," he whispered.

"He knows," she told him.

***

"What the fuck, Autumn?" He screamed at her, hitting his hand against the trunk of a tree. Autumn jumped, impulsively stepping away from him, though she knew how he was feeling. She was so angry at herself and at Marley she wanted to rip the tree from the ground with her bare hands. She'd known when he'd raised his voice in the kitchen and she'd dragged him outside to talk there instead that this was going to be a tense conversation. They'd stomped their way wordlessly through the field, straight to the spot where they'd happily rehearsed their medley together for so many hours.

"He knew," Autumn said now. "He knew as soon as I said I'd been up with you."

"Why didn't you tell him he was wrong?" he said incredulously.

"I couldn't lie to him," she replied. He punched the bark again, then hid his face in his hands. Autumn wanted to ask him to stop hitting things. She wanted to tell him he was making her nervous. She knew no matter how angry he was he would be ashamed if she told him the physical manifestation of his anger was frightening her, but she couldn't bring herself to do it. Perhaps it was because she knew this was half her fault. Maybe it was because she knew how hard she was having to work to stop herself from taking out her frustration on the things around her.

"You've ruined everything," Marley said from behind his fingers. Autumn felt anger bubble up.

"*I've* ruined everything? I'm pretty sure there were two of us there."

He shook his head and paced back and forth.

"I've never done anything like this in my entire life," he said. "And then you come along with your stupid, flirty eyes and your fucking promiscuous attitude and suddenly I'm doing the worst thing I could ever possibly do to anyone."

"Don't you dare!" She didn't have the energy to tell him just how outraged she felt, and she knew she didn't have to. He already knew. He was actively trying to hurt her and she braced herself for more.

"Why?" He hunched over and put his head in his hands. "Why did we do this?"

"It was a mistake," she said softly.

"A fucking mistake? That's a fucking understatement, isn't it?"

"Stop screaming at me." She was sick of his reaction. He was being completely irrational and she wasn't sure what he was hoping to achieve, besides making her feel even worse than she already did. Perhaps that was his point.

"I hate you," he said. He'd have hurt her less if he'd slapped her across the face. She felt her cheeks flood with anger.

"Do you know what, Marley?" she said calmly. "I fucked you because I can't have sex with your brother anymore. You smell good and you look good and I was drunk and wanted to fuck you. I'm selfish. Really fucking selfish. At least I can admit that. You can scream at me all you want, but nobody forced you to do what you did. You were thinking with your dick. At least have the decency to acknowledge that."

"You kissed me," he said accusingly.

"You held my hand," she said.

"I hold everybody's hand."

"Are you honestly trying to tell me that you bear no responsibility for what happened?" she said. He kicked at the ground, glaring at her. She shook her head hopelessly and looked out across the field, hugging her arms to her chest.

"I'll never be able to make it up to him," he said sadly. He looked utterly devastated. Autumn felt sympathy for him. She willed herself to get a grip. He'd been nasty. Unbelievably spiteful. He didn't deserve her pity. She stopped herself from telling him that everything would be OK.

"He doesn't want to talk to you about it," she told him.

"That's what he always says when I fuck up," he said, sighing into the palms of his hands. "I have to try to explain."

"There's nothing to explain. There's no excuse for what we did and he's reconciled it in his own mind by telling himself we're falling in love."

Marley chuckled obnoxiously and shook his head. Autumn ignored his vindictiveness.

"He told me specifically to tell you not to talk to him about it. If you try, he'll refuse. I'll let him know that you know and if he wants to talk to you, then he'll come to you. The least we can do is leave him alone if that's what he wants. Don't even think about trying to blame me. There is no point. He knows you. He knows both of us. Forget about it, Marley. Move on. Or at least pretend to. You're an actor, aren't you? Fucking act for once. For Bowie's sake."

She turned abruptly on her heel and left him standing on his own in the field.

CHAPTER 14

Bowie died the following Tuesday, in the evening. His death did not allow Autumn the time she felt she needed to really make it up to him, even though he'd sworn, whenever he'd caught her agonising over what she'd done, that things were fine between them. If he'd had thirty years more to keep telling her that he had forgiven her, she was quite sure that she would never have believed him completely.

He knew he was running out of time and asked Autumn if she would find a way to take him away from the house for a while before it was too late. His chest pains were not as drastic, but they were present almost all the time and his breathing was heavy and raspy. He pivoted wildly between believing he had a mass close to his chest and that he'd caught an infection his body couldn't fight off because of his weakened immune system. Autumn asked him which was the better scenario and Bowie meekly told her neither. They cried together for a while, then he proposed they get out of the house. He wanted the chance to go somewhere different with her, he said. She agreed to take him to London, and they woke in the early hours of the morning to leave the house before anybody could stop them, taking the wheelchair they knew Maddie had in the back of her car from her care-working days in case he needed it later. They smoked cannabis as they strolled very slowly, hand in swinging hand, to the train station, pushing the wheelchair along as they went, his left hand on the left handle, her right hand on the right. On the train, Bowie spoke sheepishly to Autumn about his brother.

"Marley tried to talk to me about what happened," he said. "He came to me yesterday and tried to apologise."

Autumn nodded, fiddling with her coat. She wasn't sure what he expected her to say. "I told him I didn't want to hear it," he said. An uncomfortable silence fell between them. She stared out of the window and worked hard to force the image of Marley's face, in ecstasy above hers, from her mind. The image haunted her, day and night, even more so whenever she saw him, which was, at least, less frequently, since he was making himself exceptionally scarce.

For a talented actor, Marley was doing a tremendously bad job of pretending that nothing had happened between them. He spoke to her only when he really had to and openly scoffed at the things she said. One evening over dinner, he'd ploughed his way through such an extraordinary amount of alcohol that Ben had tried to take a bottle of rum away from him.

"I think you've had enough, son."

"Leave me alone, Ben," he'd said, seething, and yanked the bottle out of reach. None of the Whittle children ever called either of their parents by their first names. The table erupted in outrage. Bowie was so incensed by his twin's disrespect that Autumn had to grab him by the waistband of his jeans, fearing he might throw himself across the table to attack Marley, even as weak as he was. Emma berated both boys and they all finished their meal in silence. Marley took himself to bed immediately afterwards.

Autumn and Bowie let the others discover their absence with a note left on the kitchen table, and answered Emma's frantic phone calls as they climbed cautiously up out of the Tube station. They were fine, they assured her. They just needed some time to themselves. Yes, they'd be careful. Yes, they would call if they needed anything. Yes, they'd check in with her every hour or so. They'd be home later that evening, and, yes, they said, they loved her too.

They'd planned to grab breakfast on the way into the city, but Bowie didn't much feel like eating, so they bought two cappuccinos and took them along the towpath. They sat together, Bowie in the wheelchair and Autumn on the grass with her head in his lap, and watched the world go by. They found deserted alleyways whenever he wanted to smoke to ease his pain. Autumn kissed him ardently whenever the moment took her, and he dragged her onto his lap whenever he could, burying his head into her hair and inhaling her perfume. They drank cheap red wine out of a brown paper bag and bought ridiculously decadent cupcakes at a tiny, plant-based café they found in King's Cross. Bowie gave Autumn his icing, the only bit she ever actually wanted, and she gave him her sponge.

They sat in front of the gates at Buckingham Palace, mimicking the members of the royal family. They fed pigeons in Hyde Park. They waited fifteen minutes or more to hear Big Ben chime five times. They talked about calling Larry Ross and asking him if they could have two tickets to watch his show that evening, but Bowie said that he was too tired. Autumn knew he was lying. The show had been raucously reviewed, but Bowie hadn't wanted to hear anything about it. It was just too painful.

"Shall we get a hotel?" he asked.

"We don't have any stuff." She looked at him, raising her eyebrows.

"Who needs stuff?"

They checked into the first place they found with a vacancy. It was a basic box room with barely any furniture. They brought pizza and sweets with them to eat, and Bowie asked for a room on the top floor so they could smoke out of the windows without being caught. Autumn watched the sun begin to sink over the rooftops and wrote notes for the final edit of her book on the hotel's headed paper, while

Bowie slept off his exhaustion. She woke him up as the sun was setting, knowing he'd be upset if she let him sleep away their precious time together.

For reasons they'd never know, they managed to make love. Somehow, he'd been able to lay back as Autumn brought him twice to climax before things went back to the way they'd been recently.

"How are you doing this?" he'd murmured halfway through the second time.

"Magic," she'd whispered, kissing him.

Afterwards, they lay wrapped in one another, dreaming up the future they might have had if things had been different. They talked of the cottages in the countryside, orchards and vegetable patches, two rescue pigs, a flock of chickens, and the mongrel they'd adopt. Autumn told him that their musings were hurting her heart, but Bowie asked her to indulge him a little longer. It would all only ever exist for him in his imagination, he said. Couldn't she allow him that? She nodded, and they dreamed up winter nights beside a real log fire, shared pans of homemade mulled wine, a library stacked so high that Autumn would need a ladder to reach the books on the very top shelf, and three kids, who loved their parents as fiercely as Bowie loved Emma and Ben.

Autumn had to make a confession. "I'm awful with kids."

"You'll be all right if you ever have your own," he said.

"Perhaps if I had you by my side. We could parent ten children and still manage to give them everything they wanted. But without you? With anyone else . . ."

She swallowed the lump in her throat. She was determined not to let tears ruin what she was quite sure would be their last night alone together.

"You'll find someone else," he said. Every now and then, Bowie would throw her a line like this. He was curious to know where she might go and what she would do once he no longer tied her to England, but Autumn couldn't bring herself to think about it. She knew her lack of willingness to discuss it made him worry about her, but she couldn't help it. She hated him speaking of the life she would live when he was gone.

"I'll never meet anyone like you," she said. She instantly regretted saying it. He was quiet, thinking for a moment, and she anticipated his answer anxiously.

"Perhaps you already have," he said musingly.

Autumn knew that part of Bowie liked to believe she had fallen in love with Marley. She was possessed by a desperation to correct him almost all day every day, but had so far chosen to respect his request that they should pretend nothing untoward had happened between his lover and his brother — up to now. This was the first time he'd brought it up and it was her chance to set him straight.

"I haven't," she said. "And I never will."

Autumn was cautious. Their day together had been perfect so far, and the chances of her clumsy mouth ruining it were high, so she thought carefully before she spoke again.

"We made a mistake," she added, in barely more than a whisper. Bowie's reply was delivered softly and with caution.

"I think Marley was meant to meet you first that night."

She sighed and swallowed hard. She was desperate for him to have complete faith in her again.

"Please don't, Bowie," she said, hearing the words come out of her mouth with surprising strength. "You don't even believe in any of that stuff."

Philosophical as they were, they'd talked frequently of fate and destiny, ghosts and the afterlife, and Bowie didn't have the slightest belief in any of it. When he died, he was adamant that he would cease to exist. She had not been sent by something divine to give him a reason to live longer, as his sisters and his mother frequently suggested. Her appearance in his life had been nothing more than a romantic coincidence and he'd insisted, until now, that their meeting had been a simple, happy accident.

"Or perhaps I was meant to bring you together? Maybe that's the real reason it all happened this way," he continued, ignoring her. She pushed him gently away. He rolled onto his back, studying the ceiling.

"You've both grown so much these last few months. If you'd met that night, you'd have been over before you even started. Instead, this way, you've fallen in love."

"He's not in love with me," she said.

"He's the male version of you." He pressed on as though she hadn't said anything. "Haven't I always said that?"

"And I'm not in love with him." Her heart fluttered unhappily. She felt uneasy. Her protesting made her feel uncomfortable. "And even if I were, do you really think we would ever do that to you?" Saying it made her conscience feel a little clearer somehow.

"Do what to me?" he asked. He hitched himself up onto his elbow and leaned over, holding her face in his hand. His fingers shook a little as he spoke. "Autumn, I'll be dead."

His candour made her weep. Bowie had been unable to talk of his impending death for a number of weeks now, and, even in the months before, he'd only ever mentioned it if it were absolutely unavoidable. He had come to terms with it, and she knew what that meant. He was really going to leave her. She grabbed his hand and pressed it against her cheek, pulling him towards her. They wrapped their arms around one another and cried.

"Please let me say something to you," he said. "You'll hate it, but it's really important."

She nodded, resolving to let him tell her whatever it was he felt he needed to, without interruption, even if she didn't like what he had to say. It was the very least that she could do for him.

"You can protest all you want, but I know Marley better than you do. Better than anybody. I know him better than he knows himself. He loves you and if you ever find yourself loving him too, then be together. Please. Ignore anyone who tells you that it's wrong. You could have sixty years or more together and you have my blessing. It won't take away from these months we've had. If there is an afterlife, which there isn't, but if there is, I'll be partying with the greatest musicians of all time. I'll be waiting to hear about all the fun you had without me. I'll be glad you found comfort in each other. So, do whatever it is that makes your heart happy. Don't give any thought to what I might hypothetically think about it. Promise me."

She sobbed into his chest and told him that she promised. She was surprised to find that she meant it.

"Can we make this an official rule?" he murmured. She nodded. "Are you sure? You know that those rules can't ever be broken? They're binding."

She laughed softly, in spite of herself.

"What are we up to?" he asked.

"Six," she said.

"Rule Number Six." He kissed her cheek tenderly. "Do what makes you happy."

"I love you," she whispered, holding him tighter still.

"I love you too," he said.

***

The next day, his brothers picked them up from the train station and helped Bowie back into his bed, and he never got out again. When she looked back on their charmed day in London, the third best day they'd ever spent together (after their cinema date and the day they'd spent in rehearsals at the theatre), Autumn knew that Bowie had poured every last bit of strength he'd had into their little trip, and it was a comfort to her.

That afternoon was the worst of her life, without question. Bowie had exhausted himself and his body was unforgiving in making sure he knew it. He lay rigid with pain, crying out for help from anyone who would listen. His legs were in agony, his back was sore, his head was pounding. It hurt when he moved, and it hurt when he didn't. Breathing was painful and thinking about anything except for how much pain he was in was impossible. He kept clutching his temples and telling them over and over again that it was in his head, he could feel it, he was going to forget who he was and who they were. He was in equal parts hurting and terrified, and it was horrifying to behold. They took it in turns to sit beside him, holding his hands when he could bear their touch, trying to remind him that the pain always passed eventually, but she knew that none of them believed he would get better this time, any more than she did. The cannabis was no longer working and nor were their words of comfort. There was something different in the way he writhed. He was still adamant he did not want professional palliative care and insisted nobody could look after him in this vulnerable state better than they could. Maddie was using every single scrap of knowledge she had about end-of-life care to try to make him comfortable, but nothing really made him feel any better. Autumn knew that it was finally time to say goodbye.

In the early evening, he started begging them to kill him. He had been howling incessantly for hours. It was torturous to listen to. Autumn closed her eyes and tried her hardest to ignore his pleading.

"Just do it and it will all be over," he said, utterly desperate to convince her. "Autumn, please."

She shook her head, but could not look at him.

"Autumn, help me. Please." He gasped the words over and over and over again.

In the end, she could bear it no longer and had to leave him by himself. She was dangerously close to helping her boyfriend end his life and she needed time to think without his desperate interruptions. She marched out of their room, past his vacant and devastated parents. They were sitting on the sofa, listening to him scream. They stood up and went in to him, as she'd known they would. Autumn stepped outside, taking her helplessness and the rage it inspired out on the front door by slamming it behind her with enormous force. She leaned back against it, caressing it apologetically.

"Rough night?" asked Marley. He was sitting on the steps. She hadn't seen him in her turmoil. She nodded dolefully and sat down beside him. He lit a cigarette, holding it out for her to take.

"Thanks," she muttered.

"You're welcome," he said. There was genuine warmth to his tone for the first time since their night together. He was trying to tell her that their ever-present awkwardness was not appropriate tonight. They stared absently out across the garden. It was starting to rain and she could see fog in the nearest fields. She willed it to creep over her. It would soak her irritated skin and hide her from the rest of the world. It would give her sanctuary from the overwhelming temptation she felt to help Bowie end his life. She knew that his continued existence depended on her establishing several reasons why it would be wrong to end his suffering firmly in her fragile mind. She was sure that the absence of his screaming would help. But even in the silence, she could think of only one. It was illegal. That was all she had left.

"We have to help him," she whispered. Autumn had long believed that legality was not an indicator of morality. It was legal to do lots of things she did not agree with and illegal to do many things she felt should be allowed. Bowie could no longer bear his pain and he should be freed from it. If he were a dog, they'd have ended his suffering weeks ago.

"How?" Marley asked, his voice drenched in caution.

"We have to find a way to help him go," Autumn said decisively, with more confidence than she was feeling.

Marley reacted violently, leaping away from her as if she'd slapped his face. He was shaking his head combatively.

"No, Autumn, no, no, no."

"Marley, we have to listen to him," she said.

"We can't," he said. "I can't."

"Marley—"

"Do you know what you're asking me to do?" he said. "Have you really thought about it? Really? Bowie's my whole fucking life. You're asking me to destroy myself."

"Do you know how selfish you sound?" She stood up to confront him. "Can you hear yourself?"

"I can't do it," he said.

"You wouldn't have to," she said. "You just have to let us. Maddie and I."

"I can't stand by and watch either."

"Then we will," she said firmly. "Say your goodbyes and leave him."

Marley moved towards her, protesting, but whatever he'd been about to say was interrupted by a high-pitched, strangled cry from Bowie's room. Marley slouched down onto his haunches and held his face in his hands. His shoulders shook.

"Is this the way you want him to go?" she asked him, his torso heaving with distress.

"W-what's the alternative?" he murmured into his palms. "What do we need to do?"

"Maddie will know how," Autumn said. "And then it'll all be over for him, all the fear, all the pain. He won't have to feel any of it anymore. And that's all he wants now. It's all he's wanted for months."

Marley lost his balance, collapsing into a sitting position on the tiled floor of the porch. He drew his knees up to his chest and turned his head to sob hysterically into the sleeve of his shirt. Her heart ached for him. She sat down beside him, pulling his shuddering body into hers. They held on to one another, listening to Bowie's pleas of distress, as the fog rolled in around them.

***

Together, Autumn and Marley told Bowie their plan, plied him with vodka to calm him down, and convinced the family that they should all get some sleep. Bowie had been in the same level of distress for many hours now, they said. If it was going to get worse, it already would have. Autumn and Marley promised to come and get them if Bowie needed them.

When Maddie came to bid her brother goodnight, Autumn caught her eye. She stared at her meaningfully until she was sure she understood. Maddie nodded gently and left. She went to bed with the others, but met Autumn and Marley ten minutes later on the stairs.

"I'm not sure I can do this," she whispered.

"Don't say that, Maddie." Autumn grimaced. "We've already told him that we will."

"I always said I'd never do it unless everyone agreed," she said.

"They'll never agree," Marley said. His voice was low and hoarse. "Mum and Dad will never agree, never. We have to do this without them."

"We need you, Maddie," Autumn said. "You're the only one who knows anything about his drugs. We can't risk this going wrong."

They held hands as they filed into the bedroom. Bowie was sleeping, but his eyes fluttered open when he heard them come in. He smiled when he saw Maddie was with them and reached out to hold her hand.

"Thank you," he said.

"Bowie—"

"I'm ready, Maddie," he answered before she could say any more. "I'm tired."

Maddie nodded, turning to the two of them. "You'd better say your goodbyes." She walked unsteadily to the doorway. Autumn let Marley step forward. He sat beside his brother, bereft. Bowie looked at his twin with wonder in his eyes.

"Thank you," he said. Marley smiled weakly, taking Bowie's hand.

"I don't think I can stay," he said.

"That's OK," Bowie said. "I love you."

"I love you too."

"Forgive yourself, Marley? Please?"

Marley tried to speak, but Maddie re-entered the room. Autumn willed him to say whatever it was he wanted to say anyway, but Marley clamped his mouth shut, instead leaning down to kiss Bowie on his forehead, nodding gently as he did. When it felt as though an age had passed, Bowie pushed him, firmly but tenderly, away. Marley loitered at the bottom of the bed. Autumn stepped forward.

"Hi," she said stupidly. It made him smile.

"Hi," he said. She didn't know what else to say. No combination of words would ever convey the enormity of what she wanted him to know. She threw herself on him instead.

"I'll love you for ever," she heard herself say.

"I know you will," he said.

He let her lay with him for a few minutes, then urged her gently to go. She moved to stand beside Marley. Bowie gestured for Maddie to come to him. In her hands, she carried boxes of sleeping pills, numerous boxes of pain relief tablets, and a cup of clear liquid. She placed them on Bowie's bedside table and perched on the side of the bed beside her brother. She was crying silent tears. They belied her composure.

"Don't thank me again," she said before Bowie could speak.

"Sorry." He stroked her arm. "You won't get into trouble, will you?"

"No, darling, but you need to take them yourself. And I think you should write a note. I'll take the blame for leaving too many pills lying around."

"Please don't do that." Bowie shook his head. "Mum and Dad will never forgive you if they think you've had anything to do with this. Promise me you won't. Tell them I've been stockpiling them and I took them myself. Promise me."

"OK." Maddie soothed him. "We will, Bowie, I promise."

"What will happen?" he said. "What will it do to my body?"

"It won't do you any good to know that," she said softly.

"Will it hurt?" he asked. Maddie shook her head.

"You should take these first, then these, then drink this vodka down. You're going to feel drowsy pretty quickly, so you're going to have to do it all as fast as you can. It's an overdose, but the sleeping pills will knock you out."

Bowie nodded, his eyes flitting fearfully to the pill packets. Maddie kissed the back of his hand.

"It isn't going to hurt," she whispered. He nodded again and swallowed, turning to look at Marley, pacing the floorboards restlessly.

"Marley," Bowie said softly. Marley stopped and looked at him. "If you're going to leave, then you should go now."

Marley walked to the door, then stopped. His face crumpled. He looked at Autumn, then at Maddie, and finally at his twin brother.

"I'm staying," he said.

He strode determinedly towards the bed and threw himself down on it with childlike abandon. He scooted closer to Bowie and helped him to sit up. He ran his hand lovingly over his brother's face and kissed him on the top of his head. Bowie smiled and let his head fall heavily against Marley's shoulder, scribbling a note on a notepad Maddie had given him and tossing it onto the bedside cabinet when he was done. Once they were settled, they looked at Autumn. Maddie held her hand out to her, gently pulling her towards the bed.

They looked between each other, each of them certain someone else would put a stop to this, but nobody did.

Bowie swallowed a handful of sleeping tablets first, then dropped the painkillers onto his tongue as if he were eating sweets. He was sinking into drowsiness in just a few minutes. He held on to the three of them, repeatedly asking them to tell his family how much he loved them, and promising their crying faces that they would be all right. As he slipped into unconsciousness, Maddie promised him, in answer to the fear in his eyes, that he wouldn't feel any additional pain. It would all be all right now, she whispered. She waited until he was sleeping soundly before she let herself sob. They sat beside him and waited.

"How long will it take?" Marley asked, cradling Bowie's head where it had fallen against his chest.

"I honestly don't know," Maddie said.

They lay motionless for half an hour or so. Bowie's breathing slowed, and then became more ragged. Autumn held his hand tight, allowing herself to hope that Maddie's plan hadn't worked. Bowie was, at least physically, still alive, but the grief she felt was already desolating. She was scared stiff. She watched as the rise and fall of his chest grew shallower. Eventually, he let out a deep sighing breath and he never drew in another. Marley stuffed the corner of the bedsheet into his mouth and released a sound like nothing Autumn had ever heard before. She knew it would haunt her for ever.

They wept and wept, and then Autumn and Maddie peeled Bowie from Marley's arms and laid him on his back in a nest of pillows. He was still warm to the touch. They tucked his bed covers around him with great care and reverence. Marley curled into a ball on the floor, crying out his brother's name over and over and over again.

"Please, Marley." Maddie knelt before him and stroked his head tentatively. "Mum and Dad will hear you, and this shouldn't be how they find out. Please."

He reached out and grabbed his sister by her arm, pulling her in to clasp her to him. He begged her, in urgent whispers, to kill him too.

"Please. Maddie, please. I can't do this. Oh God, Bowie. Maddie. Please help me."

Autumn's loss was utterly incapacitating. She was unable to do or say anything. She sat on the end of the bed and watched Maddie try to soothe her brother through her own tears, but Marley was adamant that he wanted nothing but to die. Autumn forced herself to speak.

"We should leave him," she said to Maddie. "Let's leave him here with Bowie."

Maddie froze, thinking deeply, and then suddenly relented. She held Marley's sobbing, quivering form to her chest, told him she hoped that he would make the right decision, and then released him gently. She took Autumn's hand and pulled her out into the hallway.

"Let's give him until the morning?" Maddie whispered, her voice hoarse from sobbing. Autumn nodded and they sat side by side on the sofa, staring silently into glasses they'd filled with neat gin. Neither spoke for over an hour.

"I'm glad it's finally over." Maddie's voice shattered the silence. Autumn wasn't sure where she had been, but was shocked back into the present. Maddie's words broke her heart. Bowie was really gone.

"Me too." It was a lie. She was not glad. She would never be glad.

"His suffering has consumed us all for years," Maddie continued. She was searching for something positive to say. Autumn knew her attempts were futile. There was no silver lining. She resisted the urge to tell Maddie to stop talking.

"I'm glad I was finally able to do something to help him. It doesn't feel wrong," she added.

Even in her stupefied state, Autumn knew Maddie was trying to tell her something. She didn't have the energy to ask her to explain, but managed to raise her head expectantly, bracing herself for what her friend had to say.

"Did Bowie ever tell you that I'm not their biological sister?" she asked. Autumn's mind went instantly blank. She shook her head. "Dad isn't actually his dad. His real father left Emma when the twins were only four and Bluebell was two. My mother left Dad for someone else when I was one. Dad met Emma when the twins were seven and Bluebell was five. I don't remember life before them, but apparently there was one."

Autumn was blindsided by this revelation and yet, through the fog of confusion and grief, everything made so much sense to her now. Her mind raced through the differences — both in appearance and attitude — between the siblings, Ben's unwillingness to contradict Emma or to intervene in matters relating to Bowie's health, and to Marley's outburst at the dinner table a few nights before, when he'd called Ben by his first name. Bowie's violent response seemed suddenly justifiable. Autumn felt sad for Ben. It must have been very painful to hear Marley talk like that.

"When Marley called Dad 'Ben' the other night, you didn't react. I felt sure that you knew."

"I was confused by it, yes," Autumn said. "But, no, I never knew."

Maddie smiled meekly.

"When Dad and Mum told me the truth when I was six, I was devastated," she said. "Bowie, Marley and Bluebell promised me that nobody would ever know, that they would never tell anybody, but I felt sure that they would break their promises when they grew up and fell in love. I guess I was wrong. It was so important to me that I was a legitimate part of this family, that I was as much their sister as Bluebell."

"He never told me, Maddie." Autumn listened to Maddie talk about how zealously Ben loved Bowie, Marley and Bluebell. He had never once failed them in his fatherly duties, even when they'd been disrespectful to him. Autumn marvelled at this man, who'd devoted himself to loving his wife's children with a ferocity that she had never seen from her own father, and at Bowie, who had, as it turned out, understood perfectly well how it felt to have had a dad who didn't care, but never revealed this to her because that would have meant breaking the promises they'd made as siblings to Maddie.

"I'm so proud to have been his sister, Autumn," she whispered. Autumn put her arm around her friend.

"And he was so proud to be your brother," Autumn said.

"We created this life together," Maddie said. "All of us. We forgot about the people who'd forgotten about us, so we could make ourselves into this incredible family."

Autumn could barely believe it. Somewhere out there in the night slept the man who'd conceived Bowie and Marley, and he had no idea, nor any desire to know, that at least one of his sons had lost his fight with life tonight.

"It isn't over," Maddie added. "It won't die with Bowie. My parents are terrified you'll leave us, Autumn. They love you and they don't want you to leave, but they'll never tell you because they don't want you to feel obliged to stay."

Autumn knew now why Maddie had chosen to disclose their family's secret. She was afraid that Autumn might leave and she wanted her to know that her family was more opaque than it seemed. For Autumn, pondering what she might do after Bowie died had been too painful, but she had always been fairly certain that she would, in all likelihood, leave the Whittle home as soon as she could. She would run right back to her old life and try to pretend that none of it had ever happened. She didn't know how she'd be able to get over it any other way. She was ashamed to acknowledge, even now, as she sat conversing calmly with his sister, that she was fighting the urge to bolt from this house, but she couldn't leave until she knew what Marley's decision had been. She had to know, for better or worse. Every now and then as they sat, Autumn had to fight an overwhelming urge to rip the bedroom door open. Waiting to know, powerless over the outcome, was excruciating. She felt such sadness for Marley. If he had killed himself, he'd died all by himself. If he hadn't, he was still all alone in there, with Bowie's lifeless body beside him. It broke her heart.

***

As the sun lit up the hallway with soft morning light, Maddie and Autumn walked, hand in hand, to the bedroom door. Maddie pulled it open tentatively. The medication had moved. Marley was laying on the bed beside his brother. As they stepped fearfully across the floorboards towards him, he turned to look at them. The packets were untouched.

They threw their arms around him, sobbing with relief.

CHAPTER 15

"I used to believe I really knew who I was. I thought I'd be that person for the rest of my life. But then I met Bowie, completely by chance. He asked me if I wanted to eat vegan cake with him, and, even though I had no real interest in indulging a man that night, I somehow found myself saying yes. Bowie chased me with the same intensity he ploughed into everything he ever wanted in life. By the end of the night, I was shamelessly hooked on every single aspect of him. He spent the next few months forcing me to question everything I thought I knew about men, love and relationships. He didn't even know he was doing it. Or maybe he did. I'll never know for sure.

"Bowie was wickedly shrewd. A master manipulator. He could coerce anyone into doing almost anything with his charm and gentleness, but all he really wanted was for us to be our best selves. To follow our hearts. To put everything we have into the things we love. To forgive each other, accept each other, teach each other and to work towards making a better world for the people who aren't as lucky as we are.

"By doing the thing he loved most, making music, Bowie left behind a legacy. People will continue to fall in love with the music he made. He had so much love to give, it poured out of him and into everything he cared about. When we lost Bowie, we lost a creative genius, a defender of the innocent, and a fiercely loving friend.

"Before he died, Bowie asked me to tell his parents and his siblings that he loved them, despite the fact he'd barely gone a day of his life without telling them himself. This is the man we're here to say goodbye to. A man who loved others so deeply that they were his only concern in his last few hours on this earth. He told me once that if he had to face being sick every day for a thousand lifetimes or lose Ben or Emma, Marley or Bluebell, Maddie or Pip, he would bear this disease gladly. Bowie could not stand the thought of those he loved being in pain. He was glad that he was the one facing death. He was the bravest person I've ever met. I will never be the same because of him. Everything I thought I knew has changed because of him.

"I know you'll agree that the world will be a poorer place without him. All I can do now is honour him with my own actions. I know that the best way to do that is to love the way he did. I hope that you'll join me in doing so. It's the only thing this wonderful man would ever have asked of any of us."

Autumn folded up the piece of paper she was reading from and took a step towards Bowie's coffin, running her quivering hands along its smooth sides in the same way she used to caress his face. She kissed the burnished oak that hid from view the only man she had ever loved.

"Goodbye, my love," she said. "And thank you for everything."

CHAPTER 16

Before she flew home, partly from a desire to escape the Whittle home and partly out of an ill-advised need to make a connection, Autumn called her mother, Katherine, to let her know she was on her way to visit. Could her mother pick her up from the train station, she asked. Katherine thought for several minutes and eventually told her no, she couldn't. She always spent her Friday afternoons drinking wine with her friend, Pam, and there was no way she could let a mate down. Autumn had no idea who Pam was, but, apparently, she had been there for her mother through some fairly recent difficult times. Katherine told Autumn she'd have to get a taxi.

Autumn called her sister.

"I'll do it for a tenner for petrol?" Lilly said. Autumn agreed. A taxi would've been cheaper, but her sister was unemployed, and Autumn suddenly felt eager to see them. She valued family ties differently now. She wasn't sure how long she would stay, but promised herself she'd hold them both in her arms and tell them they were important to her, regardless of the outcome.

She ran to her sister's car as soon as she saw it pulling into the dreary grey car park. It was the same electric-blue Renault Clio they'd shared when they were teenagers. Her mum and Pam were in the back. Autumn reached impatiently to open the door and readied herself to greet them, but Lilly pulled the car playfully forward. Autumn sighed and shook her head, smiling and jogging heartily after it. She grabbed the door handle, hauling it open before Lilly could pull away again. Katherine and Pam cackled loudly in the back seat. Autumn felt ridiculed, but she shook the feeling off. She knew she was being oversensitive. If Bluebell or Maddie had joked in such a way, she'd have found it funny, so she forced herself to laugh along with them, blowing a kiss to her mother and pecking her sister on the cheek. Their familiar voices, the smell of the washing powder they had always used and the lingering whiff of her mother's hairspray overwhelmed Autumn's senses and made her feel nervous.

She'd spent most of her time on the train debating whether she should tell them about what she'd been through. She decided that she wouldn't, but, when her sister asked her how she was, she found herself blurting the whole sorry tale to them. It felt good, and she realised that she'd needed someone to talk to who was not a Whittle. Since the funeral, speaking with his family about Bowie had been extremely distressing.

The women in the car gasped and made sympathetic noises as she told them about Bowie, how she'd met him, and what had happened to him. She waited for them to ask her why she hadn't called them when she'd first flown back to England, but they didn't. She was both relieved and a little disappointed. When she ran out of words, there was silence. She wasn't sure if they were absorbing what she'd said, or if they'd stopped listening, just didn't care, or were waiting for her to continue. Her mother broke the silence.

"Did he leave you any money?"

"Mum!" Autumn was aghast.

"We pronounce it 'Mam' here," Katherine said pointedly. She'd never been able to bear anything other than the northeastern pronunciation of her title. "This boy of yours was from a posh family, wasn't he? You said they lived down south and your accent has changed. You sound posher."

Autumn shook her head, but didn't say anything to deny the Whittles' wealth. Subdued, she asked her mother to stop it, self-consciously dropping the 't' at the end of her sentence, as she had as a child, in the hope that it might appease her. She hadn't noticed until now how diluted her accent had become. She was still distinguishable as northern and the Whittle men had teased her relentlessly about how she pronounced certain words, particularly 'moor, 'year' and 'purple', but there was no denying that the way she spoke was quite noticeably less northern than it had been.

"And you said he was a fancy musical bigwig in New York. He didn't leave you anything?"

"No." She shook her head. "He didn't."

She didn't bother to go into the fact that she had no need for Bowie's money. They'd have known if they'd ever bothered to follow her career. Nor did she elaborate on the details of Bowie's estate. It was none of their business. He'd left everything he had to his mother besides one lump sum he'd ringfenced for Maddie, with the stipulation she should use it to help her buy a home. Autumn had told Maddie herself, at Bowie's request.

"Bowie wanted you never to feel you might have to give up your work being a social-care-working hero because you couldn't make ends meet," she'd said.

If Maddie had refused to allow him his wishes, and, true to form, she had objected vehemently to accepting anything — Bowie had arranged for his money to be kept in trust for any children she might have, or released to her later in life if she changed her mind. Maddie had been overwhelmed by her brother's wishes.

"I told him once that I might not return to care work because of the money being so bad," Maddie had told Autumn, struggling to process her guilt. "I didn't really mean it. I would never want to do anything else."

"Bowie would've wanted you to have the money anyway," Autumn said. Marley nodded his agreement. Autumn and Maddie shared a sad smile. Marley nodded again, drawing in a jittery breath and accepting his sister's hand when she reached to squeeze his. He could not force an expression across his frozen face, but he knew how important it was that he reassured Maddie, and Autumn was grateful that he could summon the strength from somewhere. They were all aware that Bowie's gesture was only in part about Maddie being able to continue as a care worker. Without Maddie stockpiling a cocktail of his meds for months to help release him from his pain, he'd have suffered for far longer, or risked an even bleaker outcome by trying, and potentially failing, to take his own life. Bowie was sending Maddie his thanks by taking away her worries for the future and, in doing so, releasing her from the dependence on her parents she found so difficult to bear.

Emma attempted to split the remainder of Bowie's savings equally between everyone else, but they resisted, encouraging her to give his money to charity instead. Bowie cared deeply for others and it seemed like the right thing to do. They suggested a list of causes to Emma one rainy afternoon, and she agreed to split the money between an organisation helping young people with lymphoma, a charity that brought music to disadvantaged youths, and a vegan animal sanctuary, in Bowie's memory.

"Can we stop at a corner shop?" Autumn asked her sister now, winding down her window and biting back tears. "I need cigarettes and wine."

* * *

They sat themselves around the blue plastic table in her mother's sea-blue kitchen and each lit a cigarette. Katherine eyed her eldest daughter critically.

"I thought you'd given up," she said acerbically.

Autumn sighed. "I've been through a lot, Mam."

"Huh! You don't know you're born," Katherine muttered.

It was fair to say that Autumn's mother hadn't had the easiest time. Autumn's grandmother had been a teenager when she'd given birth to Katherine on the bathroom floor and, in very different times, the family had been publicly shunned. Katherine had been raised on the very same housing estate where she'd raised Autumn, and where she still lived. She'd never met her father, nor even knew who he was. The man her mother had gone on to marry had been violent and he'd tried to molest Katherine several times throughout the years. Autumn's family had seen history repeat itself, as so many families did, in all the wrong ways. When Katherine and her mother had confronted her stepfather together, there had been an altercation involving a knife. Katherine had left home and moved in with her boyfriend, Autumn's father, and his family. She'd become pregnant with Autumn's sister, Summer, at fourteen, but the baby had died as a result of complications in labour. Autumn had been born a year later. They'd lived with her father's family until she was eight and, although her memories of that time were not very clear, she seemed to remember that her mother had seemed constantly scared.

On the day they'd moved out, her mother had shown her happily to her brand-new bedroom in a little two-up, two-down with a box room, a few streets away, before telling her that her father would not be joining them. Mummy's friend, Aaron, who'd lived next door to Autumn's father's family, would be moving in instead. Autumn had never liked Aaron. He shouted all the time and he'd never said hello to her. She'd seen him fight with her father, and, in spite of her dad's disinterest in her, her irrationally intense love for him had made her a fiercely loyal child. She'd stayed that way until the day he'd refused to save her from sexual assault. As it turned out, Aaron's shouty and violent nature in the early days had been a prelude. He'd gone on to start hitting her mother, then her.

On Autumn's thirteenth birthday, Aaron had given her a lager and lime laced with ecstasy to drink and then her first kiss. He'd pressed her against the wall in the hallway before she could stop him and shoved his groin against hers. Autumn had hit out at him and pushed him away. The next day, she'd overheard him telling her mother that he was worried that Autumn might accuse him of doing something he shouldn't have. Autumn had listened to her mother telling him not to worry, that her eldest daughter was an attention-seeker and she wouldn't ever believe anything she had to say about Aaron 'in a million years'. Autumn had known then that Aaron had meant to harm her, safe in the knowledge that even her own mother wouldn't believe her. She'd spent the next three years making sure they were never alone together, often going to bed with boys she'd barely liked just to avoid being home alone with him. For a long time, she'd traded hand jobs for a safe place to sleep.

At sixteen, she'd returned home from shopping one day with her mother and walked in on Aaron having sex with a pretty eighteen-year-old on the family sofa. He'd told them he was leaving them there and then. Katherine had never got over it.

Autumn studied her mother now, her face framed by the smoke they were creating with their sucks and blows. There was a scruffiness to the way she inhaled her cigarettes. Autumn chided herself in her mind. There was no real difference between smoking roll-ups on a porch in the southern countryside and puffing away in the kitchen of a council house twenty miles from Newcastle, but she couldn't help but feel that the act, when indulged here, reeked of boredom and desperation. Katherine had not taken care of herself and looked much older than she was. She had given her children her thick brown hair and green eyes. Years of smoking had blackened her teeth and she'd had fine lines around her mouth and across her cheeks for as long as Autumn could remember. The several brown sunspots on her face were the result of a love of tanning booths.

"I was beautiful once, but age catches up with everyone," she'd often told Autumn. "You wait. You're gonna look like me one day."

Autumn was self-aware enough to know that flippant comments like this, spewed at her on a fairly frequent basis from the tender age of five, had contributed to her unhealthy relationship with her own body.

Katherine caught her staring, and Autumn turned her face away and nudged her sister.

"Tell me about your life, Lilly."

"No." Her sister shook her head. "Boring. Tell me about yours. About Bowie and New York. Tell me about this love affair."

Autumn felt a sudden rush of affection for her sister and reached out to take her hand, a gentle gesture she'd grown accustomed to performing, without a second thought, with Bowie's family. Lilly flinched noticeably at her touch, but didn't pull her hand away. She felt cold to Autumn.

"Can we put the heating on?" Autumn asked her mother.

"No," Katherine answered abruptly. Autumn was not surprised by her answer. It had always been the same. Katherine didn't need to elaborate. They couldn't afford to keep the house warm and Autumn knew that.

"I bet your boy's folks never worried about putting their heating on." Lilly laughed lightly, drawing her hand away.

"No." Autumn shook her head. "They didn't. But the house was big and it was still cold all the time."

"Got any photos?" Lilly inquired. "Of the house? Or your bloke?"

Autumn felt immediately on edge, but nodded her head. Katherine, Lilly and Pam scooted towards her until they were all surrounding Autumn. She took out her phone, skimming through hundreds of photographs she had taken of the best and worst summer she'd ever had. It was painful to look back on happier times, but she couldn't seem to stop. Seeing Bowie's face hurt her heart. She'd wiped him from her screensaver on the day he'd died so that she wasn't tempted to stare at his picture, and subtly avoided looking for too long at Marley, who, in her grief, looked more like Bowie to her now than he had even on the evening they'd met.

"He's so handsome, Autumn," Lilly said. "God, they look alike too, don't they? The brothers, I mean. I can't believe they're not identical."

"Yeah." Autumn nodded. "They're very much alike, especially in photographs. It was much easier to tell them apart in real life."

"That must have been hard work." Katherine laughed. "Making sure you didn't take the wrong one to bed."

Unbidden, the mental image of Marley's face forged its way into her mind, his lips slightly parted, his head thrown back in ecstasy. She closed her eyes and shook her head to erase his features from her thoughts. When she summoned the nerve to look up at them, they were all watching her, their faces tinged with suspicion.

"I bet loads of women want to bed them together," Katherine said. Autumn smiled in spite of herself, remembering with fondness their frivolity on the night they'd discussed the very same thing, the night they should have been at the ball. The night she and Marley had . . .

"Mam, that's gross." Lilly frowned.

"'I wouldn't kick either of them out of bed, together or separately!" Katherine laughed, louder than was necessary. Autumn winced through a smile and lit another cigarette.

"Was he good?" Pam asked. "This Bowie bloke? In bed?"

"I'm not sure that's a very appropriate question," Autumn replied, trying, in vain, to keep her voice even so as not to start an upset. Autumn didn't know Pam, and the woman had barely said a word to her all afternoon. Still, she wasn't entirely surprised by this stranger's nosiness. On this estate, everything was everyone's business, especially when it came to who was sleeping with who. They hopped in and out of each other's beds with a frequency that would make even Bluebell blush.

"I bet he was shit." Katherine took a cigarette. "Posh boys always are. They don't have to work as hard to keep their women. Not women like us, anyway."

'Women like us?' Autumn was suddenly incensed. She had been doing well to keep a lid on her reactions to their ignorant questions and lack of compassion, but she felt herself seethe in response to her mother's statement before she could stop herself. Could it be that her mother still thought that Autumn was anything like her? Katherine was uncaring, uncouth and ungracious. She was underprivileged and uneducated, that was true, but she was also cold, lazy and self-righteous. She rarely thought of anybody but herself. Yes, poverty may have played a part in making her the person she'd become, but Autumn had been raised on the same streets, in almost identical circumstances, and she would never have said something so spiteful to someone who was grieving. Katherine's casual nastiness made Autumn feel about as irate as she'd ever felt.

"I'm nothing like you," Autumn said. Her words were cold and harsh. Her mother's eyes narrowed in a way that used to make Autumn feel afraid.

"You'll always be like us, my love. You can run as far as you like, but you'll always be an estate girl at heart."

Autumn willed herself to remember who she really was inside. To remind herself she was the woman she'd been becoming for more than a decade. She was a woman who cared about more than what was happening to her personally. She was the kind of person who was happy to make herself uncomfortable by confronting her own privilege. She would never go out of her way to make someone else feel upset because of the way she was feeling about herself or her own life. She would never want anyone to feel she was indifferent to their presence. She hoped nobody would ever be afraid to tell her how she'd made them feel. She never wanted anybody to feel lonely when she was in the room. She wanted people around her to know she cared about the things they had to say. She was nothing like them. Not at all.

"You've always thought you were too good for us, Autumn," Katherine continued in a bitter tone. "We've never been enough for you. Well, it stops right now, do you hear? You don't get to come back here, expecting tea and fucking sympathy because your precious posh boyfriend went and died on you and left you with nothing. You act like you're better than we are, with your fancy American shoes and the way you always look down your nose at us. I'm tired of it."

Pam snickered nastily in support of her friend. Autumn, biting back tears, poured herself another glass of wine in silence — it was her fourth, if she had been counting correctly. It had been a mistake to come back here. She felt vulnerable enough already and could have protected herself from walking into this living nightmare. She felt like a fool. And yet, somehow, deep down, she recognised that she also felt lucky; she had been one boyfriend away from being stuck here herself. She mightn't have developed such a hard shell, mightn't have become so fucking determined to get away from them all. It might've been so easy to have fallen in love with the youngest lad of a family of six and become stranded here, on these streets, like everyone else. If things had been different for Autumn and she had wound up stuck at home, she was in no doubt that she'd have felt the same way as her mother by now: jealous of the privileged, ashamed in private, but ludicrously proud in public, full of bravado that she was happy to be a poor, uneducated northern lass. She too would have been convinced that someone with Autumn's affiliations was trying to be somebody she was not. Autumn could see, all too clearly, in her mind's eye, how her mother saw her. She thought she was a snob.

Autumn supposed she *was* being snobbish. She had been judging them, when she really was no better than her family — no better than anyone. At some point she'd come to believe that she was, but she could see now, despite her anger, that they were all a victim of circumstance, a product of their privilege or lack thereof. She could hardly expect anything else from her mother except resentment, the snooty thoughts she'd indulged in had almost certainly translated into facial expressions, and Katherine had become defensive. She was quick to anger, sure, but it was in part Autumn's fault this time.

Her thoughts moved to Bowie and she wondered what he'd think about the way she'd inwardly judged her mother, about the ego she had grown in his presence, without his permission. He'd tell her she was wrong to look down on anyone.

Autumn was close to apologising, but then Katherine spoke again, and what she said cast all of Autumn's pity and sensitivity into the wind.

"You've given that posh little prick and his family more time and attention in the last six months than you've given us, your family, in thirty years. You barely bloody knew them. It was me that gave birth to you, Autumn."

"Shut up, Mum!" Grief and pent-up rage were swallowing her and she could feel herself losing control.

"It's 'Mam'!" Katherine roared back at her. "You're not posh, you never were and you never will be, so stop talking like you are."

"Don't fucking talk to me like that," Autumn got to her feet. She moved towards her mother, knowing that all it would do was provoke her. It had been a long time since they had physically fought. They had been quite evenly matched when Autumn was in her teens, but her mother was a fair bit wider now and Autumn was so much thinner. Still, every fibre of Autumn's being wanted to take everything she felt out on this woman, right here, right now. This woman who had cheated on her father. This woman who had always favoured her sister. This woman who had made her feel so utterly worthless. This woman who had allowed her stepfather to beat her, who refused to believe she had been sexually assaulted. Who'd been happy to see her leave home because she couldn't wait to turn her bedroom into a gym. Who'd tried to invalidate everything that Autumn had worked so hard for, hadn't bothered to read her book, and who cared more about how she pronounced her words than if she was making a success of herself. This woman who still dared to call herself her mother when she barely knew the meaning of the word. This woman who could stand in front of her and insult a family who had supported Autumn more in the last six months than she had in thirty-two years, and the only man she had ever been in love with. A man who had shown her more care and affection in such a short time than this woman ever had. A lovely, sweet, unashamedly kind, dead man.

Autumn was consumed by a deeply dangerous rage. As she lunged at her mother, she wondered what Bowie might think of her if he could see her now. If she had ever dared tell him about her family and the kind of anger they stirred up in her, would he even have believed she had it in her? She knew he wouldn't. She had once been angry at him for hitting a wall in her presence. She remembered the guilty expression he'd worn that morning when he'd promised her he'd just been overcome with emotion and realised she was being a hypocrite. It only made her angrier at her mother. As far as she was concerned at that moment, this was all Katherine's fault. Autumn felt her mother's hand reflexively slap her across her face. Before Autumn could grab her by her hair, Lilly wrapped her arms around her waist from behind and wrestled her out of the room. She dragged Autumn upstairs and into her bedroom, then sat with her back against the door and refused to move, even when Autumn kicked her. Lilly let her scream for a while and then, when Autumn showed no sign of calming down, shouted at her.

"It's not us you're mad at, sis," she said. "Stop it, babe. Please."

Autumn let herself sink to her knees, holding her hands over her heart and howling, slowly and sadly. Lilly watched her sister cry, her own lips quivering at the rawness of Autumn's anguish, and then pulled her into a hug.

They held on to one another until Autumn had calmed down. When they eventually found the emotional strength to stand up together, the evening had drawn in and their mother was long gone. Before she left, presumably with Pam, she'd called to warn Autumn that she'd better be gone by the morning. Autumn could come home again only when she remembered who she really was, she'd said. The sisters climbed into bed together.

"You should have chosen the other one." Lilly spoke wryly into the silence, stroking Autumn's hair with all the grace of a person unaccustomed to demonstrating affection.

"The other brother. You'd still be sitting in a mansion now, instead of here with me in this freezing-cold shithole."

Autumn rolled her eyes, but didn't say anything. She knew her sister didn't mean to be insensitive. There was no need to tell Lilly that the Whittles had begged her to stay with them, that they'd approached her, both collectively and individually, and implored her not to leave. It was hopeless to point out that falling in love with Bowie had been the cataclysmic conclusion to an evening out she hadn't even wanted, rather than a rational choice she had made. Pathetically, Autumn found herself declaring instead that the Whittles' home was a country estate, not a mansion. Her mind was racing, but these were the only words she managed to muster.

She wanted to tell Lilly that she'd been feeling deeply depressed and that she needed help. She was desperate to confess to someone, anyone, that grief and guilt were preventing her from sleeping, and that she was already missing Marley more than was appropriate. She wanted to tell her sister that she'd been spurred by a missing period, sickness, and a strange intuition, to take a pregnancy test. That it had been positive, and that she didn't know whose baby she was carrying. She thought about the horrified stare and look of judgement her confession would likely induce and shook violently against her sibling's shoulder instead. Eventually, she encouraged Lilly to go to sleep, then she kissed her on the top of her head, collected her things and took a taxi to the airport in the early hours of the morning, trying to ignore the terrifying truth of what was growing inside her.

* * *

Bowie had only ever been in her apartment twice, but she still saw him everywhere. He was on the sofa they'd made up on, in the bed they'd slept in, and all over the mug he'd thrown up into, which was sitting, clean and dry, on the drainer beside her sink. Autumn held the cup to her cheek and cried for him, before taking it to bed with her. She hid under the duvet, grasping the cup to her heart, and hoping that she might find peace in slumber.

Restless, she thought carefully back to a time when she'd felt depressed like this before, remembering how she'd found it possible to sleep in those days only by imagining that she was no longer alive. Nothing mattered when you were dead, she'd reasoned back then. She allowed herself to pretend for a moment that she did not exist. Nobody knew for sure where she was. She was entirely alone. Again.

She felt herself relax a little at last.

* * *

Autumn's eyes opened a full forty-eight hours after she'd closed them. She had eight missed calls from Emma and multiple messages from various members of the Whittle family. Her sister had tried to call her, too.

She was hungry, thirsty, and really needed the loo. Despite an ache in her back that made her want to crawl to the bathroom, she forced herself to walk. She could hardly bear the touch of her T-shirt as it brushed across her breasts. She really wanted to be sick. She'd never known her body to feel so sensitive. Suddenly, she felt incredibly pregnant.

She weed, and then stood under the shower, scrubbing the skin on her stomach viciously as she washed, silently urging the ball of cells hidden inside her not to be real. She stared up at the ceiling, urging the universe to help her out of this mess. She'd heard that lots of women had miscarriages in the very early stages of pregnancy. Whomever he or she belonged to, this baby had been conceived barely four weeks before. Autumn let herself hope that she'd miscarry. It would make everything so much easier. She felt a twinge of guilt.

"Nobody wants you." She spoke to the foetus lurking in her belly. She sat down in the shower stall, hugging her knees to her chest and wondering what Bowie would want her to do if he were here. *Keep it.* She could almost hear his voice in her head. There was no question in her mind at all what his response would be. He'd have asked her to keep it even though Marley might be its father. And Marley? She knew right away what he would want her to do, too. It might be Bowie's, and he would never advocate aborting a part of his brother. She spent less than a second pondering what the others would want from her. He or she was a Whittle. Bowie and Marley's family would want her to have it, no question, and would love it dearly.

"I don't want you," she said, correcting herself. She couldn't keep it. It was too complicated.

She texted Bluebell to tell her she was safe and in New York, and then stared at her phone, waiting for what she knew was the inevitable. Emma rang her right away.

"Autumn! Is everything all right?" she asked urgently.

"I'm fine," Autumn said. "I just needed..." She paused. What did she need? She didn't know any more. "Something." She finished hopelessly.

"Yes," Emma said. "We understand that, darling."

"I'm sorry, Emma." Autumn's apology was heartfelt. She knew that they'd wanted her to stay close by, but she couldn't bear to listen to them telling stories and sharing memories of Bowie. She had a baby to abort and needed to do that alone, though she wasn't sure that she'd feel much differently even if she hadn't had this added complication. "How is everyone?" she asked.

"Missing Bowie," Emma said. "Missing you."

Her tone made Autumn feel guilty. She felt irritated by the pressure Emma's comment put her under, but then reminded herself that this poor woman had no idea what else Autumn was going through.

"I miss you all too," she said. "How's Marley?"

She couldn't help herself. She had to know how he was coping.

"Still here," Emma said. "Barely. But still here, so far. Autumn, there are times when he breaks his heart so hard it's as if he might literally cough it out. There is no getting through to him. He won't go anywhere near Bowie's bedroom, won't let any of us mention his name in his presence, won't let us sort through any of his things or move any of his stuff. He barely speaks and I can't get him to eat. He keeps telling me he wants to die but he's too afraid to kill himself. He says he can't get the image of Bowie and the way he looked that night out of his head, but he won't agree to go to therapy either. I don't know what else there is to do but wait."

Autumn had been battling ugly flashbacks too. When they'd found Marley alive after the night his brother had died, she and Maddie had left Marley lying on Bowie's bed. He had been clinging to Bowie and begging him to come back. Holding each other up, Autumn and Maddie had crept into his parents' bedroom to tell them he had gone. His mother had known the second she'd seen them step into the room. She'd screamed and bolted out of bed, pushing aside a trembling Pip and Bluebell — who'd heard Marley wailing, and beaten their mother to Bowie's bedside — to throw herself manically onto her lifeless son, clutching desperately at his face, his arms, his neck, and sobbing into his pyjamas. She'd read and re-read Bowie's suicide note, clutching it to her heart and shaking her head in disbelief.

Before they'd called anyone, Maddie had explained that it was better for everyone, including Bowie, if they didn't tell anyone he'd committed suicide. She'd explained that would lead to a coroner's inquest, which could take months. Instead, she'd insisted they call the family doctor, who she'd been sure would sign off Bowie's death on the basis he had been very sick. That would mean they could bury him sooner. Emma had objected at first.

"I want to know what he took and what happened to him," she'd said. "I need to know if he was in any pain."

"Then he'll have to have an autopsy," Maddie told her. Emma shook her head, and that was that. There was no way she'd let them cut Bowie open, so they hid his suicide note and did as Maddie said.

They gave her some time with him, given Emma and Marley plenty of time to kiss Bowie and hold him in their arms, to touch every bit of the man they could not imagine living without, and then Maddie called Bowie's GP and an undertaker. When the funeral director arrived in the afternoon, he found Emma, Marley and Ben still hysterical with loss. Ben was gradually coaxed into Pip's arms with gentle encouragement and support from his kids, but they had to physically pry Emma's arms from around Bowie's neck and Marley's fingers from Bowie's wrist as they pleaded with Autumn, Maddie and Bluebell not to take him from them, not to leave him all on his own, he needed them, he was cold, they said. Autumn would never forget the way Bowie's body rocked rigidly from side to side when she helped Maddie and Bluebell drag their devastated mother and brother away from him, nor how cold his skin felt against her fingertips. The GP's medical certificate of cause of death concluded non-Hodgkin's lymphoma Autumn never found out what happened to the suicide note after it was hidden.

Autumn pulled herself back into the present. Emma was still talking about Marley.

"I can't lose another child. I can't. I just can't, Autumn."

Her words caught in her throat. As Autumn listened to the sound of her crying, she tried to imagine what it must be like to love that fiercely. She let her fingers roam tentatively across her pelvis and told Emma it would all be OK, but she knew that her words sounded empty. She wasn't actually sure that any of them would ever feel OK ever again, especially not Emma. Still, she didn't know what else she could say.

"I hope so." She sighed. "I'll let you go, my love. You know where we are if you need us."

"I do. Tell them all I love them."

"I will. And they know," Emma said. "I'll call you again in a couple of days. We love you, darling. Bye."

* * *

A fortnight later, Autumn found herself inexplicably craving the outside world. She dressed and let her feet carry her to the nearest coffee shop.

"Hey, it's your season," said the barista. Autumn blinked at him blankly.

"Excuse me?"

"Autumn, right?"

He seemed so sure of her name, but Autumn didn't recognise him.

"I gave you a free coffee that time you forgot your purse. Months ago now. Back in winter."

"Right!" Autumn said. The morning she'd met Bluebell. A couple of months before she'd met Bowie. January then. It seemed like years had passed. "I remember."

"You haven't been back here in a while," he said. "Been busy?"

"A bit, yes," she said. She winced.

"Can I buy you another drink?" he asked her coyly. "I'm almost done for the day. I could join you for a coffee?"

Autumn nodded numbly. He was cute and she was feeling lonely. His name was Toby and he was a medical student. He had thick, black, curly hair and nice teeth. He was from Los Angeles. He had two brothers and a sister, and called his mother every day. He asked Autumn about herself, but she deflected his questions flirtatiously. She let him hold her hand across the table for an hour or so, then invited him back to her apartment. She dragged him through the front door by his shirt collar and slammed his back against it. He kissed her hungrily.

Autumn had been by herself in New York for almost a fortnight, though she knew that Walter knew she was home. He'd left a note tied to her staircase, along with a number of donations of ham sandwiches that she'd had to throw away. She would get around to speaking to him at some point, but she had been busy. She'd spent the first week editing the second draft of her second novel and telling herself there was no pregnancy. The book was with her publisher now and she'd had nothing to focus on since, other than how desperately alone she felt, and how time was running out for her to make a decision about whether she'd show up at the clinic appointment she'd made for the following week.

It had been weeks since she had felt any sexual urge at all, but she'd masturbated, with thoughts of Bowie in her mind, for three days in a row. She was frustrated and had been left feeling empty. She'd needed more. Someone to hold her. She'd gone out looking to meet someone, but she knew as soon as Toby kissed her that she'd made a mistake. He was nothing like Bowie at all. His lips were rough, his kisses uncaring and self-centred. He reached clumsily for her groin as though he'd never touched a woman before. His hands on her felt wrong. The way he touched her was wrong. She produced a condom from her bedside table and made sure he put it on, then jammed her eyes shut, forcing herself not to think about how wrong it all was until he was finished.

Afterwards he wanted to hug her, but Autumn asked him not to. He looked offended. They lay side by side in uncomfortable silence and she wished he would just leave.

"Why did you invite me here if you aren't interested?" he asked her.

She lied. "I was. I am."

He shook his head and rolled his eyes.

"You know, if this were the other way around and I'd treated you this way, you could post my name and where I work on social media, and I'd get lynched for being a misogynist," he said. He was right and she nodded. "It isn't right to treat anyone like they're disposable, Autumn. Anyone."

"I know," Autumn said. "I am sorry."

She wanted to tell him that her boyfriend had died, but thought it might sound preposterous in the circumstances. She wanted to confess that she was struggling to cope, that dark thoughts danced through her mind and she didn't know how to stop them. She wanted to ask for help, but he was angry with her and had every right to be. He didn't even know her. She offered him the money for the drinks that he had given her, but he shook his head and hastily pulled his clothes on, clearly upset. She apologised again, but he ignored her. She let him leave her there, listening to his footsteps as he headed for the door. She felt emptier than she ever had before.

"I'm sorry," she whispered, talking to Bowie. He'd told her never to do that, never to imagine that he might be there to accept an apology for anything she did to try to move on, but she'd still found that it helped her to speak to him. She did it all the time. Autumn heard Toby pull the door open.

"Good luck, man," he said. She barely knew him, but she knew that he was not the type to call a woman 'man'. He was talking to someone else. She sat up. By now he'd made his way down the stairs, but he had left her door open. He had let someone into her apartment.

"Walter?" she called. She heard the door click closed behind whoever it was. Walter was a little hard of hearing, but that didn't reassure Autumn's pounding heart. She felt low enough to wonder if it might be easier to just let the intruder kill her, but she pulled a bedsheet up and around her in a hopeless attempt to protect her dignity. She had no idea where her dressing gown was, or where that guy had thrown her clothes. She winced as she moved, feeling sore and bruised. Toby had taken her clumsily, and her mind had been so distant from the act that she had barely realised it until now.

She yelled out a warning. "I have a knife in here."

Marley pushed the bedroom door open with his boot and stared at her.

"Put some fucking clothes on," he said.

* * *

She dressed slowly, pulling on a pair of jeans and a baggy white T-shirt Bowie had given her. She could hear Marley moving around in the kitchen and she knew he'd found the alcohol in her cereal cupboard.

She braced herself to face him. He held out a mug of red wine and they stared, silently, at each other. She deliberated momentarily, then took it. What could be the harm? Her appointment was in just a few days. She sipped it, watching him going through her cupboards, presumably in search of food. She didn't have the energy to tell him she hadn't bothered to buy anything since she'd first got back. She barely ate these days. She had the prominent hip bones and ribcage to prove it.

Marley looked a mess. His hair was shaggy and overgrown, his skin unhealthily dull, and he smelled like he hadn't been near a shower in weeks. He turned suddenly and leaned back against the kitchen counter, eyeing her over the cracked tumbler he was drinking neat gin from.

"How did they let you on a plane looking like that?" she asked.

"I've been back for three days," he said. "Which you'd know, if you'd bothered to answer my mother's calls."

Autumn grimaced. She'd been ignoring Emma's calls for over a week. Autumn had justified her behaviour to herself. Emma's voice made her feel even more sorrowful and Autumn couldn't bear how much she was missing this woman. Whenever they spoke, two things happened: first, Autumn would feel so incredibly desperate to make Emma happy that she would contemplate telling her that she was having a baby, and, secondly, she would start to reason that perhaps it wasn't so complicated after all. She'd start to wonder exactly why it was that she couldn't simply tell them that she was having Bowie's baby, move back to England and have this child. It would make them happy and she'd started to feel as if it might make her happy too. She was certain that her mental turmoil was, at least in part, due to the reality of the termination she'd arranged. She had no choice, because she had no way of knowing whose baby she was carrying, but she felt like she was decaying from the inside out. If she could guarantee that the baby belonged to Bowie, she was fairly certain she would keep it, but it wasn't that simple, wouldn't ever be that simple. The reason for that complication, that confusion she was feeling, was standing in front of her right now, drunkenly sinking glass after glass of any liquor he had managed to find. She wondered what he might do if she were to tell him the truth. Could she depend on him to keep their secret? To submit to acting as uncle to a child he may have fathered, for the rest of their lives? She could not be sure and it wouldn't be right of her to ask that of him, nor would it be fair on the person growing inside her. She couldn't see how she could bring a human into the world and tell them their father had passed away, when he could, in fact, be sitting across from them at the family dinner table.

"You're a shitty person, Autumn." Marley slurred his words. "My mum is devastated."

"Why are you here?"

"Couldn't bear being in that house anymore," he said. "Ran off. Called them when I landed. Told them where I was."

"Aren't they furious with you?"

"Yeah." He nodded. "But glad that I can check in on you. We thought you were dead, Autumn."

He sank his gin, glaring at her. "You owe my parents more than this," he said. "After everything they've done for you."

Emma had once promised Autumn that they would never throw the love they had shown her back in her face, but Marley clearly had no qualms about doing so on their behalf. Especially not in the state that he was in.

"You're one to talk," she said. "Don't you think you owe them more than what you're putting them through?"

He laughed bitterly, tipping the last of the gin into his glass. Autumn was sure he was close to collapse.

"You're scaring them," she said. "And you're scaring me."

He swallowed hard and shuddered, swaying unsteadily from side to side. He was tall and imposing, but he looked like a lost and frightened little boy. She was suddenly overcome with a longing to hold him in her arms. She had missed him so much.

"Please don't drink any more," she whispered instead. Her gentleness had the desired effect. His face softened. He put his cup down on her countertop, took a pack of cigarettes from his pocket and held one out to her. She hid the mug of wine he had given her behind her back and accepted his offering. She wasn't sure quite how she could get out of smoking it and didn't want to think about why it seemed so important to her that she did.

"Who was that guy?" Marley asked. Autumn had been hoping he wouldn't. She inhaled from the cigarette, held the smoke in her mouth for a few seconds and then released a cloud of it dramatically into the air. That was not how she typically smoked and she was glad that he was drunk and unlikely to be paying too much attention.

"Just some guy," she said.

"Classy." He leered at her. She glared at him.

"Don't you fucking dare," she said. She suspected that his comment was driven by jealousy rather than judgement. There had been something possessive in the way he'd told her to put her clothes on when he'd burst into her bedroom.

"I'm trying not to fall apart here," Autumn said.

It was the closest she'd come to telling anyone she wasn't coping. That she'd had frightening moments where she'd thought about throwing herself out of the window, or slitting her wrists, or jumping in front of a subway train. She willed him to ask her if she needed his help. His eyes met hers. She saw recognition in them, a deep understanding, and then he shrugged any compassion he might've shown her away.

"You can't use your groin to fight depression," he said. "Trust me, I've been trying."

"What do I do then?" she asked, stubbing out her cigarette without a second drag. "How am I supposed to do this, Marley?"

"You wait," he said. "Either it will beat you eventually, or it won't."

"I don't want it to beat me," she said. "I want to live."

"Then don't kill yourself," he said. "It's that simple."

He rocked on his feet again and looked as though he might be sick. Autumn moved to steady him this time. She placed one hand on each of his upper arms, hoping that he wouldn't fall forward and bracing her elbows protectively in front of her stomach in case he did. She stared up at him. He was taller than she remembered. She saw his eyes focus on her lips in response.

"Don't." She turned her face away. He sighed, pulling her into an unsteady hug. She leaned rigidly against his chest at first and then let herself relax into his embrace. She felt immensely cared for, just as she had whenever Bowie held her. She wound her hands around him and over his back. He cradled her tightly, stroking her hair. She started to cry.

"I'm not him," he whispered.

"I know," she said, burying her gulping sobs in his coat.

"You can pretend I am whenever you need me to be," he said. "I won't mind."

She knew that the offer, although weird, was coming from the right place. She grabbed his hand and led him to her bedroom to get some sleep. He let her push him down onto the duvet and tried to persuade her to get into bed with him when she took off his shoes and socks. She refused, instead kneeling on the floorboards beside the bed to stroke his hair. He watched her intently and then closed his eyes.

"I miss him so much, Autumn," he whispered. He drifted off to sleep.

***

Autumn sat beside him all night. Every now and then, he'd stir and look at her. Sometimes he'd murmur something unintelligible. She'd reach out to stroke his cheek gently and he'd smile and slip swiftly back into a deep, drunken slumber.

At first light, Autumn clambered to her feet and stretched out her limbs. Her back ached and her hips were sore. She'd longed, hour after hour, to lie on the mattress beside Marley, but had resisted climbing into bed beside him. Still, she had not felt strong enough to tear herself away from him to sleep on the sofa. He had not exactly been great company, but his presence had already been a comfort to her lonely heart.

Autumn craved food for the first time in a while, so she pulled on her jacket and searched for her purse. She would make breakfast for them both. It would give her something to do while she waited for him to wake and they could talk seriously about how they were going to survive this when he did. She swallowed her pride and called his mother from the supermarket.

"Are you OK, Autumn?" Emma asked, forgoing any greeting.

"I'm fine. Everything's fine. Honestly, Emma. I'm just so sorry."

Emma accepted her apology with a sigh saturated with irritation. Autumn was surprised to hear such exasperation from such a typically forgiving woman, but she couldn't blame Emma.

"What are you two trying to do to me?" Emma asked. There was a tinkle of amusement in her tone this time. "You and Marley? You're trying to kill me, aren't you? Damn you both. It's a conspiracy. It's the only explanation that makes sense to me."

Autumn heard herself laugh out loud. She apologised again, from the bottom of her heart.

"Marley is sleeping in my apartment," she added. "And I'm quite sure that we're both going to be fine. Eventually."

Emma sounded incredibly relieved. "In all seriousness, my love, you are both going to need therapy."

"I know that now," Autumn said.

"It's been really helping Ben and I to look at things," Emma said. "To focus on the things we did have and do have, instead of the things we don't."

"I'll get some help. And I'll make sure Marley does too."

"Did he say anything about coming home?" Emma asked hopefully.

"No," Autumn said. "Just that he couldn't stand being in the house any longer."

She knew that it would hurt Emma to hear it, but thought it best not to lie to her about his frame of mind.

"Maybe we should come back out there?" Emma wondered this aloud. "Although I don't know if I can bear to leave Bowie just yet, in all honesty."

They'd been given permission to bury Bowie's body in their garden. Autumn hadn't even known such things were possible, but, apparently, they were if you had the right permissions. It had seemed like a lovely idea at the time, sweet and sentimental, but the temptation to sit beside his headstone when they missed him was overwhelming, and Autumn was quite sure that feeling that he was so close by would not be of help to any of them in trying to move forward.

"Bowie's gone," Autumn said softly. Emma inhaled sharply. "Marley needs you now."

She had listened to Emma lecture her on the importance of appreciating the difference between what you had and what had gone, and she knew Emma would never forgive herself if Marley hurt himself while she sat by the headstone of the son who was already lost to her.

"Yes," Emma whispered. "You're right. Of course, Autumn, love, you're right."

Autumn reached the till, her hands full of avocados, tomatoes and seeded loaves.

"Hang on a minute," she muttered to Emma. "How much is that?"

"That'll be fourteen dollars and thirty-six cents."

"Autumn, where are you?" Emma asked, suddenly anxious.

"Buying breakfast." Autumn smiled enthusiastically at the cashier, handing her a twenty-dollar bill and hoping that the young lady serving her would forgive her for continuing her conversation. She wasn't normally so rude, but this was important.

"Did you leave Marley on his own?" Emma asked. Something in her tone made Autumn spin on her heel.

"Yes," she said. "Why?"

Somebody behind Emma was shrieking hysterically. Autumn was fairly certain it was Bluebell.

"Emma?" she shouted into the telephone. She was suddenly afraid.

Emma gasped. "Autumn, run! Go home now, and run."

***

Autumn howled for help, taking the stairs two at a time, as a stream of concerned strangers followed her up to the very top floor of her building.

"My friend has hurt himself," she shouted. "Please help me."

At least, that's what she feared. As she'd sprinted from the supermarket, Emma was screeching something about a sorrowful text message Marley had just sent to Bluebell, and begging her desperately to run faster. Autumn hadn't heard much. She'd taken her phone away from her ear and focused everything she had on reaching him as quickly as she could, quite sure that Emma was still waiting on the end of the line.

He'd used the deadbolt inside to stop her from opening the door. She threw herself at it in desperation. It didn't move at all.

"Marley!" She screamed his name as she kicked the door. Fuelled by her love for this man and the terror she felt at losing him, she had beaten everybody to the top floor by quite a way, but others were joining her now. A stout man reached her first, pulling her back by her arms.

"Move right away," he said. He threw himself forward and, although the door shook, it did not open.

"Call an ambulance." Autumn shouted at the top of her voice. Walter, who had been watching from the door of his apartment, stepped out into the hallway.

"You'll never break it down if it's deadbolted," he said. "It's reinforced steel."

The man thrust himself at it again. Nothing happened. Autumn shook her head, holding her hand out to prevent him from trying again. They were never going to get to him this way. They needed to persuade him to open the door.

"Marley, please, it's me, let me in. It's Autumn. Please don't do this."

She listened hard, but could hear nothing. She knew there was a real chance he might already be dead. An image of him, his body rocking rigidly from side to side the way Bowie's had, came into her mind unbidden. She felt her legs buckle and her hands flew protectively to her stomach. A middle-aged man caught her before she fully passed out and fell. The crowd watching her gasped. As she came round, someone called out for her to be taken to the hospital.

"No, no, I'm OK," she said, hoping to silence them. She was convinced she'd heard Marley's voice, she was sure of it. He was there, just behind the door. Somehow, despite her shakiness, she found her feet and, at her insistence, two strangers supported her gingerly back up the staircase.

"Marley, I know you're there. I heard you. I know you can hear me. Please open the door."

She laid her hand flat against the steel, willing him, with all her heart, to speak to her again.

"I can't," he said. He sounded sad and frightened.

"Yes, you can, my love, you can."

"It's too late," he said weakly. She panicked at this.

"Marley! Please." She hit the door with the flat of her hand.

"No."

His voice was so weak she could barely hear it as she knelt on the concrete floor and wailed.

"Open the fucking door!" He fell silent. Autumn was filled with a terrible desperation. Marley, her best friend, was dying. The door was all that separated them. She pounded on it with the palm of her hand, willing it to break open and, before she could stop herself, she heard herself screaming.

"I'm pregnant. I'm fucking pregnant and I need you."

Her hand flew across her mouth. She listened, but could hear nothing. She laid her hand on the cold metal again and began to howl, hoping against all hope that he had not slipped into unconsciousness. She was feeling faint again.

"Please let me in," she said through sobs. "I need you, Marley. Please, please don't leave me. I can't do this on my own."

She heard his fingers graze the lock and shuffled back in shock and relief, swiping at the tears streaming down her face.

"Just you," he whispered from behind the door. "Promise me. Only you, Autumn."

"I promise," she said urgently.

The man beside her moved to betray him, but Autumn shook her head, no. It was not worth the risk. Once she was inside, she'd be able to open the door for the paramedics when they arrived.

"I promise, Marley. Just me. Please. Open the door."

Slowly, the door opened just a crack and she slipped rapidly inside. He was standing in the middle of the room, his face entirely expressionless. He had slashed his wrists and was holding them out to her as though they were a gift. He was fully clothed but soaking wet. She presumed he had been laying in the bath when he had hurt himself. He was covered in blood.

"Jesus Christ!" she murmured, walking warily towards him. She was still carrying her phone and the line was still connected to Emma.

"Emma, I'm with him now. The paramedics are coming. I'll call you back."

She disconnected the call, reaching out to grab him by his arms.

"I'm sorry," he said dumbly. "I woke up feeling so sad, Autumn."

"It's OK, Marley," she said. "Come here."

She sat him down on her dressing-table stool and held her fingers tightly around his wrists, whipping her top over her head and using it to hold his skin together as best she could. His blood oozed through her fingers and dripped persistently onto the floor. Outside, she heard sirens approaching.

"It hurts, Autumn. I don't feel very well," he said. "I think I might need to lie down."

"No." She shook her head vehemently. "No, Marley, you mustn't. Just focus on staying awake, for me, OK?"

He nodded woozily, then swayed to one side without warning. Autumn reached for him, but he was too heavy and he fell to the floor. She straddled him, picking up his wrists and raising them up with her hands. His eyes had closed.

"Marley! Marley! You have to stay awake!" She was bawling into his face. He groaned in response, and she whimpered.

"Please don't die. I need you, Marley."

His eyes were suddenly wide and he looked at her as though he was seeing her for the first time.

"Is there really a baby?" he mumbled. She nodded. With no energy to speak left in him, he nodded too, looking at her intently. She knew that he was fighting with all of his might now.

She held on to his wrists and cried.

***

"Is it true?" Emma asked Autumn directly. They were sitting side by side in a deserted hospital canteen, surrounded by chairs mounted upside down on plastic tables. It was the middle of the night. The Whittles, in varying degrees of jet-lagged hysteria, had arrived an hour or so before, and Autumn had led them to Marley's bedside and left them alone. She was more tired than she'd ever felt in her whole life and wasn't able to cope with the noises they were making: crying, sobbing, exclamations of love and relief. She'd told them she was going to get herself a coffee and, although she'd bought one, it was sitting untouched on the table in front of her. She was looking out at the city lights from the window, picking thoughtfully at the congealed blood beneath her fingernails, when Emma had come to join her. Autumn hadn't yet been able to bring herself to look at her. She forced herself to respond with a sombre nod.

"Look at me, my darling."

Autumn shook her head, staring down at her nails. She knew Emma would be ready to fall in love with this baby that she thought was Bowie's, and couldn't bear to see that in his mother's eyes. Emma stood and knelt down at Autumn's feet, taking both her hands in her own. Autumn avoided her gaze. Emma sighed.

"Nobody knows but me, Autumn. I'll keep it that way if you want me to."

"Marley knows," Autumn said.

"He won't tell anyone either, my love," Emma said. "He will know that this decision is yours to make. We both do. Even if Bowie were alive, this would still be your decision, darling."

A whole host of emotions flooded through Autumn's body. She had known that Emma, liberal as she was, would never seek to remove Autumn's right to an abortion if that was her choice. Still, she'd expected her to try to influence her decision. As far as Emma knew, this baby was the only bit of Bowie they had left.

"I know what it's like to be pregnant and scared witless," Emma said gently, sitting back down beside Autumn. "Bowie and Marley are the best thing that ever happened to me, but they weren't part of my plan. Oh God, Autumn, if you could've seen the way I reacted when I found out I was having two. I absolutely lost my shit. I howled as if the world was ending. The truth was, I'd barely talked myself into having one baby at that point, I didn't know I would love being a mother *so much* and I knew I might be doing it on my own . . ."

She stopped. She had forgotten herself and she frowned down at the floor. Autumn knew she was searching for something to say that wouldn't reveal that Ben was not Bowie and Marley's biological father, and that Maddie wasn't her daughter by birth.

"I know that Ben isn't their dad, Emma," Autumn watched Emma leaping to the wrong conclusion. "Bowie didn't tell me. Maddie did."

"Ah." Emma breathed a sigh, looking relieved. "That's different, then. Bowie's biological father was a selfish man. I loved him, but not half as much as he loved himself. I chose to go ahead and have the twins, despite what I knew about him. I hoped that having them might change him, but I was always prepared that it might not work out that way. I knew I might end up on my own with them one day and I was one hundred per cent sure that I would find a way to manage by myself if I had to. I loved being a mum so much that I went on to have Bluebell even when things didn't improve between us. They were all accidents, but I wanted them. I wanted them so much nothing else mattered. That's the conclusion you need to come to. We'll be there, but when your baby cries, or they're being bullied, or they're ill, or scared of monsters under the bed, or someone breaks their precious heart, it's their mother they're going to want. He or she should be all you care about from the moment you choose to keep this baby. If you can't give it at least that, then you're not ready. Nobody can, nor should, tell you how you feel in your heart of hearts."

"What if I choose the wrong thing?" Autumn aired her greatest fear, her eyes wide with panic.

"You can't, Autumn, not if you listen to yourself. Don't be distracted by anything or anyone else. Deep down, you already know what it is you want."

They fell into a comfortable silence. Autumn thought carefully. More than once in recent weeks, every time she had felt despair about what would happen next, her imagination had strayed to the fantasy life she'd dreamed up with Bowie in the bed they might have conceived a baby on in a hotel somewhere in London. To the cottage and the vegetable patch and the library full of books. Every time, there had been a baby Bowie resting on her hip. There was no question in her mind anymore — if there was a way to guarantee that this baby was his, she would keep him or her in a heartbeat.

For the first time now, as she sat with Bowie's mother in the chilly canteen, she let herself wonder what she might do if she knew, for certain, that Marley was her baby's father. She realised, to her surprise, that she would probably still want to keep it. They would have to tell the Whittles what they'd done, but that uncomfortable conversation didn't warrant her terminating this pregnancy.

Really, it was the unknown she was afraid of. She couldn't know who had fathered her baby until after she'd given birth. But she could know, eventually. There'd be months of internal torture, but she would get her answer, one day. It was complex, sure, but it didn't have to be. She wondered if she might be overcomplicating things. If the baby was Bowie's — and it probably was, because they'd made love twice around conception time versus three minutes of whatever that thing was with Marley — then there'd be no harm done. If it was Marley's, they would deal with it. But it probably wasn't.

"I need to get back to my boy, love." Emma stirred beside her. She sank Autumn's cold coffee theatrically, raising her eyebrows at her cheekily. Autumn groaned in disgust. Emma smiled warmly, holding her arms open and inviting Autumn into them. They held one another tightly.

"I have no idea what you're thinking," Emma murmured into Autumn's hair. "But will you let me tell you one more thing? People usually want most whatever their head is trying its best to talk their heart out of."

Autumn pulled away, smiling meekly.

"Are you coming too?" Emma asked. Autumn nodded. She didn't need more time to think. She knew what she wanted to do.

***

Marley had made a terrible mess of himself. He'd calmly drawn a bath, then sat in it and slit his wrists with a kitchen knife. It looked as though he'd attempted to make vertical cuts, but he'd managed crooked slashes instead. He swore that he could hardly remember what he had been doing and his despair had completely taken him over. He'd have bled out eventually, but it would have been a slow death. Autumn felt such terrible guilt about leaving him alone, knowing how depressed he was. Marley begged and begged her to stop blaming herself. He'd inexplicably found a strength he hadn't had before. After they'd stitched him up, he'd confessed to the hospital counsellor that he'd been exploring different options to end his life since he'd been back in New York. He'd been on a suicide mission, he said. It wasn't her fault. Nevertheless, Autumn knew she'd never make that mistake with someone so vulnerable ever again.

"How are you feeling?" she asked him the following morning. Knocked out by sedatives and painkillers, he'd been sleeping when she'd visited with Emma the evening before, so she'd curled up on a bench outside of his bedroom and tried to rest herself. She had insisted to the Whittles that she'd needed her own bed and had planned to return to her apartment, until she'd remembered that the entire place was smeared with Marley's blood. She hadn't been able to bring herself to go home.

"Hungover to fuck," was his immediate response. She smiled. His skin was pasty, he looked utterly exhausted and Autumn could see that he was shivering. He swallowed a few times, his mouth obviously dry, and rubbed his lips together. She poured him a glass of water, but he struggled to hold it when she offered it to him.

"Here," she said, holding it to his mouth.

"Thanks," he mumbled, taking a sip. He looked down at his bandages. "Well, that was a botched job."

"I'm so glad." She sat down in the chair by his bed.

"Me too." He nodded, closing his eyes. "When I used to threaten to kill myself when Bowie was dying, I really thought it would be easy. I had all these ideas in my head about how I would do it. There was never any mess the way I imagined it. Or fear. Or pain. It was never going to be painful. Turns out, it isn't like that."

She reached out to touch his hand. He wrapped his fingers around hers, opening his eyes.

"This isn't a movie," she said. "If you try to kill yourself, you leave a mess."

They sank into an awkward silence. She could feel his pulse in his hand as she held it. She marvelled at the strength of it. Yesterday, for more than a minute, she had been quite sure that he'd died in front of her on her living room floor. She'd held his wrists together and felt his heartbeat fade to a point where she couldn't feel it anymore. She had gone insane with hysteria. Losing Marley, watching him die so soon after Bowie, would have been too much for her to live through, she was quite sure of it.

He was staring at her. She knew what he wanted to talk to her about. She narrowed her eyes at him sadly, urging him to talk. He fidgeted uncomfortably under her gaze.

"We never have to tell anyone about what happened," he whispered.

"Marley—"

"I know it might not be the right thing to do. I'm just telling you that we could keep it between the two of us. Everyone would just think it was Bowie's—"

"It might be Bowie's," Autumn said. "You do know that, don't you? Close to the end, a couple of times . . ."

Marley paled, so Autumn stopped. The last thing she needed was him fainting on her. She wondered if he'd suspected she and Bowie had managed to make love in the days before he'd passed away, and concluded he probably hadn't. His face confirmed her suspicion. He was learning for the very first time just how complicated this really was. She eyed him sheepishly, allowing him a moment to come to terms with everything.

Eventually, he shrugged. "It's still an option."

"No, it isn't," she said. "This is an actual person we are talking about. We can't do that to them."

"He'd be so loved. He'd never want for anything. Do you know how rare that is?"

She did know, all too well. Her baby would never yearn for a safe place to sleep or know what it felt like to be hungry or wonder whether anybody actually cared for them.

Regardless of which twin was the father of her child, Autumn thought this must be the luckiest foetus that had ever existed.

"What about you?" she asked. "How could you pretend to be its uncle when you might be its father?"

"I could do it," he said. "It would be hard, but I would do it."

"Well, just because we could doesn't mean that we should," she said. He sighed and shook his head, pointedly drawing his hand away from hers. His head dropped back onto his pillow in defeat.

"Don't you get tired of doing the right thing all the time?" he asked after a minute. "Can't you just be a dick for once like everyone else?"

Autumn laughed, covering her face with one hand and reaching out to grab his hand gently again with the other. He accepted her gesture but couldn't raise a smile for her. In that moment, the unfairness of their situation washed over Autumn. Because she was a woman, Marley had no choice but to accept whatever it was she chose to do with a baby that might be half his. It was indisputably her right to choose, of course it was, but that didn't make it fair.

"I was a massive dick the night I got us into this," she whispered. Between her turmoil over what to do about her pregnancy and her grief over Bowie, for a while Autumn had found their betrayal shamefully easy to forget. She'd realised more than once, to her horror, that she'd even felt sorry for herself. She'd had to remind herself that she'd been irresponsible and deserved the torture that came with the consequences of their mistake.

"We," he said, correcting her. "There were two of us there, remember?"

"I kissed you first." She forced herself to stare into his forlorn eyes. She couldn't remember making that first move, but she had always trusted that Marley had been telling her the truth when he'd spat those words at her the morning after their indiscretion.

"I'm so sorry, Marley."

"We were both to blame." He shook his head, his eyes fixed on hers. "I practically asked you to kiss me. I was a split second behind you. It was just mutual stupidity. Autumn, please. Please don't cry."

She held her face in both hands, shaking her head and sobbing inconsolably. She was overwhelmed by a sudden want for Bowie. She was frightened of how strongly she felt it. Nobody had warned her that her heart, to protect her, would, in quiet moments, force her mind to forget that he was gone every time she thought about something else for even a minute. The gut-wrenching, terrifying realisation of his absence she'd spent weeks trying to accept so that she no longer had to feel the shock of his death over and over again had been halted almost as soon as she'd realised she was pregnant. Now, she felt devastated all over again. He was really gone. Marley had misinterpreted her distress and she was glad.

"Only you can decide," he said. "But I'll be there. I'll get up in the night and change nappies if that's what you want. I'll teach him to play the guitar. I'll help him to become a good person. I'll be there all the time for you both, I promise. You won't ever be on your own, Autumn."

"We'd have to get a test and if this baby is yours, we'll have to tell them all what we did," she said decisively.. He bit his lip and nodded slowly. It was impossible to imagine how his family might react. Autumn had tried. The only conclusion she'd felt able to draw was that they would forgive them both eventually.

"At least we can tell them Bowie knew," he said. "I'm not sure how that makes it any better, but it does."

Somehow, the knowledge that he'd known, and forgiven them, did make it better. Autumn knew that his family, through their anger, would take solace in the fact that their betrayal was not a secret that Bowie had died without knowing. She nodded, willing herself to admit, out loud, that she wanted to keep this baby. Marley studied her inscrutable expression, squeezing her hand in encouragement. She nodded again, with more conviction this time. He drew in a dramatic breath and moved to hug her, pausing to look at her once more.

"Do you mean . . . ? Are we really doing this?" he asked her breathlessly.

She allowed herself to sink into his arms, mindful not to hurt him. He held her tighter than anyone ever had before.

"I think we're doing it," she said, with a faltering smile. "I think we're having a baby."

CHAPTER 17

Because she believed it was important for her child to know his family and where they had come from, Autumn agreed to go back with the Whittles to England, promising a sullen Walter that they would continue their weekly telephone conversations just as they had before. No doubt believing it was where she would be most comfortable, Emma and Ben put her back in the bedroom she had shared with Bowie, and she hated it. The bed was new, but she couldn't bear to sleep where Bowie had once slept. Where she had watched him die. For weeks, Autumn sat herself on the cold floor behind her bedroom door every evening and waited until everyone had gone to bed, before dragging her duvet to the sofa to get some sleep. A horrified Pip returned home early one morning to find her sniffling and crying on the couch. She was almost five months pregnant. He led her upstairs by the hand and insisted resolutely that she take his bed, waking Marley in the process. The next day, they offered to take Bowie's bedroom and give her theirs.

"You can't do that." She shook her head at Marley. He'd yet to set foot in there. There was no way he'd be able to sleep.

"I can," Marley said. "And I will."

He lasted all of fifteen minutes. Autumn took herself upstairs for an early night, choosing Marley's bed as her own because the smell of him was a comforting reminder of Bowie, but he knocked on her door before she'd even shut her eyes properly. He'd been crying.

"I can't do it," he said. "I know this might be weird, but can I sleep in here with you?"

She nodded sleepily, holding her arms out to invite him to climb under the duvet and accept her comfort. She held him close, stroking away his tears with her thumbs. It was the only time she let him sleep with her, but she found herself gazing longingly at him more than once during her pregnancy. Most of the time, it was because she yearned for Bowie's touch. Other times, she was ashamed to admit, it was Marley she longed for.

* * *

As a family, the Whittles had had the best of times trying to decide on a name for the baby. Though the discussion descended into argument more often than not, it was everybody's favourite topic of conversation. Their suggestions were varied and, at times, ridiculous.

"What about Astro?" Bluebell had asked more than once.

"No!" they'd chorus every time she tried to suggest it.

"But it's such a good name," she said.

"What about Apple?" Pip asked, making Autumn laugh. He smiled at her. Laughing was not something they did an awful lot of anymore, and he looked pleased with himself.

"Molly?" Maddie suggested. Bluebell rolled her eyes.

"With parents called Bowie and Autumn, you can't possibly be suggesting she's called something plain like Molly?"

"This is Autumn's decision," Marley told them all.

"It has to be the perfect mix of weird and . . . not weird," Bluebell said musingly. "Like Fern. Or Wilf. Or Ivy."

"I like Ivy," Autumn said. Marley scrunched his face up.

"I thought it was my decision?" She biffed him with a rolled-up newspaper.

"It was, until you suggested naming your baby after a fucking plant," he said.

Bluebell frowned. "I'm named after a fucking plant."

"I rest my case," he said.

***

Time was — very slowly — healing Autumn's heart. She cried for Bowie constantly in the months after his death, but the baby she was growing was most certainly helping her to heal. She'd kept her promise to Emma and was seeing a therapist. She'd thought she would hate sifting through the inner workings of her mind with a stranger and was genuinely surprised to find that the weekly sessions helped her feel calmer. Together they were talking through not only her grief over Bowie's death, but how rejected and inadequate her family made her feel. They'd discussed how this might have given her a frantic and desperate desire for control and had almost certainly contributed to the issues she had with eating. It might also be why she had shunned friendships and relationships for so many years. They hadn't yet figured out why Bluebell and Bowie had been different. Autumn wasn't sure they ever would. Marley had found a therapist that was helping him too. He'd insisted, at first, that the sessions weren't easing his agony at all, but his depression had been lifting, little by little, over time. Autumn knew, beyond a shadow of a doubt, that there were days when her baby was all Marley was living for, but she'd noticed, after a while, that he took part in family frolics again. He would tease her and the others, and say things he knew would make them smile. But Emma could not relax.

"I want to hear him laugh again," she whispered to Autumn one afternoon. "When that happens, I think that's when I'll know he's really on the mend."

Autumn was thrilled to be beside him when that happened. It was a Saturday morning and they were reading their phones in their separate beds.

Marley moaned. "I'm hungry."

"Want some breakfast?" she asked, sitting up.

"You're pregnant," he said.

"And? That doesn't mean I'm suddenly incapable of making a cracking breakfast."

Marley was watching her uneasily. She rolled her eyes, annoyed. She was sick of everyone treating her like a piece of crêpe paper.

"Do you want breakfast or not?" she said.

"Yes," he said. She knew he wanted to ask her if she was sure, but he didn't dare.

"What do you want?" she asked.

"Sausage sandwich, please. Brown sauce, plenty of it."

"OK, coming right up." She pulled on her dressing gown and headed to the kitchen.

She returned twenty minutes later with his sandwich and a cup of decaf coffee for each of them. Marley sat up in bed, dramatically licking his lips.

"There's a condition to this sandwich," she said, holding it over his head.

"I knew this was too good to be true," Marley muttered. "Go on."

"You need to give me the best bit."

"The best bit?" He stared at her quizzically.

"The bit right in the middle," she said. "The bit where the melty butter meets the perfect bite of sausage. The bit with all the sauce and the softest bit of the bread. The bit everyone makes sausage sandwiches for. That bit."

He gasped theatrically. "You can't take my best bit. Why didn't you make your own sandwich?"

"I can't eat a whole one," Autumn said. "I feel sick. I just want that bit. That one tiny little best bit."

"But that's the bit I want!"

"That's my condition." She held the sandwich higher. Marley sighed, the corners of his mouth curling into the start of a smile.

"Fine," he said.

She handed him the plate and perched on the edge of his bed, watching him eating the crusty edges of the bread and waiting, expectantly, for him to stuff the rest of it in his mouth before she could stop him, but he didn't. He held the best bit out for her to take from his plate.

"Think very carefully about this . . ." he said. She grabbed it without a moment's hesitation, jamming it into her mouth before he could say anything else. He stared, aghast, at the empty plate in his hand. She collapsed in a fit of giggles, chewing her way through a mouthful that was far bigger than she could swallow. In the end, her high spirits won him over. Once he started laughing, they found they couldn't stop.

***

Throughout her pregnancy, Autumn and Marley spent all of their time together. He'd become fiercely protective of her. He wouldn't tolerate anyone telling her off, asking for her help or doing anything she might not like. If they did, Marley would leap to her defence. He watched her constantly and never stopped asking if she felt OK. Nobody said anything about it. She expected they all believed he was doing the right thing by his brother's baby. Autumn did sometimes wonder if it were more than that though. She suspected Marley thought the baby was his. One evening, six weeks or so before her due date, they were sitting on the porch with cups of tea and watching the sun set over the trees — their smoking and drinking days far behind them — and she'd dared to ask him how he was feeling about the paternity test.

"I don't really want to think about it," he said. "What's the point? Whatever happens, the baby wins. If he's Bowie's, we don't have to tell anyone about what happened and he gets to know his father was an absolutely amazing man. If he's mine, he gets to have a living father. We'll have to tell everyone what we did, but it'll be worth it if he gets to have his dad."

Autumn was ashamed to admit that she hadn't thought about it like that. She'd always hoped her baby was Bowie's, but if he were Marley's, it would most certainly be better for him. Or her. Autumn had decided not to find out the baby's gender, but somehow the Whittles had concluded she was having a boy. Now, Autumn too had defaulted to referring to her baby as he and him.

"You have to stop calling it a him," she said. "What if it's a girl?"

"It isn't." He shook his head. "I can feel it."

* * *

Autumn's baby boy decided to arrive a month early. Nobody was surprised by his prematurity. He'd already shown them that he had a real attitude problem by giving her endless complications. At times, it had felt as though he hadn't been sure that coming into the world was what he wanted to do after all. That had been sheer torture for Autumn. From the moment she'd made the decision to keep him in that dingy hospital canteen that night, she'd wanted him with a ferocity that was terrifying. She was already so overprotective and irrationally cautious that she'd spent the last six months of her pregnancy traipsing to and from the hospital, sometimes because there was blood in her knickers, sometimes because he'd not made a single movement for more than twenty-four hours, sometimes because she just 'had a feeling'. Everything had always checked out fine. Still, she'd wondered if she might deserve to lose him. What if the universe was against his existence? What if he too was taken from her now? She'd chewed herself up about it every single day. Luckily, Marley had become her main source of strength. He'd worked tirelessly to help her to keep calm, though he had later dared to admit, once the baby was swaddled safely in his arms, that he'd been seized by the same fears.

Labour was nothing like she'd thought it would be. She'd expected everybody to jump into action the second she told them she had a contraction, but they hadn't believed her. For an entire afternoon, she'd felt like the lead character in a horror movie as she tried desperately to alert everyone to a lurking danger, but nobody would listen. It was too early, they'd said. Sure that overcautious Autumn was overreacting after so many false alarms. With more than four weeks until she was due, everyone seemed adamant that this was just another mini drama.

It was Maddie who believed her in the end. She implored her family across the dinner table to pay attention to Autumn, who was plainly terrified and had been struggling through labour pains all day. Emma told Autumn she was sorry she hadn't listened to her earlier, and bundled her and Marley into her car. The others all wanted to wait at the hospital, but Autumn asked them not to come. They were all disappointed, but Ben, in particular, was noticeably crestfallen.

Autumn and Ben had grown even closer than before. She felt as though he was pouring all of the love he had for Bowie into Autumn and her unborn baby. The depth of his fatherly love was helping Autumn to heal. The little things he did mattered the most to her, things her own father had never considered important. Knowing how old she was without having to check, asking her how her writing was coming along, and talking to her about articles he'd read that he knew would interest her. She had never been sure what it was she was yearning for when it came to her own father because he had never really given her anything much at all, but now she realised that all she'd ever wanted was for him to take an interest in her as a person. That would have been enough. Ben had promised her more than once that she would never want for fatherly affection or support again. He had adopted her into his heart, in the same way he'd adopted Bowie, Marley and Bluebell.

None of that meant she wanted him to be there when she pushed a baby out of her vagina. Emma would be there, but that was different; she was a woman and she'd been through this. Autumn needed her. She wasn't particularly thrilled about Marley being there, but as he might well be the father of her child, she told herself he should be, even though his presence made her feel self-conscious.

"I need a bra," she told Emma as they rushed through hospital corridors. Her heavy breasts flapped uncomfortably as they hurried and she was anxious about being topless in labour because of Marley.

"Let's have the baby first, Autumn," Emma said.

"I'm going to need one though," Autumn said. "I can't do this without one. Please."

"Marley, can you go home and get Autumn a bra?" Emma asked her son. He looked mortified by his mother's suggestion. "Or maybe you could nip to the twenty-four-hour supermarket and buy her one? It's just along the road."

"Um, OK . . . What size?"

"30C," Autumn said curtly.

"If I say that to someone that works there, are they going to be able to sort it out?" he asked nervously.

"Yes!" they said together, with growing exasperation.

"Will they think I'm weird?"

"Probably!" Emma said. "Go on, go!"

"Any particular colour?"

Autumn sighed irritably. "Marley, go and get me a fucking bra."

***

He bore the brunt of her anger throughout that evening. She screamed, scratched and bit her way through the first hour of pushing as though she were possessed. She dug her nails into his hand as he held hers and told him, irrationally but in no uncertain terms, to leave her alone whenever she caught him looking at her. Eventually, he moved away from her vicious despair to stand by the window, calling out supportive comments to her as and when he judged them welcome. This had been a happy compromise for both of them, until the midwife gave her a status update she hadn't been expecting.

"I can see the crown of your baby's head now, Autumn," she said encouragingly. Autumn had stopped pushing, her face furious.

"Only its fucking head? I can't do this." She collapsed back onto the pile of pillows.

"You can do it," Marley said. Autumn grabbed his sleeve and dragged him closer to the bed.

"Almost there now, darling girl," Emma said. "Just a few more big pushes."

"I've changed my mind." Autumn whimpered, looking desperately at Emma in reply. "I don't want it anymore."

"Come on, Autumn." Marley stroked her hair back from her face lovingly. "You can do this. I know you can. You're the strongest woman I've ever known."

She braced herself and bore down, feeling more movement now. The midwife, presumably of the belief that Marley was her baby's father, motioned for him to stand beside her, but he pretended not to notice.

"You can watch — if you want to." Autumn gasped in a breath.

"Are you sure?" he asked. She nodded and he moved to stand at the bottom of the bed. Autumn was pushing again.

"How are you doing this?" he asked her.

"Marley, darling, that's really not very helpful," Emma murmured. Autumn cried out then, pushing harder. She'd had enough. She just wanted the baby out. And then, all at once, he was. He'd rushed from her insides and she'd never felt relief like it. She'd given Marley permission to cut his cord, and watched as the midwife passed him her son. Marley stared at the tiny pink miracle in his arms, his mouth opening and closing at the wonder of this new person, his eyes blinking back tears. Autumn would never forget the look on his face when he dragged his adoring eyes off the wriggling newborn he was holding to tell her she had a son. In that moment, Marley looked more like his brother to Autumn than he ever had before. A deep sob escaped her throat. How she wished Bowie was here. She called out his name, collapsing back onto the bed. Beside her, she heard Marley burst into tears. He stepped forward, laying the baby on Autumn's chest.

Bowie's brother and mother wrapped their arms around Autumn and her baby son, and they'd cried and cried, all three of them together, over his tiny blonde head.

Emma had tried, many times, to describe the way Autumn would feel the first time she saw the child she'd created, but she had been right when she'd eventually concluded with the words, "I can't even explain. Just wait." Before she'd held her baby boy that first time, Autumn had been entirely deluded. She'd believed that she could imagine what Emma had gone through when they'd lost Bowie. As she stared at her son in her arms, the true reality of Emma's loss smacked her in the face. In that moment, she couldn't fathom how she would ever survive if anything happened to this tiny little person. She had been embarrassingly ignorant. She didn't know how Bowie's mother was still standing. When Emma drew closer to give Autumn a hug before she held her grandson for the very first time, Autumn held her much tighter than usual.

"Thank you," Emma whispered. She ran her fingertips through the baby's wispy blonde hair. Autumn, weary but deliriously happy, told her that she was welcome. Emma paced the room with the baby, her face frozen in a grin, chattering happily to the bundle of joy she was holding, telling him all about the family he had waiting for him and how badly they were going to spoil him. Autumn reached for Marley's hand, overwhelmed with emotion.

"We're going to be OK," he whispered, leaning in to kiss her forehead. She nodded. In the past six months, they'd become experts at speaking openly to one another about something nobody else knew anything about, and braver when it came to showing each other affection. They knew they didn't have to worry about his family. The Whittles had no reason to suspect anything untoward had occurred between the two of them. Marley had loved Bowie with unabashed ferocity and, as far as they knew, would never do anything to hurt his brother. The idea that her child might be his would not cross their minds. Marley would die to protect his brother's baby as readily as he would a child of his own.

His protectiveness of Autumn would be chalked against that and they both felt safe in this knowledge. The Whittles knew that what Autumn and Marley had gone through together in New York had given them a unique closeness.

They were best friends. She was closer to him than she was to anyone else. Still, their bond did not come close to the bond that the twins had shared, and Autumn knew — though her own heart was on the mend — his would never heal. Bowie's absence was at the forefront of his mind every minute of every day. Their mother's loss was similar in a way and Emma and Marley had become ever more inseparable as a result. Autumn reasoned that it was only possible to feel such pain if you'd lost someone who was, woven into the very fabric of who you were as a person.

Over the course of her healing, Emma started to suspect Marley, Autumn and Maddie might have helped Bowie along. She became obsessed with the notion, asking Marley about it at least once a day.

"You can tell me the truth," she would say. "I know that your commitment to Bowie was a complicated love story, that you really meant it when you said you'd do anything for him. And I know you're liberal monsters. I raised you that way. I won't judge you, I just want to know."

She was convincing, but Marley never faltered.

He stuck to their story like glue and so did Maddie and Autumn. They never talked about it, but Autumn assumed they'd concluded — like she had — that Emma would torture herself if she knew the truth. That she would never forgive them, never look at them the same again, never respect the fact Bowie had been more than ready to die. The truth wouldn't help her, it would only hurt her. It was better if she never knew.

* * *

"I want to call him Ben," Autumn said. Marley smiled at her in the rear-view mirror. It was the afternoon after the birth and they were going home. They'd dressed him in a tiny white all-in-one and matching hat. Despite sending him an obsessive stream of texts to remind him, Marley had forgotten to bring the scratch mittens. Autumn was sitting in the back seat, holding his hands carefully to prevent him poking his beautiful little eyes out. She thought it best not to mention this to Marley.

"I thought you hated traditional names?" he said.

"I don't hate them," she said. "I just think they're boring. But 'Ben' isn't. 'Ben' has meaning. To you, to Bowie, to me. Benjamin, maybe, so we don't get confused."

It just felt right to her. She desperately wanted them all to know how important they were to her. She knew that the family must be terrified that she might take the baby away from them, but Autumn had never wanted anything more than to stay. She was well aware that having a baby would be hard work and was already completely overwhelmed. She needed them. All of them. All of the time.

She'd expected them to be with Marley when he came to pick her up, but he'd been alone and she felt a little disappointed. She knew they'd be excited and she'd been looking forward to seeing them all delight in her son.

"They're all as high as kites," he said ruefully. "I told them they'd overwhelm you and could wait one more hour. I had to scream at them to make them listen, so they won't be talking to me when we get home."

She knew that his solitude was not just for her sake. He'd walked into her room with his arms already open and ready to receive her son. He wanted him to himself for a while longer. He'd been crying, she could tell, but didn't ask him about it. She couldn't even begin to imagine how conflicted and overwhelmed he must be feeling. She'd watched him carrying the baby to the car. His eyes not straying once from her son's perfect little face.

"This is easy." Marley grinned. Autumn raised her eyebrows at him and laughed. Benjamin, if that was to be his name, was sleepy and satiated now, but Marley had not yet had the pleasure of hearing how loud he became when he wasn't.

"They're going to fight over him," he said. She looked down at her newborn, peeping out at her from under his hat. His eyes were big and blue, like Bowie's. They made Autumn feel as though she were in a dream.

"What a lucky little person you are," she told him, "to have so many people who love you so much already."

***

Marley sat Autumn in an armchair opposite the sofa so that she could watch his family carefully pass her baby between them. She had to fight the urge to snatch him back. She reminded herself that he was in the hands of people who would give their own lives for him. It didn't make her feel any better. Marley handed her a coffee and perched himself on the arm of her chair. He couldn't take his eyes off Benjamin either.

She was suddenly afraid of everything. Scared that the baby might be hurt, that something might be wrong with him, that she would do something to harm him without meaning to, that somebody else could upset him, that he might disappear as quickly as he had appeared.

"Well, hello there, little Astro," Bluebell said when it was her turn to hold him. Everybody laughed.

"Actually, Autumn has a name for him," Marley said. They turned to look at her and she swallowed hard, unsure anymore if this would actually be all right. Ben was not her dad, he was theirs. Perhaps Maddie would want to name a child of hers after him. Or Pip. Or any of the others. She faltered, but Marley nudged her.

"I'd like to call him Ben," she said, her eyes darting to the man who was the closest thing to a father she had ever had. He looked utterly astounded.

"Benjamin, actually. If it's all right with all of you, of course?"

One by one, wide smiles spread across their faces. Emma blinked tears from her eyes. Marley winked at his mum.

"Oh my . . ." Ben cleared his throat. "Well . . . Oh my goodness."

"I think it's a great idea." Maddie nodded. "A really beautiful sentiment."

"Me too," said Pip. "Bowie would love it."

"He does look like a Ben." Emma kissed her teary husband on the cheek.

"I still think he looks like an Astro." Bluebell smiled playfully. "But Ben? OK. I think I'll allow it."

CHAPTER 18

"Please, Autumn, let's wait a bit longer?" Marley clamped his mouth shut stubbornly. Ben was six months old and adored by absolutely everyone, including Katherine and Lilly, who had visited Autumn and Ben at the Whittle's home several times. Lilly adored her nephew. His existence had brought her and Autumn closer together. Katherine and Autumn were still not close, but were both eager to set aside their differences so Ben could know his northern grandmother. Katherine spoiled him rotten with her time. When she wasn't at the house spending precious hours with him she was researching the best educational toys, the best schools in the area and 'how to be the favourite grandparent'. Autumn — who cared only about giving her little boy as much love as she possibly could — had not been expecting such enthusiasm from her side of the family and was thrilled. Her son was the centre of everyone's universe. Everything they did they did with him in mind, especially Marley, who had become her coparent before she'd known what was happening and had time to stop it.

Now, six months to the day since Benjamin had been born, Autumn was chasing the two of them around Bowie's old bedroom. They'd eventually mustered up the courage to sleep there again because it gave the three of them the space they needed and shielded Benjamin's midnight meltdowns from the rest of the house. Autumn was trying, albeit without much success, to get Marley to let her swab inside his cheek with a tool she'd received in the post from a DNA-testing company. Marley was not happy. "Please, Autumn, don't make me do this yet."

"I have to," she said determinedly. "I need to know, Marley. For my son."

It was also for Marley's own good. He was completely besotted with Ben. She was concerned that he had already begun to raise her baby as if he were his own. She didn't feel it was right to let that continue if he weren't. She cornered him, but he folded his lips in on themselves and shook his head, not giving in. She poked playfully at his face with the swab. Reluctantly, he opened his mouth, eyeballing her resentfully as she scraped it around his mouth.

She faltered as she bagged up the equipment to send off, giving her head a little shake. She'd put this off far longer than she'd intended to by allowing Marley to successfully convince her she needed time to settle into motherhood. She'd given herself long enough. She needed to know. Marley needed to know. And, one day, Benjamin would need to know. That was the most important part of all of this.

Benjamin had become her everything. Just looking at him made her emotional. She couldn't stand to be separated from him, missing him terribly, even when he was only sleeping. She'd loved Bowie, loved his family now too, but could never have imagined that she would love anyone as much as she loved this baby. She could stare at him for hours. His cries were enough to send her into a frenzy. It was as if he consumed her whole heart. She felt she might never need anyone else again as long as she had him. He was a generally calm, patient and good-natured baby. Emma insisted that his temperament was exactly how baby Bowie's had been.

Autumn tried not to think about Bowie too much because it made her feel so incredibly sad. He couldn't have had any idea of the adventure they would embark on in his absence. Emma had convinced herself that he'd have changed his mind if he'd known about the baby coming, that he'd have worked harder to somehow keep going. That was an incredibly painful potential truth for Autumn to come to terms with. His mother was particularly fond of telling Autumn how Bowie would have loved Benjamin with all his heart. Autumn couldn't bear to let herself dwell on how terribly tragic it all was, not with a newborn to look after. Her therapist advised her not to, at least for now, and Autumn reminded Emma of that whenever she tried to strike up a conversation with her about the son she missed so horribly.

* * *

By the time the test results arrived, Autumn had begun to wonder if it might be better for everyone if Marley was his father. He had kept his promise to her. They slept together in their separate beds and when the baby cried in the night, Marley walked him up and down without a word of complaint. He changed his nappies, mopped up his sick and cooed him into fits of giggles constantly. Benjamin was as easily soothed by the touch and smell of Marley's skin as he was her own. His eyes lit up at the sight of the man they all called 'Uncle Marley' and Autumn was quite sure Marley loved her son with the same intensity as she did. It scared her. If Ben wasn't his, he'd be devastated.

Emma tossed the results envelope absent-mindedly at Autumn one morning at the breakfast table, turning immediately away to fuss over her grandson. Marley's eyes searched for Autumn's over his cereal bowl. She gave him the slightest nod and swept the envelope off the table with as much subtlety as she could. Despite Marley's protests in private throughout the day, she insisted they wait until everyone else had gone to bed before reading its contents. The consequences of these flimsy sheets of paper were potentially calamitous and she didn't want to risk anyone witnessing the aftermath by accident.

At midnight, she picked up her sleeping son from Marley's chest and put him in his crib. Then, together, they sat side by side, on the end of Marley's bed. He had once told her that baby Benjamin got to win, whatever happened, but that didn't feel true to her anymore. The results would either break her dear friend's heart, or they would open the most immense can of worms. They allowed themselves a few more moments of blissful ignorance and then Marley ripped open the envelope.

He stared at the results in shocked silence for a moment and Autumn concluded Benjamin was Bowie's. She knew that hadn't been what he was expecting, that it wasn't what he wanted, but she was relieved.

"Marley—" She reached to touch him.

"He's mine," Marley whispered. "Shit. Autumn. He's mine."

Autumn shook her head. No. It couldn't be. She'd had sex with Bowie twice and Marley only once around the time Benjamin was conceived, she'd been reminding herself of that the whole time. Autumn's eyes darted to her sleeping baby. Marley's did the same.

"He's my son," he gasped out. "I have a son."

Autumn took the papers from him. He was telling the truth. He'd read it right. He was Benjamin's father. They sat, motionless and emotionally charged, watching their baby in his crib. Neither said anything for the longest time.

"I feel like we've lost him again," Marley said eventually. Autumn knew what he meant. Benjamin had been their last hope at keeping a little bit of Bowie. Now, that was gone. There was nothing left of the man she had loved, not even a little bit of him. She realised she was crying. Marley was, too.

"He'd be devastated." Autumn spoke her mind.

"He's not here," Marley said. "He's gone, Autumn."

Autumn nodded, swallowing her sobs. Marley put his arm around her, pulling her into his chest. She held him. Marley. The father of her child. She was sure she'd never get used to that.

"I thought I'd be happy, but I'm not," he said.

"Me either," Autumn whispered.

"It's better for Benjamin."

"We have to tell everyone," Autumn dared speak aloud the part of this they were most afraid of. "Oh my God."

She had hoped their transgression would never be revealed. One by one, she ran the respective Whittle family members through her mind and tried to gauge their reaction. She started with Ben, then Maddie, then Pip, Bluebell, and, finally, Emma. Each was worse than the last.

"Can't we just not?" Marley asked. Autumn recoiled, but immediately forgave his suggestion. He wasn't thinking straight.

"We have to," she said. She felt him nod, then shake a little bit. He urged her gently away from him and stood, stepping forward to peer into the crib. Autumn watched from afar. She was ashamed to note she felt a little bit possessive. Until now, Benjamin had been hers and hers only. She didn't want to share him, even with Marley. But then she saw the way he looked at him, as though he were seeing him for the very first time, and she was flooded with love. Nobody could love Benjamin more than Marley loved Benjamin. Her little boy was lucky to have him. She gave them a moment and then she joined him, her baby's daddy, beside her sleeping son.

"Congratulations," she whispered, kissing him on his cheek. His lip trembled and he threw himself at her, burying his head in her hair. She held on to him, coaxing him eventually into bed, where they lay, sleepless, beside one another, all through that night. She held him to her, crying softly and trying to convince him they were going to be all right. She cried for Bowie and the son they'd never had, the one she'd thought she had carried and given birth to. She cried for his family, who would be so terribly pained when they heard how she and Marley had hurt him. Mostly, she cried for Marley, who, she knew, was in more pain than ever before.

* * *

They hardly touched their breakfast and it didn't go unnoticed. When Emma asked them why, their eyes flickered to, and lingered on, each other.

"What?" Emma asked with unusual sternness. Autumn saw Marley go rigid with fear. He was incapable of speech, so Autumn spoke for him. There was no time like the present, after all.

"We need to tell you something," she said. Her voice sounded stronger than she felt. She tried to avoid looking at Marley, but could see even from the corner of her eye that he was hyperventilating. She planted her gaze on her son, instead. He was sitting in his highchair eating a rusk. She ran her fingers through his hair, enjoying a few more moments of peace before inevitable carnage. Before she could say anything, Pip spoke.

"Are you two fucking?" he asked angrily. Autumn had already known that was the conclusion they would jump to, and she braced herself. The truth was so much worse. She trawled the table. They all looked furious. She searched frantically for a way to get out of telling them the truth, but there was none, so she set her face with a stern expression and spoke.

"No, we're not, but what we're going to tell you isn't going to be easy for you to hear."

She saw Ben's eyes flick to baby Benjamin, then to Marley, then back to Autumn. They stared at each other, then he closed his eyes, and waited. She wondered if anyone else suspected, but she doubted it. Ben was the only one besides Bowie who'd known Autumn and Marley snuck around the house alone after dark. The others were oblivious. Autumn sighed.

"On the night of the ball, when you all went to bed, Marley and I couldn't sleep. We were drinking in the living room and things got a bit silly and—"

Maddie gasped, dropping her fork with a clatter on her plate. She put her head in her hands and shook it.

"What?" Bluebell said, staring between her sister and Autumn.

"We had sex," Autumn said. She forced herself to face her best friend when she said it. Bluebell opened her mouth to say something, then closed it again. She turned to Marley and did the same thing. Autumn saw her shoulders stiffen and her eyes fill with tears.

"You did what?" Emma looked furious.

"Wait," Autumn said. She wished Marley would chime in and help her, but he was staring at Benjamin and she thought he might die if she tried to force him into anything else, so she left him be. "Marley is Benjamin's father," she added.

Bluebell wailed and burst into tears. Pip slammed his hands on the table and stood up, stepping threateningly towards a terrified Marley. He reached for the collar of his brother's shirt.

"Pip!" Maddie screamed. Poised, Autumn picked up Benjamin and swept him from the room. She ran into their bedroom, the room she'd shared with Bowie, grabbing a holdall she'd packed just in case. She was putting her coat on when Emma caught up to her.

"Where are you going?" she shouted.

"Away," Autumn said. Emma stepped desperately towards her, holding her hands out to her quiet and obviously startled grandson. Behind her, through the open door, Ben was pulling Pip off Marley.

"Come here, Benjamin," she said.

Autumn held him closer. "Stop it."

"You're not taking him." Emma's tone was sickly-sweet.

"Yes, I am," she said. She rushed around Emma and into the living room. Marley was standing against the wall, his hands raised in submission, while Ben tried to push a desperate and screaming Pip away. Maddie was standing bravely between her two remaining brothers. Bluebell was crying hysterically and hadn't moved from the kitchen table. Benjamin's little eyes watched the people he loved in dire distress and his bottom lip curled outwards and down. His cries pulled Marley out of whatever stupor he was stuck in and he dropped his hands and strode towards Autumn. She held Benjamin tighter, worried he would take him from her, but he didn't.

"Let's go," he said, grabbing a set of car keys off the workbench.

"Marley!" Emma shouted, giving chase. Marley pushed open the front door, pressing the remote and directing Autumn and Benjamin to the car that flashed. It was Ben's silver estate.

"Son." Ben was following, too. "Please stay. Come on, we can talk this through."

"Not now, Dad," he said. "They're too emotional. It's not their fault, I know, but Pip will kill me and Autumn is terrified you'll take the baby and kick us out."

Autumn hadn't told him that, but it was her fear. Even in the chaos, she felt immensely grateful to have someone standing beside her who understood her completely. They climbed into the car. Autumn watched Emma hit the bonnet with her fist and then dissolve back into Ben's arms. Benjamin cried harder, holding his hands out towards where his grandma had been.

"Marley!" Maddie shouted, throwing herself at the car. "Don't do this. Don't walk away from your family."

"Maddie, this is my family, too," he said through a lowered window. He pointed at Autumn and Benjamin. "I'm coming back, OK? After everything has calmed down. Take care of Mum."

"Marley, look at her." Maddie sobbed. "She's losing Bowie all over again. They all are. They can't face losing you, too, or Benjamin, or Autumn. Please, don't go."

Marley put the key in the ignition and started the car, but Autumn stopped him before he could put it into gear. Above the roar of the engine, she could hear Emma shouting Benjamin's name, over and over again. In the doorway, Bluebell was perched on the steps, hugging her knees to her chest and bawling. Pip was sitting on his haunches on the porch behind her, his head in his hands, his shoulders heaving. Marley's hand twitched beneath Autumn's palm, but she squeezed him tightly until he looked at her.

"We can't go," she said. "We can't leave them like this."

* * *

Ben collected his distraught family and ushered them into the living room, then came back to speak to Autumn and Marley about terms. They would leave if anyone got physical, they said, or if anyone shouted and upset the baby. Benjamin wouldn't be sitting with anyone besides Marley and Autumn. At the end of the conversation, whatever happened, they felt it best they moved out for a little bit, until everyone came to terms with the enormity of what this meant. They agreed, so Autumn and Marley trudged back into the house. Benjamin was, mercifully, asleep by this point, otherwise Autumn would most certainly have had to wrestle to keep him with her. He loved his family immensely.

She sat on the seat of the cuddle chair and Marley perched on the arm. The family were sitting and standing in various positions around the living room: Bluebell, Emma and Maddie on the sofa, Pip by the fireplace, Ben pacing the floor behind the couch. Autumn and Marley waited for someone to speak.

"How could you do this?" Bluebell whispered.

"We never meant for it to happen," Autumn said. Bluebell ignored her, glaring at her brother.

"How could you do this to Bowie?"

"I don't know," Marley said. "I'll feel guilty about it for the rest of my life."

"I can't believe you let us think we still had a little bit of him." Maddie shook her head. "All this time."

"We thought Benjamin was his," Marley said. "We really did."

"And then what?" Pip said. "You'd just never tell us?"

"Well . . ." Marley faltered.

"No, we wouldn't have told you," Autumn said. "Because the only other person who needed to know about it was Bowie, and he did know."

They turned, one by one, to stare at her.

"Bowie knew," Autumn said. "We told him right away."

"Oh, my poor boy." Emma sobbed, holding her heart. "He suffered that all by himself. No wonder he was sick."

Marley almost growled. "Don't you dare."

"He forgave us," Autumn added.

"But he didn't know there was a baby?" Maddie asked. Autumn shook her head.

"No," she said quietly. "He didn't know there was a baby."

"Well, thank God he's not alive," Pip said.

"Pip!" Bluebell shouted.

"What? He'd be fucking devastated."

Beside her, Marley shook. Autumn reached out to take his hand. They'd known this would be difficult, they'd talked about it lots in the night and her action was a purposeful reminder of their combined strength. Yes, this was awful, but they would be OK, whatever happened. Before her, Bluebell was seething.

"I can't believe you have the cheek to touch him in front of us."

"He's the father of my child," Autumn said.

Bluebell cackled nastily. "Only you could somehow manage to make this seedy little fuck sound somehow classy," she said. "But, I suppose, coming from where you do, you've had enough practice at pretending."

Maddie and Ben gasped Bluebell's name.

"That's enough." Marley stood. "Autumn, let's go."

"Please don't go." Emma wiped fat tears from her face. "Marley, please stay."

"I have to, Mum," he said.

"I can't bear it." She sobbed as she stood before him to block his path, knotting her hands in his shirt. "I can't stand it, Marley."

"We have to go, Mum."

Beside her, Autumn saw Ben uttering something audible only to Marley's mother. She watched his mouth. He seemed to be saying, "Tell them, Emma, tell them."

"Tell us what?" Autumn asked, loud enough to be heard above the rabble. They fell silent, turning to watch Autumn, who was staring at Ben. "Tell us what, Ben?"

Ben sighed, gesturing to the sofa.

"Sit down, all of you. Sit down now. There's something Mum and I need to tell you all."

"Let me put Benjamin in the bedroom?" Autumn said. The cuddle chair she and Marley had been sitting in was by the bedroom door. She'd be able to stop anyone who tried to take him and she felt as though he'd sleep longer in his crib, so she carried him into the bedroom, laying him down with a blanket of Bowie's he'd been sleeping with since his birth. She stroked his cheek and took a moment.

"I love you, Bowie," she whispered. "We all do."

All at once, Autumn felt calmer.

"Bowie?" she said.

She let herself imagine how incensed he'd be by the idea that she believed the ghost of him was sending her strength from the afterlife.

"I know, I know." She smiled ruefully and shook her head, letting a tear fall from her eye at the vivid memory of him. "I know, there's no such thing as an afterlife. I know."

She kissed her son, watched him for a few seconds more, then returned to the living room, where everyone had resumed their original position. She could tell nobody had spoken since she'd left.

"Right," Ben said. "This isn't how we do things in this family, fussing and fighting like this—"

"You said you had something to tell us." Marley interrupted her irritably.

"And I do," Ben said. "We do. Emma?"

Emma sighed and shook her head, her lips pursed stubbornly.

"If you don't tell them, I will," he told her.

"They're going to use it as their excuse." Emma rubbed her temples. Ben stopped pacing and sat beside her, taking her hand gently in his.

"Maybe it is the reason," he said. Emma snatched her hand away, wiping a tear from her eye. She looked resigned. "You have to tell them."

Emma sighed and then spoke, her voice small and gentle. "Bowie and I had a conversation about this once when he was very ill."

"After the night of the ball," Ben added. Emma glared at him. "It's important they know all the facts," he said, gesturing for her to continue.

"Yes, after the night of the ball," Emma continued. "The night that you . . . I'd mentioned how very fortunate it was that you two got on so well and he'd smiled and raised his eyebrows in that way he sometimes did. When I questioned him, he told me he hoped the two of you might fall in love when he was gone. That you would be perfect for each other, but you'd both be too stubborn to see it for yourselves. He told me he'd been encouraging the two of you to spend time together, hoping you might find comfort in each other when he'd gone. I laughed at him; it was so preposterous. I couldn't believe what he was suggesting. He told me that if it happened, I had to leave well alone. He said he loved you both and he wanted you to be happy. He'd forced you to spend time together, just the two of you. He engineered all this. He loved you both and he desperately wanted you to love each other, too. Really love each other. He wanted you to give to Marley what you had given him, Autumn, and for Marley to feel what he felt about you. He had come to believe, beyond a shadow of a doubt, that his purpose in life was to bring you together, to make sure you had each other when he was gone."

Emma paused for breath.

"He had no idea how it would happen, I suppose," Ben said. "But I'd say he achieved his objective, even if it wasn't in the way he'd intended."

"That's the most fucked-up thing I think I've ever heard," Marley said.

Autumn could barely believe her ears. She'd known Bowie had died believing she'd fallen in love with Marley, but she could never have guessed he'd wanted them to be together with such single-minded and selfless conviction. That was why he'd been able to forgive their betrayal of him so readily. He'd felt responsible, in part, for orchestrating a sequence of events that had contributed to it happening. Autumn found herself sobbing uncontrollably. Marley put his arm around her, kissing her on her head.

"I have something to add to that," said Bluebell, her voice meek with shame. Autumn couldn't bring herself to look at her friend, but she felt Marley move to give his sister his attention. "He said the same to me."

"And me," Maddie added. All eyes turned to Pip. He nodded, swallowing hard.

"So, who are we to rage against something Bowie wanted for you both?" Ben said. "How can we go against what he asked of us, when he's the only victim here, and he wanted it for you more than anyone else?"

Autumn felt sadder for Bowie than she ever had. She wished she could've been his more devotedly. He'd deserved more from her than she had given him. Even now, even in this circumstance, she knew Bowie's heart was so incredibly pure, and his love for her and Marley so endlessly deep, he'd be happy they'd created a little person they loved so much.

"Well . . ." Marley paused. "God, I don't know what to say."

"None of this excuses what you've done," Pip said. "You should have kept your dick in your pants, Marley."

"I know that." Marley nodded.

"You didn't deserve Bowie," Pip continued. "Either of you."

"None of us did," Maddie said. "He was the best of us."

They sat in contemplative silence, crying with varying degrees of violence. Autumn held on to Marley and allowed herself, for the first time in a while, to pretend he was Bowie. He rocked her backwards and forwards, the way Bowie used to, and she was fairly sure he knew what he was doing. She let him comfort her, despite the watchful eyes of his disappointed family. She didn't care what they thought anymore. She knew what Bowie had thought and that was all that mattered to her.

* * *

They agreed to stay, though Autumn was quite sure they didn't want her there anymore. She retired to her bedroom early and let them talk as a family, trying not to pine for Marley by distracting herself with some reading. It was after midnight before he came to bed. He forfeited his own mattress without invitation, throwing himself on hers instead.

"Hey," he said softly.

"Hello." She smiled sadly.

"Are you OK?"

"Not really. Are you?"

"Not really." He shook his head. "They've calmed down, but they'll never look at either of us in the same way again."

"We knew it would be ugly."

"I know." He sighed. "How's Benjamin?"

"He's just had a feed." She closed her eyes. "He's apparently oblivious."

"Good." Marley sighed again. "Do you want to talk?"

"About this?" she asked. "Not really, but I will if you want to."

"Let's do it another day?"

Autumn nodded. She knew what he wanted to talk about and she didn't know what to say. Things had been weird between them for a while and Emma's revelation of Bowie's wishes had confused her further. Bowie had been gone for fourteen months and Autumn had not shared a single sexual experience with anyone since her unsatisfying and unpleasant encounter with the coffee barista in her apartment a month after Bowie's death. Recently, she'd found herself beginning to feel things she was uncomfortable feeling whenever she was lonely and longed for someone's touch. Marley was featuring in her fantasies more often than he was not.

Her feelings for him left Autumn confused and bewildered. She couldn't tell him. She couldn't tell anyone.

"I think I should move out," she said into the silence. Marley, who had been snoring softly, snapped to attention.

"What? Why?"

"Because they'll never forgive me," she said. "Or you, if I'm here reminding them of what we did every single day."

Occasionally, for fun, Autumn allowed herself to think back to the day they'd met. He'd seemed so different then, bouncing enthusiastically behind his brother after his gig, cocky and very clearly aware that the women waiting for him by the door expected to sleep with him. She could never have imagined then what she and this stranger would go through together. They had both changed so much. They'd grown up, and raised each other along the way, but they'd come to rely on each other, and it was time to move on. Fate, or whatever silly thing it was she was starting to suspect might control these things, felt the same way, it seemed, and it had intervened just a week or so ago.

Before he'd grown too ill to sing, Bowie had convinced Marley to record some of the songs they'd written together, insisting Marley would take comfort in listening to them one day. Between them they'd handled everything, the instruments, editing, production and singing. Marley had gone along with it largely because he'd wanted to make Bowie happy, considering it precious time he got to spend with his ailing brother before they were forced apart. In his turmoil after Bowie's death, he'd forgotten all about the demos they'd created until not so long ago, when he'd received a call from an agent who said she'd been forced to listen to their songs via a Spotify link her assistant had been sending her over and over again for weeks. She thought Marley was wonderful and wanted to represent him. Bowie, they discovered as they hastily investigated, had uploaded their music to a profile bearing only Marley's name. He'd commissioned a company to promote the tracks and tasked his theatre friends, Phil and Clara, with managing the account. He'd instructed everyone involved not to approach Marley or his family about the profile until the music had gained some traction, by which time he hoped his brother would be mourning his death less intensely. He was right about that. Luckily, he'd also accurately predicted that Marley's reaction would be to demand Bowie's friends remove the music immediately and to tell the agent to leave him alone. But the agent had been briefed on Marley's situation, too. She went back to Phil, who forwarded Marley a voice note Bowie had recorded and sent in the final days of his life, alongside strict instructions on exactly when it should be passed on to his brother. Marley, who'd listened to it once in private, played it for the family one evening at the dinner table.

"Stop being stubborn," Bowie said. "I know you're angry, but you're not punishing anyone except yourself. Not everyone is capable of creating things. If you have something magic inside you, you owe it to the world to set it free."

Autumn reeled. Those words were familiar.

"I can't take credit for the poetry," Bowie continued. "Autumn said those words to me once. Remember, you're not the villain in this story, Marley. You saved your little sister. It's just that the system sucks. But things are changing — I can feel it in my bones."

Bowie was right — things were changing. Brave women were coming forward and publicly calling out the conduct of not only Vincent, but other men in similar industries. The internet was awash with accusations, the media was swirling and ready to swoop. The message was clear. Their time was almost up. Bowie continued.

"I know your life has probably ground to a halt. That pains me more than this damned cancer ever could."

Autumn and the Whittles passed sad smiles around the table. Bowie had known somehow that his brother would still be here, but that he'd be languishing in some sort of purgatory, surviving for the sake of everyone else, refusing to really live. Marley still wrote, but rarely played his songs to anyone. He never saw friends, went to the pub or partied with Pip like he used to. Apart from one evening with a sex worker he'd admitted to hiring the day before he'd tried to kill himself in Autumn's apartment, he hadn't been near any women, in all that time. He did absolutely nothing for the sake of himself anymore. He was living for his family, none of whom could figure out how to pull him from the funk he'd settled himself in. Luckily, Bowie knew just what to say.

"Please, Marley, do it for me. Forget everything except how much you love making music and go for it. Nobody deserves it more than you do. You're my hero, OK? I love you, bro."

Marley hadn't said much this past week in wake of the revelation, but he'd stopped insisting Phil and Clara take down the tracks, and Autumn knew he'd asked the agent to give him some time to think about it. She felt like this might be his shot and it was part of the reason she thought it was best if she and Benjamin moved out. Marley had been stuck for so long and she was confident her prominent presence in his life was holding him back. Now that he knew he was Benjamin's father, it would get worse. How could they hope to meet other people, to have lives that did not start and end with their child, if they lived together while they raised him? Moving out would give Marley the time and space he needed to start creating things again, she was sure of it.

Autumn stood and went to Benjamin. She loved to watch him sleep. She wondered if anyone had ever watched her when she was at peace, the way she had her son. The way she did his father. Marley gave her the space she was seeking from him for only a moment, then clambered out of the bed and strode to her.

"Don't do this." He fell to his knees in front of her. She laughed, but he held on to her around her waist and did not smile. She pulled him up off the floor and into a hug.

"Marley, there's a life out there for both of us," she said, holding him tightly.

"You're my life now, Autumn, you and Benjamin," he said. She sighed, and her fingers sought out wrists she'd once held together. She stroked her thumbs over his scars delicately and, despite a dangerous proximity she usually tried hard to avoid, dared to look up at him.

"I'll never do anything like that again," he said. "I promise. But I still don't want you to go."

"I know you don't."

She looked deep into his eyes. They were bigger and bluer than she'd ever seen them. She forced herself to look away, but he put his hand under her chin and tilted her head so that he could look at her again. He was trying hard to read her expression.

"What's going on in that complicated head of yours?" he asked her. She didn't know how to answer. He watched her. "You look like the sky today," he murmured. "All messy and perfect."

Whenever there was uncomfortable silence between them, which there was much more frequently these days, Marley found something poetic to compare her to: the sky, the trees, the birds. It was an effective diversion tactic. She typically found some way to brush him off, but she didn't have the strength tonight. She was trying hard to ignore how perfectly parted and inviting his lips looked when there was a knock on the door. They jumped apart a second before Bluebell appeared, her eyes small, her face crinkled and red.

"Autumn, can I talk to you?" she asked. Autumn nodded, bidding Marley goodbye with a squeeze of his hand and following her friend into the living room. She wondered fleetingly if this was an ambush, but the house was silent and she knew, somehow, everyone was in bed. They sat side by side on the sofa, their knees drawn up to their chests. Bluebell was trying hard to control her crying, without success. Autumn wanted to comfort her, but she didn't know if she'd be shooed away.

"I'm sorry," Bluebell said eventually. "For being such a witch."

"Don't apologise." Autumn shook her head. "I deserved worse."

"You didn't, though, Autumn," Bluebell said. "I know how hard the whole thing was for you. I know how much you loved Bowie. And I knew how he felt about you and Marley, what he was planning, before I said those nasty things—"

"It's no excuse," Autumn said. "Bowie didn't deserve what we did to him. We were wrong. We did the worst thing we could possibly do, though I can't say I regret it, not now we have Benjamin."

Bluebell nodded. "He's all everyone is living for now. His birth gave everyone hope. Without him, I'm quite sure Marley would be dead. Mum wouldn't ever have gotten over it. He brought them back to life. I always said you and I met for a reason."

Despite the seriousness of Bluebell's comment, a little laugh escaped Autumn's lips. It was just like her friend to bring this all back to fate. The insinuation no longer irritated her. She was willing to concede her friend might be right. She mused for a moment.

"You know," she said, wondering even as she spoke if this was the right thing to say. "Bowie was special — so kind, attentive, clever and funny — but there's no way I could have known that in the beginning, and I always wondered what it was about him that made me fall in love. I was his from the moment we met. Even after all this time, I still don't know. I've racked my brain. There was no reason I can see or touch or feel. There's no explanation. Of all the men I've ever met, and there have been a few, why him? Why Bowie?"

"Why do any of us choose anyone?" Bluebell asked. "Except that it's written somewhere?"

They sat for a moment in comfortable silence.

"Perhaps it *was* to bring you to Marley," Bluebell said. "So that you could have Benjamin. That little boy absorbed so much of our pain."

Autumn faltered. Perhaps she was right. Her son had given them all something new to live for.

"How do you feel about Marley?" Bluebell asked. Autumn winced. She didn't know herself. "If you *do* love him, it might be a good idea to declare it now, while everyone is still reeling anyway."

"I don't know what I feel," Autumn whispered. It was the closest she'd come to admitting aloud that Marley was not just her friend. Bluebell sighed and didn't encourage her. Autumn stood. "I should go to bed. Benjamin will be up again soon wanting milk."

Bluebell nodded, shuffling to the edge of the couch and standing to meet her. Autumn noticed for the first time that she was carrying a box.

"I wasn't sure I was going to give you this, but Bowie made me promise I would. He said I'd know when the time was right. Well, it's now."

She gave the box to Autumn. It was about the size of a shoebox, with a metal clasp and intricate carvings on each side. It was made from solid oak, and smelt old. Autumn turned it in her hands.

"I love you, Autumn," Bluebell said, pulling her into a hug. "And I always will. No matter what."

* * *

Autumn considered opening the box in the living room, but she thought she heard Benjamin stir and hurried back to her bedroom. Marley was standing over the crib, stroking their baby's hair. Benjamin was fast asleep again.

Without a word, Autumn perched on the end of the bed. She placed the box before her, opening it with great care. She knew Marley was watching her and was grateful for his silence. She thumbed through the tightly folded scraps of paper she found inside with curiosity. She recognised her own handwriting.

I'll never know why boys with blue eyes are not my thing, unless those eyes are blue, and belong to you.

The words on the page took her breath away. She'd written them about Bowie, not long after they'd moved to England. She picked up another sheet.

If the words are yours, then the writer is yours, too.

And another:

Rip my heart out and hit me with it. It's yours anyway.

And then another:

If you love him, love him with your whole heart.

She couldn't take credit for that one, she'd seen it written on the door of the stall in the bathroom she'd used in the café that Bowie had taken her to on the night they'd met, and it had been all the encouragement she'd needed to pursue him. Keeping notes of words like this had always given her strength, or changed the way she thought about things, and Autumn was prone to leaving them all over the place. She had been too consumed in Bowie's final weeks, and in the time since, to ever wonder what had happened to them. Bowie had been collecting them for her, dozens of them. Some she barely remembered writing. Suddenly shaky, it struck her he might also have left her a note. She opened the box properly, tipping it upside down on the bed. Something was taped to the lid inside.

I never read them, I promise. I did add one more though. It's at the bottom. I don't know when you'll get this, but whenever it is, I still love you, Autumn. And if I can be with you from here, and you know I don't believe that I can, but if I can, then I am. Always. Bowie.

She sank to her knees on the floor. It was just like him to do something like this and she had always wondered why he hadn't. He had hidden it with his most volatile sister. The woman who'd be most hurt by what Autumn and Marley had done. Perhaps he'd known Bluebell needed to see it, too. Autumn closed the box and held it close to her heart for a second. Marley was still standing there, in the middle of the room, watching her.

"Are you OK?" he asked. She nodded, but couldn't speak. "What is it, Autumn?"

"It's a box of my scribblings," she said. He frowned.

"Right . . . ?" He prompted her to elaborate.

"I never put them in here," she said. "Bowie did. And he left me his own."

Marley didn't move and she was grateful. He stood where he was, letting her come to terms with her discovery. She pored over the notes on the bed, ignoring her own writing and searching for his. The last one she picked up wasn't hers, and it wasn't a poem, it was a list of six things. He had crossed out the first four and underlined the last two.

Rule Number 5: always tell people that you love them when you do.

Rule Number 6: do what makes you happy.

Autumn dissolved into floods of tears, slamming the box lid shut and holding it to her chest again. This man had known her better than she knew herself. She buried her head in the duvet on the bed in front of her, shaking uncontrollably. She knew that Marley would come to her and she knew what would happen when he did.

"It's OK, Autumn." He pulled her away from the covers she was clinging to and into his chest. Autumn let herself rest her head against him for a minute, then turned her face to look at him. He gazed back at her the way he always did these days, as though she was the best thing he had ever seen. Marley was in love with her. Autumn had known for a while. Sometimes he muttered her name when he was sleeping, and his eyes danced over her whenever she entered a room. She basked in his gaze these days and had been doing so for several months. Now, in the dim light of their bedroom, fresh from a declaration of undying love from Bluebell, Bowie's biggest fan, the harshest critic she'd ever have to face, and riding off her lover's encouragement from beyond the grave, Autumn was ready to be honest with herself. She wanted Marley. Every bit of him. For ever.

There would never be any doubt about who moved to kiss who this time. She pressed her lips to his. He groaned in surprise and obvious desire, and pulled away. He whispered her name.

"I'm falling in love with you, Marley," she said. He stared at her, confusion written all over his face. She nodded, rising up to kiss him again.

This time, he did not resist.

THE END

THE CHOC LIT STORY

Established in 2009, Choc Lit is an independent, award-winning publisher dedicated to creating a delicious selection of quality women's fiction.

We have won 18 awards, including Publisher of the Year and the Romantic Novel of the Year, and have been shortlisted for countless others. In 2023, we were shortlisted for Publisher of the Year by the Romantic Novelists' Association.

All our novels are selected by genuine readers. We are proud to publish talented first-time authors, as well as established writers whose books we love introducing to a new generation of readers.

In 2023, we became a Joffe Books company. Best known for publishing a wide range of commercial fiction, Joffe Books has its roots in women's fiction. Today it is one of the largest independent publishers in the UK.

We love to hear from you, so please email us about absolutely anything bookish at choc-lit@joffebooks.com

If you want to hear about all our bargain new releases, join our mailing list: www.choc-lit.com/contact

Milton Keynes UK
Ingram Content Group UK Ltd.
UKHW040835030924
447825UK00010B/76

9 781781 897812